READER REVIEWS

2003

"I couldn't put this book down. Dave Hunt does a wonderful job with this fictional book, originally written as a screenplay. It presents some [fascinating factual ideas] within a fictional setting. The explanation Dave Hunt provides...for UFOs and Aliens is actually quite reasonable and believable.... Well done. It has remained my favorite book since I first picked it up. Good job Dave Hunt!" —IW

2002

"First published in 1989 but perhaps more up to date than today's newspaper. I seldom read fiction but I got into this. The best fiction book I have ever read." —TG

2000

"A great book to learn about aliens and UFO invasions. **The Mind Invaders** gets down to the truth about physics and fortune tellers.... One of Dave Hunt's best!" —EY

2000

"**The Mind Invaders** is a must read! I picked up this book by accident. However after I began reading it I simply could not put it down! Dave Hunt weaves a tale of intrigue, suspense and super-reality that may give answers to the complex question of UFOs, ascended masters, and the netherworld that surrounds us. This is simply quite a compelling work of fiction that is more reality and truth than one may want to admit. I highly recommend it to all." —DF

1999

"An excellent novel, a must read, a hard book to put down! This is the best fiction novel that I have ever read.... A very realistic book—something that could happen, or may be happening now. Thanks, Dave Hunt for such a good book." —AR

"We cast this message into the cosmos . . . this is a present from a small, distant world. . . . We hope someday, having solved the problems we face, to join a community of galactic civilizations."

— *Jimmy Carter, president of the USA*
June 16, 1977—from message on Voyager spacecraft

"I am personally convinced that superior beings from other spaces and other times have initiated a renewed dialogue with humanity. . . . I do not know what they look like, how they live or even what their goals are with respect to humankind . . . [but] I have complete faith in their wisdom and benevolent intentions toward man and living things on earth."

— *Andrija Puharich*
medical scientist who held more than
50 patents

"[Eventually] psychokinetic functioning will be reasonably well accepted. It knocks down the previous model of the human; there is something more fundamental than the material we are made of.
We can [psychically] control, external to our bodies, the matter that is around us, and control internally the functioning of our bodies, by the way we think."

— *Ex-astronaut Edgar D. Mitchell*
addressing members of Congress

"If we believe in telepathy, we believe in a process which makes possible the invasion of a personality by someone at a distance. It is not at all likely . . . that sane and intelligent spirits are the only ones to exert [such] influence. . . . There is no reason why others cannot do so as well."

— *James Hyslop*
Columbia University professor of logic and ethics

"I had great difficulty to control my thoughts. There was a demon in me. . . . "

—*Carl Gustav Jung*
psychiatrist

MIND INVADERS

A NOVEL

originally titled THE ARCHON CONSPIRACY

DAVE HUNT

The Berean Call

BEND • OREGON

Based on an original screenplay by Dave Hunt and T.A. McMahon

Scripture references are taken from the King James Version of the Bible or from the New English Bible, © The Delegates of the Oxford University Press and the Syndics of the Cambridge University Press 1961, 1970. Reprinted with permission.

The author's free monthly newsletter, THE BEREAN CALL, *may be received by sending a request to the address below, or by calling 1-800-937-6638.*

To register for free e-mail updates, to access our digital archives, and to order a variety of additional resource materials online, visit us at: www.thebereancall.org

THE MIND INVADERS

Copyright © 2005 by DAVE HUNT
Published by The Berean Call
PO Box 7019, Bend, OR 97708

ISBN: 978-1-928660-35-4
Library of Congress Control Number: 2005935596

Previously published © 1998 by Harvest House under ISBN: 1-56507-831-4
Originally published as The Archon Conspiracy © 1989

PRINTED IN THE UNITED STATES OF AMERICA

the MIND INVADERS

contents

A Note from the Author

The collapse of communism in Eastern Europe and breakup of the Soviet Union brought a new cooperation between Russia and the West. Former communist countries joined NATO. Even China experimented with modified capitalism. World peace seemed a realistic hope.

Forgotten was the warning from Anatoly Golitsyn, one of the highest KGB officials ever to defect, who in 1984 had predicted this very scenario. When the West, duped by "peace," had fallen far behind militarily, the trap would be sprung.

While Congress canceled America's best defense projects, Russia (hypocritically accusing the United States of pushing the arms race) prepared for war. Her growing fleet of SS-18 Typhoon nuclear subs (too silent for us to track) prowled offshore with their nuclear missiles programmed for American cities. Russia continued to arm Syria, Iraq, and Iran and held periodic joint maneuvers with Syria for the planned attack upon Israel. The frequent practice of preemptive strikes against the United States (using dummy warheads and fake targets)—and the increased railing against America by the Orthodox Church and Communist Party—hardly pointed to peace.

While the State Department and White House slept, the CIA continued its clandestine war with the KGB's successor, the Federal Security Bureau (FSB). Then a lucky break gave America sudden superiority in the most incredible weapon: psychic power. And that is where our story begins.

The setting is in the near future. Except where public figures are clearly identified, any similarity to persons living or dead is not intended. Similarity to future events is. It could happen soon.

the MIND INVADERS

1

Contact!

Y ou're nearing Omega! Steady now. Let yourself go. We're taking you deeper . . . deeper. . . . "

To Ken Inman, already deep in a self-induced trance and strapped into the secret apparatus he had invented, the metallic voice seemed to originate inside his head. Transmuted by electronics from Ken's brain waves into an amplifier, the robotic voice seemed to come across vast distances of space and time. It echoed eerily throughout the laboratory from a speaker directly above a second figure wearing a white lab coat and poised over the controls of a bank of electronic monitoring equipment. Beneath the thinning gray hair there were beads of perspiration on the man's broad, high forehead, and the owlish look behind the steel-rimmed glasses betrayed signs of growing nervous excitement.

Eighteen years before, while still in his mid-teens, Ken Inman had graduated *summa cum laude* from Stanford University. A child prodigy in math, he'd gone on to earn, at age 19, a double Ph.D. at Stanford in both electrical engineering and computer science—a feat unprecedented and unlikely ever to be duplicated. After establishing his own highly successful computer software company, which he still managed, Ken had branched out into psychic research. It was a decision that greatly disappointed some of his former professors, but one that Ken had not made lightly. He convincingly argued with his critics that parapsychology offered more potential for benefit to mankind than any other field. Not a hint, however, did he ever drop of the secret research that had begun to obsess and finally possess him: the search for psychic contact with highly evolved, nonphysical intelligences.

After five intensive and solitary years of work on the project, Inman had brought in his close friend, brilliant and pugnacious Stanford University professor of psychology Frank Leighton. Together they had experimented tirelessly in the pursuit of something they were both convinced was bigger than the A-bomb, the law of gravity, and the theory of relativity rolled into one. And now, at last, contact had apparently been made!

"We are the Nine. Trust us! We got your Voyager message . . . we've come to help. . . . " The alien voice sounded soothing and hypnotic.

Though in a carefully controlled altered state of consciousness, Inman felt a sense of exhilaration. *The "Voyager message"? Incredible! So they're out there.* The thoughts raced by in rapid succession as he felt himself being drawn into a vortex of magnetic consciousness such as he had never imagined existed.

Breathing heavily and fighting to control the tremor in his fingers, Frank Leighton darted probing glances at the deeply tranced figure before him. The massive reclining chair into which Ken was strapped was completely covered by a thick Plexiglas pyramid reaching almost to the laboratory's high ceiling. A maze of wires led from a close-fitting plastic helmet on Ken's head and from numerous positions on his body to an imposing array of electronic wizardry directly beside him. From there, two large computer cables fed into the monitoring equipment located outside the pyramid. The entire setup was mounted on a pentagram-shaped metal platform. This "launching pad for journeys into inner space," as Ken and Frank affectionately called their secret laboratory, was located about ten minutes from Stanford University.

"You are entering the superluminal. Relax!" The voice sent cold fingers of panic clutching at Leighton's throat and chest. *This is it—the payoff to years of hard work!*

Ken lay motionless, his face now a death mask. The monitors showed that the trance state had quickly deepened far beyond anything previously attained. Pulse rate and blood pressure had dropped to 35 per minute and 80/40, respectively. For a moment Leighton verged on panic, cursing the paranoia of secrecy that had forbidden the presence of a medical doctor during these dangerous sessions.

"We've been watching your development—we're here to help you take the next step, but there's a mental barrier blocking us. Open up! There's nothing to fear."

In spite of the assuring words and mesmerizing cadence, something chilling had interjected itself into the metallic voice coming over the speaker. Leighton felt the hair on the back of his neck rising. *Keep calm! Get hold of yourself! It's the electronics that makes it sound weird. Steady, Ken.* Leighton's eyes swept from Ken to the needles and graphs and back again. He wiped a damp hand across his forehead.

"To reach the Omega point where human intelligence interfaces with the Infinite, you must drop the barrier surrounding the self. Drop the barrier!" The commanding voice compelled obedience.

To his consternation, Leighton noticed that Ken had begun to fight his way back to normal consciousness. Convulsively he struggled against the straps holding him in place. A hollow moan escaped the rigid mouth. Blood pressure and pulse rate took a quick upward jump. Leighton watched helplessly as the monitors signaled a weakening of the deep trance state.

"Drop the barrier!" The otherworldly voice had lost its seductive quality and had taken on a harsh, authoritarian tone.

"Nooool!" The cry erupting from Ken's throat sounded more animal than human. He was fighting his restraints desperately now, like a drowning man trying to come up for air.

"You must open yourself. Drop the barrier . . . the barrier . . . " The voice was louder, more insistent, but disjointed, as though the connection were being maintained with great difficulty.

"Nooool!" A terrifying scream ripped the air. "Oh God! Nooool!"

The bank of monitoring needles fluctuated madly for a few seconds, then began a steady ascent back to normal—and beyond. Cursing under his breath, Leighton pushed a button and the Plexiglas pyramid began to tilt in a smooth motion over onto its side and away from him. The contact they had dreamed of, worked for, and had achieved at last, was slipping away.

Ken's eyes opened wildly and his head moved erratically as though he were desperately searching the room for something or someone. Panic was clearly written in every contorted feature as he strained in vain against the heavy straps holding him. Blood pressure and pulse rate had both shot up above 200. Now they began a slow descent as his eyes at last focused on Leighton, who was working swiftly to remove the electronic connections from his body before undoing the control straps.

"Ken, I don't believe it! Why did you hold back—just when you reached *Omega*? Why?"

"Uh—hold back? Did I?" Even in his still-disoriented condition, Ken was shocked by the reproach in his colleague's voice. Deliberately he shook his head to clear it. "What are you saying?"

"We were there, and then you started *fighting* it. You don't remember?"

"Fighting? I don't know. It felt like something was trying to take over my mind. It was horrible!" A shudder shook Ken's body. He clutched his head with both hands, sickened and bewildered, struggling to recall the details of a horrendous nightmare that seemed to hover just beyond his grasp.

Impatiently Leighton reached over to the recording console beside Ken and alternately punched the "rewind" and "fast forward" buttons. Garbled sounds punctuated the tense atmosphere. At last he found what he was searching for. "Here it is. We were making history! Listen to this!"

"You're nearing Omega! Steady now. Let yourself go. We're taking you deeper . . . deeper."

At the first sound of the voice, Ken's body jerked convulsively and a groan escaped his contorted lips. Leighton pushed the pause button momentarily, then released it.

"We are the Nine. Trust us! We got your Voyager message . . . we've come to help. You are entering the superluminal. Relax! We've been watching your development—we're here to help you take the next step, but there's a mental barrier blocking us. Open up! There's nothing to fear."

Leighton watched his colleague carefully. Ken's body shook uncontrollably as the insistent voice continued.

"To reach the Omega point where human intelligence interfaces with the Infinite, you must drop the barrier surrounding the self. Drop the barrier!"

"Drop the barrier!" The voice seemed to fill the room.

"Noooo!"

The sound of his own voice screaming hysterically was like an explosion inside Ken's head. The pain jerked him violently against the restraining straps. Reaching out in panic, Ken turned off the recorder and started pulling frantically at the buckles.

"Wait! I'll get you out." Leighton put a firm hand on Ken's shoulder and pushed him down.

Ken was trembling. He had the eyes of a trapped animal. "*Something* was grabbing at my mind again!" He took several deep breaths, exhaling slowly, trying to calm himself. "It's horrible! I never expected this, Frank! Who are these *Nine?* Why did I sense danger—something *repulsive?*"

Methodically Leighton unstrapped him, shaking his head in unmistakable disapproval as he did so. "I don't understand what you're saying. It's just incomprehensible!" The fear and confusion in Ken's eyes caused Leighton to ease off a bit. "Can you handle any more?" he asked. "You ought to listen to the rest of it right now—while it's fresh. You might remember something."

Ken settled back in the chair and nodded reluctantly. "Okay. Let's give it another try." Leighton turned the recorder back on.

"You must open yourself. Drop the barrier . . . the barrier . . . " The voice was fading in and out.

"Noooo! Oh God! Noooo!" It was a scream wrenched from the pit of hell. Ken gripped the arms of his chair, trying to hang on to his sanity until the terrifying but indistinct images passed.

Leighton turned off the recorder. "We lost the pattern right there. We worked for years for this moment." Gone was the momentary empathy he had felt. The stakes were too high. There was no excuse for what Ken had done. Once again he made no attempt to disguise the disappointment and resentment he felt. He was peering over his glasses at Ken, but not with the detached clinical expression so maddeningly familiar to the students in his graduate psychology courses at Stanford. A great prize had slipped through their grasp. Frustrated anger was boiling inside of him.

"Why did you fight it? *Why?*" Leighton's question loomed like a palpable presence in the room. "We had it, Ken!"

"I told you. It was like . . . like something *alive* and terribly *alien* was trying to take over—to possess me! I can't explain it . . ." Ken's voice trailed away.

Leighton shook his head adamantly. "Ken, they said they got the *Voyager message* and came here to help us. Do you realize what that means . . . the opportunity we just blew?"

"So it's my fault, is it? I'm sorry, but you don't know what it was like."

"I was watching every flicker of those needles," Leighton insisted, "and I'm telling you there was no indication of any harmful effect on any of the monitors until you began to resist! That's when things went wrong!"

Ken bristled. "I resent being blamed for this, Frank! You think I screamed like that for no reason? That's not like me, but I heard it—and so did you."

"You're not expressing anything concrete, Ken—just vague and subjective feelings that reflect only your own internal state of mind, but not what was actually happening." Leighton's tone had become clinical, as though he were analyzing a patient or a student. "I was watching the monitors and there was nothing . . . "

Ken cut him off angrily. "I don't care what the monitors showed! I was being sucked into something *hideously repulsive* beyond description! I can't explain it, but it was *terrifying!*"

"I hear what you're saying, Ken, and I'm trying to sympathize with your feelings. I'm sure they were real to you. But I've got to understand what actually happened. We can't let it happen next time. You were at the Omega point—a dream come true—and then you pulled yourself out."

"You think I'm not just as disappointed as you are? I conceived this thing and brought you into it! So get off my back!"

"Okay, okay," Leighton half-apologized. "We'll try again whenever you're ready. It should be easier next time . . . "

"*Next time?* Yeah, maybe . . . but I'd rather not think about it right now." Ken's pleading eyes and contorted face reflected the panic of unreasoning terror.

"You can do it!" said Leighton soothingly. Now it was *his* turn to panic. Surely Ken wouldn't back out? "You'll get over this with a good night's sleep. Maybe this was a fluke. Maybe next time will be a breeze." Frank put his hand on Ken's arm only to have it brushed off.

"*Maybe*—maybe you'd like to trade places with me next time."

"I'd be happy to, if it made any sense," returned Leighton earnestly, "but you trained yourself for years: psychedelics, yoga, Zen . . . How long would it take me? Come on, Ken—I've never known you to be a quitter!"

"Get off my case, will you? I'll try again—of course I will. But I—I need some time."

Ken stood resolutely to his feet, his tall, athletic frame towering over his companion. They were quite a contrast. Leighton obviously liked his liquor and rich foods too much. "I've got to get out of here!" muttered Ken, as much to himself as to Leighton. He shook his head again, then held it in both hands, wincing at the pain and confusion. Still shaking his head, he staggered out the laboratory door and slammed it behind him.

Leighton made a few hesitant steps to follow, then stopped. He stood still, the sound of the slamming door echoing in his memory. Caught up in a whirlwind of conflicting thoughts, he surveyed the lab that Ken's genius and perseverance had built. It had become his own magnificent obsession as well.

We've made contact! The thought brought a fierce exhilaration. He went quickly to a phone on a nearby desk and punched a number—a number that he never called except from locations where it couldn't be traced to him.

The phone rang and rang. Finally an efficient female voice on the other end answered, "CIA."

Leighton cleared his throat. "Hawkins, please."

"Who shall I tell him is calling?"

"Tell him it's Herbert George Wells—with the big news he's been waiting for."

Appointment with Death

U pon leaving the lab, Ken instinctively drove toward the coastal hills. So many times he had gone there in the past to wander in the woods and think tough problems through to a solution. This time, however, when he found himself on the winding mountain road that he knew so well, and facing the late-afternoon sun that was about to sink into the Pacific just beyond the range he was climbing, he could not remember how he'd gotten there. Nor could he remember—somewhere along the route—pushing James Taylor's *Sweet Baby James* into the tape deck. Its nostalgic sounds blared at him from the quad stereo of his Mercedes SL-600.

In spite of the wealth his computer company had brought him, Ken was far too dedicated to his goals to have time for the many luxuries he could so easily afford. The Mercedes was the one symbol of success he allowed, the one possession that possessed him. It was his pride and joy. Yet now he had the bizarre feeling that this finely tuned machine, which had always been instantly responsive to his lightest touch, was fighting him, like some living, breathing, untamed animal. Even that strange realization seemed vague and unreal. Only one thought obsessed him now: the terrifying imperative to escape from an elusive but dread memory. That haunting nightmare became steadily clearer and more painful as the eerie voices hammered the same phrases repeatedly and loudly inside his throbbing head.

"You've reached Omega . . . Omega . . . the superluminal . . . superluminal . . . superluminal . . . " It was more than a memory. The metallic, menacing commands seemed to be emanating from his very soul, as though he now belonged to "the Nine," whoever they were. Each stabbing sound heightened his desire to escape and the panic of knowing he could not. His brilliant mind, the genius that intimidated the proudest intellects—what good was it all now?

A strange transformation was taking place in his physical perceptions. The Mercedes that he had been battling began to feel more and more like an extension of himself. Then the two of them were somehow one shared being—flesh and machine fused into the same essence. His arms were now frozen to the steering wheel, moving as it moved in wild maneuvers; and his foot and leg were part of the pumping accelerator that goaded the pulsating hulk to its limits. At the same time, on another level, he knew he was acting irrationally, but that wild surge of power seemed his only hope for retaliation against the haunting voices. Even if it meant his own destruction. That would silence them! The thought was insane and he knew it, but still his foot ground into the floorboard in obedience to some inner command.

"We Nine will guide you. You must open yourself . . . open yourself . . . "

The road had narrowed and steepened sharply, becoming a seemingly endless succession of dangerous curves winding along the edge of a deep and precipitous gorge. The brilliant blue of sky, the trees rushing by with the setting sun slanting through their branches, the surging power that engulfed him—it was exhilarating. He'd had that same feeling at the first moment of contact with "the Nine." And now, as then, ecstasy metamorphosed into fear and confusion. On a blind curve the Mercedes swept effortlessly around a laboring truck laden with hay as though it were standing still. It was a deadly chance that he would never take in his right mind, but something irresistible was now in control. The realization that he was more than playing with death—that he had an actual appointment with it—seemed vague and unimportant.

Is this all a dream? In stunned and frozen fascination, he watched as a huge cobra slithered out from under the dashboard and up between his legs. It stared at him with unblinking, hooded eyes, then wrapped itself quickly around his left arm. Ken screamed in terror and clawed desperately for its neck, but his free hand found only empty air. Yet it was there. Its eyes stared hypnotically into his, and its darting tongue flicked menacingly.

His terrified preoccupation with the hideous serpent was shattered by the sudden sound of squealing brakes and a blaring horn—and the terrible realization that he had wandered across the narrow road's double line and into the lane of oncoming traffic. In one instant the deadly serpent vanished and in its place, filling his vision, were a truck and trailer loaded with huge redwood logs heading directly toward him. The truck driver braked and swerved frantically. Ken pulled the steering wheel desperately to the right.

For a split second Ken thought he'd made it—until the truck's huge bumper struck the left rear fender of his car with a deafening impact, flipping the Mercedes over the guardrail and sending it catapulting nearly 500 feet down a precipitous, rock-strewn slope. The crumpled mass of twisted and pounded metal dropped the last 20 feet straight down into a dry creek bed in the bottom of the canyon. Landing with a sickening crunch that Ken never heard, the car sat wedged into the narrow crevice between two massive boulders.

The steep terrain and tall trees made it impossible to call in a helicopter. When paramedics finally reached the wreckage, they found Ken unconscious and still strapped in by the seat belt that would have to be given credit for saving his life—*if* he survived. In spite of the enormous blood loss from multiple compound fractures and the piercing of a lung by one of his broken ribs, there was a barely detectable pulse. It took more than an hour to cut him out of the twisted metal tomb and haul him up the cliff. Intubated immediately and respirated by hand with the ambu bag, he was still clinging to life by the slenderest of threads. Using a large-bore needle, the paramedics started an IV of normal saline, as the racing ambulance reached the hospital in Palo Alto.

There the blood transfusions began in concert with emergency surgery. Two of the best surgeons in the country—Dr. Harold Elliott and his assistant—worked heroically but, by their own estimation, futilely. The patient had fixed dilated pupils and no spontaneous respiration. Yet his CT scan was normal, indicating that the coma was not due to intra-cerebral hemorrhaging.

"Diffuse brain injury—possibly secondary to hypoxia," Elliott's assistant muttered matter-of-factly with a scowl. "Worst possible diagnosis. We're probably wasting our time."

"Hmm . . . maybe," was all Elliott replied as he cut and sewed rapidly. He was thinking of another and possibly even more hopeless explanation for the coma—a nonmedical one that his assistant would scoff at, so there was no point in mentioning it.

"We could schedule an MRI—if he survives long enough," suggested the assistant.

"Perhaps," said Elliott, preoccupied with other thoughts. The patient's name was well-known to anyone who kept current with the local news. *The guy's an outspoken promoter of Eastern mysticism and psychic powers. As involved in that stuff as he's been, he could be heavily demonized. That could explain his peculiar unconscious state . . . maybe.*

By the time the two surgeons had put their instruments down, Ken's fiancee, Carla Bertelli, had arrived at the hospital. The young woman that now nervously paced the waiting room floor had gotten her master's degree in journalism at the University of California, Berkeley, seven years after Ken's double doctorate. They had met when Carla attended a guest lecture series Ken had given on parapsychology at the university. It had been love-at-first-sight for both of them. She had admired his genius, sense of humor, and especially his suave humanism and clever put-down of all religions that reinforced her own rejection of the Christian faith in which she'd been raised. And he had seen in her, in addition to everything else a man could ever want in a woman, that rare tenacity of purpose that reflected his own. At first Ken had made frequent trips to date Carla. At times, however, it might be a two-hour drive each way between Palo Alto and Berkeley, depending on the traffic. Ken was already putting in 16-hour days developing computer programs.

When he added psychic research on top of that, there wasn't much time left for romance.

From her Italian father, Carla had inherited her olive skin and large, dark, almond-shaped eyes. Her Irish mother had endowed her with auburn hair and long-limbed beauty. Winsomely affectionate, stubbornly determined and loyal, Carla was a dream-come-true for the dedicated young scientist. Pursued by other suitors, she had kept faith with the man she loved, even when he had become too involved with a double career to have the time or energy to make the long drive except on rare weekends. Carla was much like Ken in that respect: Once she'd determined upon an objective, there was no turning aside. It was that way with everything. She had turned down several promising offers from modeling agencies in order to pursue the career in journalism that had been her calculated goal since high school.

Carla spent two years with *The Wall Street Journal* and another two with *The Washington Post*, then decided to free-lance. She had found day-to-day reporting on corporate takeovers and Wall Street scandals less-than-challenging and had set her sights on a Pulitzer prize. To be free to pursue the big story when it came along—that was now what she wanted. Ken had eventually flown to the East to tell Carla how much he missed her, and it took little persuasion to convince her to move back to Palo Alto. She'd never lost the deep interest in parapsychology which Ken's electrifying lectures had earlier aroused, and under his tutelage she had begun to write articles on the subject. It was an enthusiasm that her editors had not shared at first. Divulging information that no one else knew, Ken had fed her selected data about his own secret research and introduced her to the most famous scientists in the field. It was not surprising, then, that the young woman who was soon to marry Ken Inman had already become recognized among the world's journalists as one of the top experts in parapsychology. Indeed, she had given a new and badly needed respectability to such reporting.

Carla leaped to her feet apprehensively the moment the tall, graying doctor in green surgical scrubs walked into the waiting room and looked around. She was attracted immediately by his face—it had to be the kindest she could remember ever seeing. "Is he? . . . " She had already learned from Emergency the details of the accident and the grim prognosis and didn't know how to finish the question. "Will he? . . . "

"I'm Doctor Elliott." She felt her outstretched hand enveloped warmly in both of his. "He's in a coma but clinging to life—barely. We've done all we can. There's a slim chance he may survive, but the damage is so severe we'll just have to wait and see." He paused for a moment and put a sympathetic hand on her arm. "We haven't determined the cause of his coma," he added solemnly, "and that's not good."

"May I see him? We were getting married next month."

"I'm sorry. No visitors until we get him stabilized in the intensive care unit. We don't know how long that will be. Why don't you leave your phone number at the nurses' station? They'll notify you when it's okay to come in. There's really no point in waiting around here. The best thing you can do now is to get some rest—and pray."

Carla looked momentarily startled. *Pray? Are you really serious? I'm counting on Ken's determination to live—and your medical skill. How can I trust a doctor who mixes modern science with Dark Ages mumbo jumbo!*

"Thanks," she responded, a bit icily in spite of her attempt not to show her feelings, "but I don't believe in prayer—and neither does Ken." She didn't mean to be ungracious, but honesty about what she believed was very important to her. No false impressions, no compromise of principles . . . especially when it mattered so much.

"Well, I believe in God," responded Dr. Elliott softly, looking her straight in the eye, "so I pray for each of my patients, and you'd be amazed how often He graciously answers prayer. And in this case it—it wouldn't be honest if I gave you the impression that there's any other hope."

Exit "the Nine"

Prayer was a major part of Dr. Harold Elliott's life—a fact that drew varied reactions from his colleagues, from shrugged shoulders to veiled hostility. This was not due to his critics' lack of interest in alternative methods of healing. The hospital, in fact, sponsored seminars in everything from yoga to shamanistic visualization and was considered to be on the cutting edge of holistic medicine. The problem with Elliott was his polite but uncompromising insistence that the God revealed in the Bible was the only true God and that He alone could intervene miraculously, and then only as He graciously chose—there were no techniques that could guarantee miracles.

Elliott was considered narrow-minded for his flat rejection of pseudoscientific techniques such as hypnosis and biofeedback—which he bluntly called "religion masquerading as science" and would not tolerate. No one could fault him, however, for the surgical skill that had earned him an international reputation. And even those who called him a dogmatic fundamentalist grudgingly admitted that among his patients there had been an amazing number of medically inexplicable recoveries.

Each Thursday evening Elliott's large home was the site of a prayer meeting that often went on until after midnight and usually drew 30 or more participants from among his wide circle of Christian friends. Of course, Dr. Elliott's patients (first names only)

23

were routinely included on the carefully compiled and updated prayer sheet which the members were given as a reminder for their own daily intercession. Ken's name was added to the lengthy list at the regular weekly gathering when it met three nights after his accident. In fact, he became the major focus of earnest prayer that evening.

"I have a special burden for this young man," Elliott had explained at the beginning of the meeting. "For years he's been a brilliant, outspoken enemy of Christ, advocating Eastern mysticism and psychic powers. It's hard to believe that anyone that heavily involved in the occult wouldn't be demonized to some extent.

"He's still in a coma, yet the brain scans show no hemorrhaging. Ordinarily, that would most likely indicate diffuse axonal injuries, or hypoxia—conditions which are virtually hopeless. In his case, however, I suspect a nonmedical reason—some kind of demonic involvement. Let's make Ken a special prayer project around the clock and see whether God in His grace will intervene—at least to restore consciousness so that he can hear the truth and make a rational choice. I think he's been too heavily deceived to have been able to do that up to this point."

In response to this appeal, the group had spent nearly an hour in earnest prayer for Ken, when Elliott's wife, Karen, called him out of the living room into his nearby study.

"Hal, it's ICU again!" she whispered as she handed him the phone.

"This is Dr. Elliott," he said, hopeful that there might be some further good news. The patient had shown some gradual improvement in his respiratory status over the last few hours. Elliott, in fact, had ordered decreased sedation because of momentary flickers of consciousness.

"Doctor!" said the excited voice on the other end of the line, "I think you ought to get in here and see your patient, Inman. We've been following the weening parameters. I extubated him at 19:20. He's been breathing better at 20 per minute, blood pressure stable at 130 over 80, and his pulse in the 90s. His post extubation blood gas was within normal limits. He rested peacefully for about an hour, no distress—and then something frightening happened. Eerie, inhuman voices began coming out of him!"

"He's still in a coma?"

"Yes—but I'd swear I've seen him move! Doctor, I took the liberty of putting in a videotape. I thought this should be recorded."

"I'll be right there—and keep that tape running."

Elliott put down the phone and turned to his wife. "Honey, I need you to come with me!"

As the two of them hurried through the living room toward the front door, Dr. Elliott paused to explain to the prayer group their sudden departure. "I've just had a call from the hospital. Ken is still in a coma, but he's improved somewhat. They've taken him off the ventilator and he's breathing on his own. And now strange things are going on that could be demonic. . . . Karen's coming with me. Please back us up with prayer—for his complete deliverance and healing."

The intensive care unit consisted of 12 patient rooms arranged in a rectangle and surrounding a central nurses' station. While there were solid walls between them, the rooms all had glass fronts, allowing for observation of each patient. Over the beds in four of the rooms were TV cameras connected to monitors on which the most critical patients could be more closely observed from the central station at all times.

It was a terrified and bewildered ICU charge nurse who, along with three assistants, was apprehensively watching Ken Inman's TV monitor when Dr. Elliott and his wife arrived.

"Are we glad to see you, Doctor!" she exclaimed. "I've seen a lot of psychotic patients and plenty of weird behavior—but nothing like *this*."

Elliott glanced from the TV screen showing Inman lying in bed, to the other monitors that continuously exhibited his current medical status. "Nothing unusual at the moment," he observed. "Let's take a look at him."

The charge nurse walked the few steps with Elliott to Inman's room. "It's been quiet for the last 20 minutes. But even worse than the voices, there's *something* in there with him! You can *feel* it!"

They were standing now just outside the room and looking through the glass. Inman was clearly in view. His right leg and left arm were in casts. Because of the punctured lung, there were chest tubes protruding. Suddenly the comatose patient's right arm flailed about, then dropped limply at his side.

"Did you see that!" exclaimed the nurse.

"Get back to your station," said Elliott. "My wife and I are going in there. Make sure that tape is still recording!"

All was quiet when Dr. Elliott and his wife entered the small room. The doctor drew the curtain across the glass front, then approached the patient. A quick evaluation indicated that he was still in a coma and, after the brief improvement, sinking. The bedside monitors indicated a serious deterioration in his status. Karen prayed silently. As Elliott leaned over and pulled back the lid of one eye, Ken's face suddenly contorted into an evil, mocking expression. At the same time his lips began to form words and a taunting, guttural voice muttered, "Keep your hands off! He's ours!"

While Karen continued to pray, now audibly, Dr. Elliott commanded the entity that had spoken: "In the Name of Jesus Christ, tell me who you are!"

An ominous silence was the only response. "In the authority of Jesus Christ . . . " began Elliott, when he was interrupted.

"He's ours!" came a sneering voice, this one clearly different from the one that had first spoken, but once again seemingly emanating from the patient's mouth. "You can't save him!" said a third voice derisively. Ken's face, which had seemed lifeless moments before, contorted again into hideous expressions. His unbroken right arm suddenly flexed violently in a threatening motion toward Dr. Elliott, then dropped back onto the bed. A chorus of voices joined in mocking, jeering laughter that exploded from Ken's now-leering mouth.

"Father God," prayed Elliott aloud, "in the Name of Jesus I cry out to You for this young man. Please deliver him from the powers of darkness." Then once again he commanded firmly. "In the Name of Jesus Christ, tell me who you are."

"We will not!" came the instant reply in a defiantly contemptuous tone.

"In the Name of Jesus Christ of Nazareth and through the power of His blood shed upon the cross for sin—tell me *now* who you are!"

Hellish groans issued from Ken's throat, and then came the grudging admission: "We are the Nine . . . the rulers of the darkness of this world." Ken's body was shaken violently as though by some internal struggle. His tongue shot out repeatedly, like the forked tongue of a snake; his eyes opened wide, then took on a hooded reptilian malevolence; and his right arm flailed about furiously once again. Hal and Karen both sensed a heavy, serpentine presence that seemed to be the embodiment of evil more ancient than the pyramids. "This one belongs to us," cried a new and more commanding voice in a burst of fury. "He has been ours for many years."

Again Elliott turned to prayer. "Lord Jesus, You are the Creator of this universe who became a man to die for our sins. Your Word says that through Your death upon the cross You 'destroyed him that had the power of death, that is the devil, and delivered them who through fear of death were all their lifetime subject to bondage.' Lord, we ask mercy and grace for this one who lies near death and is helpless to combat the evil one who now holds him in his grip."

"He is ours!" shrieked the defiant voices. "He is not a Christian! He rejected Christ! You can't take him from us!"

"You have deceived him. Now come out of him, in the Name of Jesus Christ, and enter no more into him." Elliott pulled out a handkerchief and wiped the perspiration from his brow.

"We will kill him first—and you too, and your family. Leave us alone, and we will not harm him."

"You lie, you deceiving spirits. Your threats don't frighten us. You have no power. Satan, your master, was defeated at the cross by Jesus Christ. You know you have to come out, so do it now!"

"I'm leaving," said a weak voice. Ken was shaken again like a rat in a terrier's mouth. Then he lay motionless, enveloped once more by ominous silence.

"That was a trick," said Karen. "No demon came out."

"I know," replied Hal.

The ensuing battle was long and draining. Together Hal and Karen had been through similar struggles with demons many times before. Hal had been raised by medical missionary parents in Sri Lanka when it was still known as Ceylon. As a young man, he had participated in exorcisms led by his father, a physician who had inspired Hal also to enter the medical profession. After getting his M.D. degree, Hal had returned to the mission field—this time to East Africa, where he had met and married Karen. Their ministry there had often involved casting out demons. Returning to the United States to put their four children through university, they had been astonished to find as much demonism in North America as in any Third World country. In the West, however, demon possession took a more sophisticated form and was often called by various psychological names instead of being recognized for what it really was.

Ken's exorcism turned out to be the most difficult the Elliotts had yet experienced. At times the comatose patient's body was thrown violently around on the bed. The demons loudly accused Elliott of medical malpractice and warned that he would be put in prison for causing Ken's death. Yet one by one, grudgingly, the demons came out, as Hal and Karen continued to invoke the Name and authority of Jesus Christ.

When the last one of "the Nine" departed, an immediate change came over Ken. Color began returning to his cheeks, and his eyes opened briefly. He stared momentarily at the two bending over his bed, then closed his eyes and dropped off into a deep sleep.

"Praise God!" exclaimed Hal and Karen in unison and bowed together in prayer to give thanks. Then Elliott threw open the curtain. The ICU charge nurse, who had been observing the exorcism in astonishment from the control station, met the doctor and his wife outside Inman's room. Her face was ashen. "Incredible! I can't believe it!" was all she could say.

"I think he's had a major healing!" said Elliott confidently. "If he continues to improve, as I'm sure he will, I'm going to move him out of here to a regular post-op room. Call me as soon as he awakens. I want to be kept advised of everything."

The nurse was still badly shaken. "Is this thing over?" she asked anxiously. "I mean . . . ?"

"It's finished—completely," said Elliot, "so relax. And I want the Surgical Review Committee to see that video, so be sure to set it aside, okay?"

"You really think you want them to see it?" asked the nurse. She looked as though she were about to faint.

"Of course I want them to see it. Why not? Say, are you all right?"

"I'm okay—just concerned about you. You know some of the criticism you've been getting, and the stories in the surgical lounge. This video isn't going to help!"

"Oh, I think it will," responded Elliott. "It could do them a lot of good to see this. Might even stop some of the rumors and replace them with facts."

Unconvinced, and with the strain still showing in her features, the nurse agreed reluctantly. "Okay, doctor, I'll set that tape aside. It'll be there anytime you want it."

"Now, about the patient," added Elliott, "I think we're going to see a remarkable recovery from this point on."

Out of the Darkness

When Ken awakened about eight o'clock the next morning, he felt as though he were ascending slowly out of a dark pit. Mercifully, the mocking voices and hideous images seemed more memory than reality and faded away as the room in which he found himself came steadily into clearer focus. The sun was slanting in through a large window to his left. Its welcome rays were glinting from a metallic apparatus standing just to the right of his bed. He had difficulty turning his head far enough to see it clearly, but the realization slowly dawned that it was an intravenous pump—and that it was connected to *him*.

I'm in the hospital! The thought seemed impossible to connect with himself. *How did I get here? What happened?* He had a vague recollection of leaving his lab and driving his car somewhere, but beyond that everything was blank no matter how he struggled to remember. In utter exhaustion he gave up trying to understand for the moment and just lay there staring at the ceiling and trying to get back in touch with his body. A dull, throbbing pain seemed to envelop him. He could move his right arm—the one with the IV in it—but his left arm and right leg seemed to be weighted down. Lifting his head up slightly with great effort, he could see that those limbs were encased in casts.

Ken became aware that someone was moving around near the head of his bed, just out of his line of vision. "So you're awake!" said a pleasant feminine voice. "How do you feel this morning?"

"I'm trying to figure that out. I'm not sure this is really *me*. How did I get in here?"

"I'm afraid your car went over a cliff. You were more dead than alive when they brought you in." Now the nurse came into view and stood there looking at him with obvious empathy.

"A cliff? Really? I don't remember being near any cliffs!" Ken tried to adjust his position and groaned at the pain. "Was anybody with me . . . anybody else hurt?"

"No, I don't think so."

"When did it happen?"

"This is your fourth day in here—and the first time you've been conscious. You don't know how lucky you are! You've improved so much in the last ten hours. It's just incredible! I'm going to slow the IV and see if you can take some clear fluids. The doctor's moving you along as fast as you can go."

The nurse reached for the controls. "I'm going to raise your head up a bit. There. Now let's see how this goes down."

It was painful swallowing at first. After several swallows, however, the pleasant liquid with a slight lemon taste went down smoothly and seemed to soothe his throat. He managed most of the glass, then lay back exhausted. As he dozed off, he heard the nurse's voice drifting through a fog: "I'll be back soon. We're going to move you out of intensive care to another room."

"How's the miracle patient doing today?" At the sound of the enthusiastic voice, Ken turned his head painfully to see a white-garbed physician bursting exuberantly into his room. The lean, energetic man—looking much younger than his 56 years—seemed to take in Ken's entire situation at a glance. It was obvious that he was pleased, very pleased, with what he saw.

"Doing? I'm plotting my escape—that's what I'm doing," retorted Ken, managing a wry smile. He was propped up in bed and drinking from a glass of water that he was holding with his one good hand. "When do I get out of here? And what do you mean by *miracle*?"

"Well, you *are* on the mend! There's no better medicine than a good sense of humor," said the doctor, ignoring his questions for the moment. "I can see we're going to have to tie you down!" Elliott stood there for a moment grinning at his patient approvingly. At last he said quietly, "A *miracle*, my friend, is something that only God can do—and you're it!"

The tall, wiry figure bent over the hospital bed to lay a hand gently on Ken's good shoulder. "By the way, I'm Dr. Harold Elliott. You can call me Hal. I'm the director of Trauma Surgery. My assistant and I tried to put you back together the other day."

"Were you able to do it?" asked Ken, eyeing with interest the tousled black hair with streaks of gray and the intense but kindly face so near his own. He glanced at his pain-racked body. "It looks like you had a lot of mending to do. Seriously, doctor, what's the, uh . . . prognosis?"

"Yesterday—practically hopeless. Today—excellent. Complete recovery. And that, my friend, is one of the biggest miracles I've ever seen!"

"Boy, are you ever hung up on 'miracles'! The luck of the Irish is what I'd call it."

Elliott let out a short, good-natured laugh. "The 'luck of the Irish' wouldn't even come close to what you needed! And you can't argue with me, because you weren't even conscious and don't know what happened. And that's what we've got to work on a bit. Starting from right now and going back in time, tell me what you can recall."

"*Touche*—end of discussion. Bing, bing, bing. You're not a doctor, you're a bulldozer." Ken decided he was going to like Elliott. "What do I recall? Well, it hasn't been exactly what you'd call partying it up—just average, run-of-the-mill hospital fun and games." His eyes met Elliott's, and they both laughed. The resultant pain brought a sharp moan from Ken. "The nurse just took my IV out and moved me in here from wherever I used to be . . . and promised me something a bit more solid for lunch. She said I'd run my car over a cliff. . . . "

"Do you remember that?" Elliott interrupted.

"I've tried, but so far—well, I—I can't remember any of it. Do I have amnesia?"

"Hardly. You told the nurse your name and address this morning. Temporary loss of a small time segment. Nothing to worry about. What you and your car went through was horrific and just as well forgotten, but that's not the worst of it. What's the last thing you remember before it all goes blank?"

Ken shook his head slowly. "Well, I remember driving somewhere in the coastal range, but it's vague. I don't know whether it led up to this accident, or whether I'm just remembering something earlier. I used to drive up there a lot."

"It'll help if you try to think where you were when you got into your car."

"I was trying to remember that when you walked in. I think I was at the lab with my associate. And I don't have a good feeling about whatever happened there, but I don't know why—and I'm sure it's irrelevant."

"Irrelevant? You think so?" Elliott's tone became very serious. "That's what put you in here! If you hadn't gotten involved in psychic research you wouldn't be lying in that bed."

"Doctor, with all due respect, you don't know what you're talking about."

"As a matter of fact, I do. Your associate, Frank Leighton, called the hospital yesterday, concerned about your condition. Insisted on talking to me. You were still in a coma. Said he'd been involved with you in psychic research. When I asked him about contact with spirit entities, he tried to change the subject."

"Why would you ask *that*?"

"You know why. Anyone as deeply involved as you've been with either drugs, mysticism, or psychic phenomena—and you've been into all three—is bound to have made contact with spirit entities."

Ken smiled wearily, and there was now a new respect for Elliott in his voice. "So you do know a bit about my field."

"You've been playing with fire for a long time," said Elliott. "I've followed your research and exploits in the papers—and you finally got badly burned. What I want to know is how much you remember about trying to contact so-called 'highly evolved' extraterrestrial intelligences."

"I think you're playing games with me," responded Ken testily, suddenly wary of Elliott. "Frank wouldn't give out information about our research."

"I'm not trying to get at your secrets," said Elliott. "I'm trying to help you remember what happened when you made this 'contact.' It's very important."

Ken hesitated for a moment. "Okay," he said at last, "but I'm going to chew Frank out for this. Yes, we were trying to make contact, and all I can remember is . . . there were these voices in my head. Not like my own thoughts, but from somewhere else . . . and audible! It's hard to explain." He fell silent.

"Leighton didn't tell me," said Elliott matter-of-factly.

Ken stared at him. "Then how did you find out? And why did you say my research put me in here. Why?" His eyes pleaded for an explanation.

Dr. Elliott's belt pager was beeping. He said a few words into his cell phone then turned back to Ken.

"Excuse me," said Elliott, "I've got some other patients to see. And, anyway, you need to get some rest before we talk anymore."

"I'm not letting you off the hook, Doctor. You made some pretty strong statements that I want clarified—okay?"

"You can count on it. I'll get back here this afternoon, and then we'll talk some more. In the meantime, have a good sleep!"

Living Proof

When Dr. Elliott returned a few hours later, he was accompanied by a woman who was apparently not a nurse—at least she wasn't in uniform. The doctor closed the door behind them. Then he pulled up two chairs and they both sat down next to the bed.

"Ken," he said to the patient, "I want you to meet my wife, Karen. She works with me on cases like yours."

"You are a nurse, then?" Ken liked her immediately. She exuded the same warmth and the same quiet confidence as Elliott—and her smile was contagious.

"I'm an RN—long retired," she responded. "But I don't get involved with Hal's medical work anymore—only special cases like yours."

Ken looked from one to the other questioningly. Then he glanced at his aching body. "It looks pretty medical to me."

"It's a whole lot *more* than medical, Ken," declared Elliott. "Medically—well, you should be dead. God had His hand on you, that's for sure. Otherwise you wouldn't have survived."

"Look, Doc, with all due respect, as I already said, I'd rather you keep *God* out of this."

"You sound a lot like your fiancee."

"Carla! You've met her?"

"Once—briefly," said Hal.

"I've been asking the nurses where she is."

"She's been in and out several times, but you were still in a coma. They've been trying all day to reach her to let her know you're conscious—just got her a few minutes ago. She's on her way over."

"It'll be great to see her! We're getting married next month," announced Ken proudly.

"Congratulations!" said Karen.

"Now look," said Ken, turning to Elliott, "you seemed to know some stuff you shouldn't have, and you said my psychic research landed me in here."

Dr. Elliott nodded. He leaned over from where he was sitting beside the bed and put his hand gently on Ken's shoulder. "This isn't going to be easy for either of us, but you have to know."

Seeing the apprehension in Ken's eyes, Elliott hastened to add, "It has nothing to do with your prognosis." Ken looked immediately relieved, and Elliott continued. "The duty nurse called me last night. You were in a coma, yet you were emitting strange voices and you were writhing on the bed. Karen and I and several nurses all witnessed it." He paused.

"So what was going on?" asked Ken.

"There's no easy way to tell you this," said Elliott solemnly, "so I'll just be blunt. You were demon-possessed."

Ken was indignant. "Come on—I don't even believe in demons!"

"You don't have to believe in cholera for it to kill you," put in Karen quickly.

"You're mixing metaphors," retorted Ken. "You can identify cholera germs."

"You can also identify demons," countered Hal. "There isn't time to beat around the bush. Human beings don't have psychic power—it's demonic—and your involvement in it nearly got you killed."

"Wait a minute!" protested Ken. "I'll bow to your expertise in *medicine*, but I resent it when you try to straighten me out on *psychic research* as well. Isn't this a little out of your field?"

"Not at all," returned Hal quickly. "I grew up in Ceylon and spent much of my life in Africa. I've done a lot of psychic research both overseas and in America, and I can tell you there's no difference between what Western parapsychologists are trying to reproduce 'scientifically' in their laboratories, and what's been going on in the Third World in dark seance rooms and primitive jungle huts for thousands of years."

"That doesn't prove *demons* are behind it," said Ken firmly.

"We've proved it many times," interjected Karen. "In *every* case when we cast out the demons the so-called psychic powers ended. And we've faced witch doctors with powers that would dazzle Western parapsychologists."

"That would scare them to death!" added Elliott.

"It's not *demons* you're casting out," said Ken, "it's just that your brand of dogmatic fundamentalism is so negative that it destroys the positive atmosphere needed for psychic power to manifest itself!"

"That doesn't speak too well for psychics, then, does it," quipped Karen, "if false suggestions from 'dogmatic fundamentalists' can strip them of their powers!"

A faint smile on Ken's lips acknowledged that the point was well-made. "You said I was possessed with demons . . . and you knew I'd tried to make contact with extraterrestrials. . . . "

"We have a prayer meeting in our home," began Elliott, "and you were our main focus last night for several hours."

"So you prayed," Ken interrupted impatiently, "I woke up from the coma, and you call it a 'miracle'—and throw in the 'demons' as a bonus. Is that it?"

"Not quite," said Elliott. "The charge nurse called me in the middle of our prayer meeting, told me about the voices coming out of you—and that you were moving while in a coma. Karen and I came right over while about 30 people in our home kept praying for you. When we got here, the voices claimed you belonged to them. They were in the process of destroying you."

"*They?*" asked Ken apprehensively. "Who are *they*?"

"They called themselves 'the Nine.'"

"The *Nine?*" The color drained from Ken's face. He closed his eyes and winced with pain as memories surfaced, unbidden and horrible.

Elliott waited patiently. Finally Ken said weakly, "Go ahead. I'm listening."

"You wondered how I knew you'd tried to contact 'highly evolved' extraterrestrials," continued Elliott. "When we commanded 'the Nine,' in the Name of Jesus Christ, to tell us how they had taken possession of you, they confessed they'd pretended to be ETIs ... and said you'd fallen for it."

"They really said that?" He looked stricken, like someone who had just been robbed or was watching a fire consume his house and all of his possessions.

Dr. Elliott nodded soberly. "It's the perfect scam that the whole scientific community is being set up to fall for. Maybe your experience will serve as a warning."

"It's not a scam," said Ken. "It makes good sense. Just imagine what it could mean if such entities would share their incredible technology and psychic secrets with us! Every human problem could be solved!"

"And you made contact?" asked Elliott politely.

"I think so, but it's vague. Something went wrong, and I tried to fight them off. I have a hazy recollection that Frank couldn't understand and was upset with me. That must be why I left the lab. It felt like they were trying to take over my mind."

"They did take over—and tried to kill you. Eyewitnesses reported that your driving was insane."

Ken shuddered. "I wish I could remember what happened." He lay there in silence, looking from Hal to Karen helplessly. "Their name," he asked at last. "How did you come up with that?"

"You know, of course, that 'the Nine' are widely known in occult circles." Ken nodded. "It's an identity demons often assume," continued Elliott. "'The Nine' are even mentioned in the Bible. But we didn't assume that was who they were. In the Name of Jesus Christ, I commanded the seducing spirits that possessed you to identify themselves."

"And they said, 'We're the Nine,' just like that?"

Dr. Elliott shook his head. "They screamed obscenities and threats—to kill you and us. Karen and I have been through this many times before. The group was praying, and we didn't back down."

Hal paused for a moment. Ken was listening intently. "Your case was unique," he continued. "And that's why it offers the kind of proof you want. Remember, you were in a coma. Vital signs very weak. Yet the veins were standing out on your neck, and loud voices—not your own—were speaking through you. It just happens that every bit of it was recorded by a TV camera over your bed in the ICU. When you're stronger, we'll put it on your TV for you—if you want to see it."

Ken was stunned. "You're not kidding me? You really have that video?"

"Absolutely."

"I've got to see it!"

"You will. It's all there: the sneering voices, the unbelievable contortions your body was going through while you were comatose. Not the least of it were the expressions your face took on—it was beyond description!"

"That could have been a purely psychological phenomenon," suggested Ken, groping for another explanation. "The 'voices' represented splits of my deep psyche, and the thrashing around was an unconscious release of psychic energy."

"Give that a little more thought, Ken," said Elliott firmly, "and you'll realize it's absurd. Why doesn't your subconscious—and everyone else's—do that sort of thing all the time? The fact is, when the last demon came out, your coma ended—that fast." Elliott snapped his fingers. "You're going to heal so rapidly now that it will boggle the entire hospital staff! You'll be written up in medical journals—and the skeptics still won't believe it."

Ken was shaking his head. "I've got to see it before I'll believe it!"

"You will, but you need some rest now."

Ken looked tired, but he desperately wanted to understand. "You don't like my theory about the unconscious or splits of the psyche, but don't you think it's a bit archaic to talk about *demons?*"

"Is love archaic?" asked Karen. "Or justice or beauty or truth? Some things never change—and good and evil, God and Satan, angels and demons are in that category."

"I could give you lots of reasons for calling them demons," added Hal. "But you desperately need to sleep. For one thing, they admit that's who they are. And they cry out in rage, then fear, when they're confronted with the authority of Jesus Christ . . . then they grudgingly obey. You'll see it all for yourself. Then you can decide."

Dr. Elliott and his wife stood up to leave. "We've stayed too long. You get some sleep."

"Yeah, I will," sighed Ken wearily.

Hal patted him affectionately on the arm. "We'll be back tonight with that video."

Ken's eyelids drooped and closed as he fought to stay awake to ponder the shattering pronouncements of these two obviously intelligent and sincere people. He would have dismissed them as fundamentalist fanatics had he not been in that hospital bed. That fact gave unwelcome credence to what they said. And the video! *I can't believe it. There's got to be another explanation. But what if they're right? What if they're right!* That unwelcome possibility hounded him to the very edge of unconsciousness.

the
MIND
INVADERS
6

Changes

I t was a still-apprehensive but very excited Carla Bertelli that the charge nurse led into Ken's room about an hour after the Elliotts had departed. They found the exhausted patient still sleeping soundly. "You may sit beside him and wait," the nurse said softly, "but be careful not to awaken him. He needs all the rest he can get."

"He's out of danger and—he's going to be okay?" Another nurse had already assured her of that, but Carla had to hear it again. It was almost too wonderful to believe.

"Oh, definitely. The doctor's very pleased."

Carla let out another sigh of relief and sank down in a chair that was right beside the bed. There was another one next to it. So he'd already had two visitors! She wondered who they could have been. Never mind. She was only too grateful to be able to sit next to the man she loved and wait, no matter how long. It had been so hopeless, but now she could allow herself to be intoxicated once again with the euphoric anticipation of the wedding they had planned with such happy excitement. The dream she had shared with Ken and that had seemed shattered only a few hours earlier was now alive again. In fact, it was less than 24 hours since she'd last visited him in intensive care and been told by the nurse that things didn't look at all good and that she should keep in touch.

When she'd come home for lunch and found the message on her answering machine to call the hospital, she'd dreaded picking the phone up and dialing. The last thing she had expected to hear was the wonderful news that he was out of danger and on his way to a very remarkable recovery. *It's really happening!* she kept reminding herself, as she turned her eyes now and then from Ken to take in the bedside table with the profusely blooming potted azalea she'd sent, the broad vista of lawn and trees through the window, the starkly modern hospital paraphernalia reminding her that he was being well cared for. *He's alive and getting well! It really is true!*

Her thoughts were interrupted by two doctors leading a group of interns, all of them dressed in green surgery garb, who suddenly marched in and gathered around to view the patient. They passed from one to another the chart showing Ken's impossibly sudden transition from an apparently hopeless coma to normal consciousness. So absorbed were they in trying to understand what they apparently regarded as a unique case, they scarcely seemed to notice her sitting in the chair beside the bed.

"I assisted Dr. Elliott when the patient was brought in from emergency," commented one of the surgeons softly. "Normal CT, fixed dilated pupils, no spontaneous respiration—more dead than alive." He hesitated, then added, "I can't tell you how surprised I am. . . . There's just no way!"

"Incredible!" said one of the interns as he looked over the chart, then let out a low whistle of astonishment.

After a brief silence the other surgeon turned to his colleague and said in a confidential tone, "I suppose you've heard that Hal's prayer group was involved, and there are rumors about an *exorcism!* I get a bit uncomfortable . . . "

Carla was hanging onto every word, but with a few more exclamations of awe interspersed with medical jargon, the doctors were gone.

The austere hospital bed, the stark furnishings of the room, the antiseptic odor faded away momentarily as Carla's memory paraded before her—vivid scenes of the delicious moments they had shared. She saw Ken once again lecturing at the University of California,

Berkeley, the night they had first met; she relived some of their weekends together; she smiled happily as she remembered how nervous he'd seemed the night he had proposed—then was ushered abruptly back to present reality when Ken moaned softly and began to stir. Suddenly he opened his eyes and was staring at the ceiling. "Darling!" she whispered, leaning over the bed to stroke his forehead.

Now he saw her. "Carla!" He could say no more.

She held his head in her hands, covering his stitched face with soft kisses. "I love you! Oh, I'm so happy, so happy you're alive!"

"I love you, Carla!" he managed to say and reached up to embrace her with his one good arm.

"They told me you're going to be fine!" Carla bubbled on ecstatically. "I never gave up. I knew you'd make it! What's the latest from the doctor?"

"He says everything's going to be okay." Carla was now standing beside him, holding his hand. He looked up at her. "It's so great to see you!" They smiled into each other's eyes, and she stooped down to kiss him again.

What if Dr. Elliott and his wife are right? Even in this rapturous moment he couldn't escape the troublesome thought that had been tormenting him. *What if they're right! How can I ever explain that to Carla? What will she think?*

"They told you what happened?" he asked. "I mean . . . isn't it incredible?"

"I can't believe it. Last night I thought you were dying—and now look at you! You've got color in your cheeks and the old sparkle in your eye!"

"I'm so glad you weren't in the car! I still don't know how it happened. I love you, darling, so very, very much! I'm sorry for what you've been through. It must have been hell. . . . "

"It was unbearable! I kept from breaking down by playing the investigative reporter—just had to find out what happened. But it never made sense." She paused. "Would you rather not think about it?"

Ken shook his head. "No, go ahead. I want to hear."

"I even talked to the truck driver. He said you were on his side of the road, and he did his best to miss you."

"I don't remember anything. The doctor thinks it may gradually come back to me."

"I hiked down and saw the car—what was left of it after they cut you out." She dug around in her purse and came out with an audio cassette. "This was in your smashed stereo deck—still in good shape." She held it up so he could see it.

"*Sweet Baby James?* That figures."

"I checked to see if it would still work," added Carla, "and it does. Are you curious at all to know where it had stopped?"

"I don't know if it means anything, but where was it?"

"Just before the end of 'Fire and Rain.'" She put the cassette on the top of the bedside table next to the flowers she'd just brought in. "We'll leave it right there—until the happy day you carry it out of here!"

He was looking at her appreciatively. "I've never known you to be so *sentimental*. I love it!"

She squeezed his hand. "Darling, it's more than sentiment. If you saw what was left of your Mercedes, you'd know why I had to hold onto something for hope. There's no way you could have survived."

Ken looked suddenly troubled and bewildered.

"I'm sorry, darling," said Carla. "I shouldn't have mentioned that."

"No, that's okay. It just bothers me that I don't remember any of it. I've got to know what happened—how it happened."

"You were driving like a maniac, the reports said. Of course, you always did, but at least you were a safe maniac." She brushed some strands of stray hair back from his forehead. "From what the highway patrol told me of eyewitness reports, this time your driving was completely insane. I just don't understand it."

"That fits," sighed Ken reluctantly.

"Fits what?"

"What Dr. Elliott said."

"Well, what did he say?"

"I need to think about it some more."

"Darling?" She was frowning. "He's that praying surgeon. It's so unprofessional to mix medicine with religion. It's like he thinks prayer could actually make a difference. He even told *me* to pray! I felt like saying, 'Come on, Doc, get into the twentieth century!' A group of doctors was just in here while you were asleep, and some of them don't like his approach, either."

"Did they say so?"

"I got that impression."

"Why were they here?"

"They were checking you out like some rare specimen—really boggled by your sudden recovery. Called it impossible."

"So Elliott was right. He said the whole hospital staff would be coming in to see me and that I'd be written up in medical journals."

Carla was frowning. "They said something about an *exorcism*. Ken, did that doctor go through some hocus-pocus?"

"Is that story going around the hospital? I'm really upset!" declared Ken angrily.

"Well, look at that! Am I dreaming, or has the world's greatest electronic genius really come back from the dead?" It was Professor Leighton's booming voice coming from just inside the door.

"Frank!" exclaimed Ken. "Come on in! Now we've got the best man and the bride. All we need is a preacher."

"A judge," corrected Carla. "It would be wonderful, but honeymooning with a plaster man in traction isn't exactly what I was anticipating. I can wait a little longer. How long will it be?"

"The doctor didn't say *how* long . . . but he said I would be out of here a lot faster than anyone could imagine."

"Look, I don't want to barge in on you two. . . . " Leighton was starting to back away.

"That's okay, Frank." Ken looked questioningly at Carla, and she nodded her assent.

Leighton was clearly excited as he approached the bed. "I've got a lot to tell you, Ken! But I can come back."

Ken looked at Carla again. "No, it's okay. It's good to see you."

Leighton hesitated. "There've been some incredible developments in just the last two days. We've established solid contact."

"You've *what*?"

"I couldn't wait, Ken! You were in a coma, and they didn't give you much hope. . . . "

"You did that all *alone?*"

"I brought someone in—someone I've known about for several years."

"*I* brought *you* in, and now without even consulting me—"

"I couldn't consult you!"

"Who is it?"

"If you're worrying about leaks, forget it. He's a Jesuit. A *priest.* Nobody keeps secrets better—you know, the confessional and all that. So don't worry. And he's the best natural psychic I've ever seen. You won't believe what happened the first time I hooked him up on the 'launching pad'!"

"Frank, I've got to talk to you about that. There are some dangers that I think we have to go over and work out before we go ahead with any more research."

"We can't hold up, Ken! It's urgent. Every day counts! We think the Russians could be on the verge of a similar breakthrough."

"The *who?* What in the world do the Russians have to do with this? And where did you get that kind of information?"

Frank looked uncomfortable. "We've got to talk—alone. I'll come back tomorrow. You'll be feeling stronger."

"Yeah, we may really have something to talk about after I see a certain video that you and Carla have to watch, too."

"A video?" they both asked at once.

"I'm sorry, but you'll have to leave now." A nurse had entered the room and was motioning the two visitors toward the door. "I really let you overstay."

Carla gave him a long kiss. Still hovering over him, she whispered, "What's the video about?"

"I'll tell you later, sweetheart. It's too involved to get into right now . . . " he murmured, then fell once again into a deep sleep.

Dr. Elliott and his wife returned after visiting hours that evening, when they knew they wouldn't be disturbed. The doctor had an orderly connect a VCR to Ken's television. After closing the door, he inserted the cassette he'd picked up at the nurses' station.

"Now, I've got to warn you," said Elliott solemnly, "this may be more than you can handle. If it gets to be too much, I'll turn it off. You're sure you feel up to it?"

Ken gave him an accusing look. "Are you trying to talk me out of it? Is there something fishy about this tape?"

"You'll see what I mean." Dr. Elliott picked up the remote and turned it on. They watched the whole thing together—nearly an hour of intensive, and at times very frightening, spiritual warfare. Elliott had to turn it off frequently for Ken, who was seeing himself on the screen saying and doing the incredibly bizarre, to be able to handle it. Each time it was interrupted, however, Ken would insist, after gaining control of his emotions, that the video be turned on again.

When the exorcism was complete and Elliott had turned off the television, Ken lay quietly for a long time, stunned by what he'd seen. The whole thing, from beginning to end, just as Elliott had warned him, had been too much to handle—like living the plot of a horror movie. He had seen *himself* on that screen with his own eyes, heard it all with his own ears, and there was no denying what was obviously all-too-true. The voices issuing from his own mouth had sounded frighteningly familiar and had made him relive tortured memories from the lab and the car once again. What had shaken him the most, however, had been the astonishing variety of hideous expressions his face had taken on repeatedly—and while he was in a coma! At those times the feeling that something supremely evil was in control had become overwhelming—an evil so palpable that it had nauseated and repelled him. Yet, at the same time, there had been something fascinating about its abhorrent wickedness that had drawn him strongly—a perverted but almost irresistible appeal that had left him feeling ill.

The Elliotts prayed silently as they waited patiently for Ken to express himself. He made several attempts but broke down each time. When at last he was able to speak, he surprised himself by the stubbornness he expressed aloud, which was not at all what he really felt inside.

"I've seen it with my own eyes, but I still don't believe it. It challenges my whole worldview—not just mine, but the consensus of the entire scientific community. It can't be true. There's got to be another explanation."

"You wanted proof," Dr. Elliott said gently. "Let me remind you that you were in a coma, with vital signs almost nil. After showing some apparent but temporary improvement, you were sinking. Some alien beings—it couldn't have been your conscious or unconscious mind—were animating your body. You can't escape that, Ken. And if that means the scientific consensus is wrong— well, remember you're talking of *materialistic* science, and this obviously involves something outside the physical dimension."

Ken was silent again, thinking, desperately trying to find a defense for his cherished beliefs, but knowing within his own heart that there was none. *Those voices—what they say—and the way they hate and fear the Name of Jesus Christ and reluctantly submit to His authority—that can't be explained as deeper levels of my psyche, or archetypal images from the collective unconscious, or anything else I'd like to believe. Elliott's right! They're right!* The humbling thought kept hammering at him. *I can't believe it! It can't be true! I've got to know what Frank and Carla think. They've got to see this. But what other explanation is there?*

"Come on, Ken!" chided Elliott. "You're a scientist. So why not face the facts? You saw it with your own eyes. The entities you made contact with in your lab possessed and tried to kill you. Why is it so hard to admit they might have been demons?"

"I don't know," said Ken wearily. "It's just that it undermines everything . . . " After a long, painful silence, "Okay, supposing I go along with your scenario, Doctor. So what's their game plan?"

"Deception, destruction," said Karen, "but all under the guise of helping mankind establish a New Age of peace, love, and brotherhood."

"And the Name of Jesus—why does that silence them and force them to obey?"

"We're rebels, Ken," said Elliott quietly. "We want to be our own gods, just like Satan, and that brings us under his power. The penalty is separation from our Creator forever. But He loves us so much that He became a man to pay the sentence His own justice demanded. In dying for our sins and resurrecting from the dead,

Jesus Christ put an end to Satan's power. Forgiveness and deliverance is available as a free gift of God's grace to all who willingly repent and accept His death upon the cross as the penalty for their sin."

"You couldn't have gotten me to listen five seconds to what you've just said if I hadn't gone through this hideous experience and seen that video for myself." Ken seemed almost persuaded. He looked at Hal and Karen earnestly. "Frank has to see it—and Carla. I want to know what they think. Can I borrow it?"

"Of course." Hal slid open the drawer beside the bed and dropped the tape in. "I'm putting it right here. It belongs to the hospital, so tell them they can make copies if they want to, but I have to have the original back again."

"You're worried about Frank and Carla," said Karen solemnly. "What about yourself? What are you going to do with Jesus? 'The Nine' won't let you go this easily. You need His protection."

Ken hesitated. They could see the inner conflict mirrored in his eyes. "I guess you can tell, whether I admit it or not," he confessed at last, "that you've shaken me." He closed his eyes wearily and lapsed into painful silence again.

I can't, just like that, throw out beliefs I've spent a lifetime building—and I'm not going to. I can't deny that tape, and what they say about Jesus makes a lot of sense, but still . . . With great effort Ken opened his eyes and turned to the Elliotts. "You can't imagine how hard it is even to admit as much as I have. I've got some big decisions to make, but I'd like to know what Carla and Frank think. . . . " He was fading.

"Sure, Ken, sure," said Elliott. "We'll see you tomorrow."

A CIA Operation?

I'm not happy about this, Frank. Not a bit!" said Ken for the third time.

The morning sun was streaming through the open window. Ken had been enjoying the sound of the birds outside and the scent of fresh-cut grass—and feeling ravenously hungry and impatient for breakfast. Suddenly Frank had been standing beside his bed. He'd gotten permission from the RN on duty to drop in early before visiting hours. An emergency had affected Ken's business, he'd told her, and he'd promised to take only five minutes—ten at the most.

"There's nothing to worry about," responded Frank again, reassuringly. He pulled over a chair next to the bed and sat down. "I told you Del Sasso's a Jesuit—a *priest*—and you know, they're . . . uh, trained to keep secrets. I trust him completely."

"That's not what I'm worried about. I want that research stopped—at least for now. It's *dangerous*. Look what happened to me!"

"You had an accident, Ken, that's all. It could have happened to anyone. Maybe you fell asleep?"

"I don't fall asleep at the wheel—and certainly not at five in the afternoon. Come on, Frank! Do you know what the eyewitnesses said about my driving?"

"I haven't heard."

"I was driving like a maniac. I don't do that! I don't take chances on blind curves, drive on the wrong side of the road. . . . There's a connection, but I can't prove it because I don't have any memory of what happened. What state of mind was I in when I left the lab that day?"

Frank seemed embarrassed by the question. He stood up and stared out the window for a moment. At last he admitted, "You were very upset. You'd had a bad time in trance. I should have kept you there until you calmed down, but I had no way of knowing this would happen."

"I don't think we should carry on any more experimentation—at least not for now, under these circumstances!"

"It's so out of character for you to say that! This was your magnificent obsession! Ken, Del Sasso has established a permanent contact. We're moving forward. This partnership with 'the Nine' will accomplish everything you've dreamed of and more!"

"Partnership? They tried to kill me!"

"That's a wild statement, Ken. I don't understand this sudden negativism. It's not like you at all. Del Sasso had some problems, too, at first. The entities told us to cut the power under the platform. The electromagnetic emanations were putting the brain hemispheres out of sync."

"I don't buy that. They were trying to take over my mind."

"You've become obsessed with that delusion."

"It's no delusion. Look at me! That's why I'm here!"

Frank began to pace back and forth in growing agitation. "We could argue about that, and it wouldn't prove anything. The simple fact is that when we followed the Archons' directions and cut the power, Del Sasso tuned right in. That was the one flaw in your design."

"I built that equipment, and I don't want it used until I get out of here and have checked it over myself and am satisfied that it isn't the doorway to—well, demonic possession!"

Frank stopped beside the bed and stared down at Ken in astonishment. "Are you out of your mind? Where did you get such a ridiculous idea? Since when did you believe in *demons*?"

"I'm not saying I believe in them. I'm only throwing that out as a hypothesis that we can't afford to overlook."

Frank made no attempt to hide his exasperation. "You keep talking like that, Ken, and I'll have to put you in a psychiatric hospital for treatment! You sound like you got some wires crossed—and jumped the track!"

Their eyes met and what Ken saw frightened him. *I think you just might do it.* The thought was terrifying. *I'm lying here helpless! I never knew how vulnerable a person could be—completely at the mercy of the shrinks who set the criteria for "sanity" in society.*

Frank's voice brought him back from theoretical possibilities to present reality. "Look, Ken, we have to come to an understanding. You've had one goal in mind, but from the very beginning I've seen a different potential. This research is absolutely vital to the defense of the Western world. Stopping it would be an act of sabotage—treason against our country! If the Russians get this power first . . . "

"You're paranoid about the Russians! The cold war ended years ago. Maybe 'the Nine' you've joined in partnership with are the ones you ought to be worried about!" *Shall I give it to him? Will it just give him more reason to say I'm insane?* After a long silence, Ken pointed to the bedside table. "There's a videocassette in that drawer. I'd like you to watch it and tell me what you think."

"I'm sorry, Dr. Leighton. You'll have to leave now. I've given you 11 minutes. The patient is exhausted." Leighton wondered how long the nurse had been standing just behind him and what she'd heard.

He opened the drawer in the bedside table and took out the videocassette. "I'll watch it," promised Leighton, waving the tape as he headed for the door. Ken had already dozed off again.

"I'm sorry, Miss Bertelli, he's just had lunch and he's taking a much-needed rest." The nurse in charge had seen Carla heading directly toward Ken's room and had hurried over to cut her off. "You'll have to wait in the lounge down the hall until he awakens. I'll call you."

"But yesterday," Carla protested, "they let me go into his room and sit there until he woke up." The nurse's stern expression didn't change. "I won't make a sound," pleaded Carla. "I want him to get his sleep as much as you do."

"I can't vouch for what someone let you do yesterday," said the nurse in an antiseptic tone. She seemed as unbending as her stiffly starched uniform. "Dr. Inman's visiting schedule has gotten completely out of hand, and we have to restore a semblance of order. The man was practically dead 36 hours ago, you know. This is a hospital, not Grand Central Station."

"You've really got a grouch on duty today," Carla told Ken when he had awakened and she was finally allowed into his room. "She says it's getting to be like Grand Central Station around here. How come everyone else gets in and I have to wait? Who's been here?"

"Only Frank that I know of—and Dr. Elliott, of course. Maybe she's upset because Frank talked her into letting him come in to see me before breakfast."

"Why was Frank in here so early? Was there something that important?"

"Not really. He wanted to tell me what was going on—and I wasn't happy about it. I don't want any more research going on until I get out of here. He made a sort of guarded threat to have me committed to a psycho ward."

Carla was furious. "That doesn't surprise me! I've gotten some information about Frank that makes me suspect his motives. Did he ever tell you that he'd been with the CIA?"

"No, but there are probably lots of things about him that he's never told me. It must have been a long time ago—he's been at Stanford for nearly 20 years."

"As I started to tell you yesterday before they threw me out, I've been doing some investigating," said Carla. "Just imagine what was going on inside of me—wondering *why* you were driving on the wrong side of the highway in the path of a logging truck. Frank wouldn't cooperate. He stonewalled me—very politely, but very firmly. Protecting secret research is one thing, but it was more than that."

"He's brought in a psychic to work with *my* invention. He thinks he's competing with the Russians."

"I heard him mention the Russians yesterday. That fits perfectly with what I found out! Listen to this! I wasn't going to let Frank sweet-talk me. I had to know what was going on over there with you in the hospital. So, on a hunch, I used some connections and got a listing of the phone calls from your lab during the time you haven't been there. At 4:10 in the afternoon on the day of your accident—it must have been shortly after you left—he placed a call to Langley, Virginia, and there have been quite a few since."

"Langley? CIA headquarters?"

"Exactly. So I did some more digging—through some of my friends at *The Washington Post*. I found out that he wasn't just someone with casual ties—an informant, perhaps—but a graduate in the mid-fifties of the CIA's 'West Point' near Williamsburg. 'The Farm,' as they called it, involved covert action training. The guy's been seriously involved for years, Ken—and obviously he still is!"

"*Maybe*. Not *obviously*. Past involvement years ago, okay—but some phone calls . . . that's no proof. I just don't see Frank as a CIA agent."

"You're not supposed to. The best agents are the ones no one would ever suspect."

"But parapsychology? It doesn't fit."

"What do you mean 'it doesn't fit'? Darling, you know the CIA's interest in psychic research."

"Well, there have been some published reports, but I've never known how true they were to the actual facts."

"Don't be naive! Frank knows—you can be sure. And I think that's why he got involved with you in the first place."

"But he's been teaching at Stanford all this time," protested Ken. "And working with me. I've never seen anything, as long as I've known Frank, to indicate he was involved in some clandestine activity on the side."

"Shall I remind you where Stanford is located?" Carla persisted. "Right next to Silicon Valley, with one of the heaviest concentrations of foreign agents in the country. I don't think his duties at Stanford would inhibit—rather they'd probably enhance—whatever role he's been playing with the CIA."

"You've been reading too many spy novels, sweetheart," laughed Ken. Even as he said it, however, he remembered wondering why it had been so easy to persuade Frank to join him. In fact, now that he thought about it, Frank had initiated the idea, but that hadn't seemed significant at the time.

Leighton was back early that evening. A different nurse was on duty and he didn't have any trouble getting in for his usual "five minutes, ten at the most." Ken was awake, feeling somewhat stronger and trying to sort out some hard decisions, going back over what he'd seen on that terrifying video. What had Frank thought of it? What would Carla's reaction be when she saw it? Then suddenly Leighton came barging into the room and unceremoniously interrupted his private thoughts without so much as a solicitous "How are you doing?" or a polite "Good evening."

Leighton seemed in a hurry and didn't pull up the usual chair to sit down. "Was this some kind of joke?" he asked, waving the videocassette at Ken and then tossing it on the table beside the bed.

"What do you mean?"

"It's blank. Nothing."

"Frank, I don't know what kind of game you're playing, but that's unacceptable."

"I'm telling you it was a blank tape."

"And I'm telling you it wasn't when you took it out of here. It belongs to the hospital, and it was a very important tape to me, too. I want it back."

"I just gave it to you. You can check it out yourself."

Frustrated anger that Ken had suppressed for so long now came to the surface suddenly. "Whatever you're up to, you didn't have to wipe out that tape!"

"I know you've been through a terrible ordeal." The response came back clinical and sympathetic. "You're not yourself, Ken. That's clear enough from the trouble we've had communicating since you came out of your coma. I don't want to overstay and tire you further." He pulled an envelope out of his inside coat pocket and put it on the table beside the tape. "You'll want your lawyer to look this over. It's a contract for the purchase of all of the equipment in the lab, including any patents and all rights of any kind, for $1.3 million. I think that's a fair price. There's a cashier's check for that amount. I'd like to pick up the signed contract tomorrow evening."

Ken was stunned. "Where did you get that kind of money? Is the CIA involved in this?"

"I've made some lucky investments. Look, Ken. You want to put everything on hold, and I want to proceed. We're at a stage where it's urgent and vital to go ahead without any interruption. If you feel like getting back in when you're fully recovered and your old self once again, nothing would please me more. I took the liberty of notifying both your CPA and attorney. They each have a copy of the contract and will be stopping by first thing in the morning. In the meantime, get some rest, old buddy, and take care."

"So this *is* a CIA operation, and if I don't agree to their terms they've got their ways. Is that it?"

Frank was already walking out the door.

the
MIND
INVADERS
8

At the Crossroads

D o you have another copy of the tape?" asked Ken anxiously the moment Dr. Elliott and his wife stepped inside his room later that evening.

"Is there a problem?" asked Elliott, instantly apprehensive.

"Is that the tape you gave me?" Ken nodded toward the side table.

"Why, yes," began Hal, picking it up and examining it. "It certainly looks like it. There's the hospital label. Why? What's wrong?"

"Leighton says it's blank." Ken's eyes told the story.

"There's one way to find out," said Elliott. He took the tape and hurried from the room. When he returned a few minutes later he looked grim. He handed the cassette to Karen. "Somebody's erased it!" he said angrily.

"I loaned it to Leighton. I never dreamed . . ." Ken looked stricken. "I should have known."

"Don't berate yourself," said Hal. "We never let the original out of the hospital without making a copy, and I slipped up." He turned to his wife and shrugged helplessly. "I can't believe it! If there was ever a tape I wanted the Committee to see . . . "

"It's another one of those lessons we keep learning," said Karen solemnly. "We're in a spiritual battle, and we let our guard down."

"I wanted Carla to see that video!" Ken's voice shook. "If she could have seen it herself it might have persuaded her."

"Does that mean *you're* persuaded?" asked Karen hopefully.

"I'm persuaded that what I saw on that video was—well, genuine. As for what it ultimately means, I—uh—I'm still thinking about that. I wanted Carla's reaction to it—and Frank's."

"The whole group's praying for Carla," said Hal. "And for you. 'The Nine' aren't going to let you go without a fight—in fact, we suspect something's going on that involves much more than just you and your presumed 'accident.'"

"What do you mean?"

Hal pulled up a chair next to Karen's and sat down. "Look, Ken, I'm not trying to build a case, but the New Testament warns about increasing demonic activity in the 'last days' just before Christ returns—involving seemingly supernatural powers—to set up the world for the Antichrist."

Ken rolled his eyes. "*Last days? Antichrist?* I would have laughed you right out of here the day before yesterday. Of course I couldn't laugh then—and would have been dead if you hadn't cast those demons—yeah, that's what I think they were—out of me. But *Antichrist?*"

Karen looked at him sympathetically. "I understand. But did it ever occur to you that this device you invented—the one 'the Nine' used to possess you—could be just the thing for Satan to use to deceive the whole world?"

"Are you kidding?" protested Ken. "Don't you think you're getting a bit melodramatic?"

Hal dug around in the drawer of the nightstand next to Ken's bed and took out a Gideon Bible. "This isn't my own idea or someone's speculation, Ken. Here's what the Bible has said for the past 2000 years. Listen to this: 'Now the Spirit speaketh expressly that in the last days some shall depart from the faith, giving heed to seducing spirits and doctrines of devils.' That's 1 Timothy 4:1." He pulled his chair closer to the bed and held the Bible in front of Ken so that he could see it for himself.

"Now listen to what Jesus said," continued Hal, "in Matthew 24, when His disciples asked Him what signs would mark the last days before His return: 'Take heed that no man deceive you.... For there shall arise false Christs, and false prophets, and shall show great signs and wonders; insomuch that, if it were possible, they shall deceive the very elect.'" He turned the pages to another passage. "Look at this. Here in 2 Thessalonians chapter 2 the Apostle Paul also warned about deception in the last days. Concerning the Antichrist, he wrote: 'And then shall that Wicked be revealed . . . whose coming is after the working of Satan with all power and signs and lying wonders.'"

Dr. Elliott closed the Bible and put it on top of the nightstand. "Those are only some of the prophecies about the 'last days.' In Revelation 13, the Apostle John even warned that ultimately the whole world would worship the Antichrist—and Satan as well, who will give him his seemingly supernatural power."

"That's incredible stuff—way out of my league," said Ken. "It sounds like science fiction. I never read the Bible in my life."

"Why not broaden your education a bit?" Karen challenged him. "You can't dismiss the Bible on hearsay without reading it— or because it challenges some of your 'scientific' ideas."

Ken was quiet. At last he said, "I feel so helpless just lying here. Leighton's been carrying on the research without me—claims he's established contact with 'the Nine' and is working in partnership with them to save the world. Almost sounds like what you just read."

"Ken, he may not have wiped out that video," suggested Hal. "*They* may have done it. He could be completely under their power."

"I don't want anything to do with entities that tried to kill me. I told Frank to hold up on the research until we can be certain what's really going on. But he refuses, even though I'm the one who designed and built the equipment and the lab. He says it's urgent to keep ahead of the Russians." Ken pointed wearily to the envelope Leighton had dropped on the table beside his bed. "In there's a contract and a cashier's check Frank left to buy the lab from me for $1.3 million! What should I do?"

Hal and Karen exchanged astonished glances. "I'll call the group, and we'll have special prayer about this," said Hal. "Does Leighton have that kind of money?"

"No. And this is too fast to get a group of investors to put it up. Carla thinks the CIA is backing him, that he's been working for them all along."

"That makes sense," agreed Hal. "It's pretty common knowledge that the Russians—like the Soviets—have been involved in psychic research—presumably far ahead of us. So I can understand Leighton's urgency and the CIA's involvement."

"But if all psychic power is demonic like you claim it is," queried Ken, "then does it really make sense? I mean, would demons give help to both the Russians and Americans—against each other?"

"Why not?" responded Hal. He stood up and looked out the window at the expansive lawn rimmed with shrubs and flowers softly illuminated by colored floodlights, then to the glaring artificial brightness of the parking lot, and the darkness beyond. "Out there in the 'real' world, that's the way it works. International bankers back all sides in every war. They don't care who wins, so long as everyone remains dependent upon their finances. Why would a 'psychic war' be any different? Satan could care less—so long as he retains control."

There was a long silence. At last Ken suggested, "But even the international bankers don't want to destroy the whole world—that would put them out of business. I thought they wanted a one world government for their own selfish reasons."

"That's true," agreed Hal. "And that's what the Bible says Satan will attempt through the Antichrist—to bring peace and prosperity under a new world order to prove that mankind can make it on its own. If we really are in the last days, then there will be a push for worldwide unity—peace, love, and brotherhood. The Russians and Americans are going to have to come together—along with the Chinese and everyone else."

Ken's expression had changed from skepticism to concern. He shook his head wearily. "You've really got me confused. I don't want to believe any of it. It's like a nightmare." Then he added, "I care about Frank a lot—in spite of the way he's obviously taking advantage of my being out of the picture right now. I'm sure he believes he's doing what's right."

"You may be too generous with Leighton," suggested Dr. Elliott solemnly. "He impresses me as someone who's hungry for power, and that sets him up for any lie that promises it. Truth has to be more important than anything else, and we're going to be praying that you'll pursue it with your whole heart."

"Dr. Elliott has scheduled you to start physical therapy today," said the nurse cheerfully when she came in to take Ken's temperature and a blood sample first thing the next morning. "Do you feel up to it?"

"Do I feel up to it? Are you kidding? I want to get out of here! Nothing personal, you understand. When do we start?"

"They'll come and get you about 9:30. You want your usual disgustingly healthy breakfast this morning?"

"You got it. I eat that 365 days out of the year. That's what keeps me in such good shape that I have to get banged up now and then and go into a hospital just to bring me back down to normal."

Ken had no sooner finished his breakfast when a nurse ushered in his lawyer, Phil Gold. Moments later, Gordon Stuart—his CPA—walked in.

"We've both studied the contract," Gold assured him. "It's all legal and in order if you want to accept it. That's up to you. I have no idea whether $1.3 million is a fair offer or whether you want to sell at any price."

"Your tax base is less than $100,000," cautioned Stuart. "There are tax consequences to think of with that kind of profit. If you want to sell, there might be better ways to go about it than taking all cash."

"I don't know what I want to do but I don't want to sell it. I may want the whole thing destroyed."

They both looked at Ken as though he were out of his mind.

"Why not let Leighton take it off your hands—and pocket the cash?" suggested the lawyer. "If you don't know what to do with $1.3 million," he added with a laugh, "I could make some suggestions."

"It's too complicated to explain."

They stood up to leave. "You've got to make your own decision based upon your personal goals," said his CPA. "But from just a legal or accounting standpoint, other than some tax planning we don't see any reason to turn it down."

Carla was flabbergasted when she came in later that morning and learned of Leighton's offer. "Don't sell at any price!" she warned. Then after thinking it over, she added quickly, "There's a hot story building here!" She was obviously very excited. "I've got to get to the bottom of it. I smell the CIA. Something big is brewing. I'd like to know what the Russians are discovering. We know they've been involved in the same research."

"I don't know about the Russians, and I don't care. All I know is that Frank has made some kind of partnership with the entities that tried to kill me. That's what I'm concerned about."

"Tried to kill you?"

"Sweetheart, I was literally a man *possessed*. That's why I drove like a madman. I'm remembering pieces of it now!"

Carla looked at him sympathetically. "You were in a coma for three days. I wouldn't rely on *memory* for what you think was going on at the time of the accident."

"I've got more than memory to go on." Ken turned away. Outside, the mockingbirds were pretending they were canaries, and a gentle breeze wafted the aroma of a bouquet of spring blossoms through the open window. It was such a beautiful day. *Here I am, miraculously alive, with the woman I'm soon to marry beside me—and instead of being ecstatically happy, I'm afraid!*

He turned back to look earnestly into her face once more. "Carla, you remember when we went to see *The Exorcist*? We couldn't imagine that any intelligent person could be so gullible as to believe William Blatty's claim that it was based on a true story. We lost a lot of respect for J.B.Rhine, the 'father of American parapsychology,' when we learned that he'd investigated the case and said it was genuine. Remember?" He paused for breath and courage.

"I remember—and it scared me to death even though I knew it was nonsense." She laughed. "And you were scared, too! But what made you think of that?"

"There *is* such a thing as demon possession. I wouldn't have believed it, except that it happened to *me*."

"*Demon possession?*" Carla's eyes flashed in sudden anger. "So that's what they meant about *exorcism!* And you let Dr. Elliott—that *praying* surgeon—talk you into that? How an intelligent man can perform highly technical surgery that shows his commitment to science one minute and stoop to medieval hocus-pocus the next is beyond me!"

"He didn't talk me into it, Carla. He gave me the proof—a video of my *exorcism*."

Carla was standing now, hands on hips, indignant, ready for action. "So that's the tape you mentioned. Where is it?"

"It's right there on the table, but it's blank now. I loaned it to Frank and somehow it got erased."

"So Elliott performed *exorcism?*" The look she gave him said, *You've sure been brainwashed!*

"You think I've flipped—brain damage from blows to the head, lost it all in the coma, something like that. Sweetheart, you didn't think there was anything wrong with me until I said this."

"When did this—this *exorcism* take place? It had to be here in the hospital, and that's a violation of ethics!"

"Please, Carla. Don't get on the warpath now. You and your Irish temper!"

"Yes, I am upset—and with good reason! That a doctor would take advantage of a patient's weakened condition to push his religion is criminal!"

"Sweetheart, give me a chance to explain. It was the night the nurse called to tell you I might not make it. I wasn't in a 'weakened condition'—I was in a deep coma and sinking. Dr. Elliott and his wife came in and talked to the—call them *entities* if you don't like the word 'demons.' Commanded them in the name of Jesus Christ to come out of me. It was all recorded by a hospital video camera over my bed! I saw the whole thing—it really happened. It was horrendous!"

"So that sneaky Elliott convinced you of this," said Carla evenly, holding back the anger with great effort. "He should stick to surgery and forget the 'clergery.' He's a charlatan. He should lose his license!"

"Carla, I saw it myself! And their voices—I recognized them. They were the same ones I'd heard in the lab and in my car. They called themselves 'the Nine'—exactly the way they introduced themselves to me when I first made contact. Elliott had no way of knowing that. I heard the voices of nine separate entities. They were real!"

"Of course they were, but they weren't *demons!*" Carla reached out and took his hand and stroked his forehead. "Come on, honey, there are *scientific* explanations. You know what they are. With your conscious mind submerged in a coma, deeper levels of your psyche were released—splinters of your personality, or archetypes from the collective unconscious. Frank could give you a dozen psychological explanations. When these archetypes were suddenly integrated, you came back into the conscious level."

"My coma wasn't *psychological*. I was at death's door from physical trauma to my brain and body suffered in a horrible wreck that you yourself said I couldn't possibly have survived! What I saw and heard on that video wasn't Elliott and his wife putting me through Jungian depth analysis. They were commanding these *demons* to come out of me in the name of Jesus Christ. And they did come out! That's what healed me."

"Darling, if you buy that, you've got to take the whole package—angels and God and *Jesus Christ!*" Carla turned away and began pacing back and forth beside the bed. "You're a scientist," she continued in frustration, "and there are *laws of science* that you just don't break."

"*Laws of science*," he repeated. "I've said that a thousand times without realizing the giant ego behind it. Science doesn't *make* laws—scientists *discover* the laws that God established. We can't break them, but He can—and that's a *miracle*."

"So you *have* bought the whole package!"

"I didn't have any other choice. If only you could have seen that video!"

"That wouldn't have changed anything, Ken." She stopped pacing and stood there close to the bed looking down at him with pity. "It's so *wrong* what that doctor has done—taking advantage of your weakened condition to brainwash you! To see this happen to the man I love just kills me. Ken, darling, you know there's no God or Satan or demons. Religion is a cop-out that keeps people from taking responsibility for their lives!"

Ken shook his head. "I used to believe that, Carla, but it doesn't wash anymore. Last night I took the Bible out of that drawer. I'd heard a lot of intellectual garbage spouted against it, but I'd never read it for myself. Once I'd started, I couldn't quit until I was absolutely exhausted. I read the whole book of Mark—all about Jesus Christ, who He is, why He came, His death for our sins, and His resurrection. There's a verse in the front of this Bible that has been translated into 1100 languages. It's John 3:16."

"My mother taught it to me when I could barely talk," interjected Carla. For a moment she softened at the memory of the woman she had loved and admired almost to the point of worship—the one person who truly had lived the Christianity that her father's hypocrisy had caused her to denounce.

"I never heard it before," continued Ken eagerly. "I learned it last night. Let me see if I can still say it: 'For God so loved the world, that he gave his only begotten Son, that whosoever believeth in him should not perish, but have everlasting life.' It was the best news I'd ever heard—and I believed it."

"So did I, as a child," said Carla, "but not anymore."

"Listen to me, Carla! I can't explain it, but something happened. I found forgiveness and peace and joy like I never knew could be possible!" There were tears in his eyes.

For a long time Carla stood beside the bed and stared in stunned silence at the man she passionately loved. At last she leaned over and kissed him lightly on the lips. "You look awfully tired, honey," she said. "Get some rest, and think this thing through again when you're feeling better." Then she turned to leave. As she headed for the door, Ken heard her say under her breath, *I've got to get out of here before I explode. When I find Elliott!* . . .

A Parting of the Ways

When Dr. Elliott stopped in alone on his late-evening rounds, he found Ken cheerful in spite of the new concerns that were weighing heavily upon him. Leighton had come by earlier with his lawyer and a notary public as witnesses to certify Ken's shaky signature on the two copies of the contract. Ken was surprised that he now felt a great sense of relief. For Leighton, however, he felt an oppressive heaviness and concern. As for Carla, he knew her well enough to realize that there was little hope to salvage their relationship unless he renounced his newfound faith in Christ. That realization was almost more than Ken could bear. At the same time, however, he had a new joy that seemed to be independent of circumstances.

"I didn't have the strength to fight Frank and the CIA," Ken told Hal. "It wouldn't have done any good, anyway. While I'm laid up in here, they could copy everything I've done and build their own model. There's no way I could stop them. At least I got some cash out of the deal."

"I don't see what else you could have done," said Hal sympathetically. "Now put that behind you and leave the results in God's hands."

"That's not so easy when I feel responsible. If my invention is the means of bringing Frank—and who knows how many others—under demonic control, how can I feel good about that?"

"That device won't do it, Ken. Whatever you invented, it's not what you and Leighton think. It's not the ingenious electronics that makes the connection with 'the Nine.'"

"How can you say that?" asked Ken.

"Witch doctors have been in touch with 'spirit guides'—which is basically the same idea—for thousands of years," said Elliott dryly. "Demons have a variety of disguises designed to appeal to everyone. The 'extraterrestrial intelligence' mask is for science-fiction buffs and scientists who imagine that time plus chance could produce godlike beings out there on some planet light-years away." Elliott shook his head in dismay.

Ken paused to think it through. "When you said something like that the other day, I didn't like it, but now it makes a lot of sense that today's parapsychologists are just civilized witch doctors. I think you're right—it's the same thing under another label."

"Exactly," said Hal. "Whether they call themselves 'the Nine' or 'Ascended Masters,' or whatever, demons have perpetually been in contact with mankind through assorted yogis, witch doctors, mediums, and other shamans. So don't be racked by guilt. The device Leighton foolishly paid $1.3 million for is no better than a Ouija board or a crystal ball."

Ken looked at Hal and laughed. "You mean all my supersophisticated electronics was just window dressing—and I didn't know it?"

"Right. There are dozens of divination devices, and that's all you designed—just one more. On the other hand, 'the Nine' may have special plans for your version because it seems so scientific and sophisticated. That could be the ideal catalyst to set in motion a fulfillment of the prophecies concerning the entire world becoming deceived enough to hail the Antichrist as its savior."

Ken turned his head and stared out the window in silence. At last he looked at Hal and said, "It sounds like a science-fiction plot, but it also makes a lot of sense. I think I'm beginning to understand. It's not that the deception itself is so convincing, but that human pride is so blind. I can see why it appealed to me." Then he added somberly, "The thing that's troubling me most of all—well, you know what it is."

"I understand," said Elliott sadly. "Carla cornered me in my office this afternoon. She was livid—claimed I'd brainwashed you, vowed to report me to the hospital administration for practicing 'clergery' instead of surgery."

"She'll do it. That's Carla—you can count on it. When she decides on something, there's no turning back. I hope it doesn't affect your position here."

Dr. Elliott smiled. "She can complain all she wants. It won't matter. I haven't done anything unethical—or that I wouldn't do again. So don't worry about it." He reached out and put his hand on Ken's shoulder. "She didn't spell it out, but I got the impression she's breaking the engagement—and I feel at least partly responsible. I can't believe that I'd let a video get out of this hospital—especially one that important—without having a copy made!"

"We've been over that. She says it wouldn't have convinced her, and I'm sure that's true. You have to understand where she's coming from. She mockingly refers to herself as a p.k.—you know, a preacher's kid. Her father is still a pastor of a *huge* church, but from what she says, he must be the ultimate hypocrite. She's bitter about that. When she met me—well, I was an atheist and had all of the intellectual and supposedly scientific arguments to support her rejection of everything she'd been taught as a child."

"And now you've pulled that prop out from under her."

"She never *needed* any propping up. She's a very strong person. Carla won't compromise—and she knows I won't."

"A lot of people are praying for both of you," said Hal. "Don't put any limits on what God can do."

"I'm trying to learn. Karen came in this afternoon and read to me from the Bible. I really appreciated that. There's so much to take in, and it's suddenly like I can't get enough. She was reading from, I think it was Peter. Something about faith being tested. I hope I can stand the test."

"None of us can on our own without Him," Dr. Elliott assured him. "Faith isn't some power we wield to slay spiritual dragons—or aim at God to manipulate Him into answering our prayers. Faith is trust in God in submission to His will. That means letting Him do things His way!"

"I've been seeing that, but it helps when you explain it. There's something exciting about—well, this whole thing of faith that I used to think was only for uneducated people who couldn't think for themselves." Ken ran out of words, but his eyes had a new light that spoke volumes.

"Hey, you've come a long way since I saw you last!" exclaimed Hal. "It's always exciting to see someone 'born again' and starting to grow!" He could only squeeze Ken's arm as they looked into each other's eyes with a new sense of brotherhood.

"I'm grateful to you and Karen for not giving up on me!"

"God didn't give up on us," responded Hal when he'd recovered his voice. "That's what's so fantastic—to know that the Creator of the universe loves each of us personally. I can never get over the wonder of it. So it makes sense to surrender ourselves into His hands, because He happens to be quite a bit smarter than we are— and He really does love us. So His way is always best. Once you're thoroughly convinced of that, everything else takes care of itself."

Ken nodded. "I'm convinced. It's the only thing I've ever found that really makes sense. And I used to think that 'faith' was some kind of irrational leap in the dark!" Even as he spoke, there was an inner joy that transcended the sense of impending loss that he now felt so strongly.

Carla came in late the next morning to say goodbye. Her eyes were red-rimmed and swollen in spite of the heavier-than-usual makeup. She was strong, but her love for Ken was strong as well. He'd been dreading this moment, and it had driven him to try his hand at prayer. It had been a rather clumsy attempt, but already he'd experienced a lightening of the burden and a strengthening for the battles ahead.

"Ken, I don't want this to deteriorate into an emotional catharsis," Carla began. "We both know that a barrier has come between us." She had to turn away to hide the tears.

"Carla, I love you so much! I'd do anything that I honestly could."

"Except renounce your new beliefs—and I wouldn't ask you to do that."

"I hope you can respect my beliefs."

"I respect you and your right to believe whatever you wish, but I can't respect what you now believe. I once believed it myself—and I know it isn't true."

"I could argue that," said Ken softly, "but I don't think that would help either of us right now."

"I love you, Ken—as much as ever. I want you to know that." Their eyes met, and for one brief moment they shared their anguish together.

"And I love you, Carla, even more than I ever have before. That's why this hurts so much. Our love for each other—we can't let that be destroyed." Their eyes met again briefly, in wordless empathy for each other's pain.

Carla was the first to break the silence. "Love has to have help, Ken. You know that. Even the closest relationships have their times of strain. It wouldn't work to start out this far apart in something that's so important to both of us." She lost her voice, and there was another long silence before she was able to continue. "It just wouldn't work," she repeated. "It just wouldn't."

"I wish you'd give us some time." Ken's eyes were pleading with her, but she couldn't meet his gaze.

"There'll be plenty of time," she said in a faraway voice, "whatever good that will do. It would be agony for us to be near each other. I've already made up my mind. I'm moving back to D.C. I've got lots of connections there."

Now Ken had lost his voice. There was another long, traumatic silence.

"I just can't believe it," Carla added at last. "You were the ultimate atheist. What happened to all those arguments?"

He took a deep breath. *God help me!* "Carla, I don't think there is such a thing as a convinced atheist. I always knew that God existed. You can't honestly pretend the universe just happened by chance! I just didn't want to face the consequences—that I was morally accountable to my Creator."

Carla cut him off. "Ken, I didn't come here to have you preach at me. I've heard plenty of that most of my life!"

"You asked me a question. Please, listen to me! There's not a doctor or nurse in this hospital that can deny that I'm a living miracle! You can't deny it!"

"Oh, can't I? My father preached *miracles*. And, oh how he preached against *sin*." Derisively she spat out those two contemptible words. "And you know what he did? He committed adultery—not just with one woman but with who knows how many. Eventually he ran off with his secretary and divorced my mother. When she finally faced the horrible truth, it killed her. She died of a broken heart."

"I'm sorry," said Ken, "but that doesn't prove—"

Carla cut him off again. "Prove? I'm giving you the *facts*! My father has a *huge* church today. His lifestyle doesn't seem to keep him from 'success' in the self-righteous *Christian* world!"

"But Carla, there are plenty of Christians who are just as nauseated by your father's hypocrisy as you are. And your mother—you've told me what a saint she was—she was a Christian. So how can you condemn Christ because of your father?"

He fell silent. What else was there to say? She had turned away, unable any longer to bear the pain of looking into his eyes. She pulled the strap of her purse over her shoulder and prepared to leave.

"I wish this hadn't happened this way," she said. "I didn't come here for a discussion or argument—just to make a simple statement . . . and say goodbye."

"We love each other!" Ken pleaded. "We can work our way through this." Then he remembered the audiocassette she'd brought in and tried to get it from the bedside table, but it was just beyond his grasp. Out of the corner of her eye she saw what he was reaching for but made no move to help him.

"'Fire and Rain.' James Taylor. You brought it back from the wreck," he reminded her. "'More than sentiment,' you told me—it was a hope you held onto. Do you remember the words?" She nodded almost imperceptibly. "I was humming it this morning," he continued eagerly, "and thinking it had to be more than coincidence that the stereo was playing *that* song when I went over the cliff."

He began to sing it softly, *"Look down upon me Jesus, You've got to help me make a stand. You've just got to see me through another day. My body's aching and my time is at hand. I won't make it any other way."* He reached out to touch her, but she pulled her hand away. "Please, Carla! I played that dozens of times when I claimed to be an atheist and never thought of what the words meant. We've listened to it together. You never told me you found the words offensive. I've only believed in Jesus like that song suggests. Why has that brought a wall between us?"

"Stop it, Ken! There's no point in prolonging the agony we both feel. You know that neither of us is going to compromise what we believe so deeply, so let's get this behind us." Abruptly she stood up and walked resolutely toward the door.

"I love you, Carla!" he called after her. "I love you!"

For a moment Carla's face broke as she paused and half-turned. "If you love me, then do me one favor: *Don't ever waste your time praying for me!*"

Through a blur of tears he watched helplessly as she walked from the room and out of his life.

The FSB Connection

For some time, hope for genuine cooperation between the West and Russia had pervaded the climate of international politics. That all the former communist nations in Eastern Europe had been accepted into NATO, made this hope seem reasonable. In the meantime, however, a covert and desperate rivalry between the CIA and FSB (successor to the KGB) that was never reported in the press had reached new intensity. If an outside observer had been able to look in on a certain clandestine psychic commando base secluded in the deep woods an hour north of Moscow, he would have found its activities and goals to be in complete contradiction to the peace initiatives being outwardly promoted by Russia's new "democratic" leaders.

On a blustery day in late April, two years after the sale of Ken Inman's secret laboratory to the CIA, Russian Army colonel Alexei Chernov, commander of the secret commando base, stood watching a platoon of his elite troops. They were practicing *Hwarangdo* on a soggy field that still held a few patches of snow in the almost-perpetual shadows of the 12-foot-high wall marking the highly classified installation's southern periphery. Chernov was a powerful brute of a man with the arrogant cockiness of a professional fighter. In superb physical condition, he appeared to be much younger than his 52 years. Having lost both parents in the Battle of Stalingrad, he had come up the hard way—through life and in the army as well. He was a survivor in every sense of the word.

On this particular day, statuelike, with arms folded, Chernov remained longer than usual on a path behind a hedge that made it possible for him to watch his troops unobserved. A nasty situation had developed at the base that occupied his thoughts and kept him from seeing what he appeared to be looking at for so long. At last he seemed to remember that he should be elsewhere. Spinning around, he traversed a muddy parade ground and turned onto a walkway that led between two long brick buildings. He seemed to be heading for the largest structure on the base, straight ahead of him. Two soldiers armed with automatic weapons patrolling just in front of it prepared to salute, when the colonel suddenly turned off to his right down another walk that led to what appeared to be a gymnasium.

A large red sign in front of the guarded building declared in bold Cyrillic letters: BEKTEREV RESEARCH INSTITUTE— AUTHORIZED PERSONNEL ONLY. The inside was a maze of corridors lined with offices and laboratories of various sizes and degrees of importance. In the center was a large and elaborate psychic research laboratory to which all corridors eventually led. It consisted of a main room with several auxiliary rooms adjoining, each of which had at least one window of one-way glass opening onto the lab. Thus it was possible from a number of angles to observe the laboratory activity without disturbing the concentration of those involved—and of course without those participating in the experiments knowing they were being watched.

One-way glass from floor to ceiling between the main control room and the lab provided a broad view of all activity from a location that was elevated about ten feet for better observation. Inside that vantage point, the scientist in charge, Viktor Khorev—a slim, prematurely graying and scholarly looking man of about 40—was directing two assistants through a final check of a complex bank of instruments. By reason of diligent, hard work and an undeniable brilliance, Dr. Khorev had established himself as the top Russian involved in advanced psychic research so secret that even within the Kremlin itself only a handful of leaders knew about it. His only apparent flaw was a troublesome habit of independent thinking that didn't fit well into the Russian military system—a flaw which so far had been largely overlooked in recognition of his great value, particularly in relation to his present work. In the lab below, two other scientists—Pyotr Dobrovsky, a relative newcomer, and Dmitri Petrekov, Viktor's close colleague and confidant of several years—were connecting the last wires to a man who, from the perspective above, looked undersized and vulnerable where he reclined at a slight angle in a special padded armchair.

Viktor followed intently the quick, sure movements he observed below. His own composure was a studied professionalism. Beneath the surface, however, like each of the other scientists, he was very much aware that the experiment they were about to begin—an experiment which he had not wanted to perform—would very likely end in disaster, as had the two immediately previous attempts.

"We're ready down here!" crackled Dmitri's voice over the intercom.

"I want to know the instant anyone detects the slightest abnormality—anything!" ordered Viktor over the microphone in front of him, where he was now seated at the main control panel. "Is that clear?"

"Right!" came Dmitri's prompt response from below. The two assistants seated beside Viktor nodded without taking their eyes from the panel before them. There, on dozens of graphs, needles were already tracing out brain waves, heartbeat, blood pressure, oxygen level in the bloodstream, and other vital data.

"You're cleared for trance state, Yakov," said Viktor quietly. In spite of himself, his voice reflected his own reluctance and apprehension.

The psychic, securely strapped into the huge chair, nodded almost imperceptibly. He was already well on his way to out-of-body readiness. His hands, which had gripped the arms of the special chair, had now gone limp. Total relaxation marked every visible muscular capability.

"Yakov. Listen carefully." Viktor was speaking in a slow and even-paced cadence. "At the word *STOP*, you will instantly come out of it! Is that clear?"

"Yes." Yakov's voice was barely audible.

Viktor pressed a button on a special panel to his left. On the screen immediately in front of the psychic was projected a slide of a group of several buildings surrounded by a high wall. Then the scene changed to the central structure of the complex.

"That is your target, Yakov. The location is in the coastal hills south of San Francisco about 12 miles west of Palo Alto, California. Agents in the field indicate it's a CIA installation involved in advanced psychic research—perhaps similar to our own." Viktor's voice was deliberately hypnotic now. "Enter the target building and gather all possible data in the time we can allow. If you have any trouble of any kind—even the slightest—communicate it to me immediately. Is that clear?"

Yakov nodded slowly. His eyes glazed over and on their surface the target structure was now dimly reflected. The heavy lids drooped and closed.

Viktor pushed another button and the screen began to reflect a computer-enhanced digital conversion of what Yakov himself was seeing in his presumed out-of-body journey. The picture was taken directly from his brain waves through an ingenious electronic enhancement process that Viktor himself had only recently developed. Indistinct and intermittent at first, the image slowly became clearer and more recognizable. Everything was being recorded on videotape directly from the instrument projecting the picture as Yakov was seeing it in his brain.

The image became sharper as the building was approached. There was a sense of floating through space. With a slight jerk and a momentary blackout, the target was penetrated by Yakov and the view was now of its interior. The inside walls seemed to have little substance as Yakov's probing mind repeatedly passed through them in the process of traversing corridors and entering rooms.

Suddenly two shadowy figures approached from the background, one from each side of the screen. For a fleeting moment the face of the figure on the right, who seemed to be in a long, hooded robe, became clearly delineated. He had never appeared in previous experiments of this nature. Viktor let out a grunt of recognition, however, when the face of the man on the left came briefly into view. Though his features were slightly distorted, he looked unmistakably like Stanford University professor Frank Leighton, recently a rising star in international psychic research circles. His presence was quickly recorded on a computer.

"I'm inside—nothing special to report yet." Yakov's words came slowly and with great effort. "I sense that the central lab is off to my right."

Suddenly the hooded figure blocked Yakov's progress, pointing threateningly at his invisible position. In the next moment, the image projected from Yakov's brain became a whirling kaleidoscope of distortions, a phantasmagoria of gyrating substance and line. The needles monitoring the psychic's vital signs went berserk.

"Help!" Yakov screamed in terror. "I'm being pulled in! *They've got me!*"

"Stop!" Viktor yelled into his microphone. "Stop, Yakov! That's an order! *STOP!*"

Yakov's face had become a death mask of agony. His body began to convulse, straining desperately at the straps holding him. Suddenly there was a blinding flash as Yakov was torn loose by some incredible power and thrown across the room. Hitting the opposite wall 30 feet away with a frightening impact, his shattered body seemed to hang for a moment before dropping to the concrete floor like a slab of raw meat.

"See to him! Now!" Viktor yelled into the mike, then turned to run for the stairs leading to the lab below.

Dmitri reached Yakov's crumpled body quickly and recoiled in horror. "*Moy Bog!*" he gasped, and stared down helplessly. Rushing up to take command of the emergency, Viktor could only stand transfixed beside Dmitri. The violence wreaked on Yakov was clearly far worse than in the two previous "accidents." There didn't appear to be an unbroken bone in his body. Yet his left hand gripped a felt pen of American manufacture that the investigators later would not be able to identify as belonging to Yakov or having been in the building prior to that moment.

As Viktor, Dmitri, and Pyotr—the three scientists on the project—watched in frozen terror, that lifeless arm began to move. In clear, block letters it printed a brief sentence in Greek on the bare floor. The scratching of the felt pen added a final eerie touch to the macabre scene before them. Then the silence of death.

Still in shock, Viktor struggled frantically to gather his wits. "Get a computer translation of that message," he told Pyotr, who pulled a pad from his pocket and, scarcely knowing what he was doing, managed to copy the strange writing. With apprehensive backward glances, he hurried from the lab.

Viktor turned to a stunned assistant. "Yuri! Get Colonel Chernov here immediately."

In the gymnasium, the colonel was seated in yoga position on a raised platform facing about 40 newly inducted elite troops, also in lotus position. He had just led them in a 20-minute meditation. The last "OM" faded into the walls. Each recruit, like the colonel, was wearing a black *gi* with Federal Troops insignias. Chernov stood suddenly and extended his arms with fists clenched toward the men.

"Open your eyes," he commanded and motioned for two assistants to bring a heavy slab of concrete and hold it out in front of him. "You are about to witness bio-energy extension," he explained. "You will be taught to project this energy beyond your bodies. Meditation is the key for developing it."

"Hiyah!" With a quick karate jab, Chernov's hand smashed through the six-inch-thick slab, sending concrete splinters flying.

"You assume it was my hand that smashed the concrete, but your eyes deceived you." Chernov paused dramatically to let the recruits think that over. "In fact, my hand made no contact. The invisible force extending from my hand shattered the slab. That force, when you learn through meditation how to focus it, acts as a protective shield over the entire body."

A thin smile tugged at the corners of his mouth as he reached for a delicate glass beaker and slid his right hand into it. He motioned for two other men to bring another concrete slab and hold it up in front of him.

"Hiyah!" The Colonel's glass-encased fist lashed out with lightning speed and again the demolished concrete slab splintered into a hundred pieces. Stepping back in triumph, Chernov let the delicate glass beaker, still intact, drop from his hand to the floor, where it shattered upon impact.

Arriving from the laboratory still in shock, Yuri quietly entered the gymnasium and stood respectfully at the rear, anxiously trying to get the colonel's attention. There was no mistaking the look of terror on his face. At last Chernov noticed and quickly motioned for him to come forward.

"Yakov has been killed!" Yuri whispered breathlessly.

Chernov's eyes blazed with anger. Without asking further details, he put his assistant, Major Rusak, in charge and immediately hurried from the gym, followed closely by Yuri.

By the time Chernov entered the lab, Viktor was back in the control room going over the data and shaking his head in puzzled unbelief. Seeing the colonel, he came down to join him beside the body.

"This man was your responsibility, Dr. Khorev!" barked Chernov.

"No!" Viktor responded firmly. "I was not in favor of risking another life. That was your decision."

"The Committee gave the order."

"But on your insistence."

Though so frail in comparison, Viktor stood his ground almost nose to nose with his powerfully built superior, staring him down with unwavering eyes. The colonel had long found this unbreakable man's individuality and unorthodox behavior maddening. Watching at a safe distance while directing the rest of the staff in shutting down equipment and gathering ripped wires and debris, Dmitri felt a growing sense of dread.

Chernov's mind was made up. He'd had one passion for months now: to nail Khorev's hide to the wall—and this was more than sufficient justification. "Yakov's death has jeopardized the program. *You* let him die! Why?"

"He didn't *die*," Viktor snapped back. "He was *killed* like the others—by *something* beyond our control. I told you that we were warned, but you wouldn't let me tell that to the Committee."

"Warned? That's fantasy!"

"Colonel, listen to this tape of Yakov's last words." Viktor quickly went to a nearby control panel and pushed a button.

Yakov's voice came over the speaker. "Help! I'm being pulled in! *They've got me!*"

Turning off the sound, Viktor demanded, "*They've* got me. Who are *they*, Colonel? Certainly no one in this lab. He was out of body inside that CIA lab in California. That's who *they* are, Colonel! *They* got him—just like they got the two before him—and that's why I didn't want to risk another man, but you insisted!"

"He was incoherent at that point," objected Chernov, pointing to the writing on the floor. "Look at that gibberish."

"Yakov was dead *before* he wrote that!"

"Impossible!"

"We have the data recorded on the monitors."

"He was ripped out of the wires," said Chernov. "You've got nothing when he was lying here!"

"Look at his body—and his mangled left arm. Even if he'd still been alive, he couldn't have written anything!"

At that moment Pyotr returned and handed a piece of paper to Viktor. "Here's the translation of your *gibberish*, Colonel. It was written in Greek." Viktor held it out for Chernov to see for himself, then began to read aloud: "Death to Prometheus. Archon."

"This is the *third* warning, Colonel."

"Prometheus? Archon?" growled Chernov. "If those are code names for American agents, we'll hunt them down—if it takes the whole FSB worldwide network!"

"You might try looking first on Mount Olympus, headquarters of the gods," suggested Viktor caustically, making no attempt to soften the derision in his voice, even though he knew how dangerous it was to bait Chernov. "Surely you remember from your wide reading that in Greek mythology Prometheus stole fire from the gods and they punished him. It's quite obvious that Archon has punished us!"

Chernov's face became livid. What he lacked in education he made up for in native cunning. Viktor's stinging sarcasm would be repaid not with brute strength, but with a false accusation he would find difficult to deny. "You're saying the *gods* did this? Doctor, the Committee meets tomorrow to inquire about the two previous deaths—and now we have a *third*. We'll see how amused they'll be with your fairy tales!" He turned abruptly and stormed out of the lab.

Dmitri's concern had turned to dismay. He was terrified for his friend. "Come, take a look at this," he said, motioning Viktor toward the shattered chair. As they bent over it together, Dmitri whispered: "He's a dangerous man, Viktor, and he intends to destroy you. Don't make it easier for him!"

Viktor's mind was wrestling with the immediate puzzle before them. "The colonel is right," he said softly. "Dead men don't write messages."

"But we all saw it happen!"

"Yakov was dead, Dmitri. And even alive his brain could not have commanded his arm in that condition to move. So what happened couldn't have been Yakov's subconscious. That's the established theory we've been clinging to in spite of the evidence. But we can't escape the truth any longer. If it wasn't his unconscious mind when he was dead, then it needn't have been when he was alive! Something else is in control—even when we don't realize it!"

"What do you mean?"

"We're being watched and manipulated by some higher intelligence. Archon, whoever or whatever that represents, is letting us know that it holds the key to psychic powers and is not happy with the way we're using them."

Dmitri was too stunned by this revolutionary idea to reply. "I'll tell you what else it means," suggested Viktor. "Archon must exist outside the material dimension, but with the capability of invading it at will!"

Instantly Dmitri put a cautionary hand on his friend's shoulder. "You keep talking like that, and you'll end up in a labor camp!" he whispered.

They both glanced anxiously around and noticed a soldier standing in the doorway and straining to hear what they were saying.

"What are you doing here?" Viktor demanded.

"We've come for the body, sir."

"Well, take it then," he barked, then said to Dmitri, "I feel like some fresh air."

Viktor turned to the rest of his staff, who still seemed to be too shocked to function. "I think it would do us all good to get out of here. Get some rest. Tomorrow is the hearing, and you should all be prepared to give a clear account of what you've witnessed."

Outside, the two comrades found a bench in a secluded place, where they kept their faces turned away from buildings that might hide eavesdropping devices poised in their direction. Earnestly Viktor tried to persuade his friend. "Listen to me, Dmitri! Everyone admits that if life could start on earth, it could happen on other planets too. There has to be intelligent life out there, and finding it is a significant part of the space program—for us and the Americans. Isn't that true?"

"Of course," conceded Dmitri, wondering what this had to do with Viktor's unthinkable performance with Chernov.

"We've had contact with intelligent life from beyond earth! Can't you see that? But it isn't the kind we were expecting, and we didn't find them through probing outer space. They've come to us—in *inner space*. We haven't seen their bodies because I don't think they have any!"

"Watch your step!" responded Dmitri. "*Think* it, if you wish, but don't ever *say* it—not even to me. If the Committee ever suspects you think nonphysical intelligences exist—well, don't expect me to visit you in Siberia!"

"Forget the Committee and give me a hearing, comrade. You're the only one I can talk to. Now, suppose these entities do exist . . . "

"What entities? Your thesis is pure fantasy. We saw two figures on the video. You think they were *nonphysical?*"

"Dr. Leighton, of course—you recognized him, too, I'm sure—was physical. He could be in charge of the lab. But the other figure—the hooded one—the force came through him. I'm sure of it! Since when does the CIA wear such robes? That was an *Archon*— dressed like *death!*"

Dmitri looked around apprehensively. "Keep your head down when you talk," he hissed. "You're getting careless. They have devices."

"I know the devices. We're too far away—so long as we face away from the buildings." But he leaned closer to Dmitri as he continued. "Now listen to me. I don't think the Americans have the capability of doing what we just saw today! *Archon* killed Yakov and the others. *Archon* is not a code name for the CIA! I don't think Archon has a body of its own; it uses the bodies of others. Maybe it kills CIA agents, too. It must have its own purpose. Who or what is *Archon*—and what is it up to? I've got to find out!"

From where the two friends sat they could see a military van drive up to the front door of the lab complex. Feeling strangely detached from the horror they had just experienced, they watched as two soldiers emerged from the building carrying Yakov's crushed remains. They shoved the body into the vehicle, climbed in, and drove off.

Dmitri pleaded earnestly with Viktor. "You can't bring Yakov and the others back by sacrificing yourself! What is the purpose of angering Chernov? Don't do it! And if you want to survive to pursue your research, then don't try to be a hero. Just tell the Committee what they want to hear!"

"I have a plan," said Viktor cryptically. And when Dmitri's eyes asked to know what it was, Viktor only shook his head.

MIND
INVADERS
11

For the Record

T he committee overseeing Psychic Warfare Research had already been scheduled to meet for a full hearing to inquire into the cause of the previous deaths of two psychics. Now they had a third death on their hands. Understandably, the atmosphere was extremely tense. Viktor did his best to appear in command of himself (although a certain amount of nervousness was expected as a matter of respect) when he was called at last into the small conference room down the hall from the laboratory. It was a closed hearing, with only the four Russian Army officers present—two generals and two colonels—as judge and jury. So secret was the subject matter that not even a stenographer was included. The officers made their own notes as the hearing progressed, and, of course, it was all recorded on audiocassettes.

Although Viktor had not been consulted in its composition, he knew exactly what Colonel Chernov's written report stated because he had been given a copy late the evening before. It was the usual head-in-sand nonsense that echoed the materialistic line, and it angered Viktor. It would take all of his self-control to go along with it. The new democratization had changed little at this level of operations.

He and Dmitri had talked late into the night, and he knew that his friend was right. It would be suicide to attempt to get the committee to understand what he suspected. The only sensible course was to parrot Chernov's report, his supposed "findings," which was simply what the colonel knew his superiors wanted to hear. Dialectical materialism was still the controlling ideology despite exaggerated reports to the contrary. Defending established dogmas was far more important than discovering the truth, even though officially that state of affairs was now denied and relegated to the past. Some things were simply a part of human nature no matter what regime might be in power and what ideals it might espouse.

All of his life under the former Soviet system, Viktor had nourished, and suppressed, a bitter hatred of the necessity for sheer survival's sake of never expressing one's true opinions. Perpetually torn between hypocrisy or prison, he had always swallowed his pride in the end and opted for the former—though sometimes by the narrowest of margins. And now—under the new "freedom"—so little had changed. Deep in his heart he maintained his integrity, and he knew that the day would eventually come when the dam would burst and pour forth a flood of cherished convictions that would send him to prison with his head held high—at last. On this occasion, however, Viktor had a preeminent motive for controlling his tongue. His plan depended upon surviving this hearing—a plan that he dared not disclose, at least not yet, even to Dmitri, the one man on the entire base that he trusted.

Customarily only one witness was called in at a time, and no discussion between witnesses of any testimony was permitted outside the hearing. No one working in the lab was to know what anyone else had testified. Viktor waited in the corridor for more than two hours while Chernov made his presentation before the Committee. As the colonel exited and Viktor entered, neither man looked at the other. That was customary—an indication that there was no collusion between them. Even the slightest change in expression, the interplay of a glance, could be cause for suspicion.

Viktor came to attention in front of General Nikolai Gorky, the steely eyed chairman. Seated to his right, behind the same slightly raised table, was General Aliyev. To Gorky's left sat the two colonels—Ostapenko and Lutsky. There was no attempt to set him at ease. Upon the shoulders of these men lay the responsibility of preparing the Russian Republic for the deadliest warfare ever conceived, a responsibility that they carried with the utmost solemnity. The only man in Russia who fully comprehended what they were involved with was the FSB director himself. There was no room for error, and anything at the secret base that was the least out of line had to be dealt with harshly and immediately.

Viktor knew by experience that he was just a pawn on the chessboard. Like all of the others, including Colonel Chernov, he was a man who knew far too much. His survival depended solely upon his ability to continue to produce what was vital to the program. If he ever failed in that, he would end up somewhere in the gulag—if they decided to let him live at all. He also knew that by now the unbending superiors he faced had already come to their conclusions based upon Chernov's bullheaded input, and he must not say anything that would rock their boat. He had survived this ordeal four times before and was determined to do it again.

General Gorky was shuffling through some papers and barely acknowledged Viktor's presence when he entered. Finally he found what he wanted and looked up to stare Viktor coldly in the eye. "Dr. Khorev, the autopsy declares cardiac arrest to be the cause of death in both cases—and now in the third as well. We all understand that the type of experiment these men were involved in—so-called 'out-of-body' journeys for the purpose of intelligence gathering—puts a great strain on the heart. Were there any warning signs to alert you? If not, why not? And if so, why did you not stop the procedure in time?"

"Sir, as you know," began Viktor, choosing his words carefully, "my medical assistant, Dr. Chevchenko, who is present during all of our experiments, was brought into the program two years ago because of his many years of experience as a cardiac expert and surgeon. He detected no sign to indicate an imminent heart attack in any of the subjects, nor could he find any indication after carefully going over the graphs with me several times since. We simply had no warning that anything was wrong, and thus there was no way we could have aborted the process in time to save the lives of these men—comrades who were very close to me and so important to what we are all dedicated to accomplish."

"Then how can you explain what happened?"

"I have asked Dr. Chevchenko, and he has no explanation. He is giving first priority to establishing additional safeguards, but he has come up with nothing as yet. We will keep working on that, but I think we all recognize by now that these experiments are extremely dangerous."

Gorky turned to his colleagues. "Does anyone have any further questions regarding the matter of medical procedures and safeguards?" The three officers shook their heads.

"Now we come to something far more serious, something that is not discussed in the official report given to you by Colonel Chernov last night. He has informed this Committee that you made some reference to 'gods.' We are assuming that was in jest, but that you were not jesting when you stated to him that we are being *warned not to proceed with this program.* I view that statement with great concern. What do you have to say for yourself?"

Viktor drew a quick breath. "Of course I was not serious about the 'gods.' While I presumed Colonel Chernov recognized that, I admit it was an ill-advised remark. I'm afraid, also, that my other statements to the colonel may have been hasty."

"Hasty in what regard?"

"Well, there—uh—could be other explanations. I may have been overreacting under the stress of the occasion. I can tell you that what we witnessed yesterday was not only awesome but terrifying—as I think the others who were present will all testify."

"You didn't answer my question. Hasty in what regard?"

"I expressed an opinion about the meaning of the message that was given under the stress of the moment and had not been carefully thought out to a conclusion."

"Have you come to that conclusion by now?"

"No, sir, I have not. 'Death to Prometheus' does seem to be a warning. Its exact meaning, however, remains a mystery—which may indeed be the intent."

General Aliyev had been shifting in his chair restlessly and drumming his fingers on the table as if to show his impatience with the lack of progress. He interrupted at this point. "There has been a consistent pattern to these so-called messages. Is that not true? For one thing, each has been signed by 'Archon.' You are responsible,

Dr. Khorev, to determine their source—and also their meaning. This Committee is waiting to hear something substantive from you. Instead, you've given us nothing but vague apologies."

"If you took a poll of the leading Russian psychologists," replied Viktor quickly, "I'm certain the consensus would be that the source of these messages has to be the deep unconscious of each psychic. That three different individuals have, in their deaths, given us messages that are so consistent in content must be attributed to the collective unconscious that is shared by all members of the race. The consistency in the presentation of the messages can also be explained on the same basis, which is why I would personally consider this to be the only possible theory."

Colonel Lutsky was shuffling loudly through some papers in an apparent show of disapproval, and Colonel Ostapenko had cleared his throat, shoved his chair back, and turned his head several times toward General Gorky. As for Gorky, his steely eyes were staring with unblinking intensity into Viktor's.

Determined to keep his train of thought and not to be unnerved, Viktor pushed on with his explanation. "In the altered state of consciousness that, as you know, is the only way we know of for engaging in these experiments, the subconscious mind controls the motor muscles. This often results in what has been called 'automatic writing.' In each case—"

"We're familiar with the mechanics," interrupted General Aliyev impatiently. "What we must know is the interpretation of the message."

"I'm leading up to that, General," responded Viktor respectfully. "To make an interpretation, it is important to consider the source—which is why I gave such a lengthy explanation to support my belief that the subconscious is the culprit, at least by all of the indications."

"Such as what?" demanded Aliyev.

Viktor was troubled, wondering why the general seemed to be resisting the very explanation he had been so certain they wanted to hear. There was no way of knowing what Aliyev or the others might have in mind if it weren't the materialistic line, and Viktor did not dare to change his planned response. This could be a trap—an attempt to encourage him to betray himself.

"For one thing, we have in each case a reference to Greek mythology." Viktor was doing his best to seem relaxed and sincere. There must be no indication that the questioning was bothering him. "Yesterday, for example, it was Prometheus—a figure that could indicate a subconscious fear on the part of Yakov that he was treading on dangerous ground. Many Russian psychologists agree with the theory of Carl Jung that the collective unconscious is rich with primitive memories embodied in archetypes, some of which have become the substance of mythology. It would be entirely consistent with this theory to expect the very kinds of 'messages' that we have been receiving. The interpretation, then—"

Gorky cut him off. "Doctor, you don't seem to understand our concern. What General Aliyev is saying is this: We have been getting 'messages' from some source telling us not to proceed. Is that not the case?"

"Yes, sir."

"Now who would most benefit if we shut down our research?"

Viktor was stunned by the unexpected direction the questioning had taken, but did his best not to betray his emotions. "The Americans, I suppose," he replied cautiously. "But I don't—"

Gorky cut him off again, and his tone hardened. "Three of our best psychics die while probing what we believe is an American intelligence installation doing advanced research similar to our own. Doesn't that tell you anything, Doctor?"

"I don't think the Americans have the capability—"

"You don't think—you don't *think!* Opinions are useless. We need facts. Your job is to figure out how they do it—and stop them!"

"We've been doing our best, General, to discover their methods through psychic probes, but I don't see how we can continue our present approach. Don't we have agents abroad who can penetrate their organizations?"

"That has nothing to do with this hearing," Gorky reminded him coldly. "Your laboratory has its own reasons for existence and its specific assignments. Are you suggesting that, in fact, it has no function that is different from agents abroad, and that we shut it down?"

"No, sir, I am not suggesting that. I understand your point and we are doing our best to fulfill our function, but we seem to have confronted a force that is beyond our present capabilities."

"Precisely!" returned Gorky. "And that is the intolerable state of affairs that this hearing is intended to address—and to resolve!" The general hesitated for a moment, as though uncertain whether something ought to be mentioned, then proceeded. "The felt pen with which Yakov wrote the message is of American make. Such a pen is not easily available in Russia. How did Yakov obtain it?"

"I had never seen it before, nor had anyone in the laboratory. I would swear it was not there prior to the incident."

Gorky held up the pen in question. "You, Dmitri, and Pyotr personally observed Yakov writing with this pen?"

"Yes, sir, and with his left hand. He happens to be right-handed, and I have never known him even to attempt to write with his left. Of course, in a trance anything is possible."

"I don't think anyone puts much importance in that, Doctor. It's the pen we want to get straight."

"It's an *American* pen!" interjected General Aliyev. "Not German, not French or English, but *American.*"

"Of course," Viktor added thoughtfully, going along completely now, "he was psychically in America at the time this occurred. We don't even know what such astral projection involves. Conceivably something from America somehow became psychically attached to him and appeared in the lab at the time he suddenly came back into his body."

"Can we be sure he 'came back'?" Gorky asked sharply. "What does Dr. Chevchenko say?"

"He does not know, sir. I'm afraid that the unknowns outnumber the knowns when it comes to out-of-body travel."

Gorky turned to Aliyev. "You wanted to say something else, General?"

"We're dealing with a force," declared Aliyev grimly, "that could make the atomic bomb look primitive. If the Americans win the race to control psychic power, that's the end! We have been assured for years that American scientists ridicule psychic power, that their government spends very little on such research, and that we are far ahead in the race—so far ahead that they can never catch us. That no longer seems to be the case. And you, Khorev, will have to shoulder the blame!"

"This is a sudden turn that has come only in the past few weeks." Viktor was reeling now. He had been so confident that he could weather this procedure. "I would not have risked Yakov, believe me, but I understood that the committee insisted upon it."

"You had another plan?" asked Aliyev derisively. "Why didn't you tell us?"

Of course, he couldn't tell the committee that they were stubborn, mulish fools who discouraged any genuine exchange of ideas, but he wanted to. Oh, how he wanted to do just that! "I don't have a plan at the moment, and, until we do I don't think it's wise to make another attempt of this nature."

"We have a plan," interrupted General Gorky. "Tomorrow, when you fly to Paris for the opening of the First International Congress on Parapsychology, there will be some additions to your delegation. Everyone—*including you*—will be under the command of Colonel Chernov, who will pose as your assistant. There must be no hint that you are not really in charge of the delegation in your public appearances together. Is that clear?"

"Yes, sir!" responded Viktor quickly, relieved to know that he was still to be allowed to leave for the West. That was essential to his own plan—or was it a dream?—that he'd been going over carefully for several months.

"I've drafted a statement which you will include in your address to the Congress," continued Gorky. "It calls for strict controls on the use of psychic power and for the free exchange of research findings. Your assignment is to see to it that this resolution is adopted. And I expect you to come back with an invitation for you and two assistants to visit the CIA's California installation. In return, you will invite Dr. Frank Leighton to visit you here."

Gorky turned to his fellow officers. "If no one else has anything further to add ... "

"Sir, the medical report," Colonel Lutsky reminded him.

"Indeed. One more question, Khorev." To Viktor's relief, Gorky's tone was no longer threatening. "Your report seemed to suggest that Yakov died prior to writing the message. Obviously impossible, is it not?"

"That was an oversight, sir. Colonel Chernov had already pointed out to me the obvious fact that the monitors had malfunctioned before Yakov was ripped from the controls. And once the wires had been torn from him, of course, we no longer had any means of determining exactly when he died. In that case we can only go by common sense and I heartily concur. The report will be rewritten and the records corrected, sir."

A Desperate Decision

Everything else was mere formality after Viktor's acquiescence to the "correction" in the medical report. The Committee spent little time questioning Dr. Chevchenko, Dmitri, and the others, whose testimony added nothing to what was already known. When Colonel Chernov returned to be apprised of the Committee's official findings, he strongly expressed once again the same suspicions that he had consistently presented in the past.

"While I have no proof as yet," Chernov declared, "I am convinced that Dr. Khorev is the main link in all three deaths. Furthermore, I also suspect that he never was a Marxist. He has always had disloyal leanings toward the West, even though so far nothing of that nature has been picked up on any of the monitors in his office or lab or apartment. I urge the Committee not to send him to Paris. He's a high risk beyond our borders—he knows too much!"

"We understand your feelings and have our own suspicions," replied Gorky. "But without Khorev to head it, our delegation would not be taken seriously, and that would jeopardize our entire mission. You don't deny that?"

"I'm thinking of the risk, sir, of having a disloyal man on the team."

"You are in charge, Colonel," Gorky reminded him icily. "Are you suggesting that you can't handle the situation? The Committee thought you were competent—in spite of the fact that we entrusted you with the investigation of these deaths, and your latest report adds no new insights."

"I apologize for the lack of progress, sir."

"We're interested in results, not apologies, Colonel. You have your assignment. Are there any further questions?"

"No, sir."

When Dmitri returned to the lab late in the day after his testimony had been taken, there was no opportunity to ask Viktor how he had fared before the Committee. Dr. Chevchenko was there, going back over the charts for all three psychics again and again, searching for some clue he had not been able to see in his many previous reviews. Yuri was assisting Pyotr in repairing the wiring that had been ripped out, and the other lab workers were going over all the electronics in every monitoring machine and recording device, to make certain that there was no hidden damage. Appearing before the Committee had given everyone a fresh motivation for working overtime to make up for the failures of the past. That burden was shared by all under the common guilt of the three deaths that tortured memories and cast a pall upon the future.

As the evening wore on, exhaustion overtook them one by one. At last, when the hands of the large clock on the laboratory wall had moved past midnight, only Dmitri and Viktor remained. By this time Viktor was down the hall in his office, where Dmitri hurried to join him. He found his friend going through file drawers as though his life depended upon it.

"These files will still be here when you get back," Dmitri suggested. "You ought to be home packing and getting a good night's sleep!"

"I am packing," said Viktor, continuing to work without looking up. "I'm gathering some papers that I'll need on my trip."

"All of *that*?" asked Dmitri, waving at an already overstuffed and very large briefcase.

Viktor wiped his brow and sat down behind his desk with a tired sigh. "I'll have time to sleep on the plane. This is very important."

"Well, tell me, good comrade, how did it go today? I've been dying to find out!"

"I think it went well, Dmitri. There were some anxious moments when I feared my trip was finished, but in the end I think they were satisfied. I went along with their totally insane idea that the Americans have been killing our best men. That made them happy."

Dmitri quickly put a warning finger to his lips and shook his head vigorously, horrified that Viktor would speak so carelessly in his office.

"Don't worry, old friend," Viktor responded, laughing at the expression on Dmitri's face. "Do you think they can hide an electronic bug from *me*? I put together my own detection equipment and I use it to sweep this office every morning. As fast as they put their bugs in, I take them out."

"You do?" Dmitri was astonished at Viktor's boldness.

"I do. It was costing them a czar's ransom. Those things are expensive. Finally they gave up. I haven't found one for weeks—and I just checked again this morning, so don't worry."

Dmitri looked relieved, but still apprehensive.

"Don't worry," Viktor assured him again, reaching into his shirt pocket to pull out a scrap of paper. Dmitri could see that it was the very one on which Pyotr had copied the message from Archon. "I've been thinking a lot about this."

"You should destroy that before it destroys you!" exclaimed Dmitri in alarm.

"I can't. I'm obsessed by it. There has to be an outside intelligence behind these messages."

"If you want to survive," Dmitri responded quickly, "you'd better agree with Gorky. The Americans were being probed, they didn't like it, and they retaliated. It's that simple. It certainly makes sense, so why fight it?"

"Certainly, certainly." Viktor's voice dripped sarcasm. "The Americans can kill any of us at will from thousands of miles away!

Do you want to be the first to surrender, or shall I? I haven't noticed Gorky waving a white flag—it's still blood-red!"

Viktor paused to let that sink in, then continued. "There's only one explanation that fits the facts, Dmitri. I've wrestled with this, but you just can't escape it. We're dealing with intelligences far more highly evolved than any Americans. I'm convinced the Archons don't have bodies, but they have incredible minds. They must be the masters of the psychic power we've been seeking. And they're not happy with what we're doing."

"Please, Viktor. Stay away from such ideas."

"Because I'm afraid of Chernov or Gorky? What about the facts? As a scientist, I have to know the *truth!*"

"There is also such a thing as being practical," argued Dmitri passionately. "It won't help the cause of truth to get yourself sent to a labor camp in Siberia! Yell your 'truth' as loud as you want up there for all the good it will do. You may convince the wolves, but nobody else will hear you!" He stood, resolutely, put both hands on the front of Viktor's desk, and leaned over until his face was only a foot from his friend's. "You may not like this, Viktor, but I don't think your theory makes any more sense than Gorky's. Take the matter of a motive, for example. The Americans have a good one. But highly evolved non-physical intelligences? What would such entities want with humans? We've got nothing to offer them—if they do, in fact, exist. And why would they interfere when we try to probe the Americans but let us proceed with all of our other experiments? I tell you, it doesn't add up! Even if he's wrong, Gorky can make a better case than you can."

That outburst ended, Dmitri sank back into his chair. Then he added in a more conciliatory tone, "And I think you're both wrong."

"You do?" asked Viktor in surprise. "Then tell me: What's your theory?"

"I can't explain it well enough yet. But when I can, then I'll tell you."

"Now you have me curious, Dmitri! But I can't wait. This thing drives me day and night. I've got to find the answer to this puzzle!"

Viktor searched around and dug some photocopies of magazine articles out of a drawer, waved them at Dmitri, then dropped them onto the pile that was overflowing his briefcase. "I've been reading some papers—like these—by an American psychic researcher named Ken Inman. He argues very persuasively for nonphysical intelligences being behind all psychic power. He has some revolutionary ideas that are quite convincing, but I can't get anything recent from him. It's all at least two years old. Supposing he's made contact with some entities—like Archon, perhaps—and that's why he suddenly says nothing anymore. This could be the secret behind the Americans' new power. They certainly didn't have such capabilities a short while ago."

"That's not like you, Viktor—accepting theories from the Americans. It could be deliberate misinformation."

"It makes sense, Dmitri! More sense than the pigheaded materialism we're stuck with over here in spite of the supposed fall of communism! You saw what happened to Yakov. That's not misinformation! I'm awed by such power. It's some kind of mind energy, and it's far beyond anything we or the Americans are capable of on our own."

"I agree with you, but you're fighting a rising tidal wave of popular opinion that you can't stop. You know the Americans—some of the motivational experts the Kremlin has brought in to help us install a modified capitalism—talk about 'unlimited' human potential."

Viktor smiled derisively. "Any child knows better than that! There are *obvious* limits, Dmitri, and what we've seen with our own eyes is light-years beyond anything reasonable."

Both friends lapsed into thoughtful silence as Viktor returned to searching the drawers of his desk for documents he wanted to take with him. At last he paused in his work and picked up the conversation again. "I've searched every encyclopedia we have and tried to recall everything I know from history or mythology to find some clue as to the identity of Archon."

"Yes? Tell me!" responded Dmitri eagerly.

"I thought this subject was taboo. Are you sure we shouldn't just drop it?"

"It's too late to play games," said Dmitri earnestly. "Don't joke about something so important. Now come out with it."

"*Archon* is the Greek word for 'ruler.' The Archons were a group of nine magistrates who ruled ancient Greece. I think these entities use the name 'Archon' to indicate that they are a hierarchy of beings—most likely a group of nine highly evolved intelligences—who rule in the psychic realm and control psychic power. They probably have such incredible powers that they would seem like gods, compared with our level of development. This certainly fits with the reference to Prometheus."

"I thought you were mocking Chernov—but you really think there are godlike creatures out there without bodies who are interested in what we and the Americans are doing in our labs? Tell that to anyone but me and you *will* end up in a labor camp under the care of *psychiatrists!*"

"Not gods in the mythical or religious sense—although they could be the basis for that idea in various religions—but highly evolved entities that our ancestors mistook for gods."

"I didn't know you were a religious man, Viktor."

"I'm not."

"That sounds like a religious idea to me. Are your godlike creatures any different from the gods of the ancient Greeks or today's shamans in Siberia?"

"This is a *scientific* theory!" retorted Viktor indignantly, losing patience with his friend. "These entities *evolved* to their present level!"

"Call it scientific, if you want," insisted Dmitri, "it's still religion. And I don't think *scientific religion* makes any better sense than any other religion. If your 'gods' were created by evolution, they're no better than the gods of the most primitive and superstitious peoples. They certainly couldn't have created the universe!"

Viktor leaned back in his chair and gave Dmitri a long, curious look. "I never knew you were interested in religion at all! This is a side of you, my friend, that I never suspected. Have you become religious recently?"

"We're talking *truth* and *facts* and what makes *sense*," replied Dmitri, deliberately avoiding the question. "All I'm telling you is that the only God that makes sense would have created the universe and we would all be responsible to Him. There could be beings He has created with more power than we have—angels or demons—but there aren't any 'gods' out there for the atheist to look up to."

"You amaze me, Dmitri. Is this related to your theory of what's behind psychic power?"

Dmitri nodded. "I've been hoping we could discuss this—perhaps when you get back. Now isn't the time."

Viktor gave him another long look. "And we always have to be so careful, don't we, with whom we speak, what we say—always with the cloud over our heads that someone will report us." Viktor's voice was rising in anger. "Materialist ideology continues to be an albatross around our necks! It stifles our research—and makes me sick! The whole human race may be in danger, and we can't pursue certain possibilities. So Marx and Lenin still rule us from their graves?"

Confronted by the hopelessness they faced, the two friends lapsed into silence while Viktor continued pulling papers from the drawers in his desk. At last he decided that he had to share with Dmitri the secret he'd been guarding closely for so long.

Viktor straightened up from his work and leaned across his desk to face Dmitri. "I've made a big decision, old friend. What is impossible here is possible in the West. They're open to considering a nonphysical extension of the universe and intelligent life."

Dmitri looked from the opened drawers to the overstuffed briefcase. The truth was beginning to sink in. "Viktor! You're not . . . ?"

"I've got to talk with the Americans. I want to find Dr. Inman. We have to compare information."

"You can do that in Paris at the Congress!" exclaimed Dmitri hopefully.

"With Chernov breathing down my neck? Even if I had complete freedom in Paris, we're only there a week. That's not enough time to scratch the surface, and Inman may not even be there. Dmitri, old friend, we've been together a long time, but I think we must now say farewell."

Their eyes met in a long silence. No words could express the look that passed between them: what it meant to trust someone in a society that destroyed all trust, where one's best friend or even a lover might be an informer. Or a friend, might turn into an informer for an advantage or be forced into betrayal against his or her will in any one of a hundred tried and proven ways. Such an existence could never be explained to those who had not experienced the nightmare of fear and the pain of biting one's tongue a thousand times a day.

Ironically, here at this top-secret base, where 24-hour surveillance of every individual was practiced in its ultimate perfection, they had found one another. It had not been easy. There had been weeks of guarded looks passing between them—covertly at first, tentative, questioning. No words. Just an occasional fleeting hint in the eyes, until each thought he knew. Then one of them—it had been Dmitri—had made the first careful remark, testing Viktor in the middle of a sentence with a whispered sarcasm about hidden listening devices. Viktor had made no verbal response, but his eyes had told Dmitri what he had sensed for some time. Eating their sandwiches alone together later that day on a secluded bench outside, they had loosed upon each other a flood of pent-up resentments against the regime, then laughed almost hysterically at the intensity of the catharsis.

Secretly and with great care not to give any outward sign to the others on the base, their friendship had grown firm and deep—and now it was to be no more. They both stood suddenly, and Viktor came around from behind his desk. There was a swift, fierce embrace.

They held each other for another moment at arm's length. "If you make the attempt and fail, you know what that means." Dmitri was somber. "I'll be praying for you, Viktor."

Viktor looked at his friend in amazement. "You *pray?*"

Dmitri nodded.

"So that's what you were telling me—you're a *believer?*"

Dmitri nodded again. "It's something very new with me, and I'm beginning to wonder how I can stay in this kind of work. Of course, once they find out—"

"I'm not a believer," replied Viktor firmly, "and I never will be. You can pray if you want, but I don't think the 'gods' will listen. Why should they? As you said, what can we offer them? The whole universe is a jungle—the survival of the fittest. I'm just trying to survive."

"I will pray that you do! And that you will very soon believe in the true God. Of course, we have nothing to give Him—except ourselves. And that's why the forgiveness He offers is a gift of His grace. He is loving and kind and gracious. You need Him, Viktor— and He will not turn you away if you call upon Him. Please remember that!"

"And you watch your step, too," Viktor managed to say, putting a hand on Dmitri's shoulder. "I'll be worrying about you!"

They embraced again briefly, tears welling up to blur their vision, voices now too choked for further speech.

Dmitri almost ran from the room. At the door he turned around and made a feeble last gesture of farewell, but Viktor was once again engrossed in his feverish stripping of files. Dmitri understood. He hurried down the hall, the void within growing in size and pain with every step. The silence had begun again.

Paris!

During the hour-long early morning ride to Sheremetyevoz International Airport just north of Moscow on the Leningradsky highway, Colonel Chernov had a great deal to say to everyone else in the small bus, but he didn't address one word to Viktor. It made him feel uncomfortably like an outsider—which indeed he was. They were supposed to be a delegation of top Russian parapsychologists led by internationally known Dr. Viktor Khorev. In fact, Chernov was in command, and out of the six "delegates" from the secret base, only Viktor and Pyotr were psychic researchers. The others were either military or Federal Security Service (FSB) officers. And Viktor had his suspicions about Pyotr.

He had requested that Dmitri, who was second in command of the lab, should come along as his assistant. Yet Dmitri had been rejected, and Pyotr, a relative newcomer, had been sent instead. Why? That question had bothered Viktor for some time. Had his too-close friendship with Dmitri been noticed after all? There was no use worrying about it now. He would be watched every minute and could look to no one for help in making his escape. It would not be easy. Chernov would like nothing better than to bring him back to Moscow as a criminal caught in the act.

"Stay with me," ordered Chernov as they climbed out of their vehicle in front of the busy airport. "I have your passports and tickets." The reminder was hardly necessary. No member of the party would see his passport again until they had returned to Russia.

It was a great shock to Viktor when they were joined by eight more "delegates" at the airport—FSB agents who would pose as "secretaries, lab assistants, and researchers." Some of them would stay in the West after the Congress to complete their assignments. "They will accomplish by other means what you have failed to do!" Chernov told Viktor pointedly. This was a terrible last-minute blow to Viktor. It had already been an impossible dream to be able to slip away from the smaller group—but from 13 of them now sharing the task of keeping him under surveillance around the clock? How could he do it? Somehow, somehow . . .

As they moved through the airport, Viktor did his best to suppress his excitement and to stifle the fear that he would be held back at the last moment by some unforeseen technicality. That he—with all the secrets he knew—should be leaving the country at last seemed too good to be true. It took all of his willpower to maintain an outward facade of calm. He steeled himself to ignore the suspicious stares that Chernov continued to aim at his bulging and very heavy briefcase.

"Open everything!" The command was barked by a grim-faced customs officer as soon as he had lifted his baggage onto the long counter. He'd hoped that an official party would be exempted from close inspection. There was nothing to be concerned about in his suitcase, but as he opened the briefcase he could scarcely control the tremor in his hands.

The customs official dug around with practiced fingers, deliberately dumping precious documents out onto the counter. A chief aim of all border inspections was to prevent the smuggling out of any information that might weaken or harm the Russian cause. The paranoia for secrecy—a carryover from Soviet days—interpreted this law so broadly as to include the most mundane facts and figures. The officer straightened up and gave Viktor an accusing look.

"What are all these papers?" The question he'd feared took his breath away. Desperately he fought a growing feeling of dizziness.

Get hold of yourself, Viktor!

"I'm part of an official delegation to a conference." Viktor gestured toward the other members of the party, who were in front and behind him. "I have to give some talks. This is my—uh—documentation." The officer stared at him coldly for a moment longer, then waved him on. It seemed to Viktor that he would never get the papers stuffed back inside, but on the third try he just managed to jam the briefcase shut. The fact that Chernov was standing nearby and watching him closely did not make it easier.

"You should have taken a suitcase for your papers!" hissed Chernov in a low voice, coming alongside of Viktor as the delegation moved through the shuffling crowds toward its departure gate. "Did you bring your whole office? You must have lots of classified documents there!"

Viktor gripped the briefcase tightly and kept walking. Any hesitation or hint of fear would be an admission of guilt. "I have support statistics in case anything I say in my two speeches is challenged," he replied firmly. "And I have lots of work to catch up on. I don't intend to waste any spare time!"

The look Chernov gave him said, *I don't believe you, but it doesn't matter. We've got you under the microscope!*

At least he had made the right decision to put the precious video of the Yakov disaster in an inside pocket of his heavy overcoat. Had it been in the briefcase, it would have been discovered. More than anything else, he wanted to show the Americans what Yakov "saw" in the CIA installation—and his brutal death. He had to know how it all correlated with what was actually going on in American psychic research. Was Leighton really with the CIA? Was that organization, like Russia's FSB, tied in so closely with psychic research? Why was Inman no longer in the news? And what about the hooded figure? He seemed to be the focus of power! Would he find the answer to these questions? Would he actually make it to the West? He *had* to—failure was not an option.

Only when the Aeroflot Ilyushin 86 jet had rattled its way down the long runway, shaken itself like a huge bird, and lifted into the air to begin climbing toward the southwest did Viktor at last lean back in his seat with a contented sigh and begin to breathe easier. The flight offered a chance to relax and time to think about a serious problem that had been troubling him. He had originally planned, at the earliest opportunity, to confide to the American delegation his desire to defect. Surely they could be counted on to get word to the American Embassy, which would in turn contact some branch of intelligence to provide the help—and above all, the protection—he would need.

Viktor had been confident that the Americans would consider him a prize and thus be willing to do whatever would be necessary to effect his escape. After Yakov's death, however, he was no longer so certain. It seemed doubtful now that he had any expertise to offer that they needed or would want. For years it had been common knowledge that the Russians were far ahead of all competitors in psychic research. That no longer appeared to be the case. Something had happened to make the Americans superior. After all, they had been probing a CIA installation when the three psychics had been killed. Could it be that "Archon," whom he had long suspected was the real power behind psychic phenomena, was represented by the hooded one? And was Archon, then, in some kind of partnership with the Americans? There was no escaping the implication of Dr. Frank Leighton standing near the hooded one in the image that had been projected on the screen from Yakov's brain just before he'd been killed.

The implications became more disturbing—for him personally and for his planned escape—the longer he allowed his thoughts to run in that direction. Leighton seemed to be looking directly at Yakov's position. Would that mean that he had known that Yakov had psychically penetrated their secret research facility? Would he not also be aware of Russian intentions and capabilities, and of Viktor's part in the program? Would the hooded one, who had made the threatening gestures and was apparently responsible for Yakov's death, be at the Congress in Paris? It seemed strange that Russian intelligence had never even hinted at the existence of such a unique figure among the American psychics. Leighton, of course, would be at the Congress. He was listed as the head of the American delegation and a keynote plenary session speaker.

If I tell Leighton I want to defect, will he turn me down—perhaps even betray me? That would be one way to set the Russian program back a few years. There's no one to replace me. What can I offer the Americans in exchange for my safety? If not insights into psychic power, certainly a briefcase crammed with information about top secret Russian research. That's my trump card—or is it? Do they really need anything I've got?

Such thoughts gave Viktor little comfort and much concern. Nevertheless, under the mesmerizing effect of the throbbing engines and despite the apprehensions churning inside him, he dozed off at last from sheer exhaustion. Almost immediately, it seemed, someone was gripping his shoulder and shaking him. With great effort, he groped his way out of a labyrinth of unconsciousness and back to the present. At last his startled eyes focused upon the unwelcome figure of Colonel Chernov, now occupying the seat beside him.

"I've been studying your speeches. Some things have to be changed." The colonel was pointing accusingly to a word he had circled in the very first paragraph. *"Telepathy."* He spat it out contemptuously. "That's a mystical term incompatible with scientific materialism."

"It's not mystical. That's the common term in the West, and my audience will be mostly Westerners."

"Change that to 'biological radio.'" It was an order.

Viktor snorted in disgust. For his own survival he had to play it tough. "Western scientists will laugh at that. *Biological radio!* The strongest brain waves hardly carry more than a meter, and the subjects in this experiment were nearly 2000 kilometers apart!"

The look in Chernov's steel-gray eyes pierced to Viktor's soul. "Let's get this straight, Dr. Khorev, so we have no more misunderstandings. I'm in charge. You're taking orders from me. Now is that clear?"

If I let him bully me and don't fight back, this whole trip could become a disaster! He'll control everything I say and do, and I'll come off as a bumbling lackey of Marxism materialism that no

one would help defect! They wouldn't want me! But what can I do?
Viktor fought to control the panic welling up inside and to conceal
any outward expression of the fear and confusion that made him
feel suddenly ill. *Get tough, Viktor, get tough—for your own survival! You've come this far. Don't buckle now!*

Steeling himself, Viktor returned Chernov's icy stare without
flinching. "And I consider myself duty bound to give you sound
technical advice, sir." It required a tremendous effort to keep his
voice even. "If you refuse to take it, then you, sir, will be responsible for holding Russian psychic research up to ridicule in front of
the whole world!"

"Don't play games with me. I know your leanings towards the
West!" Chernov's angry voice had risen above the dull roar of the
aircraft, and several other members of the delegation were stealing
curious glances in their direction. "You step one centimeter out of
line, and I'll send you right back to Moscow!"

Viktor's flashing eyes dared him. "You think Pyotr can take my
place? Without me, you don't have a delegation. Send me home and
you've lost all credibility—you might as well all pack up. I don't
think the committee would be happy about that!"

Chernov's face was red with suppressed rage. He held the page
in question under Viktor's nose and thrust a pen into his hand.
"Now do it!"

Slowly and deliberately Viktor scratched out "telepathy" and
wrote in above it "biological radio." Then he handed the pen, covered with icy sweat, back to the colonel, who was now a seething
volcano on the verge of eruption.

"Not so fast, comrade. You've got lots of other changes to
make!" Chernov flipped through the pages methodically, pointing
out Viktor's further deviations from materialist orthodoxy, each of
which he had already marked in red.

Slapping the pen back into Viktor's hand, the colonel twisted
around until they were almost nose to nose. "You don't fool me,
Khorev," he hissed. "I'm going to get you if it kills me!"

Those words haunted Viktor for the rest of the flight. What if
Chernov did send him back? The man was a maniac and just might
do it, then blame him for sabotaging the Russian mission. Already

the trip he had looked upon with such hope was turning into a nightmare. To enhance his chance to escape, he could just go along with Chernov's stupid demands and even pretend to agree with them. There was, however, such a thing as professional pride in one's work. It was one thing to pacify Chernov by making his ridiculous changes on paper. It was something else to be humiliated before an international gathering of scientists by making foolish statements in a speech. It was a terrible dilemma that he'd have to deal with when the time came.

The ride in the long black limousine from Charles de Gaulle Airport through the suburbs of Paris, then across the Seine over Pont de Neully and down the broad and stately Avenue Charles de Gaulle left Viktor gaping in awe. Moscow and Leningrad had their broad avenues as well, but there was no denying that they were drab in comparison with the graceful elegance before him. Everything was brighter here: the festive storefronts and rich window displays, the rainbow-colored umbrellas unfurled above the well-dressed Parisiens sipping wine or tea at the innumerable sidewalk cafés. The great abundance of fruits and vegetables displayed in the front of shop after shop was staggering—and nobody standing in long lines for anything, anywhere. It was hard to believe. And the trees! Everywhere along the avenues there were trees, graceful and groomed, lending an almost feminine softness to the gray of stone and expanse of boulevard.

The crowds moving along the sidewalks seemed to exude an almost tangible gaiety. He had read of it—what the French affectionately called *joie de vivre*. A vibrant enthusiasm hung in the air, a saucy, brazen individuality that seemed shocking but appealing. Viktor winced at the vividly recollected contrast: the stolid, impassive doggedness of the typical Russian shopper, who rarely found anything even in the largest stores to make him or her happy and was consistently bullied by clerks who could care less whether something was sold or not. Could Paris be on the same planet?

There was a sophistication and an obvious affluence that was utterly foreign. The heavy traffic, with so many luxurious autos he'd never seen before and whose names he now strained his eyes curiously to read—Mercedes, BMW, Volvo, Renault, Alfa Romeo— left him breathless. This was the West he'd heard about and longed to visit for himself! To be here—at last! For the moment, caught up in the kaleidoscope of wondrous images, he even forgot Chernov, who was riding in the other limousine provided by the Russian embassy.

As they entered the huge traffic circle fed by nine converging avenues in front of the Palais des Congres, the magnificent Arc de Triomphe lay directly ahead, just visible in the distance at the end of Avenue de La Grande Armee. Beyond it stretched the fabled Champs Elysees. Off to the right, the Eiffel Tower pierced the blue sky. The few photographs he had seen were enticing, but Paris in real life exceeded his dreams. Moscow, which had always looked so impressive, now seemed somber and poverty-stricken in comparison. Even St. Petersburg—that magnificent city of the czars— appeared dull and dismal in retrospect.

While Chernov was registering the delegation, Viktor took in his dazzling surroundings. He glanced through a color brochure showing some of the huge conference rooms and exhibition halls, the 3700-seat auditorium, luxurious shops and restaurants, and the thousand-room high-rise hotel that made up the huge Palais des Congres complex. Moscow had its proud hotels as well. While they looked splendid from a distance, closer inspection inevitably revealed the disappointingly shoddy workmanship. The stark contrast to the flawless proficiency now before him could not be denied. It was his first glimpse of the "evil fruits of capitalism" he had heard denounced most of his life, and to Viktor the grandeur and opulence were beyond belief—but there they were.

Chernov herded the Russian delegation up the elevator to the twelfth floor, where the embassy had reserved a block of rooms. Before giving them their separate keys, the colonel held a brief meeting for everyone in his large and luxurious suite. Viktor was certain that no one else in the group would have such quarters!

"Two people in each room," recited Chernov, as though he had given similar speeches before. "One key, kept by the senior officer. We stay together. No one goes *anywhere* alone." He was looking directly at Viktor. "And every contact with anyone outside this delegation must be reported daily. You know your assignments."

Viktor's roommate, Fyodr, was a rather suave young man of about 30. Fyodr had already tried to strike up a conversation with him in the Moscow airport while they were waiting for the plane and had ridden beside him in the limousine to the Palais. It was quite obvious that his assignment was to gain Viktor's confidence in order to catch him in an incriminating slip of some kind. It was a game Viktor had played all his life, a game in which he was confident he could best any informant—and one which he even enjoyed at times. But not in Paris. It would only add to his burdens and stand in his way.

Viktor, Pyotr, Fyodr, and Chernov—who was posing as a parapsychologist named Dr. Alexandr Pavlov, allegedly Viktor's assistant—went together to the magnificent dinner and reception for all delegates held later that evening. It was a get-acquainted time before the opening session of the First International Congress on Parapsychology to be held the next morning. The colonel never left Viktor's side as he mingled among the numerous Westerners who were familiar with his published research and were eager to meet him at last.

Suddenly Chernov stiffened and grabbed his arm. "There he is! Right out of Yakov's video! So it *was* the Americans!" Out of the corner of his eye, Viktor could see Dr. Frank Leighton edging over in his direction. At last they came face-to-face.

"Dr. Khorev, what a privilege to meet you!" Leighton shook Viktor's extended hand vigorously. "This is your first time in Paris?" Viktor nodded. "We're so pleased to have you and your distinguished colleagues here on this historic occasion!" He reached out to shake Chernov's hand as well.

"This is my assistant, Dr. Alexandr Pavlov," said Viktor. "We are very happy to be here. I'm looking forward to exchanging ideas and sharing information."

Leighton was observing "Pavlov" curiously, an undisguised look of amusement on his face. "Any relation to the famous behaviorist?" he asked with exaggerated, innocent interest.

"He was actually a great uncle," responded "Pavlov" smoothly.

Leighton continued his scrutiny for another moment, then added in an offhanded and disarming tone, "I was just thinking that you bear a remarkable resemblance to Colonel Alexei Chernov. You know him, I'm sure—the commander of the elite Russian corps of psychic combat troops. They have a base north of Moscow."

There was no mistaking, at least to Viktor, what Leighton was doing. *He's trying to shake us up . . . let us know how far ahead the Americans are . . . what incredible power they have . . . that we're an open book. If he knows who Chernov is—not by ordinary spying techniques, but psychically—then he knows everything we've been doing, and all about me as well. So why would he help me escape, or even want me in the West?*

"I wasn't aware of the existence of such a corps," replied Pavlov in feigned surprise. He looked over at Viktor, who shook his head in confirmation of the nonexistence of such troops. "Where did you get such an intriguing idea?" asked Viktor, not knowing what else to say.

Leighton threw his head back and laughed. He patted Pavlov good-naturedly on the arm. "Isn't that the way it always is? You only hear the news of what's happening in your own backyard when you're thousands of miles away."

He turned his attention back to Viktor. "I'm very eager to have you come and see exactly what we're doing. We've made some remarkable progress that I hope will contribute to international peace. You'll be getting a formal invitation to visit our country through the proper channels."

"I would be very happy if that could be arranged," replied Viktor, wondering whether the man was serious now, but seeing a faint glimmer of hope. "It is my privilege to invite you to Russia." *If only Chernov weren't hanging on every word!* "We'll have to get together before the conference is over to work out the details." *If only I could see him alone!*

"Let's do it over lunch," suggested Leighton with enthusiasm, "in a nice secluded setting where we won't be bothered by your many Western fans interrupting us. How about tomorrow? I know a restaurant—*very French*—with the most delicious food you've ever tasted. It's not five minutes walk from here, just off Boulevard Victor Hugo."

"I'd like that," said Viktor wistfully. "Tomorrow, then?"

Viktor felt Chernov's steel-like grip closing in on his arm. "My assistant, of course, always accompanies me," he added obediently. "I hope that's agreeable."

"Of course," responded Leighton, giving Chernov a penetrating look. He turned to Viktor. "I understand fully. You'll both be my guests tomorrow after the morning session. I'll look forward to seeing you then."

"Next time you won't forget to tell your Western friends that you never go anywhere without your assistant, will you!" whispered Chernov threateningly, as they rode the elevator up to their rooms when the gala reception broke up late that night. "I'm sure they'll all understand."

"Leighton seems to understand plenty," returned Viktor caustically. "Like who you *really* are, for instance—and probably everything we're doing."

"And *our* job is to find out *how* he gets that information and to prevent it in the future!"

Viktor took some comfort in the word *our*. At least Chernov was beginning to recognize how important he was and wouldn't be likely to ship him back to Moscow without sufficient reason. But how would he get away from this leech long enough to seek asylum? That was going to be far more difficult than he had anticipated! Perhaps he could slip a note to Leighton somehow. No, there was too much to explain; the risk of misunderstanding was too great. There had to be another way.

Discovered!

s one of the top parapsychology journalists in the field, Carla Bertelli had, of course, been looking forward to the Congress for months. She had planned to arrive early to relax for a few days in Paris, but a last-minute development had forced a change in itinerary that brought her into Paris the very morning the Congress opened. Eager to catch at least the closing minutes of the first day's opening session, Carla had driven desperately from Orly Airport to the Palais des Congres in a driving rain. To save precious time, she decided not to check into her room yet, which meant she had no access to hotel parking. Instead, she left the rented Volvo C-70 convertible coupe in front of the Palais in a no-parking zone. Hoping that the official "Press" documents she'd stuck in the front windows on both sides would hold off the local gendarmerie until the noon break between sessions, she hoisted her umbrella and ran up the broad steps into the main entrance.

Checking in at the convention registration desk, Carla received her official Congress press badge and hurried to the crowded conference hall. As she made her way as inconspicuously as possible down a side aisle, Dr. Viktor Khorev, the second and final speaker of the morning, was just closing his address before entertaining questions and reactions from the audience. She slipped into her assigned seat in the "Reserved for the Press" section near the front and settled back to listen. Carla had been following Khorev's research for years—that portion that was published in or leaked out to the West—trying to read between the lines to catch hints of the real data he wasn't sharing. This conference, at last, was going to provide the opportunity for a personal interview with this celebrated Russian parapsychologist on his first trip to the West, and she had some very pointed questions to ask.

Looking younger than she had expected, Khorev had an honest, open face that made one want to trust what he said. He seemed relaxed but earnest as he reached the climax of his talk. "... So this Congress—and the future international cooperation that must result from it—involves the highest stakes, the very survival of civilization. In summary, let me remind you of the following:

"1) In spite of widespread use for years—and an almost blanket acceptance by medicine, psychology, education, and crime detection—hypnosis can be used as a powerful tool to effect mind control. No one knows how it works or what force is behind it. Not only must we have international cooperation in such research, but we must also effect a means of preventing harmful use of this power.

"2) Contrary to popular belief, a subject can be hypnotized without his consent or knowledge and made to act against his will. I have given you several examples where we have done this at distances up to 2000 kilometers.

"3) The possibility of remote mental influence being exercised over the entire world is no longer science fiction. It could happen! A major purpose of this Congress, therefore, must be to prevent such an eventuality.

"4) Hypnosis is only one example. Psychic power can be exercised in many other, and even more dangerous, ways. It is the ultimate force that might very well make obsolete every conventional weapon—possibly within as little as ten years. International controls must be established before it is too late. For this we need the cooperation of all nations. Time is short!"

Khorev paused to shuffle through his notes. "I have a statement which I have been instructed by my government to deliver at this opening session of the Congress." Finding what he was searching for, he began to read verbatim. "In the name of the peace-loving peoples of the Russian Federation, I call upon the delegates of this the first International Congress on Parapsychology to formulate an agreement for strict international controls upon future research and use of psychic power, and for the free exchange of all data. Nowhere is *glasnost*, or openness as you say in the West, so desperately needed as in the area of psychic development. The Russian Federation is prepared to cooperate fully with the other nations in making certain that psychic powers are used only for peaceful purposes. Thank you very much."

The applause was thunderous, not so much because Khorev had said anything that was new to the other delegates, but because of the emotional appeal of his final statement. One by one, members of the audience stood to their feet as the clapping continued. At last, the chairman for the day—tall, thin, and personable Dr. Hans Erickson of Oslo, Norway, who had replaced Dr. Khorev at the microphone—managed to make himself heard.

"You may be seated. We're running a bit behind schedule, but I don't want to cut short the question-and-answer period, so we may go 15 minutes or so into the noon break. When I recognize you, please direct your questions to Dr. Khorev—and confine them to the topic he has just addressed."

"Yes, Dr. Jacques Rouzier, of France. Your question?" The chairman stepped aside and Viktor returned to the mike.

The French scientist was obviously agitated. "Dr. Khorev, are you implying that brain waves can travel 2000 kilometers—the distance over which your hypnosis experiment took place?"

"Obviously not. Brain waves only travel a few feet."

"Then why do you use the term 'biological radio'?"

Gripping the podium and clearing his throat, Viktor fought to control the anger he wanted to direct toward Chernov, seated nearby at the Russian delegation's table. "It's merely a matter of semantics. In Russia we use that term. In the West, of course, you call it 'telepathy.'"

Rouzier was not satisfied. Clearly he intended to press the point. "There are proven experiments of mental telepathy halfway around the world. It has been demonstrated to function outside the limitations of space, time, and matter. Would you agree?"

Swallowing hard, Viktor conceded, "I can't argue with the evidence, but of course the exact explanation is a matter of interpretation."

"But it obviously is not some form of 'biological radio'—and the use of that term is misleading in the extreme." He waited for Khorev to agree, but getting no response, Rouzier continued. "What about the involvement of intelligences who may be so highly evolved that they are beyond the physical state and exist as pure consciousness? Could they not act, perhaps even without our perception, as the couriers or transmitters of telepathic communication that would thus operate outside the limitations of our physical dimension?"

Viktor was staring angrily at "Pavlov" with an "I-told-you-so" look, and scarcely heard what Rouzier was saying. Only with great effort could he tear his eyes off "Pavlov" and concentrate upon the question, which was becoming very long, complicated—and embarrassing.

"This has become a major theory in the West," Rouzier was saying. "Do the Russians accept this as a viable possibility? The reason I ask, of course, is because in order to engage in treaties for the control of psychic powers—and I agree that it should be done—it would seem that we need, first of all, an agreement concerning the nature of that power. And if other entities are, in fact, involved, then it may not even be possible for us to exert control over it without their permission or cooperation. Have these considerations been discussed in the Russian Federation at all?"

If I agree, Chernov will ship me back as a traitor to the materialist cause! If I disagree, I will only open this topic for further discussion, which would be disastrous! There was only one way for Viktor to resolve his dilemma. Turning to Hans Erickson, he strenuously objected, "Mr. Chairman, I think we're wandering from the subject of my paper."

"Not at all," protested Rouzier quickly. "If human brain waves only carry a few feet, yet telepathy has been demonstrated across continents, then the involvement of higher intelligences from a nonphysical dimension would be a good hypothesis, would it not?"

When Khorev again gave no response, Rouzier persisted: "Have you had any indication of that in your experiments?"

Sensing Chernov's murderous look, Viktor heard himself respond, "I think you've raised some important questions, but as I've already said, the Russian interpretation would differ from that current in the West—and that could very well cause problems. It's something that I agree should be explored."

Quickly he turned again to the chairman. "There are other hands out there."

"Yes, over there," said Erickson, pointing to someone with hand raised just behind the press section. "No, not you. Members of the press will have their special chance to ask questions later. Just behind—I believe that's Dr. Mitsuo Nakamoto of Japan. Yes, Dr. Nakamoto."

At that very moment, back at the secret base north of Moscow, Dmitri was also being confronted—not by an ardent audience of fellow parapsychologists, however, but by the feared Committee Overseeing Psychic Warfare Research. This was not a general inquiry, but a private one involving him alone, and it was being held in Viktor's office for ominous reasons. There had not been time to call together the full Committee. Only two members were present.

General Nikolai Gorky, his face dark with suppressed rage, sat behind Viktor's desk, with Colonel Lutsky seated grimly beside him. Looking frail and vulnerable, but with his head held high, Dmitri stood before them. Two soldiers were guarding the door.

The general's accusing eyes never left Dmitri as he angrily pushed the buttons to operate a tape recorder on the desk in front of him.

"Well, tell me, good comrade, how did it go today? I've been dying to find out!" Dmitri's pulse almost stopped at the sound of his voice coming from the machine.

"I think it went well, Dmitri. There were some anxious moments when I feared my trip was finished, but in the end I think they were satisfied. I went along with their totally insane idea that the Americans have been killing our best men. That made them happy."

General Gorky stopped the cassette player momentarily. "You admit being in here with Dr. Khorev two nights ago?" Dmitri nodded. "And you admit that we have just heard your voice and Khorev's?" Dmitri nodded again. Gorky turned the machine back on.

"Don't worry, old friend." Viktor's voice was confident and contemptuous. "Do you think they can hide an electronic bug from *me*? I put together my own detection equipment and use it to sweep this office every morning. As fast as they put their bugs in, I take them out."

"You do?"

"I do. It was costing them a czar's ransom. Those things are expensive. Finally they gave up. I haven't found one for weeks—and I just checked again this morning, so don't worry."

Gorky pushed the pause button. "So much for your cocky comrade's competence! Unfortunately, we didn't check the tape until this morning, or he would not be in Paris now—but you may be certain that he will be on his way back very shortly."

The general fast-forwarded the machine briefly. When it began to play again, Dmitri heard those shocking words from Viktor that had been haunting him ever since. Then came his earnest but ineffective pleading.

"Party ideology is an albatross around our necks! It stifles our research—and makes me sick! The whole human race may be in danger, and we can't pursue certain possibilities because Marx and Lenin would be offended! They rule us from their graves!"

There was a long silence on the tape, then Viktor's voice again: "I've made a big decision, old friend. What is impossible here is possible in the West. They're open to considering a nonphysical extension of the universe and intelligent life."

"Viktor! You're not . . . ?"

"I've got to talk with the Americans. I want to find Dr. Inman. We have to compare information."

"You can do that in Paris at the Congress!"

"With Chernov breathing down my neck? Even if I had complete freedom in Paris, we're only there a week. That's not enough time to scratch the surface, and Inman may not even be there. Dmitri, old friend, we've been together a long time, but I think we must now say farewell."

The general stopped the machine and pounded the desk in a rage. "You, Dmitri Petrekov, knew that Khorev was planning to defect in Paris! Do you deny that?"

"I knew," said Dmitri softly, but without shame. "I tried to persuade him not to."

"You kept his secret!" Gorky was livid. "You put a traitor ahead of your own country! You're a traitor, too! Not only that—" Gorky paused as though what he was about to say was too repugnant even to express. It seemed an eternity that he stared with contempt into Dmitri's unrepentant eyes. "Tell us once again," he said at last, "exactly what it was you were searching for when you were discovered early this morning in this office."

Dmitri returned the general's stare—not defiantly but fearlessly. "I was looking for the listening device that I suspected might be here."

"And why should you be concerned about such a device?" asked Gorky coldly.

"I wanted to protect my friend," came the honest reply.

"You wanted to save your own skin!"

"You may think what you wish, sir, but I was not concerned for myself."

"Every man looks out for himself first!" interrupted Colonel Lutsky.

"Two months ago," continued Dmitri courageously, "I placed myself in the hands of God—the God I had been taught all my life did not exist. Whatever happens to me now, I will accept as His will. What I have done was with a good conscience. Viktor Khorev has been loyal and conscientious in serving his country. He was not able, however, to tell the Committee what he really believed—that nonphysical beings were involved in the destruction of our psychics—because you would not have listened to anything that was contrary to Marxist materialism."

The general held up his hand. "Stop!" he ordered. "We don't need any further proof of your guilt—much less a *religious* lecture." He was making an obvious effort to control his anger. "You understand, of course," he added evenly, "that you have no right to a public trial—which is a pity, because I'd like to make a public example of both you and Khorev. But this work must remain secret."

Gorky turned to Colonel Lutsky. "I'm taking Petrekov back to Moscow with me. I've already sent a cable to the embassy. Khorev will be on the next plane out of Paris. I'm looking forward to meeting him myself at the Moscow airport!"

At the First International Congress on Parapsychology, Chairman Erickson was recognizing a fourth questioner. "Yes, Dr. Derek Balfour of the British delegation." Viktor stepped nervously back to the mike. His questioners were being polite, but they were also obviously attempting to discredit before the world the narrow-minded materialism of hard-core Marxism that had supposedly lost its power in the new Russia. Chernov was becoming increasingly agitated.

Just as the audience microphone was being handed to Balfour, Viktor's attention was distracted by the sudden entrance into the conference hall of two burly men who made their way quickly to where Chernov was sitting. One of them leaned over and spoke to him quietly. What could be so urgent that they could not wait the few minutes until the session ended? Casting frequent glances at Dr. Khorev on the speaker's platform, the three held a hurried consultation. The colonel seemed to grow more furious with every word. Viktor felt a sudden overwhelming sense of impending disaster.

Although the two men quickly finished delivering their message to Chernov, they remained squatting in the aisle next to the colonel. It took great effort for Viktor to concentrate his attention upon Balfour's question—which itself only increased his apprehension.

"In out-of-body experiences—such as the clinically dead looking down on their bodies from above, hearing and seeing everything," Balfour's tone was just a bit patronizing, "as a *Marxist*, do you think something *physical* is outside the body looking back at it?"

Avoiding Chernov's unnerving stare, Viktor replied: "The Russian position would be to call this a projection of consciousness."

"A *physical* projection of consciousness, Dr. Khorev?" persisted Balfour. "Surely even a Marxist would see . . . "

Jumping indignantly to his feet, Chernov interrupted with an angry roar. "Is the purpose of this Congress to ridicule Marxism?"

Startled by this uncivilized outburst, the British scientist looked to the chairman for help.

Erickson stepped quickly to Viktor's side and spoke calmly into the mike. "This is Alexandr Pavlov of the Russian delegation. I think his objection is a legitimate one."

"My point is," insisted Balfour, standing his ground, "that the narrow materialism of Karl Marx should not be allowed to limit the possible explanations of psychic events."

"And this Congress," shouted "Pavlov," "should not be an excuse for attacking political beliefs! I demand an apology!"

"I said nothing that warrants an apology. My remarks were addressed to Dr. Khorev, and I would like to hear his response."

"Pavlov" would not be put off. "Mr. Chairman, I will give the British delegation and the Congress Steering Committee three hours to deliver an apology. If not, then the Russian delegation is withdrawing from the Congress!"

Chernov had now revealed that he was the one in charge of the Russian delegation. *That can only mean one thing!* Viktor felt a sinking sensation in the pit of his stomach and had to hold onto the podium as a momentary dizziness swept over him. He watched in consternation as all of the Russians, following Chernov's lead, stood to their feet and headed for the nearest exit. Viktor was stunned. He put his notes hastily back in the briefcase, closed it, and stood there too shocked to think. He looked desperately and longingly in the direction of Dr. Leighton, who seemed in a state of shock also. Should he run to the Americans right now, crying out for political asylum? Before Viktor could rationally evaluate that desperate thought, Chernov grabbed him by the arm and steered him toward the door—with the two newcomers following closely behind.

The convention hall broke into pandemonium. The growing babble of voices became a roar as delegations huddled together in earnest conversation, trying to comprehend this startling development and to seek ways to resolve it. Jumping to her feet, Carla hurried to catch the departing Russians. *I thought Khorev headed their delegation. Who is this Pavlov? He must be bluffing. They're not pulling out! What if they do? I can't let Khorev get away without an interview!*

What Carla now observed heightened the mystery. While the rest of the Soviet delegation headed for the room elevators, "Pavlov" and the two men who had been in such earnest conversation with him pushed and pulled an obviously reluctant Dr. Khorev out of the lobby and down the front steps. Carla burst out the revolving front door just behind them. The rain had stopped and the sun was trying to shine through the thinning clouds. The Russians seemed to be heading toward a limousine parked directly in front of the hotel.

Hurrying down the steps in hot pursuit, Carla pushed her way through the crowd that had gathered on the sidewalk. She was just in time to see "Pavlov" shove Khorev roughly into the backseat of the waiting car.

"Dr. Pavlov!" she called, running up to him breathlessly. About to climb in beside Khorev, Chernov paused and turned around. Carla pointed to her Congress press badge. "I'm with the official press corps here."

Chernov cut her off with an angry "Nyet!" The merciless, cold-blooded look in his eyes made her suddenly afraid for Dr. Khorev. Several other reporters had wormed their way through the crowd and were edging up to "Pavlov" and Carla, with tape recorders, cameras, and notepads ready. "Le Dr. Khorev, s'il vous plaît!" The two men who had brought the limousine began shoving the journalists back.

Carla tried to step between "Pavlov" and the open door, only to be pushed roughly aside with such force that she almost fell to the pavement. "I've come all the way from Washington, D.C.," she protested loudly, "to interview Dr. Khorev!"

"Nyet!"

Slumped in the backseat, a thoroughly dejected and confused Viktor Khorev was trying to comprehend this sudden turn of events. Why had the other members of the Russian delegation apparently gone to their rooms, and only he had been hustled out to this vehicle? It was true that he had been speaking, but surely he was not being blamed by Chernov for what his questioners had persisted in saying. *Was there, after all, a device recording what Dmitri and I said? I checked that morning, but not after I had testified before the Committee! Or has Dmitri cracked and sold out our friendship? Somehow they've learned of my plan to defect!*

With terrifying certainty, he realized there could be no other explanation for what was happening. The best he could hope for would be a Siberian labor camp—if he somehow escaped the death penalty. His morose thoughts were interrupted by the sounds of a loud commotion on the sidewalk. Peering out the open door, he could see that Chernov and the two Russian Embassy FSB bodyguards had their backs to him and were viciously pushing back some Westerners and yelling at them in Russian, while the Westerners were yelling back angrily in English and French. In that instant he made a desperate decision. *Better to make even a futile attempt to escape than just sit here!*

Clutching the precious briefcase, Viktor shoved the door open on the street side and jumped out. Recklessly he began to thread his way as fast as he could through four or five irregular lanes of heavy traffic at the convergence of Boulevards Gouvion and Pereire. Not knowing how best to plot his course because of his total ignorance of Paris, he angled toward a smaller street that he could see just beyond the swirling mass of hurtling vehicles. If he could only get in there before Chernov saw him! Brakes squealed and horns blared as swerving cars racing around Porte de Maillot tried to dodge this insane pedestrian challenging them in the middle of the wide traffic circle. Attempting to avoid Viktor, a small

Renault sedan driven by an elderly woman cut in front of a racing taxi and the two cars collided. Three more in rapid succession piled into them. Within moments, the huge roundabout was jammed with bumper-to-bumper cars and frustrated, angry drivers.

At the sound of screeching brakes followed by the rapidly repeated crunch of impacted and crumpling metal, Chernov whirled around. Over the tops of a swarm of autos he could see Viktor breaking clear of the traffic jam and entering Rue Debarcadere. Reaching the sidewalk at last, the fleeing would-be defector ran as fast as the heavy briefcase would allow him.

Following "Pavlov's" gaze, Carla caught a fleeting glimpse of the man she wanted to interview just as he disappeared in the direction of Place Ferdinand. Then she remembered that her car was conveniently parked only a few yards away. Pushing her way clear of the growing crowd, she ran quickly toward the Volvo.

Swallowed Up!

Yelling a command in Russian, Chernov raced into the street. Because of the now-stalled traffic he was able to make much faster time than Viktor and had gained considerable ground on his quarry by the time he entered Rue Debarcadere. The two FSB officers jumped into the limousine and took off with tires screaming, but had to apply the brakes almost immediately. As they turned left into Port de Maillot to make their way around the traffic circle, their progress was impeded by the mass of autos and trucks backed up behind the five-car collision.

Carla made a hurried decision. Pushing the button to retract the roof of the Volvo convertible, she backed out of the entrance to the Palais in the opposite direction from that which the Russians had taken. Then she spun her car around and angled it across the oncoming traffic on the opposite side of the huge circle from the barely moving limousine which had now disappeared from her view. Drivers swore and shook their fists at her, but because of the collision blockage, only a trickle of cars was getting through in her direction. After several near-disasters she had safely negotiated the head-on traffic and was able to turn the Volvo into the small street that Dr. Khorev and his pursuer had entered.

By this time, Viktor was badly winded and his legs were near paralysis. He seemed detached from himself, as though he were watching his own agonizing performance in slow motion from a distance. The briefcase was now an impossibly heavy burden, an unreasonable impediment to his escape. Whenever that thought surfaced, however, he gripped the precious case all the tighter and pushed on. Each time he twisted his head around to look behind him, he could see in growing panic that Chernov was gaining ever more rapidly. Should he take refuge inside one of the shops or cafés he was passing? No, Chernov would tear the place apart. If only there were a gendarme in sight, but this was a small street and they weren't likely to patrol here. What could he do?

Rue Debarcadere was too narrow to allow Carla to pass other vehicles. Fortunately, however, the sparse traffic was moving fairly well. Fifty yards into the small street, she saw "Dr. Pavlov" charging like a wild bull along the sidewalk just ahead on her right, bowling over pedestrians in his mad race to overtake the fugitive who was now almost within his grasp. Passing "Pavlov," she pulled alongside a nearly spent Dr. Khorev. Face contorted with terror and the agony of extreme fatigue, he had scarcely the strength to carry the heavy briefcase any longer, but he still clutched it desperately as though he would rather die than abandon it.

Honking her horn and waving to him from the open convertible, Carla yelled, "Dr. Khorev! Dr. Khorev!" She was directly beside him now and slowed the car to match his exhausted pace. "Get in! Hurry!"

Viktor had no idea who this young woman might be, but she was his only hope. Staggering into the street, he threw his precious burden into the open auto and with his last remaining strength dove in after it, with Chernov now only a few paces behind. Just as Carla pushed the gas pedal to the floor, the colonel, with a superhuman leap, grasped the backseat and hung on with a grip of steel. Legs flailing empty air, trying desperately to find the bumper for support, Chernov struggled against the acceleration of the vehicle to pull himself inside. For one mad moment, Viktor attempted to batter his pursuer with the briefcase, but his strength was gone.

"Drop to the floor!" screamed Carla. Still accelerating, she entered the tight circle of Place Ferdinand at more than 70 kilometers per hour and made a sharp turn to the left into Rue Brunel. The car skidded crazily, throwing the rear around and slamming the right wheel up against the curb. The force was too great even for Colonel Chernov's brute strength. He lost his precarious grip and flew through the air. Caroming off the top of a sidewalk café table, the colonel crashed through a plate-glass window. The careening car tilted, nearly turned over, then righted itself as Carla regained control and sped away.

Through the rearview mirror she saw the Russian limousine enter Place Ferdinand and pull to a stop at the curb where she had shaken off Khorev's pursuer. The driver and his companion leaped out. They were half-carrying a staggering and badly bleeding "Dr. Pavlov" back to their vehicle when Carla lost sight of them as she made a sharp right turn onto Boulevard Pereire. Almost immediately she turned right again, this time onto the equally broad Avenue des Ternes. At last she breathed a sigh of relief.

"We're going to make it! We're going to make it!" she shouted happily.

In a state of shock, Viktor was crouched on the back floor. He was still clutching the briefcase, his chest heaving in agony.

"The American Embassy!" he managed to gasp.

"That's where I'm headed. Don't worry. It's a straight shot—and not far."

Carla knew Paris almost as well as she knew Washington, D.C. Just past Place Des Ternes the Avenue narrowed and became Rue du Faubourg St. Honore. She followed its slightly skewed route as far as it went. Viktor pulled himself up onto the backseat and slumped against it, still gasping for breath. Every few moments he turned his head fearfully to search the traffic behind them for signs of their Russian pursuers. They were nowhere to be seen.

Turning right at last onto Rue Royale, Carla exclaimed exuberantly, "We've got it made—they can't catch us now!"

For Viktor, the terrifying nightmare had metamorphosed into the surrealist numbness of a dream. Directly ahead, in the center of Place de la Concorde, his eyes focused in surprise upon a huge Egyptian obelisk towering above the traffic. It all seemed unreal—like turning the pages of a schoolbook to see once again a picture of this 3000-year-old treasure of Ramses II brought from Luxor's ancient temple growing rapidly larger in his vision. Was this actually happening?

"The embassy?" It took all of his concentration to get out the words.

"Look to your right!" yelled Carla in triumph. Turning abruptly onto Avenue Gabriel, she pulled almost immediately over to the curb. A large building set far back could be seen over the top of a high stone wall surrounding it. There was an entrance for autos leading to a circular drive going up to the front of the building, but the heavy metal entry gate was closed. On either side of it paced a member of the French gendarmerie holding a submachine gun. A brass plaque on the wall read: "No. 4, Avenue Gabriel, AMERICAN EMBASSY." The defector from the Russian Federation could not hold back a sob of relief.

As Carla and Viktor opened their doors to get out of the car, the nearest policeman moved quickly toward them, waving his gun and shouting, "Parking interdit!"

Viktor shrank back into the auto, but Carla kept moving and motioned to him to follow. "Please help! It's an emergency!" she called back in French. "He's a Russian defector! We're being pursued."

"D'accord!" Quickly the policeman waved them toward a low, narrow structure built into the wall just to the right of the metal gate and, with his gun at the ready, turned to watch for their pursuers. Entering hurriedly, they were confronted by two young United States marines in full uniform.

"He's a Russian defector!" Carla explained again. "We have to get inside!"

"Yes, ma'am," came the answer in a welcome Southern drawl. The marines hardly changed expression. "Let's have the purse and the briefcase. Just step through this metal detector."

They both looked back over their shoulders toward the street several times as they half-ran across the courtyard and up the steps of the main embassy building. Over the top of the steel gate, there was still no sign of their pursuers.

"We made it!" exclaimed Carla, giving Viktor a triumphant "thumbs-up" sign as they entered through the broad doors. Safely inside at last, they were motioned by another young marine guard toward a reception counter on the right, just beyond a group of sofas and chairs. There Carla confided in a low voice to a clerk, "This is Dr. Viktor Khorev from the Russian Federation—a very important scientist. *He wants political asylum!*"

The young woman's eyes widened. "Please take a seat over there, and someone will be right with you."

Throwing back her long, auburn hair and taking a few welcome deep breaths, Carla said with a warm smile, "Well, now that we can finally relax, I guess it's time to introduce myself. I'm Carla Bertelli."

"Carla Bertelli—the American journalist?" Dr. Khorev asked tentatively.

"You mean I'm known in Russia? I don't believe it!"

"I've read some of your articles. Excellent!" He looked at her admiringly, then blurted out, "I thought you were—well, much older."

They both laughed, the tension draining. There was a brief, spontaneous embrace. Viktor held her at arm's length. There were tears in his eyes again. "You saved my life! Do you know that?"

Carla nodded. "I suppose so. I didn't understand what was happening. I guess I just acted on impulse."

Wearily they sank down together on a long sofa facing the reception counter. Viktor was shaking his head in relief. "I can't believe it! I'm free! I didn't think it would happen. How could I ever repay you? I owe you everything!"

"Well, I did have a selfish interest," said Carla, turning toward him with an impish grin. "I've been looking forward to having an interview with you for months—and I wasn't going to let anything prevent *that*."

She hesitated a moment and then grew serious again. "I'll tell you what you could do for me, Dr. Khorev—a very, very special favor."

"Yes, tell me!" said Viktor eagerly.

"How about an *exclusive* interview?"

"You mean I don't talk to any other journalists—you get the whole story?"

Carla nodded. "Is that asking too much?"

"Too much?" exclaimed Viktor. "I owe you my life. How do you say it in America?—you've got a deal? You've got a deal!"

"Dr. Khorev?" A balding and rather owlish-looking man of about 45 in an impeccable business suit had opened a private door to their left and was looking questioningly in their direction.

"Yes, I'm Khorev," replied Viktor eagerly.

The man marched over somewhat pompously, almost like a parade of one, bowed slightly and shook Viktor's hand warmly. "I'm Karl Jorgensen. Do you have any identification?"

"Yes I have." Viktor picked up the briefcase and patted it affectionately. "And I've got more data in here than you could imagine!"

Jorgensen's eyebrows raised just slightly, and a thin smile formed on his lips. "If you'll please come with me."

"And Miss Bertelli?" Viktor gestured toward Carla. "She brought me here—rescued me, saved my life."

"We must talk to you alone first of all." He turned to Carla. "If you'll just wait here for a few minutes, we have some formalities." He smiled reassuringly.

"Yes, of course." At the door, Viktor hesitated and turned around. Carla waved. "I'll be right here," she called.

When the First International Congress on Parapsychology reconvened that afternoon, the Russian delegation was conspicuously absent. The conference hall was buzzing with rumors that Khorev and Pavlov had quarreled and that Khorev had last been seen running across Boulevard Pereire into Rue Debarcadere pursued by Pavlov. It took the Congress chairman, Dr. Erickson, longer than usual to quiet the conferees and to get their undivided attention.

"I have been unable to get in touch with either Dr. Khorev or Dr. Pavlov," began Erickson. "None of the Russians has checked out of the hotel, yet I have not been able to contact any of them. I did reach the Russian Embassy, however, just a few minutes ago. Although they could not help me in locating Khorev or Pavlov, they assured me that their delegation had not withdrawn from the

Congress and would accept the formal apology that had been delivered to them by the British delegation.

"The Americans and a number of other delegations," continued Erickson, "have also expressed their goodwill and their deep concern that the Russians not withdraw from this Congress. We have reminded them how vital their continued participation in the important decisions yet to be made at this conference will be. I'm sure everything will work out. In the meantime, we must proceed on schedule.

"And now let me introduce our first speaker of the afternoon, the distinguished philosopher and mathematician as well as one of the world's best-known parapsychologists, Dr. Bernard Rogers of Canada."

The brief applause was quickly enveloped by the solemn hush of anxiety that still hung like a pall over the conference. In spite of Erickson's assurance, the Russian delegation's section was empty, and that spoke louder than the chairman's words. So somber was the atmosphere that Rogers wondered, as he looked up from his notes and cleared his throat to speak, whether his audience would be able to forget the present crisis and actually hear the important points he had to make.

"The title of my paper is 'Psychic Applications in the Search for Extraterrestrial Intelligence,'" he began. "As we all know, the existence of extraterrestrial intelligences somewhere—and probably in millions of locations throughout the universe—is no longer doubted by most space scientists. The only question is how to make contact with them. The basic problem, obviously, is the vast distances over which contact must be made."

It was at that point that the thoughts of Dr. Frank Leighton, who had begun to listen with great interest, were interrupted by a messenger presenting him with a United States Embassy envelope and a receipt form to sign. Intrigued as to what it could contain of such urgency, he hastily tore it open and read the message within, whistling softly under his breath as he took in its importance.

As Leighton's concentration was drawn into the message he was reading, the Canadian's speech became muted, as though it were reaching him from another dimension. "Traveling at one million miles per hour—40 times present capabilities, but perhaps conceivable in the not-too-distant future—it would take 30,000 years for visitors to reach earth from the nearest solar system 4.5 light-years away. Our galaxy is 100,000 light-years across, and it is 15 times that distance to the next galaxy.

"Obviously, the likelihood of face-to-face physical contact with beings from other planets is too remote to take seriously. I certainly wouldn't stay awake nights thinking about what to do if it should happen. Even radio contact would take a nine-year round-trip to the nearest solar system, and hundreds or thousands of years to any really likely locations where intelligent life might exist within our own galaxy—to say nothing, of course, of the millions of years it would take for radio contact with those in other galaxies.

"I don't want to hold Carl Sagan's Memory and his successors and the entire search for extraterrestrials—to which the world's governments have committed tens of millions of dollars—up to ridicule, but you can see that some other approach is needed. Nor do I need to tell you the one way that the problem posed by these vast distances can be eliminated. Of course, I'm talking about *psychic* contact.

"There is another even more intriguing possibility—that there are not only extra*terrestrial* intelligences out there, but extra*dimensional* intelligences as well. Exactly what this means in technical terms need not concern us at the moment, so long as we are convinced that it is a viable scientific possibility, which I have no doubt that it is. That this subject is of the utmost importance and urgency . . . "

Catching the attention of the American delegation's vice chairman seated next to him, Leighton leaned over and whispered in his ear. "There's an emergency. I have to fly immediately to Washington, D.C. Please take over for me, will you? Fortunately, I don't deliver my paper until Friday and hope to be back by then. If not—I hate to put that burden on you, but would you mind giving it for me?"

"I'll do my best," was the whispered response.

Leighton pulled a file folder from his briefcase and handed it to his obliging colleague. "It's all typed in final order, no handwritten notes." He shut the briefcase and, with a whispered word in the ear of another colleague, walked quickly out of the conference hall.

Carla looked impatiently at her watch for at least the tenth time in the last five minutes. Dr. Khorev had been behind that closed door for more than two hours. *Had something gone wrong?*

She went to the reception desk. The two young women who had been there when she and Khorev had come in had been replaced by two others. One of them looked up and smiled pleasantly as Carla approached. "May I help you?"

"Well, I hope so. I brought someone in here nearly two-and-a-half hours ago, and I've been waiting. I was told it would only be a few minutes."

"Well, let me check for you. What kind of business did this person have, or who were they seeing?"

"He was a very important Russian scientist—a defector. He needed political asylum."

"I don't recall any such person. We've had nothing like that since Iron Curtain days. No one defects anymore.'"

"You weren't here when we came in. Anyway, a Mr. Jorgensen—I believe it was Karl Jorgensen—took him through that door right over there. Said it would be a few minutes and asked me to wait. I've been waiting, and waiting. Could you check to see what is happening with Dr. Viktor Khorev—that's his name—and how much longer it's going to be?"

"Certainly." She picked up a phone and dialed. "This is Arlene out in front. There's a lady here who says she brought in a Russian *defector* a couple of hours ago—a Dr. Viktor Khorev. Do you have any information I can pass on to her? She's been waiting."

The receptionist put down the phone. "He's going to check and let me know. It could be a few minutes. Why don't you just sit down again?"

"Thanks, but I'll stand." Carla paced back and forth, a growing feeling inside that something had gone terribly wrong.

The phone rang, and she turned eagerly to the reception desk. Arlene picked up the phone and listened for a few moments, then put it down. "There is no record of any Russian *defector*—that just doesn't happen. Are you sure?"

"What do you mean, am I *sure*! I brought him in here myself!"

Arlene looked sympathetic and genuinely puzzled. "That was the ambassador's secretary. Believe me, if any Russian had come in here, she would know."

"I don't care what she says," returned Carla evenly, leaning over the counter. "She's lying. I brought Dr. Khorev in here myself!"

"Let me assure you, no one lies around here—certainly not the ambassador's personal secretary!"

"This is incredible! I want to talk to Karl Jorgensen! Get him out here!"

"I don't think Dr. Jorgensen has been in today. He usually doesn't come in on Thursdays."

"Get him out here—now!"

Shaken, Arlene picked up the phone again and dialed. After a brief conversation, she held it away from her ear and said to Carla, "Just as I told you, Karl Jorgensen has not been in all day. In fact, he's gone back to Washington."

"Listen to me! Jorgensen or no Jorgensen, I don't care. Just get someone with authority out here to talk to me!"

Arlene said a few hushed words into the phone. About two minutes later, the same private door opened and another well-dressed and polished embassy-type gentleman called to her. "Miss Bertelli?"

"Yes!" Carla hurried over to him. "What have you done with Khorev?"

He had shut the door behind him and stood with his back against it. "I think the receptionist has told you that we have never heard of a Dr. Viktor Khorev, has she not?"

"And we both know that's a blatant lie."

His face reddened. "Those are harsh words, Miss Bertelli. I could call you a liar, too."

"My word against your word—is that the game?" Carla's eyes were flashing. "How do you know my name?"

He hesitated. "You gave it to the receptionist."

"I did not—and she mentioned no name on the phone." Carla drew a deep breath. She stared at him contemptuously. "Look, I'm not a nobody. I happen to be a very well-known journalist with a photographic and indelible memory that's been recording everything."

"Don't be a fool! The Russian government will officially deny that he's missing. You've got no story."

"You're right. I'm not publishing anything—until I have the *whole* story. And I'll get it!"

"Good luck!"

"I saved Dr. Khorev's life. I'm sure you know that. He promised me an *exclusive,* and I'm holding him—and the U.S. government—to that promise! Don't forget it! And remember this, too: I know where Dr. Khorev is being taken—and if he's not treated fairly, I promise you, the whole world is going to know!"

the
MIND
INVADERS
16

Project Archon

I can't say that I'm exactly shattered. I'm too cynical for that. But it's still disillusioning when your own government—or at least those who represent it—*lie* to you! That's the sort of thing we expect from the Russians, but not from our own people!"

Angry and frustrated, Carla was speaking by phone to a close friend in New York, one of the senior editors of *Time* magazine. As she talked, she paced impatiently back and forth within the limits of the phone's short cord in her fourteenth floor room at the Palais des Congres. Perfectly framed in her window, there before her gaze at the far end of Avenue Raymond Poincare lay the majestic monument of Place Victor Hugo and the sprawling Palais de Chaillot, while just beyond arose the black filigree of the Eiffel Tower. She fixed her eyes on its familiar and stolid beauty as a frame of reference for a world gone badly awry.

"Why should you be shocked?" came the unruffled voice from the other end. "Eisenhower lied to the whole world about Gary Powers and the U-2 spy plane the Soviets shot down in 1960; John Kennedy lied about the Bay of Pigs in 1961; Nixon lied about CIA attempts to fix the Chilean elections in 1970, as well as about his tapes and—I could go on and on. Denial isn't just the name of the game; it's an honorable tradition and it's still in vogue. You don't expect the embassy boys to say, 'Yes, Miss Bertelli, we have taken

Dr. Khorev to a secret location for our own nefarious purposes and aren't going to let anyone know about it until we're good and ready, so please don't breathe a word.'"

"I know, George, I know. But it's terribly insulting and demeaning when you get lied to right to your face! I can't let my personal feelings get involved, but it still makes me screaming mad!"

"Look, Carla. I know you think you're onto something bigger than Watergate, but you're also aware of the general feeling among editors about *psychic research*. That's tabloid stuff. You couldn't get a legitimate paper or magazine to touch it with a robot. If Khorev were a physicist or a novelist or in the military or an athlete or almost anything else—but a *parapsychologist*! That's the kiss of death on your story. Most editors would say, 'Oh, another Uri Geller, huh? Well, that fad has died off, thankfully. Sorry, we're not interested.'"

"He's not a psychic, for heaven's sake. He's a scientist who checks up on psychics—and he's one of the most brilliant in the world!"

"Most if not all psychics are phonies, so why does he have to be so brilliant to check up on them?"

"George, the CIA is involved in this up to its ears."

"How do you know?"

"I'm not at liberty to reveal that yet, but I've known it for a couple of years. Anyway, it's fairly common knowledge that the CIA is involved to some extent in psychic research. If *they* take it seriously, that ought to give it some credibility."

"Oh, now you've really convinced me. Shall I remind you of some of the absolutely kooky things the CIA has been involved in, the blunders it's made, the bungled, harebrained assassination plots against Castro, Lumumba, and others—working with people like Noriega, the endless list of lies and misinformation?"

"Forget it. I've read Woodward, Agee, Marchetti, Stockwell, Snepp—all the exposés by ex-agents." She paused and frowned at the Eiffel Tower. "Okay, so if I can't get an old friend like you interested—"

"I'm interested. You know that. I'm just reminding you of what you're up against."

"Please don't. I've heard it for years. But I'm telling you, *something* is going on that's way out of the ordinary."

"Convince me."

"Well, you know why I'm over here. This is the world's very first International Congress on Parapsychology. And it's not a bunch of out-of-touch professors sitting in their ivory towers talking theory, either. These are official government representatives discussing actual applications of psychic power, and very concerned about it."

"Like what?"

"Look, I don't have time to go into that."

"That's the problem, Carla. It's always so vague."

"George, it's not vague—believe me. But please have pity on me—I'm paying for this phone call. The Russians are so concerned that in Khorev's speech this morning, addressing the entire Congress, he called for international controls, free exchange of information—and he was dead-serious when he warned about the dangers of psychic power!"

"But you think he was being hustled off to the airport to be taken back to Moscow?"

"There isn't any other explanation for what I personally witnessed and got involved in. We could have both been killed!"

"Then apparently the Russians weren't happy with his speech."

"I'm not talking about his speech. This was a prepared statement that his government instructed him to read."

"You think he changed it?"

"No, there's something else behind this. Listen. I get nothing from my friend at police headquarters here in Paris. A top Russian scientist defects, and one of their delegation has to be in a hospital here somewhere with dozens of fresh stitches in him, and there's not a peep."

"You've checked the hospitals?"

"Every last one. They really have the lid on this! The American Embassy goes so far as to tell me—*me, the person who brought him in*—that Khorev doesn't even exist. Hide a defector—that's standard procedure. But you tell the world you've got him, and the other side screams for his release. Why is nobody saying anything?

There's something I don't understand, and whatever it is, it's got to be big—really big!"

"Well, I'll admit it stinks a little worse than usual. I'll give you that much."

"And to top it off, Dr. Frank Leighton, head of the American delegation, has vanished as well. I would bet you anything that he's on the same plane with Khorev heading for the U.S. right now. And let me tell you something else—Leighton's been working for the CIA for years!"

"So have a lot of other people."

"He's not just a paid informer—he's involved in secret research that's incredible. But I can't even write about that yet. I've been sitting on it because it was passed on to me in confidence."

"Okay, what do you want me to do?"

"Just remember what I've told you and let me know anything that comes over the wires that seems to be even remotely related to this story."

"Okay. I can reach you at this number in Paris, right? Then you're back in Washington?"

"No, when this Congress ends Saturday, I'm only stopping in Washington long enough to pick up some things. Then I'm heading for California. I'll call you when I get out there."

"California?"

"I'm reluctant. It's going to be painful."

"Ken?"

"I don't think there's any other way. He's still got a connection with Leighton, and that's how I'm going to find Khorev." Her eye had wandered over to look down on Rue Debarcadere and Place Ferdinand. For a moment she had a horrifying vision through a rearview mirror of "Pavlov" bouncing off the table and flying through that plate-glass window. She shuddered—and then a smile began to spread across her face. *It serves you right, you contemptible gorilla! I'd love to know your thoughts right now.*

"Are you there, Carla? Hello?"

"Sorry—I was just thinking. One of these days, George, I'm going to hand you one incredible story! That's a promise. Talk to you later."

She hung up the phone and stood looking down upon Place Ferdinand for a few more moments, relishing the memory. Then it hit her. *Why didn't I think of this before? They're going to be looking for me! They don't know me—but they know my car!*

She dug around in her purse, found her rental papers, and hurriedly dialed a number. When someone answered, she began talking rapidly in French. "This is Carla Bertelli. I picked up a blue Volvo C-70 convertible from you this morning at Orly. Yes, I know it was for a week, but I can't drive it anymore. No, there's nothing wrong with the car, just with me. I'm incapacitated. Someone will have to come and get it. I'm at the Palais des Congres. Never mind the cancellation fee, penalties, pickup—or anything else. I don't care what it costs. And there's a 100 Franc *pour boire* if someone can get here within the hour. I'll be waiting in the main lobby near the checkout desk."

Viktor had protested vehemently at being taken suddenly out a back exit from the embassy and into a waiting limousine without being able to thank Carla Bertelli once again for saving his life. "It's extremely urgent to get you out of France," Jorgensen had insisted, "and safely to the United States before the Russians raise an international furor."

"But what about Miss Bertelli?" he had asked. "She's waiting, you know."

"One of my assistants will explain everything to her. She'll understand."

Now the sense of euphoria began to build until he thought he would burst with the joy and relief. On the way to the airport, Viktor kept running his hand over the briefcase clutched on his lap to make sure it was still there. It all seemed unreal, especially when, without going through customs or passport control, he was escorted aboard a large, sleek jet that apparently belonged to some agency of the United States government. He was treated with great courtesy and care, as though the flight and everyone on it existed for his benefit alone. It was not long before he realized that was indeed the case.

As soon as the plane had attained its cruising altitude, Viktor became the center of attention—attention that began with questions that seemed at first to reflect genuine interest in him as an individual, but which soon turned into intensive and eventually grueling interrogation. For the first hour or so, it hardly seemed to matter. He was almost too intoxicated with the wonder of it all to answer the questions that were being fired at him in rapid succession. However, the truth finally moved from surrealism to cold reality. He was indeed high above the Atlantic Ocean, speeding toward Washington, D.C., and it had at last become clear to him that his fellow passengers were all either embassy personnel or CIA agents. He was now certain that his interrogators had to be with the CIA.

"Doctor, we're sorry to be asking so many questions, but you understand why we have to be as thorough as possible. It's for your protection as well as for ours." Jorgensen had said that at least five times, but he sounded sincere and Viktor appreciated his solicitude, even if it seemed overdone. At last Viktor leaned back in his seat, completely exhausted with the effort.

The seats were arranged facing one another on both sides of the plane. Viktor was in the middle on the right aisle facing toward the rear, with five other men sitting around him. Three were obviously professional interrogators. Then there was Jorgensen and an aide. There were at least a dozen others on the plane, but he'd had no contact with them as yet, although they were apparently part of his escort. Looking around, he'd seen several men engaged in phone conversations. It was an impressive operation.

"Take us through your reasons for wanting to defect just once more, Doctor, if you don't mind." Why did they keep saying that? If he did mind—and he did—he couldn't say so. This politeness seemed so unnecessary, and certainly strange in comparison with the way the Committee back at the base, for example, operated.

"Well, as I've said," began Viktor once again wearily, "the evidence I accumulated over the past five years—and I have as much of it as I could carry in my briefcase—led me in directions that I couldn't pursue in a Marxist society where materialism has so long been the sacred cow. I don't have to tell you—that even now—there's little freedom to think for yourself—especially at certain levels in the military and classified work—and I'm starved for freedom. I need freedom for my research, which is my whole life—and personal freedom just to be a human being." He paused and shrugged. "And that's basically it."

"And the Paris Congress gave you the first chance you'd had?"

"I'm not a Communist Party member, never have been, and without that you couldn't get out of the country—and even very few Party members ever got to the West. There's just no way you can escape across the border to Finland or Turkey—at least not any way that I would dare to try. There's supposedly a new freedom—but not for people in my position. They wouldn't have sent me to the Congress if it hadn't been necessary to give the delegation some legitimacy. Every so-called 'delegate' except me was working for the FSB."

In a curtained-off section in the front of the plane, Frank Leighton, tie loosened, looking tired but clearly very excited, was seated with two other men—the embassy's top Russian expert and the CIA's Western Europe division chief. They were closely watching Khorev's interrogation on closed-circuit television.

"I don't think he's a plant," said the embassy official, for about the sixth time. He himself had defected from Russia 20 years before. Everything about Khorev rang true, not only to this expert's intimate knowledge of the Russian system, but to his intuition as well.

"I *know* he's not a plant," insisted Leighton. "He's too important to them to risk—and I need him immediately out in California!"

"There's no way you can put him to work yet," protested the CIA division chief. "So forget that." And then he added cautiously, "He wouldn't be the first big fish they've thrown our way."

"He's not a 'big fish,'" retorted Leighton. "He's their top man in psychic research! They couldn't possibly afford to use him that way. Can you imagine how much it's going to set them back to lose him?"

"I still think he could be a plant," cautioned the CIA watchdog. "He's got to be kept on ice until we can check him out thoroughly."

"What do you want to do?" demanded the Russian expert. "Treat him like you guys did Yuri Nossenko, locked up for three years in a tiny room with the screws turned ever tighter, trying to break him because somebody was afraid he was a double agent?"

"Don't keep bringing that up," countered the CIA man. "I know Yuri was your friend, but that's an isolated case, a bad mistake—and plenty of mistakes have been made in the other direction, too. Don't forget Fedora and Tophat. Their misinformation about Soviet ICBMs led us astray for years. And how about Colonel Penkovsky? Now there was the darling of British Intelligence, and our own also—supposedly the greatest Western intelligence coup of the century. And you know the doubts about him today. I just want to be sure."

"There's no way to be *sure*. Lies become truth, defectors turn out to be plants, some of our own agents are working for the other side. Moles are everywhere, and pretty soon you don't believe your own judgment and black-and-white evidence when it's under your nose." He threw up his hands. "Everything's a calculated risk."

Leighton had deliberately withdrawn from the argument. It was irrelevant as far as he was concerned. He had already placed a call to the Director of Central Intelligence (DCI) and would make his appeal directly to him. Noticing Leighton's lack of interest in their discussion, the other two joined him in leaning back and watching the television monitor in silence. Khorev was going into more details than he had before, telling about the last experiment.

"This was the third psychic we lost. He was out of his body—at least that's my present understanding—probing a target that the FSB had given us several pictures of . . . quite a large complex supposedly located outside Palo Alto. We were told it was a CIA psychic research lab."

The questioners seated around Khorev exchanged skeptical glances. In the front of the plane, Leighton suddenly sat up straight and leaned forward on the edge of his seat.

"Did he describe what he saw—any details of interest?"

Viktor nodded. "Yes, but better than a mere description, I developed a means of transferring the image in a human brain onto video film. My briefcase—someone took it from me when I came aboard—" Viktor looked around questioningly, just a trace of worry in his expression.

"We can get it for you when you need it."

"There are things in there I really need to explain," put in Viktor hurriedly.

"You'll have plenty of time for that later. Now you were saying—?"

"I've got a cassette in there of what our psychic saw. I suppose you've heard of Dr. Frank Leighton—one of your top parapsychologists. You'll see a glimpse of him on the video."

Behind the curtain, the Russian expert and the CIA chief looked at Leighton questioningly. He stood abruptly to his feet. "This has gone too far! I want the questioning stopped—*now*. I'll take full responsibility." He pulled the curtain aside, and the three of them hurried down the aisle.

"He was dead beyond a doubt," Khorev was saying as they came up behind him. "And that mangled, lifeless arm—holding a felt pen that none of us had ever seen before—printed out in Greek letters the message: 'Death to Prometheus. Archon.'"

Following the gaze of the men seated opposite him, Viktor turned around and was astonished to see who was standing there listening. Leighton leaned over and patted Viktor on the shoulder. Surprised and overjoyed, Viktor reached up and the two shook hands warmly.

"I missed you at lunch today," quipped Leighton, "but dinner will do. And I think we'll both be just as happy that your 'assistant' won't be listening in."

Viktor managed a weak smile. "You must tell me how you knew who he was."

"Oh, I'll explain that and a whole lot more in due time. Chernov's a nasty one—fills up one of our thickest red-flagged files. But you won't have to worry about him anymore."

"That's right!" exclaimed Viktor, and then repeated the words as though he were just beginning to understand his new freedom. "You're right—no more Chernov! You can't imagine what that means!" The tension drained from his face, and he joined Leighton in an exhilarating laugh.

"I was looking forward to showing you the sights of Paris," added Leighton a bit wistfully. "But how about Washington, D.C. instead? And after that San Francisco!"

"It's just too much to believe." Viktor's voice was choked. "Am I really here? Is this really happening to *me*?"

"It sure is. We're happy for you. And you can count on us for any help you may need. Now I think it's time we all had something to drink and relaxed a bit before they serve us some dinner."

In the middle of dinner Leighton was called away to a phone. It was the DCI returning his call.

"I understand you've got Khorev," said the director.

"Right. That's what I was calling about."

"Congratulations! I'll hear how it happened later. How does he look?"

"Clean as a hound's tooth! I mean, this is *Viktor Khorev*—the one and only. He's not playing any games."

"I'd tend to agree with that just because of who he is."

"We've been through his entire briefcase. You've never seen anything like the treasure of documents he's brought us. I guarantee he hasn't held anything back."

"That's a good sign. So?"

"I've got to have him immediately out in California."

"That's not the way we do things."

"I know it isn't, but this is a unique situation."

"You know I'll take some heat from some of the Old Guard."

"I know, but can't you see where Khorev could play a key role in getting the Plan accepted by the world? Think about it!"

There was a long silence on the other end. When finally the director spoke, there was suppressed excitement in his voice—excitement that he never allowed to intrude into his professional life, but which he could scarcely suppress now as the truth of what Leighton had said gripped him. "You've got him. On one condition: He doesn't leave the base. He's got to be kept there under 24-hour guard—for his protection and ours."

"I'll see to that!" responded Leighton.

"And listen: This project is so sensitive that if Khorev ever steps one centimeter out of line, he's history!"

"Do you want me to bring him to Langley to see you on my way through?"

"I'm leaving for the Middle East tomorrow. I'll stop by when I'm next out on the West Coast. This is a big break—congratulations again!"

When dinner was over, Leighton motioned for Viktor to follow him. Together they went toward the back of the plane, away from the others.

"What I'm going to talk about now is so secret," Leighton said in a confidential tone, putting his hand on Viktor's shoulder and leaning close, "that no one on this plane knows about it except me—and soon you. So don't mention this to anyone—and don't discuss your video or your work, no matter who asks. I've given the order for no one to question you any further. So if someone tries to do that, just call for me." He paused for a moment, smiling warmly at Viktor.

"I've really been treated very kindly."

"And you always will be," said Leighton solemnly. "Now I don't know what your hopes were—I mean what you expected to do in America?"

"Of course, I want to continue my research here—if there's some place I can fit in." He looked at Leighton questioningly, knowing that what he had in mind was really too much to ask—at least at this early stage. "I had hoped to be able to learn about your research, but I know it may be very secret."

"That's no problem. I'll be happy to show you everything."

"Would you? That would be wonderful!" Viktor began to feel that he and Leighton would be good friends. "I hope I can see you sometimes—I mean, I don't know where I might be taken."

"That's up to you, really."

"It is?" Viktor couldn't believe his ears, but then this was the West, and he was going to America, the land of freedom. That gave him courage to ask something else. "There's someone I've wanted for years to meet."

"Who's that?"

"Dr. Ken Inman. I've read some of his papers and find his theories particularly challenging, but he seems to have dropped out of sight. I haven't seen anything recent from him." Something changed slightly in Leighton's eyes that Viktor couldn't interpret. Now he was fearful that he had overstepped his bounds. "I'm sorry—I shouldn't be expressing myself so freely when we hardly know each other."

"No, that's quite alright. So you want to see Inman. You know, he hasn't been involved in this field for about two years."

"Did he retire? I thought he was quite young."

Leighton was thinking of a possibility that might have some real promise. "I'm sure I can arrange for you to meet him. That wouldn't be difficult. Whether he'd be willing to talk about his psychic research—that's another question. But to you—yes, I think you might be able to do what some of the rest of us have tried to do without success: stir his interest again."

Viktor didn't understand what Leighton meant and didn't know how to respond. They stood facing each other in silence. At last Leighton put his hand back on Viktor's shoulder and his tone became confidential once again.

"You may have been hoping for a little vacation, and I can probably arrange that later. There's a matter of some urgency, however, and I was wondering whether you'd be willing to join my staff at that special research installation in California?"

Viktor's eyes lit up and a grin began spreading across his face. "You really mean that? Is it possible?"

"I'll have to get security clearance for you, which isn't usually granted at this stage, but I've got a lot of confidence in you." He was searching Viktor's eyes. "You won't let me down, will you?"

"Never!" said Viktor earnestly. "This is such an honor. I never dreamed of such a thing!"

Leighton gripped his arm. "You're going to find what we're doing fascinating. Remember: No one else on this plane knows about this project, so don't mention a word."

Leighton motioned Viktor over to a seat. They sat down and Leighton leaned in close. "What we're involved in out there is the most exciting challenge I've ever faced. Let me tell you a little bit about it. The code name is 'Project Archon.'"

the
MIND
INVADERS
17

A Surprising Proposal

C arla slowed the rented car to a crawl as waves of nostalgia swept over her. The curving street, the elegant new homes set far back on acre lots, the pleasantly rolling foothill terrain and, at last, the house she hadn't seen since it had been in the framing stage—it all seemed reminiscent of a dream she had long forgotten. *It's beautiful, but I can't believe he's lived in that huge place all alone for two years! I'm sure he hasn't married—at least I haven't heard. Plenty of women would be interested in him! He probably has someone in mind if he isn't engaged by now.*

Sitting atop a steeply sloping and ivy-fringed lawn at the end of the cul-de-sac, the home was all she had imagined and hoped for— in another time that now seemed unreal. The low, sprawling silhouette of its overhanging roof of beige concrete shakes blended into the lush landscaping of stately conifers, blooming azaleas, and rhododendrons. The magnificent native live oaks that had been left in place completed the tasteful artistry, appropriate to the background of wooded hills rising just beyond. It had been little more than raw acreage and a dream the last time she'd seen it.

She had come directly from the airport—hadn't even gone to her hotel yet. At first, Carla had thought of calling from there, but that would have made it even more painful. It had to be a surprise for him—and she knew that if she didn't get it over with immediately, she might not find the courage to face him later. Courage? She felt a total lack of it as, with growing apprehension and embarrassment, she forced herself to climb those broad steps onto the front porch and ring the bell. *Maybe he won't even be home. Off on a trip somewhere—or who knows what. I should have phoned first. This is crazy!* Anxiously long moments preceded the sound of familiar footsteps beyond the door. Then it swung open and there he was, a look of shocked and openmouthed unbelief written on his face.

"Carla?"

"You remember the cartoon of the guy who went by plane, then canoe, and finally by dogsled to reach a cabin deep in the Arctic, and then said, 'Thought I'd drop by while I happened to be in the neighborhood'? Well, I just happened to be in *this* neighborhood. Only all I did was fly in from D.C.—no canoes or dogsleds."

He didn't laugh at her little joke—didn't even smile. He seemed too stunned to know whether to invite her in. It was, after all, a staggering surprise.

"Actually," continued Carla, "I'm pursuing a story. And I desperately need your help or I wouldn't be here." Her voice quavered just a little in trying to get out the carefully chosen words through a mouth that had become suddenly very dry.

That's Carla—still the same. Abrupt, honest, everything up front. That's one of the many reasons I loved her so much. Ken stood there for what seemed another eternity, trying to convince himself that his eyes and ears were not deceiving him, that it was really happening. *Carla* was actually standing there, looking more beautiful than ever, facing him on the front porch of the home they had dreamed of and planned together.

"Well, come on in," he finally managed to say, opening the door and stepping aside. "You know I'll do anything I can to help you."

"I know. That's why I came." She stepped inside, her full skirt swishing against him as she passed. Now he smelled her perfume, the kind she'd known was his favorite. He'd tried to forget her, and thought he had pretty much succeeded, knowing that was best. He had dated several other women, but none of them seemed right. And now suddenly, in spite of himself, he felt that overwhelming attraction again. *Get hold of yourself, Inman! It's finished.*

They stood without speaking, just inside the door, looking at one another. She was searching his face for scars and not finding any. "It's great to see what a remarkable recovery you made. Are you as sound as you look?"

He nodded. "Perfect condition, so the doctor tells me. And your job? I confess I haven't seen many of your articles—don't read the right journals anymore."

"No need to apologize. I wouldn't expect you to." Her eye was taking in the comfortable but simply-furnished sunken living room just off the entry hall. Its huge windows reached from floor to lofty open-beamed ceiling and looked out upon a breathtaking view of the city in the distance below. The large stone fireplace and raised hearth with its sweeping curve across the far corner of the room had been one of her many creative ideas. The plans they had worked on together had incorporated far more of her taste than his. *He finished it that way—and still lives in it!*

For a moment she could see them strolling hand in hand over the raw land, then merrily walking through the floor plan that had been laid out on the finished foundation—and finally, the last time, just after it had been framed and just before the accident, like children playing house, going through "their home" together, excited to get their first real sense of the size and layout of the rooms. She put a hand quickly to her mouth so he couldn't see that her lips were trembling. That surprising upsurge of feelings—feelings that she had assured herself were long dead—caught her completely off guard. She was amazed at their intensity.

He led her into the living room and pulled up a chair for her near his in front of the fire. They sat for a moment in another brief but awkward silence.

"Have you had dinner?" Ken asked at last. "Mom is fixing it right now." Seeing her look of surprise, he explained, "My dad died just before Christmas. I've got this big house here, you know, that we . . . " His voice caught and he turned away for a moment, then managed to continue. "Well, she's out here now staying with me. The winters are pretty tough in Maine. She'll keep the family home back there for the grandchildren, for summers. It's right on the bay—well, you remember."

Carla suddenly felt like crying on his shoulder as the guilt surfaced once again. Walking out on him when he was still in the hospital so close to death. It seemed so heartless. She threw her head back instead and laughed, that rollicking, lilting laugh he knew so well.

"What's so funny?" he asked in feigned offense.

"You! You look like you've just seen a ghost."

"Well, haven't I?" They both laughed nervously.

"Dinner is out of the question," said Carla firmly. "I'm not staying long. I just got off the plane from D.C. and came right here. It's rather urgent." She was looking around the room again, taking it all in with evident approval. "You've done a great job, Ken. It's beautiful."

"Would you like to see the rest of it?" he asked eagerly, jumping to his feet. She didn't move, as though she hadn't heard. He hesitated, looked embarrassed, then sat down again. "Well—why don't you tell me how I can help you?"

"You're still in touch with Dr. Leighton?"

"You mean Frank? Not really. Why?"

"But you could be?"

"I suppose, but I don't have any real reason. We've hardly had any contact since he bought me out. That's got to be two years."

"And he moved your equipment—that you invented and developed—to another location. Do you know where?"

Ken nodded. "I've been there once—maybe a year ago. He needed some technical advice when it was being reinstalled. But I'm out of that field completely. And Frank's very secretive now. You may have been right about the CIA."

"I was right—about that and a few other things." She stared thoughtfully at the fire in silence. "He'd really like to have you involved once more, wouldn't he?"

"He's told me that a few times." Ken looked uncomfortable. "What's this sudden interest in Frank? I heard you crossed him off your list—which surprised me, really. He could have been a great source."

"It was mutual. But *you're* still on good terms. Right?"

"As far as I know. But, as I said, we haven't really had any contact for a long time—for reasons that I'm sure you remember."

She looked a bit uncomfortable for a moment, but chose not to take up the challenge, if that was what he intended. Instead she surprised him. "Listen, suppose I said that I'm in agreement—that Leighton's involved in something *evil*?" At Ken's hopeful look, Carla held up a cautioning hand and shook her head. "Please, don't jump to conclusions. I've got different reasons than you have, of course, but I don't like what I think is going on." She paused, choosing her words. "Look, I've got certain suspicions, okay, that I have to check out somehow."

Ken got up and threw on another log. He stood there with his back to the fire, looking at her questioningly. "Why don't you tell me exactly what you have in mind?"

"I don't know *exactly*. That's the problem. I just have a bad feeling about something." She hesitated, then shrugged and continued. "It's too much to go into, really. There's a hot story, as you probably suspect. It's got everything in it—CIA, FSB, a Russian defector—and I suspect that Frank is right in the middle of it."

"The big story that comes along once in a lifetime?" interrupted Ken. "Pulitzer prize?"

"Forget the prize. This is far more important than that. I saved someone's life in Paris. You'd know his name—Viktor Khorev."

"You're kidding! How did you do that?"

"Well, I just happened to be in the right place at the right time. Rescued Khorev when he was making a break for it and just about to be caught. I got him to the American Embassy in Paris. They took him into an office for an interview, and then they denied that I'd brought him there—tried to tell me they'd never seen him!"

"This must be some bad dream you had," interrupted Ken skeptically. "You're saying they just outright *lied* to you—it was that blatant?" She nodded and Ken laughed. "The State Department doesn't know what a huge mistake it made. They've got a tiger on their tail now. And you're going to show them."

Carla smiled and held up both hands in mock humility. "Okay, okay—that's part of it. But give me credit for having some heart. I'm deeply concerned about Khorev. I don't want to see him exploited! That's happened too many times to defectors to let me feel comfortable right now. He's got to be somewhere in this country, of course, and I think Frank's got him."

"And, of course," added Ken facetiously, "incidental though it may be, there *is* a story involved—and it sounds like a big one. So you wouldn't pass that up."

"I'm not *all* heart. After all, Khorev owes me his life—and he *promised* me the exclusive on his story. But I think he's gotten himself involved in something much bigger than his defection, and he's going to be my entreé to that as well."

"I think you're probably right about him being with Frank— eventually. But I doubt that he'd be involved out there already."

"I think he is, and I've got my reasons. But again, that's too much to go into now."

"And you want me to find out, if I can, whether Khorev's actually there, and generally what's going on. Is that it?"

"I want more than that. I want to get inside that installation myself and see firsthand what's going on!"

"Why don't you just go directly to Frank? You could reach him at Stanford—that's where I'd have to call. He still teaches a course or two over there. In fact, he's head of the department now, in case you hadn't heard. He'd be glad to be back in touch with you—probably invite you out there himself, if he thought you'd give him a good write-up. Of course, he wouldn't want you to mention any of his secret work. You know how paranoid Frank is about that side of things—his fear of the Russians and all that."

Carla shook her head. "No chance of that! You don't know the way I told Frank off the last time I saw him—for taking advantage of you when you were in the hospital and stealing your life's work for a fraction of what it was worth, and for a few other things. I don't think he'd give me the time of day." She stood to her feet. "Am I asking too much?"

"Ken, supper's going to be ready in about five minutes. Do you hear me? Where are you?" His mother's voice drew nearer as she came down the hall from the kitchen. Before Ken could answer, she walked into the living room and stopped in surprise. "Oh, I didn't know you had a visitor." Then she saw who it was and put both hands to her mouth in astonishment.

"Carla—I—well, how wonderful to see you!" She rushed over and gave Carla a hug. "Would you join us for dinner?"

"It's nice of you to ask, but I already told Ken I couldn't."

"Well, I'm much more persuasive than he is. It would be such a treat! Would you?"

"I can't." Carla started toward the entry hall to escape what was becoming increasingly emotional and embarrassing. Ken hurried after her. He opened the front door. "I'll see what I can do. Where can I get in touch with you?"

"At the Hilton. But only if you can get me in out there—or have found Khorev."

She started down the steps and he followed her to the car. "Hotels are terribly expensive. You could stay here. I wouldn't hassle you. There's a suite, you know, at the other end of the house with its own bedroom, study, and bath—and its own entrance."

"I know. That was my idea, remember?"

"This house is full of your brilliant ideas, and they all worked out great—except the bomb shelter under the garage. Solid granite begins about six feet down."

"That was your inspiration."

"Well, you thought it was a good idea, too." He looked at her longingly. "You really ought to see how it all turned out."

She put a hand on his arm. "Your mother's as sweet as ever. Tell her I'm sorry I couldn't stay. And maybe you shouldn't even mention to Frank yet that I'm out here."

As soon as dinner was over, Ken got on the phone and called the Elliotts. Karen answered.

"Everything going okay?" she asked. "We missed you Thursday. Hal was going to call you."

"I missed being there. Had a touch of the flu, but I'm okay now. Is Hal in? He ought to get on the phone, too."

"No. Emergency surgery. What's up?"

"Carla's back in town! She just left here a few minutes ago!"

"Praise the Lord!"

"Well, yeah—but I'm sure she's just as far from the Lord as ever. There wasn't any chance at all to broach that subject."

"I wouldn't even think of that yet, Ken!" said Karen gently. "It's not your job to 'witness' to her. You've already tried that. She knows what's right—now it's her move. If the Lord opens the door, and she shows some interest . . . okay. In the meantime, you just need to be a friend to her, if she'll allow that. Let her see the love and forgiveness of Christ in your life."

"Well, I think it was pretty clear that she has no intention of even giving me a chance to do that. She wants me to do a favor for her, which I'd be happy to do if it was anything else." Ken hesitated. Finally he added, "I don't feel comfortable about it, but I promised her . . ."

"Promised her what?"

"She wants me to get back in touch with Leighton."

"Ken!"

"Don't worry. You know it's completely out of the question that I would get involved again in the slightest. But I promised I'd contact him to try to find out something for her. She's working on a big story."

There was a long, thoughtful silence on both ends of the line. "It was great to see her again, and there's still a lot of feeling there, that's for sure. It really surprised me—and convicted me, too. I have to confess that I've tried so hard to forget Carla that I haven't prayed for her lately as I should. But I'm going to from now on."

"I've never stopped—day and night. God has given me a real love and concern for Carla, and Hal feels the same way. Well, this *is* interesting! So you're going to contact Leighton after all this time. And at least you're back in touch with Carla. I'll notify the prayer group right away."

"Yeah, that's why I was calling."

"So she's working on a big story that involves Leighton—that's interesting! Is there anything else you can tell me to pass on to the group so we can pray specifically?"

"Not yet. It's her secret. She thinks it's the biggest story that's ever come along. If it's what I think it is—you know, if Archon is going to make the move like we've been expecting—then we'd better start praying around the clock and getting a lot of others to join us!"

Ken called Frank's Stanford office first thing the next morning. "You just caught me!" exclaimed Leighton, sounding both surprised and pleased. "It's been a long time."

"I've been wanting to get in touch, but you know how time flies. How are things going?"

"You mean here at school, or at the lab?"

"Oh, I read about you in the alumni news. I apologize for not calling sooner to congratulate you—new head of the department and all that. But actually, I was wondering about the project."

"Still worried that I'm trafficking with demons?"

"Frank, I'm not calling to push my beliefs unless *you* want to talk about it. I really am interested to know what's been happening."

"Ken, I'd love to show you." Leighton was bubbling with enthusiasm now. "When you see what we're doing and where it's leading—well, you'll forget all about those 'powers of darkness.' I can't talk about it on the phone. It's too big."

"And too secret, of course. I understand."

"Well, that's true. But, actually, we're not going to keep it secret much longer. Not totally, anyway. We've got to gradually leak it to the press. The public has to be informed."

"Really? You've come that far?"

"You can't imagine what's happened! It's interesting you called, because I was just thinking of you last night—*and* your ex-fiancée. I caught a glimpse of her in Paris last week at the Congress. She'd be the logical one to write some key articles about our research."

"Frank, this is amazing. I haven't seen or heard from Carla since she broke our engagement, but she just got into town last night and we were talking about you and the project. She expressed a lot of interest."

"Really? Listen. What about this? Del Sasso—you remember Del Sasso?"

"I never met him, but you've talked about him."

"Right. Well, Del Sasso is going to be doing some work in our main lab tomorrow. Why don't you and Carla stop in? That would give you both a good idea of how far we've come. You remember where we're located?"

"I can find it. What time?"

"It's going to be at 10:00 in the morning, so you should be here by 9:30. Actually we're doing this for someone who just arrived from—well, you'll meet him tomorrow. In fact, I was going to call you, because he's very anxious to meet you. Seems to be a great fan of yours."

"Can't imagine who that would be. Anyway, we'll be there. See you at 9:30."

"One thing, Ken. There's a lot of security around here. Just some precautions. I'll leave word so they'll let you in."

Carla was out when Ken phoned. She returned his call just after lunch.

"How would you like to see your Russian friend tomorrow?" he asked.

"Look, Mr. Practical Joker, this is too serious to kid about."

"I'm not kidding." He heard her gasp on the other end of the line.

"You're not?"

"Nope. How about if I pick you up at the hotel at 9:00 tomorrow morning? I promise not to drive over any cliffs."

There was a moment's hesitation, then, "Why don't I come to your house? I'll follow you from there in my car. I'd feel more comfortable that way. And you're really not putting me on?"

"Come on, Carla, you're making me feel bad. Where's your confidence? When you put Supersleuth Inman on the trail—well, you ought to know it's in the bag! Tomorrow you get to find out what's going on. We're both invited to watch Del Sasso do his stuff in the lab—you know, he's Frank's prize psychic. And you turned out to be right again. I'm just about positive your Russian friend will be there."

She was ecstatic. "This is fantastic, Ken!"

"Oh, that's not all," he added matter-of-factly. "Can you take any more good news?"

"If you try to make it any better than this, then I'll know you're putting me on. What more could there be?"

"Frank says they're going to begin leaking developments to the media, and he'd like you to write some key articles. How about that?"

"You just broke through my credibility barrier. I don't believe a word you've said now."

"Carla, it's all true—every word."

"So I was right on this, too. I told you Frank would be eager to get you involved again. That's what did it."

"But you and I know that isn't going to happen. And I don't want to mislead him. I'm just getting you inside there, and then you're on your own. That was our deal—right?"

"That's right."

"Okay. See you tomorrow morning out here at 9:15. I'm about ten minutes away, and we're supposed to be there at 9:30."

"I'll be there. And Ken, thanks. I really do appreciate it."

General Nikolai Gorky's office was on the third floor of the modern high-rise building the KGB had moved into during the summer of 1972 and was now occupied by its successor, the FSB. The huge crescent-shaped complex was hidden behind a thick wood just off the road encircling Moscow—much like the sequestered Central Intelligence Agency headquarters outside Washington, D.C. The architecture even seemed to have been patterned after the CIA design. Gorky was one of the few people in the new structure who had come up through the ranks in the old All-Russian Insurance Company's building on Moscow's Lubyannskaya Square that the infamous Cheka, predecessor to the KGB, had occupied in 1918. He was very happy not to be in that ancient edifice any longer. Many FSB offices were still housed there, along with the notorious Lubyanka Prison where Gorky had gotten his start as a guard and learned the exquisite art of extracting confessions by torture for whatever the State wanted—whether they bore any relationship to what the prisoners had actually done or not. He had come a long way since then to become responsible for an elite corps of commandos trained in psychic power, whose very existence was unknown even among top Russian leaders—except for the FSB director himself, the President, and the General Secretary of the Communist Party, and a very few close aides.

Gorky had always exuded a smug and seemingly justified confidence in his periodic reports to those above him. On this day, however, he was still smarting from the humiliating experience of a meeting with the two most powerful men in the Kremlin—a meeting that had gone on into the early-morning hours. He'd had to confess that the Americans had apparently killed their three most talented psychics. And on top of all that, the most brilliant and productive Russian psychic researcher had defected right under the noses of the psychic force's field commander and two of their best FSB agents and was now working with the Americans.

Gorky was in no mood to face anyone, but the matter was urgent and time was of the essence. Nor was Colonel Alexei Chernov inclined toward patience and kindness that day. The stitches had only been removed that morning. Two long scars, still ugly and red, were all-too-conspicuous for a man who needed to be able to blend into the crowd. One scar angled across his nose and down his left cheek, and the other slashed across his neck beneath the chin. Another few millimeters and it would have severed his jugular. These two proud but now humiliated and furious men faced each other in Gorky's office, each knowing that something had gone terribly wrong in their operation, but neither willing to admit it, much less to take responsibility.

"You had your orders in Paris—and you failed." The words came painfully from Gorky, knowing that failure of those under his command eventually reflected upon him.

Chernov stood stiffly erect. "There will be no more failure, except by the Americans. I had never been in favor of Khorev's method of penetrating the CIA by projection of consciousness. On the spot, we will accomplish our mission. I have no doubt about that."

"Don't be so cocky," cautioned Gorky. "You know that overconfidence can bring defeat to the superior force in any conflict."

Chernov nodded grimly and shifted uneasily. "I will not be *over*confident, just confident—and with good cause. I'm taking my two best men. Together we can accomplish the impossible."

"Are you forgetting the hooded one? From the new information we've just gotten, he's extremely dangerous!"

"We will destroy him."

"I want Khorev *alive*—don't forget that. We have confirmation that he's working with Leighton and is being housed on the Palo Alto installation. It's a fortress."

"I want to see him *dead*—and the woman, too—but you know I obey orders."

"Do whatever you want to satisfy your thirst for revenge against the woman who helped him escape. Her name is Carla Bertelli. She's got to be a CIA agent. Her career as a journalist is just a front. She's in Palo Alto already."

The general stood abruptly. "Remember: I want Khorev *alive*, right here in front of me! I want to sweat and bleed his full confession out of him *personally*."

Gorky picked up a large, thick envelope from his desk and handed it to the colonel. "These are your new identities, passports, and instructions for you and your men. They'll be expecting you at the consulate in San Francisco, but they know nothing. Colonel Lutsky is being assigned there as an advisor. You report only to him or to me. Don't fail this time, comrade!"

|nside!

T he thick fog that had drifted over the hills from the coast during the night was vanishing under the warming rays of the morning sun. The few lingering wisps of vapor lent a momentary translucence to the air, giving the leaves and blossoms on trees and shrubs a delicate, glistening sheen. It was a morning of rare beauty—which only seemed to accentuate the bittersweet mood that gripped Ken. In spite of the fact that he had long since given up any thought of recovering his past relationship with Carla, their brief meeting the night before had stirred emotions for her that he had thought were long dead and that he dared not nourish now.

Ken backed out of the garage and eased his GMC Yukon down the steep driveway just as Carla, in her rented Chrysler, came around the curve and stopped in the cul-de-sac to wait for him.

"Perfect timing!" called Ken, as he pulled up beside her. "Follow me, and we'll be there in a few minutes."

Traversing the rolling residential area through a maze of curving streets, they came at last to the main highway. Here Ken turned left and headed higher into the coastal range. As they began climbing into the foothills, a flood of memories poured over him. This was a route he purposely avoided for that very reason. Ten miles ahead was the cliff he'd gone over. He'd been up there only once since that fateful day. Looking down from the road to the chasm below, he'd been overwhelmed by a mingled awe and gratitude at the miracle of his survival. As a result of that fearful plunge that should have brought death, he had found a new life as different as night and day from what he'd known before.

A little more than a mile up the winding highway, the two cars turned right onto a newly paved road marked "Private: Keep Out." After another mile of meandering through a thick forest of young pines, the road led into a stand of mature redwoods. It was one of the few groves that had survived—through belated government intervention—the earlier indiscriminate slaughter in the 1800s of these ancient giants. Soon another much larger and obviously newer sign warned: "Restricted Government Property. No Trespassing!" Shortly thereafter, they came over a sharp rise and the trees opened up to reveal a broad meadow. Here the winding approach straightened and ran along a ten-foot-high stone wall that had not been there on the one previous occasion when Ken had visited the clandestine installation. Except for the coils of barbed wire on top, it was vaguely reminiscent of an ancient medieval castle, complete with moat.

Ken pulled left into a narrow entrance. There were no signs to indicate what kind of government operation this might be. The heavy, solid-steel gate was nearly as high as the wall and revealed nothing but a few scattered treetops beyond. Built into the wall next to the gate was a fortified guard station manned by two men carrying automatic weapons and wearing flak jackets over their civilian clothes. One of them approached Ken's vehicle, while the other remained inside, on the alert.

"Dr. Inman?" the guard asked.

"That's right."

"Identification, please." He leaned down and looked through the window, searching the interior of the car. "Is that Miss Bertelli behind you?" Ken nodded. "Would you please open the back?" asked the guard. A brief search followed, then the businesslike order to close it. Only after the same procedure had been followed with Carla did the heavy gate swing slowly open. It closed with ponderous precision the moment the two cars had moved inside.

Fifty yards directly ahead, at the end of a broad drive lined with flowers and exotic shrubs, stood the main complex—a wide, two-story building of heavy construction, few windows, and a solid front door sheltered behind a stone wall of about shoulder height. Other buildings, low and rambling, lined the wide lawn that stretched out to the right and left on either side. The installation had been greatly enlarged since Ken had visited it earlier and now formed a giant U-shape, open toward what seemed to be the only gate in the massive, high wall surrounding the property.

In front of the main building the drive widened to allow a dozen spaces for "Visitor Parking" on either side. There Ken and Carla left their cars and walked the short distance to the entrance under the vigilant surveillance of two more guards wearing flak jackets and with automatic weapons slung over their shoulders.

"Just your average psychic research lab," whispered Ken with pretended naiveté. "No reason at all to imagine the CIA could possibly have anything to do with this friendly little operation!"

"I knew *something* was going on," returned Carla softly, "but this is *awesome*—a far cry from any parapsychology lab I've ever visited!"

"May I see your bag, Miss Bertelli?" asked one of the guards half-apologetically as they approached the front door. "Just a formality." While he performed that inspection, his companion ran a metal detector over their bodies. "Okay. Go on in. Dr. Leighton is expecting you."

Leighton was waiting in the small lobby just inside the heavy carved-oak front door, which Ken suspected had a steel core. As they entered, Leighton rushed over to greet them, arms extended exuberantly. Shaking Ken's hand vigorously, he exclaimed, "You don't know what your call meant to me, Ken! It's great to be back in touch and to know that you're interested again. We could sure use your expertise!"

"And Carla—what a wonderful surprise this is!" Leighton began, turning to greet her warmly. She gave him her hand tentatively. He shook it gently, then held it in both of his for a moment. "I had planned to talk with you in Paris, but then I had to leave suddenly. And now here you are!"

Then to both of them, Leighton explained apologetically, "I hope the tight security wasn't too bothersome. It's just a precaution."

"Do I detect that same old paranoia about the Russians, Frank?" Ken shook his head in mild reproof. "I thought it was all peace, love, and brotherhood now, with arms reduction and all that good stuff."

"It is!" replied Leighton, winking at Carla. "However, we've made some reluctant concessions to the normal world of bombs and bullets—but not for long. What we're developing here will bring *real and lasting* peace to the world, not just a slogan. And I don't mean decades or even years from now, but in a matter of *months!*"

"If you can do that, Frank," said Ken sincerely, "then you've got me and everyone else on your side. I'd be very interested to know *how* you're going to do it. I guess that's what we came here to find out."

"And have I got a trip for you!" Frank's eyes were gleaming. "Buckle your seat belts and hang on."

Motioning to them to follow, he led them down a long hallway, pausing beside the first door on the right. "We'll stop in my office for a moment." With his hand on the knob, he turned to Carla. "Are you ready for a surprise? Someone in there is very anxious to see you. Can you guess?" She looked nonplussed and shook her head. It wouldn't do to let him know that she had suspected Khorev was here and had actually come in search of him.

Leighton opened the door and led the way inside. A slightly built man of medium height with dark, prematurely graying crewcut hair and Slavic features jumped up from the sofa facing the huge desk and rushed toward Carla, arms extended.

"Miss Bertelli!"

"Dr. Khorev!" There was a quick, affectionate embrace, then a momentary awkward silence.

"They didn't let me say goodbye," began Viktor at last. "I'm sorry. Of course, they explained to you."

Carla started to say, "No, they didn't," but glanced over at Leighton and some sudden instinct caused her to swallow those words. "It's so good to see you here safe and sound!" she exclaimed. "That's all that matters."

Putting an arm around Carla once again, Viktor turned to Leighton. "You can't imagine how brave she was! If it weren't for Miss Bertelli, I wouldn't be here!"

Frank motioned toward Ken. "Viktor, this is Ken Inman—the man you wanted to see. He's actually the genius who invented the Psitron."

"It's a great honor to meet you," said Ken enthusiastically, giving him a warm handshake. "I've followed your work for years—what little we could learn. I've read everything of yours that's been published in the West."

"It's a greater honor for me to meet you, Dr. Inman. Dr. Leighton has told me about your research—and your terrible accident. I only arrived last night, and I'm looking forward—"

"Let's drop the 'doctor' stuff, Viktor," interrupted Leighton good-naturedly. Viktor acknowledged the reproof with a nod and returned Leighton's smile. They had apparently been over that before.

"About five more minutes, Frank!" The penetrating, slightly abrasive voice belonged to a tall, spare, and rather attractive fortyish woman in a white lab coat who had materialized briefly in the doorway, then disappeared down the hall.

Leighton called after her, "Come back here, Kay!" She reappeared, smiling, and took two short steps into the room.

"This is Kay Morris," said Leighton. "She's in charge of our labs—and what she says goes."

"Want to put that in writing?" responded the woman with a short laugh. "That would be the day!"

"Kay's made some fantastic contributions," returned Leighton, sounding almost too effusive. Carla's investigative reporting instincts were suddenly aroused. As a bachelor, and not a very handsome one at that, Leighton had always been known at Stanford as a cold fish. Yet there was an uncharacteristic warmth between him and Kay—an intriguing chemistry that obviously went beyond the most amiable employer-employee relationship. That in itself would not have been enough to pique Carla's interest had it not been for something else she sensed as Leighton hurried on with his introductions.

"Kay, you haven't met Viktor Khorev yet. He's just come from Russia to join our team." Viktor half-bowed, and Kay's smile suddenly froze as she seemed to notice him for the first time. Quickly she recovered.

"Not the world-renowned parapsychologist!" she exclaimed smoothly.

"You're right!" went on Leighton with great enthusiasm. "This is *the* Viktor Khorev—fresh from the base we know so well just north of Moscow. He's going to be quite an addition to our staff, and I know he'll have a great deal to contribute."

"I'm sure he will," responded Kay. Turning toward Viktor, she said with less-than-ample enthusiasm, "I'm looking forward to working with you, Dr. Khorev."

Something wasn't right, but Carla couldn't put her finger on it. *Is she, perhaps, paranoid about Russians? Or does she feel threatened by a male world-class parapsychologist coming into the picture? Or are my journalistic instincts out of control? I don't know, but there's something . . .*

"This is Carla Bertelli, the journalist," Leighton was saying. "I'm sure you've read some of her stuff."

Kay managed a more convincing smile than she'd given Viktor, and seemed almost relieved to turn her attention away from him. "Yes, in fact I have. Most insightful. What a pleasure to meet you, Miss Bertelli."

"And last, but far from least," continued Leighton hurriedly now, glancing at his watch, "this is Ken Inman, who invented the Psitron a few years back and wants to see what we're up to now."

Kay extended her hand. "I think you'll be astonished," she declared with a show of real enthusiasm, "to see how far we've gotten using your incredible electronic device—and some of the innovations we've added."

"I'm looking forward to that," replied Ken.

Kay nodded to each one again. "It's an honor to meet all of you," she said cordially. Then, glancing at her watch, she added, "I'm sorry, but I have to get right back to the lab. I'll see you over there. In about two minutes," she added pointedly to Leighton, then turned and hurried from the room.

"Ph.D. in robotics from MIT," said Leighton, with evident pride. "Brilliant, efficient. The smartest thing I ever did was hire her three weeks ago. She has really gotten us organized." He hesitated as though he felt he might have waxed a bit too enthusiastic. "I don't need to tell you the connection between Kay's expertise in artificial intelligence and what we're involved in here."

He started toward the door and motioned for them to follow. "We can talk more later. The man I want you all to meet is Antonio Del Sasso, the most remarkable psychic in the world. He's already in the lab preparing himself—and Antonio's a stickler for promptness, so we'd better get over there."

Leighton led them out into the hall again and around a corner to the right. Carla was still preoccupied. Suppose there was a romance between Frank and Kay. While it was none of her business, she hoped it would bring the real happiness that, as long as she'd known him, she had sensed Frank desperately needed. Add to the strains inherent in such a relationship with one's boss the tremendous pressure Kay must be under to perform, and now the unknown elements being introduced with Viktor's entry—perhaps her reaction to Viktor had been only natural. Carla filed the impressions away for further reference and determined not to let them inhibit her relationship with this rather unusual woman.

Again Leighton's effusive voice commanded Carla's attention. "Antonio is the first one to be fully developed on the Psitron. He's been under the direction of the Archons for two years. They have a program for developing other psychics—in fact a plan for the world."

"You're in touch with *Archons?*" asked Viktor, looking at Leighton in sudden consternation.

"I thought I'd explained that."

"You invited me to join 'Project Archon,' but I had no idea . . ." Viktor seemed almost frightened.

Leighton stopped in front of a door marked "Laboratory 1". Above it a large red light was flashing the warning: "Experiment in progress." He looked at Khorev with concern. "Would constant contact with the Archons and guidance from them bother you?"

Viktor hesitated. "They have done you no harm?"

"Harm?" returned Leighton with a laugh. "Of course not! They're our mentors. That's what this whole project is all about. Forget any contact you may have had with them in Russia. You're on our side now and there's nothing to fear."

Viktor seemed relieved. "That explains a few things. I think I'm beginning to understand what I really came to the West hoping to find out."

Leighton put his hand on Viktor's shoulder and gestured toward Ken. "My good friend here once thought that the Archons were *demons* up to deviltry. I think what we're all about to witness will make it clear that they are indeed highly evolved intelligences that want to rescue mankind from self-destruction."

"I'll believe it when I see it," said Ken with a good-natured grin. "So let's take a look at what this Del Sasso can do. That's why we're here, isn't it?"

"That's right!" Leighton was beaming once again. Putting a finger over his lips for silence, he pushed the door open.

Antonio Del Sasso

arla could hardly contain her excitement as Leighton led them quietly into a large, high-ceilinged room. It seemed almost too much to believe that she had located Viktor Khorev and, on top of that, to have been so easily invited inside this top-secret psychic research installation that she was certain at the very least was being funded by the CIA—and more than likely was totally under its control! Were her hopes too high and her imagination too keenly incited, or was this the Pulitzer-prize story she had been so certain she was pursuing? Whatever it turned out to be, she must keep her objectivity in order to present the facts to the public, and she must not be swayed by Frank's persuasiveness. Evaluating psychic phenomena was a very tricky business, as she well knew. It was never easy to separate the small amount of genuine from the vast amount of fraud.

Once inside the huge laboratory, Ken looked in vain for the "launching pad for journeys into inner space" that he'd invented and that Frank now called the Psitron. It was nowhere to be seen.

Frank detected the questioning search and whispered, "The Psitron's in another lab. Del Sasso doesn't need it anymore. He goes into Omega instantly. We've started training two others on it. They're just the first. One day there'll be thousands and eventually millions with Del Sasso's capabilities in every country around the world. It's fantastic, Ken, fantastic!"

In the center of the wall opposite the entrance was a raised platform occupied only by an oversized, cushioned chair with broad arms and a high back. In appearance it was almost throne-like and looked quite out-of-place in an experimental laboratory. On this lofty perch, in yoga position, sat a man whose giant size and commanding demeanor made him an intimidating figure even in the passivity of deep meditation. The full-length monk's robe he wore, with hood thrown back, was jet-black like his thick eyebrows and heavy, close-cropped beard. There was no need for Leighton to announce that this compelling person was the highly-acclaimed Father Antonio Del Sasso.

The hooded one! Viktor was staggered. So Yakov had been inside this very installation! *Was it Del Sasso, or the Archons, who killed Yakov? Maybe there was no real distinction.* Viktor sensed that Leighton was watching him and tried his best to control his feelings.

Kay Morris gave Leighton an almost-imperceptible nod, then turned back to her relentlessly efficient direction of two assistants. One lab worker was preparing a remotely operated broadcast-quality video camera on wheels; the other was readying a computer next to a bank of monitoring needles and graphs. Ken noted that there were no wires connected to Del Sasso and wondered what was being measured.

Again Leighton sensed the unspoken question and whispered: "Antonio generates an incredible electromagnetic field and an anti-gravitational force—and some other strange forces we haven't been able to analyze. I'll explain more later."

Then to all three he whispered, "You aren't going to believe this!"

With the use of a small forklift, the two lab assistants began hauling from behind a storage wall on the far right side of the room a number of heavy articles. These they carefully spaced about 15 feet in front of Del Sasso. There was an empty 50-gallon steel oil drum, a late-model automobile gasoline engine mounted on wooden skids, a large electric motor similarly mounted, and a barbell with numerous large weights on it, which, Leighton whispered, weighed "more than 1000 pounds!"

When the objects were in place to the satisfaction of Kay Morris, she motioned to her assistants to join her behind a heavy steel shield that surrounded the monitoring equipment and controls. Then she quietly addressed the meditating psychic. "We're ready, Father Del Sasso."

A long and almost palpable silence followed. Carla and Viktor glanced at Leighton apprehensively. He flashed them a quick, confident smile. Suddenly the oil drum was lifted straight up by some invisible force. It remained motionless about ten feet in the air for a full minute. Then, with a sound like a sonic boom, it was crumpled into a ball and dropped back to the floor.

Viktor and Carla were stunned. They looked at one another and then at Leighton. He was smiling and nodding at them again. Ken's facial expression had not changed. Somber and thoughtful, he avoided looking at the others.

Now the automobile engine started with a roar and revved up to a fast and steady idle. Then the electric motor started as well. No cord or cable connected it to any source of electric power. The barbell lifted from the floor and continued slowly to rise. With a triumphant grin, Leighton threw a quick glance at Viktor and Carla. They were transfixed.

Ken's eyes, like Del Sasso's, were closed. "Father," he prayed silently, "in the Name of Jesus Christ and through His blood shed on the cross for our sins, I ask You to bind the demons who are empowering Del Sasso and that you will thereby expose the evil behind him and the true source of his power."

Suddenly the barbell hesitated in its ponderous levitation and began to wobble. Something appeared to be going wrong. Viktor and Carla looked in surprise at Leighton. His face registered stunned incredulity.

Del Sasso moved uncomfortably in his chair and became increasingly agitated. The suspended barbell jerked and dodged about crazily. Even the driverless forklift began to rock back and forth as though shaken by some unseen giant hand. The two motors sputtered and bounced spasmodically, then fell over on their sides and quit. At the same instant, the heavy barbell slammed against the steel shield protecting the control center, bounced off, and crashed to the floor. Then all was silent.

Dr. Morris and her two assistants frantically checked the graphs and computerized monitors. Leighton seemed paralyzed.

Del Sasso opened his eyes like a man awakening from a nightmare. He sat in awesome stillness for a moment, staring at Ken. Then a terrifying roar—of anguish at first and then rage—erupted from Del Sasso's throat. Jumping to his feet with eyes blazing, he pointed an accusing finger straight at Ken and screamed, *"He* did it! Get him *out!"*

Unperturbed, Ken calmly returned his gaze. Viktor looked in bewilderment and apprehension from one to the other of these two apparent antagonists.

"You'd better leave," urged Frank in a low voice. "He has a violent temper."

"I'm not afraid of him. Are you?" Ken's challenge was clear.

"Ken, I don't want a confrontation."

"Get him out *now!"* Del Sasso thundered.

"Let's all go," whispered Frank in consternation. Ken willingly went along as Frank hurriedly led the way, followed closely by Viktor and Carla.

Outside in the hall, with his back against the closed door, Frank turned to Ken once again. "Now what was going on in there? What did he mean *you* did it? *What* did you do?"

"Could he be jealous of Ken?" suggested Carla tentatively. "Ken invented the Psitron and was the first to make contact. Psychics can be very temperamental."

"He *is* a prima donna," conceded Leighton. "And he can explode. But he's never acted like this. But then, I've never known him to fail." Wiping his brow with a handkerchief, he turned to Viktor. "What do you think?"

Viktor was overwhelmed. "I don't know what happened, but I've never seen anything like this! Del Sasso's powers are . . . are . . ." He gave up trying to find the proper English superlative and shrugged his shoulders helplessly.

"If he has such great powers, why doesn't he work them on *me?* Why does he ask *you* to escort me out?" Again Ken's voice carried that unmistakable challenge.

Leighton looked at Ken in amazement. "What are you trying to say?"

"He's afraid of me, and I know why."

"You're crazy. He's not afraid of anything or anyone, I can guarantee that. And I already told you I'm not going to have a confrontation. I don't want *that* kind of a demonstration. Now what did he mean *you* did it?"

"I know what he meant, and he knows that I know. But I'm going to let him tell you. You wouldn't like my explanation."

"Somehow Ken broke his concentration," suggested Carla.

"Concentration had nothing to do with it," retorted Ken. "That's a myth."

"Then what was it?" demanded Leighton.

"Frank, I told you to ask *him*."

"I'm asking you. Did you deliberately do something?"

Ken turned away without replying and began to walk back toward the lobby. Frank and the others followed him.

"Ken, I want to know—from *you!*" demanded Frank.

Ken turned slowly around to face them. "Del Sasso doesn't have any psychic power," he said quietly, looking Frank in the eye. "You're being deceived—badly."

Frank turned to Viktor and Carla in frustration. "No psychic powers?" he repeated scornfully. "Is this man crazy? You saw it."

"Oh, we all saw power," retorted Ken. "Lots of power. But it wasn't under Del Sasso's control. I just proved that. Humans don't have the capacity for psychic power. There's no way they can develop it. That's part of the delusion. The Archons are using Del Sasso—and you. That man's *possessed*—like I was."

"Come off it, Ken! I thought you'd gotten over that fixation."

"You asked me to tell you what I did," said Ken evenly. "Okay, I'll tell you. I just very quietly, in the Name of Jesus Christ, asked the one true God to bind the demons that were putting on that show. And you saw what happened."

Leighton's jaw dropped, and for just a moment he seemed shaken and uncertain. Then his face reddened in anger. "That's a coincidence," he spat back. "Antonio is a very sensitive person. He sensed your hostility and it broke his concentration. This is a delicate procedure."

"Ken, I find your explanation childish and self-serving!" Carla wanted to distance herself from his religious fanaticism immediately.

A world-renowned journalist had an image to maintain, especially if that journalist was a woman.

Viktor was watching and listening in perplexed silence. Such a conversation could never have taken place in his lab in Russia! What did Ken mean by *possessed*? Was he referring to *demons*, and was he, like Dmitri, a *believer*?

At that moment the laboratory door burst open and Del Sasso exploded into the corridor. He immediately saw Ken and erupted with rage once again. "I told you to get him *out!*" he bellowed. "If I ever see him here again, I'll *kill him!*"

"Why?" asked Ken quietly, in a very calm voice. "Why?"

"Get out!" Del Sasso started toward them.

Ken stood his ground, staring fearlessly into Antonio's hate-filled eyes. "I'm not afraid of you. Greater is He that's in me than the *demons* that are in you."

Del Sasso let out a roar of frustrated rage. Leighton grabbed Ken by an elbow, turned him around, and started moving him hurriedly toward the lobby. Ken went along without resisting. As they turned the corner in the corridor, Leighton called back over his shoulder. "I'll see that he leaves, Antonio. I'm taking him out right now."

"Wait for me in my office," Leighton added to the others.

As he stepped into the lobby, with Frank still pushing him along, Ken heard Carla telling Viktor, "I'm glad we came in separate cars!" The words were like a knife plunged into his back.

Outside, they walked side by side in stubborn silence. When they reached the car, Frank put his hand on Ken's arm. "I can't believe you'd do this to me!"

"Do what?"

"You deceived me! I thought you were genuinely interested or I wouldn't have invited you."

"I was—and I am, Frank. And I'm concerned for you."

"I think you deliberately came here to disrupt the program. You incited Del Sasso. You've resented that I bought you out, even though I've always kept the offer open to bring you back in."

"I don't want back in. But I came here genuinely interested to see what was going on, and I'm glad I did. I've met Del Sasso now, and he only confirmed what I already knew. I'm warning you, Frank: You're heading for disaster."

"I don't know how you can say that, Ken! If you only knew the potential available to mankind, not just to Del Sasso—he's only the first—but to all of us!"

"I know the full deception of that false promise, Frank. And I know who's behind it. They tried to kill me, and they'll kill you when you've served their purpose and they have no further use for you."

"Ken, I already told you there was a flaw in your original design. It was a slight mistake that anyone could make, but it was an important one, and that was why you freaked out and drove over that cliff. The Archons identified that flaw, told us how to correct it, and we did. This isn't theory. We've *proved* that what they said was true. After we made that modification, Antonio had no more trouble—not the slightest."

"He's completely possessed!"

"I don't want to hear that again!"

"Whether you want to hear it or not, it's the truth."

"Ken, listen to me. If you would only drop your fixation about demons and take another look with an open mind."

"I took a look."

"But with the same old superstitious prejudice. Ken, we're on the verge of solving all human problems! We're going to have a new world without poverty or disease or war!"

"And with the Archons in control, right?"

"So?" Frank conceded. "Now I suppose you're going to find something sinister in that! How could it be otherwise? It's their plan and they have the knowledge and the power. They have to be in charge, but only until we've got the power to do it ourselves."

"A lack of *power* isn't the problem, Frank. You should realize that. You know what this generation has been called: 'nuclear giants but moral midgets.' Remember? And that's dangerous!"

Frank grew silent. Ken climbed into his car and lowered the window. "Who are the Archons?"

"They're highly evolved, nonphysical intelligences who've been guiding our evolution."

"They've done a lousy job!"

"That's why they're intervening now—to prevent an ecological or nuclear holocaust. If we destroy ourselves, that could set back the karma of the whole galaxy."

"What you're giving me, Frank, is basic Hinduism. Why is *that* acceptable, but Christianity is unthinkable?"

"It's not Hinduism. It's science."

"You know better than that. Karma, highly evolved Masters, magic powers through yogic trance—that's *science?*"

Frank didn't answer. He spun around and started to walk away. Ken leaned out the window and called after him. "So I'm *persona non grata* from now on?"

Frank stopped and turned to face him again. "I wish it were otherwise, but what would be the point? Another blowup with Del Sasso?"

"You ought to be asking yourself some serious questions, Frank. For example, what happened to Del Sasso's great powers? And where are the Archons? Are they so weak? They nearly killed me once, but I have no fear of them anymore. Face the facts! I told you the truth—what I actually did in the lab. I shut Del Sasso down with a simple prayer!"

Leighton looked at him with astonishment, and then with contempt. "A brilliant mind gone to ruin—that's what you are. Ever since that accident you've been suffering from religious delusions. You need professional help, Ken. I could arrange for the best psychiatric diagnosis and treatment."

"Forget about 'analyzing' me, and analyze your own situation. You're getting in over your head. You ought to stay awake nights asking yourself how you know the Archons are telling you the truth! Why do you trust them? Suppose they're not who they say they are, and I'm right after all?"

Frank stared at Ken in silence. Then he turned away once again and, without another word, hurried toward the front door.

Ken backed his car out of its parking place and drove slowly toward the gate. He felt the weight of a heavy grief for Frank, and for Khorev, too—and an overwhelming sense of foreboding for Carla. As for Del Sasso, the man was evil personified and capable of almost anything. The Archons had chosen their instrument well.

the

MIND
INVADERS
20

The Plan

When Leighton returned to his office, he found Del Sasso in a relaxed and affable mood, sitting in an easy chair deep in conversation with Carla and Viktor. They had been probing him with pointed questions about the dangers of the incredible psychic power they had just seen him display. What if it got into the wrong hands? And how could that possibility, after all, be prevented if psychic power was simply a normal human potential and thus available equally to everyone? What a frightful world it would be if every person had such dangerous capabilities—a world of sorcerers zapping one another with unlimited powers of the mind!

Del Sasso had laughed at their fears and assured them that, contrary to popular misconceptions about unlimited human potential, psychic power was a gift to mankind from higher intelligences—the Archons. A failure to recognize and honor the true source of this force was, in fact, the reason for the slow progress and frustration that had plagued the field of parapsychology worldwide since its inception at the end of the nineteenth century. The breakthrough came when this secret research center, directed by Frank Leighton, had been willing to enter into an agreement with the Archons to become, under their direction and control, the distributors of this power to the world. That partnership had catapulted the Americans light-years ahead of the Russians and everyone else.

It all made sense to Viktor. In fact, the critical questions that had loomed so large for him seemed to be in the process of being answered without even asking them. Del Sasso's explanation of the role played by the Archons was in perfect agreement with the conclusions Viktor had arrived at in Russia, and filled in most of the missing gaps in his theory. The reason for the repeated warnings, and the horrifying events in his laboratory north of Moscow when they persisted in pursuing their research along forbidden lines, now seemed clear.

For Carla, however, who knew nothing of what had happened in Viktor's lab, Del Sasso's statements were too revolutionary to accept without further proof. Of course, she had little doubt about the staggering power he had displayed, but to attribute it to mysterious nonphysical intelligences seemed to raise more questions than it answered. Who were these *Archons* that Leighton and Del Sasso spoke of in such familiar terms—and that Viktor seemed to have known about and feared? What was their intent and motive? It also reminded her, uncomfortably, of some of the things Ken had said in the hospital. While she could no longer believe in *demons*, yet, if there were highly evolved nonphysical entities out there somewhere, was it not possible that some of them could be *evil*? She resolved to keep an open mind, but not to surrender the skepticism that every journalist had to apply continually to each story being investigated.

"How did that lunatic get in here?" demanded Del Sasso the moment Leighton walked through the door.

Leighton shook his head in embarrassment and disbelief. "It's my fault for inviting him. I'm sorry, Antonio. I had no idea."

"Don't even think about it," replied Del Sasso contemptuously. "He's a fundamentalist fanatic completely paranoid about demons. I met dozens like him when I was on lecture tour for the Society of Jesus. They'd confront me at my talks, quote Bible verses that 'proved' the pope was the Antichrist. When I'd agree and say, 'Maybe he is,' they'd be speechless. You know, of course," he added conspiratorially, "that the Jesuits haven't gotten along too well with the pope for years." Then his eyes narrowed. "Don't let me see that maniac in here ever again!"

"You've got my word on that," said Leighton with conviction, seating himself casually on the front of his huge desk. "Now tell me, what *really* happened in there?"

Del Sasso leaned back comfortably and laughed as he looked from one to the other of his admirers. He obviously enjoyed his celebrity status, but he exuded a winning sincerity as well. His charm, when he wanted to turn it on, seemed almost supernatural. *Keep your feet on the ground, and your head out of the clouds!* Carla reminded herself.

"I was in Omega," said Del Sasso, "with my eyes closed, waiting for the starting signal from Kay. Then you all came in. The moment *he* entered the lab I *knew* he was there, even though we've never met. The Archons identified him as an *enemy.*"

Del Sasso let that sink in for a moment, then continued. "I tried to ignore him and carry on for their sake." He gestured toward Carla and Viktor. "But I was so tuned into the collective unconscious that his negative thoughts were like radio static jamming the frequency on which I was receiving the energy. It infuriated me. Finally I just had to call a halt and get him out of there."

"He told us he shut you down," said Carla. She wanted to hear from Del Sasso a direct response that would lay to rest Ken's fundamentalist fantasies once and for all.

Del Sasso's warm, brown eyes instantly ignited in a blaze of anger. Carla found the sudden transformation too Jekyll and Hydeish for comfort. Yet what he said was persuasive enough. "What makes a man lie like that? I knew every thought he was thinking—pitiful, archaic superstitions about *demons.*" He rolled his large eyes in contempt, then turned to Viktor. "How did the little you saw—before I stopped it—compare with the level you've reached in the Russia?"

"There's no comparison. You're so far beyond anything we've achieved—well, it's obvious that your explanation about the Archons is accurate." Viktor leaned forward and nodded his head slowly in awed assent. "It certainly confirms my own research, and explains some mysterious events in my lab that I suspect you know all about."

Such confirmation from Viktor made a strong impression upon Carla, but she still didn't know what they were talking about. Leighton could not suppress a smug expression. "So Antonio has been explaining about the Archons, has he?" Seeing Carla's puzzled look, he suggested to Viktor, "Now that you're reunited under, shall we say, more relaxed conditions than when you met in Paris, it would be a good idea, when there's time, to tell Carla some of your past experiences with the Archons."

"You've been in contact with them, too?" asked Carla, turning to Viktor in surprise.

"We've been *chastened* by them—severely," he replied somberly. "I'd like to see further evidence, of course, but so far, everything Dr. Del Sasso—"

"*Antonio*, please, or *Father* Del Sasso, if you prefer," interjected the psychic graciously.

"—Antonio has said rings true," continued Viktor. He turned to Leighton. "Perhaps I could show Miss Bertelli—Carla—" His cheeks flushed slightly as he corrected himself. "Perhaps I could show her my video."

"A great idea!" responded Leighton, looking suddenly like a man who had just remembered he had some extraordinary surprises up his sleeve. "That would give her some insights. And that's important, because eventually the power that the Archons are training us to use must be shared with the world." He turned to Carla. "That's where you come in, if you're willing, of course. We'll discuss that later. It has to be planned carefully."

Looking questioningly at Del Sasso for confirmation, Leighton suggested, "I don't think Antonio wants to go back to the lab and start over after that rude interruption."

Antonio glanced at his watch and shook his head. "I've got to get over to lab four. It's almost time for the daily transmission, and I have to get wired up." Standing to leave, he shook the outstretched hands of Carla and Viktor. "It was a pleasure to meet you. I'm looking forward to working with you both."

"I would be highly honored," said Viktor enthusiastically.

"Well, you've certainly impressed me," added Carla. "Do I understand that you're willing to give me complete freedom as an investigative reporter?"

"We wouldn't want it any other way," Del Sasso assured her instantly, looking her directly in the eyes with an expression of childlike innocence that encouraged total trust.

As Del Sasso left the room, Leighton walked around and seated himself in the oversized executive chair behind his huge desk. The very few papers on top of it were neatly arranged. He obviously ran a tight ship and was well-organized himself. Clasping his hands behind his head, he leaned far back in evident and justifiable satisfaction. "Well, you just got it from the horse's mouth. Antonio's something else, isn't he? In case you're wondering, he's still an active Jesuit priest, but not a narrow-minded adherent to Christian dogma by any means, as I suppose you can tell. His doctorate's in Oriental languages. When I first met him he was already a top psychic—developed his powers while studying Buddhism in Japan shortly after the Korean War. I knew immediately he was a natural for the Psitron. So when Ken had his accident and dropped out, I brought in Antonio. He made almost immediate contact with 'the Nine,' and it's been an incredible adventure ever since."

Leighton paused dramatically for a moment, then added, "Instead of just talking about it—since you got cheated out of seeing what Antonio can *really* do—why don't I just boggle you a bit before we break for lunch. Okay?"

"Boggle?" asked Viktor.

"Astonish, amaze, astound," explained Carla. "Sounds good. Let's go for it." Then she leaned over and patted Viktor's arm. "That's a highbrow word. I wouldn't worry about it. Your English is so much better than my French or German. And as for my *Russian*, about all I can say is 'Good morning,' 'How are you?' and 'Good-bye.'"

Leighton pushed a button and spoke on the intercom to his secretary in an adjoining room. "Hold all my calls—I won't be available until after lunch."

He selected a videocassette from among several stacked neatly in one corner of his desk, walked over to a VCR connected to a huge, curved television screen nearby, and inserted it. Picking up a remote control, he came over to join his two guests on the long sofa. As he started the video he reminded them, "If you have any questions, just let me know and I'll stop it."

The video began with Del Sasso seated in an office, eyes closed, a thin wire in his hands, which he was moving slowly in a circular motion, holding it horizontally about six inches above a large-scale map spread out on the desk before him. Suddenly the wire twisted in his fingers and pointed directly at the map. At the same instant, with his eyes still closed, his hands stopped their motion and seemed to hover. An assistant appeared from the side and put a calibrated magnifying device on the map in the designated spot. The camera zoomed in on a nearby computer where the precise latitude and longitude appeared on the monitor.

Leighton pushed the pause button. "This is one of the first practical applications of the Archons' powers. The coordinates you saw on the computer were obviously changed, but otherwise you witnessed it exactly as it happened. Army engineers are still mapping out the area, but already it promises to be the largest pool of oil ever discovered. It's in a wilderness location within the continental United States, a site that would surprise any geologist—which may be why it remained unknown. They've drilled a number of wells, tested, and capped them. The location, of course, is secret at the moment."

The next scene that came on the screen was the interior of a huge hothouse shaped like a pyramid. It was filled with a wide variety of vegetable and melon plants. Del Sasso could be seen walking slowly up and down between the long rows, stopping to hold his hands briefly over each plant. That scene merged into another showing several workers in the same location harvesting astonishing quantities of cabbages and cantelopes the size of basketballs, as well as huge tomatoes, carrots, beets, and other produce, all of prodigious size and superb quality.

Again Leighton paused to comment. "This is another practical application that will benefit the world. Everything you just saw was grown in about two-thirds the normal time and with half the usual amount of water in very poor soil, yet with a vitamin and mineral content far higher than anything being presently produced. The secret is a conversion of psychic energy innate in space, even in a vacuum. The same results can be had in the Sahara, or anywhere. I don't have to tell you what this will mean for the world."

"Now that's something worthwhile that I could get excited about!" exclaimed Carla. "Is it being done now?"

"Not yet. We need thousands of Del Sassos. They have to be trained, and that can only happen when the Plan has been revealed and accepted by the world's leaders. That will bring the dawning of a New Age beyond imagination—paradise on earth!"

"The Plan?" asked Viktor warily. "What plan?"

"We don't have all the details yet, but the Archons have a definite Plan for implementing their solution to the crises we now face. We'll get into that later. I want to show you one more example of what the Archons can do. It's something I think you'll agree could guarantee lasting peace among all nations—and even among individuals."

Leighton started the video again and Viktor gasped. The scene was now inside his laboratory in Russia. The quality of the image was almost as good as if it were being transmitted live over a clear TV channel. Yakov was being strapped into his chair by Dmitri. Viktor saw himself busily directing the operation from the control room above. The whole traumatic episode unfolded again before his eyes exactly as it had happened. He saw Yakov ripped out of the apparatus and thrown across the room to his death. Viktor groaned and looked away.

Unconsciously, Carla put a comforting hand on Viktor's arm.

Leighton stopped the film. "I'm sorry," he said. "I should have warned you beforehand. I guess I got carried away wanting to surprise you."

"No, it's okay," responded Viktor solemnly. "I needed to see it again. Sometimes it seems so unreal—like a nightmare, or something I've fantasized." He turned to Carla. "I guess you could tell that was inside my lab near Moscow?"

"That actually happened?" she asked in astonishment.

Viktor nodded. "That was the third psychic we'd lost."

"You brought the film with you?"

"I brought some film, but not that." He turned to Leighton. "Now I know what you mean by 'boggle.' I don't know what to say. So you actually knew everything we were doing?"

"Everything," said Leighton matter-of-factly.

Carla still did not understand. "How could you get an agent inside his lab?" she asked Leighton. "And how could he take that film without anyone knowing it?" Before he could respond, she turned to Viktor in bewilderment. "Did you ever suspect that one of your own men was doing this?"

"That's not how it happened," replied Viktor. "I know what Frank is going to tell us because we did somewhat the same thing, but our results were Stone Age in comparison."

Hitching around on the sofa so that he could look directly into their eyes, Leighton leaned in close. It was a gesture of confidentiality toward these two who were being taken into the inner circle. "Del Sasso took that film *with his mind*, sitting right in that lab where you saw him today." He spoke calmly, but the expression on his face was a crescendo of triumph.

"I can't believe it!" exclaimed Carla. She looked over at Viktor. He was nodding in awed confirmation.

Leighton's eyes reflected an excitement that he could hardly contain. "In our vaults here we have thousands of feet of film of secret Russian experiments, not only from Viktor's lab, but from other labs of various kinds—even films of top-secret, high-level Kremlin meetings."

Leighton lowered his voice and leaned even closer. "What I'm telling you is highly classified information. It's not to be shared with *anyone* until the Archons give the word. You could count on one hand the people outside of this base who know about it. None of the film I just mentioned—and I mean *none of it*—has been seen by anyone in the FBI, the State Department, the Pentagon. . . . Such knowledge and power will not be used against the Russians, or against any other nation, so long as they go along with the Plan when the time comes—which will be very soon."

Leighton let that information sink in for a few moments. He stood and began to pace the floor in silence. At last he began to speak with passion. "Can you see what this means? War will be impossible. Peace will be permanent, and even crime will be no more. In the New World no one will be able to hatch secret plots. There'll be no subversion, no terrorism. It will be impossible to hide any thought or deed from those in control. Paradise will be restored."

"'Those in *control*'?" asked Viktor pointedly. He suddenly looked apprehensive. "Who will that be?"

"The Archons at first, of course," declared Leighton without hesitation. "Then those who have been chosen by them as channels of their power."

"And if some nations refuse to accept this new order?" suggested Carla.

"What's the alternative?" shot back Leighton. "They'd be insane not to go along. The rewards for cooperation are virtually unlimited. Every nation will have its own psychics—thousands and even millions of them—with powers like Del Sasso's. For the average person, this will bring about an entirely new way of perceiving themselves and the world around them—a transformation that will follow naturally from the daily and routine display of what used to be thought of as impossible. I think you can appreciate from even the little you've seen on the video that such power as this creates a radical change in consciousness, an entirely new way of looking at reality that removes the illusion of limitations that have needlessly enslaved us as a result of our past conditioning. The new conditioning process will come about through the very display of this power. That in itself will produce a new worldview and, as a result, a new world."

Viktor had scarcely heard their exchange. He was still so stunned by what he'd seen that he could hardly find words. "This is absolutely staggering," he murmured, more to himself than to the others. "I thought it was the Archons that killed Yakov, and my superiors insisted it was the Americans. Who was it?"

"It was both," replied Leighton simply.

"Why?" interjected Carla. "Why would they help Del Sasso, and kill the Russian psychics?"

"For the same reason that Viktor defected to the West: Marxist materialism still dominates. It refuses to admit the existence of entities without bodies. The Archons—well, you have to believe in them to work with them."

"I still don't understand the favoritism," persisted Carla. "What's their purpose?"

"They want to help us, and that means the whole world eventually. But at this stage they're working through the Americans because we're the ones who made contact and have faith in them." He looked at Carla sympathetically. "That was Ken's problem. He wouldn't trust them."

"But who are they?" she asked.

"That's almost like asking what is gravity or energy. I don't have a complete answer to that question, and we probably never will because they're so far beyond us. Basically, as I've already said, they're highly evolved beings who have advanced beyond the lower states of bodily dependence. From their higher dimension they've been guiding mankind's evolution for thousands of years. There's no death or time in their dimension, and they say we've reached a critical phase that requires their direct intervention to prevent us from destroying ourselves."

"I don't doubt the need for their intervention," murmured Carla, not entirely convinced. "But I'm not sure I like the way they're going about it."

"You won't question their wisdom or ability once you've worked with them. I guarantee that."

Viktor still seemed stunned. "Such staggering power. How does it work? Why do they need to channel it through humans—not just one, but thousands and even millions of Del Sassos?"

"They haven't explained that. I don't think it's so much that they *need* to work through a human channel. I think it's more a case of wanting us to be responsible for ourselves." Leighton began to pace back and forth again, pondering his words as he spoke. "The impression I get is that they don't want to do everything for us. We've got to learn to do it on our own so we can be independent of them eventually. So they do need Del Sassos. Millions of them have to be trained. That's our only hope for survival. Time is short, and they must have the cooperation of the world."

He stopped in front of Carla and stood looking down into her upturned face, studying her carefully. "That's where you come in. It's a very delicate situation. If we don't break this news just right, it could cause worldwide panic or skepticism. One is as bad as the other. We have to generate *belief* and genuine *trust*, or it won't work. Right now Del Sasso is our one link, our one hope. If something should happen to him—well, I don't even want to think about it."

That night Ken and his mother attended, as they regularly did, the weekly prayer gathering at the large home of Hal and Karen Elliott. There were, as usual, a number of "praise items" that were enumerated at the beginning of the meeting by the leader of the group, Roger Andrews, a local attorney. It was considered no less important to give thanks for prayers that had been answered than to make new requests, of which there were always several important ones.

When Ken's turn came to make his prayer needs known, he stood to address the group. "We've had Carla Bertelli and Frank Leighton, as you know, on the prayer list for a long time," he began earnestly. "I'd like to update you so you can pray more specifically. Carla is back in town and may be getting involved with Frank's psychic research program—the same one that got me demonized and almost killed. Praise God, that what Satan meant for evil, God turned into good. And that's how I came to the Lord, as most of you know."

"Thank you, Lord! Praise God! Thank you, Jesus!" The short expressions of thanksgiving were murmured softly around the room. Most of those present had prayed earnestly the night that Hal and Karen had gone to the hospital to cast the demons out of Ken, and they had watched with joy and excitement his rapid growth in the faith.

"The psychic who took my place," continued Ken solemnly, "is heavily demon-possessed. I don't think there's any doubt about that. I'm afraid Carla is so impressed by what she thinks are psychic powers that she'll be sucked right into the whole delusion. She needs to have her eyes opened to the truth. Please pray specifically that she will become *disillusioned*—that the mask will slip enough for the real evil behind this to become obvious to her."

He started to sit down, then remembered Viktor. "Please pray also for the top Russian scientist in psychic research who has joined Leighton's team. I think he has some doubts. Pray that the Lord will deliver him also." After a moment's pause, he added thoughtfully, "Of course, they'll both have to be willing. It's a choice they have to make. So just pray that God will do everything possible to confront them with the truth so they can at least make an intelligent choice. Right now they're under heavy deception, which can only get worse as long as they remain under the influence of Leighton and his team."

There were, of course, many other prayer requests, and the meeting, as usual, went on until nearly midnight. These people had come to the firm conviction that prayer involved more than briefly stating a string of casual requests. There was a fervent earnestness and persistence in their prayers as they not only laid before God the many needs, but appealed repeatedly to Scripture and God's grace and love in support of their requests.

Though the hour was late, the participants lingered when the meeting at last broke up. Don Jordan, the FBI's West Coast Director of Counterintelligence and stationed at the local office, shook hands warmly with Ken. "Good to see you again, brother. I'll sure be praying daily for those requests you mentioned." He took Ken by the arm and said in a low voice, "Could we step outside for a moment?"

When they were away from the house in a corner of the dimly-lit backyard, Jordan said, "I wonder if I could ask you something. You said a Russian scientist has joined Leighton's team?" Ken nodded.

"No Russian that would qualify for such a job has been in the country that I know of," added Jordan, "which means he's got to be a high-level defector—and a *very* recent one that I don't even know about. Is that correct?"

"That's right. Carla didn't give me any details. She only mentioned that it happened in Paris two weeks ago at the First

International Congress on Parapsychology. She apparently played a key role in helping him make his break."

Don shook his head in disbelief. "That means only one thing: Leighton's operation must be under some government agency, and I suspect it's the CIA. Nobody else could have a top-level defector that quickly. It usually takes months, and even years, for clearance. You're sure about this?"

"Absolutely. I was there and saw him myself."

"There's nothing like bureaucracy," said Don with a resigned shrug. "The left hand never tells the right hand what it's doing. You'd think *somebody* would have told us that a brand-new Russian defector was going to be working in our area. The Russians may very well make an attempt either to recover or to kill this man. But does anyone tell me? No, I just happen to find out by accident!"

"Do the Russians normally go after defectors?" asked Ken in surprise. "You don't read about that sort of thing."

"It rarely gets into the news. If he's a big enough fish—which this man sounds like—they'd go after him if they knew where he was. That's precisely why defectors with high-level classified information to give, or covert ties, are given a new identity and disappear at least for a few years, until they're not 'hot' anymore. I don't think there's any doubt that the Russians will find out where he is—and that means we've got problems!" He shook his head again in disbelief. "I can't believe the CIA wouldn't tell us."

"Maybe they planned to tell you. He just got there last night. Anyway, it's like a fortress out there," added Ken. "I don't think the Russians could possibly get at him."

Don smiled and shook his head. "The Russians have an elite corps that handles just such jobs, and they're *very* efficient. I'm going to call my office right away."

"The CIA must know what they're doing."

"I wouldn't count on it—not if *my* life depended on it." He put a hand on Ken's shoulder. "And you're sure your ex-fiancée helped this defector escape?"

Ken nodded. "That's what she said."

"If the Russians know that—and they probably do—then she's in big danger. Revenge is a powerful motive, even for the FSB. Do you know where she's staying?"

"At the Hilton, as of last night."

"I'll have someone check on her now and then. That's the best I can promise. The CIA should really have someone assigned to her day and night."

Cat and Mouse

I t was very late when Carla, with a restrained yawn, finally stood to her feet to say a reluctant good night. Frank and Viktor stood up stiffly as well. It had been an emotionally exhausting day for all of them. Del Sasso had retired earlier with a bad headache, which had become a frequent occurrence for him lately and gave Leighton a great deal of concern.

"This has been incredibly informative and fascinating," said Carla, "but I just have to get some sleep. Don't expect me before noon. What about you, Viktor? Where are you staying? Do you need a ride?"

"I'm staying out here—in one of the guest apartments. It's nicer than anything I've ever lived in."

"It's for his own protection," added Leighton. "If we gave him a new identity and let him disappear, he'd be of no value to the Plan. But as the top Russian scientist in this field, with an international reputation, his endorsement will mean a lot. So we're guarding him in here where he'll be safe until the Plan has been implemented. Then anywhere in the world will be safe for everyone!"

Carla gave Viktor a quick hug. "It's been wonderful seeing you again, and knowing that you're in such good hands—and that you'll be involved right away in the kind of research you were hoping to get into."

"I can never thank you enough!" he responded. "Without your courage, this wouldn't have happened! I hate to think where I'd be right now."

"Well, don't forget our little arrangement."

"Never! And I'm so happy that you're going to be part of this project, too. Is that right?" He looked questioningly to both of them for confirmation.

"I certainly hope so," said Leighton, turning to Carla. "Are you accepting the assignment?"

She had been moving slowly toward the door as they talked. "I'll be back tomorrow to get a closer look and a few more questions answered." Carla paused for a moment, then added cautiously, "I'd be crazy to turn down an opportunity like this! Yes, I'd like to accept the challenge, Frank—provided I can keep my independence as a journalist."

"That's understood," Frank reminded her, "so don't even mention it again."

As the heavy steel gate swung shut behind her and she turned her car onto the access road, Carla breathed a long, satisfied sigh. *Wow! What a day! Incredible! Do I want to take the assignment? I guess I played that cool! Here I thought it would be so difficult to find out what was going on. Instead I'm invited—almost begged.* It was all beyond anything she would have dared to hope for. Yet, in spite of her exhilaration, there was a gnawing pang of doubt. Something bothered her.

Was it too good to be true? Or was it the fact that Del Sasso, who could be so charming and sincere, had shown another side that was frighteningly vicious? And the Archons—were they really highly evolved intelligences or simply deeper levels of the human psyche? Frank had assured her that he had personally met them and that she would, too, eventually. He'd also said that their actual identity wasn't all that important and was probably beyond human comprehension, anyway. After all, the potential for bringing peace and prosperity to the world was what really mattered, and there seemed little doubt about that. And yet, she hardly knew how to pinpoint the unsettling feeling that something wasn't quite right.

It was a longer drive back to the highway than she remembered. The remoteness of the narrow road and the intense darkness under the tall trees heightened another anxiety that she had managed until now to suppress entirely. Suppose the men who had pursued Viktor and from whose clutches she had literally snatched him tried to find him? That would not be unlikely. Of course they wouldn't be able to reach him inside that CIA fortress. In their frustration, might they not try to take revenge on her?

Suddenly the unexpected glare of headlights in her rearview mirror startled her back to present reality. She tried desperately to suppress the impulse to panic. Surely it was paranoid even to consider the terrifying fear that now had her heart beating wildly. But who could it possibly be? No one else had been leaving the research center after her. She'd heard one of the guards at the gate make that remark to his companion. And the road dead-ended there. Cars didn't materialize out of thin air. Had someone been hiding in the woods, waiting for her? She pressed the accelerator harder and her tires squealed in protest as she skidded around succeeding curves. The pursuing car quickened its pace accordingly.

By the time she reached the main highway, a feeling of helpless terror gripped Carla. She pulled onto it without stopping—directly into the path of a fast-moving car. The screech of brakes, a long skid, and it had careened briefly off and back onto the roadway. Blinking headlights and blaring horn signaled the driver's anger. At least there was someone between her and what she was now convinced were determined pursuers. She remembered Ken's invitation, but resisted the temptation to turn off onto the road leading to his house. That would be the day! She'd made the right decision two years ago, and now that she had gotten what she wanted from him it would be insane to have any further contact. Seeing his incredible performance at the lab had made that crystal-clear once again. He had developed into an impossible fundamentalist fanatic, just as she had feared he would.

All the way down the mountain the car that had followed her on the access road made no attempt to get directly behind her again. When the highway left the foothills and leveled off in the valley, the intervening car turned off at an intersection. Now the other car hung back. But by the time she had made several turns in town and it was still behind her, there could be no doubt of its occupants' ultimate intentions.

If she continued on to her hotel, they would know where she was staying! Should she drive directly to the police station? That would accomplish nothing except to make her look foolish. *Think, Carla, think!* She willed the terror-driven thoughts into submission. Yes, she had it—a plan—a way that she could get to another hotel without her pursuers knowing it. There was no way to lose them by trying to drive faster than they did. She would go into her own hotel first. If they followed her into the parking garage, however, she would be trapped. To avoid that, she pulled up to the front door and gave her keys to the bellman. As she did so, she noticed that her pursuers had parked just down the street and turned off their lights.

Inside the lobby Carla checked at the desk for messages. There was one call from her editor friend in New York. She hurried to the elevator. Once in her room, she would phone another hotel for a reservation, gather her things, and call a cab to meet her at the rear service entrance. An elevator was waiting with its doors open. She stepped inside and, with a sigh of relief, pushed the button for the eighth floor. Two men stepped in quickly beside her just as the doors closed.

She fought off the first wave of panic and tried to think rationally. From what she'd seen as they had entered and could now observe out of the corner of her eye, they didn't look like Russian agents—or did they? How could one be sure? They were fortyish and, in spite of their business suits, looked unmistakably muscular and very fit. She tried to assure herself that they couldn't possibly be the occupants of the car that had followed her. Then she remembered that she had carelessly stood waiting for her mail at a portion of the front counter where a side door, through which they might have entered, was not visible. *Idiot! And they didn't push a number for their floor! They're obviously planning to get off at the eighth with me! What to do now?*

The elevator stopped at the sixth floor and a young couple got in, looking a bit embarrassed and hastening to explain why they were out and about in their pajamas and bathrobes. "The ice machine wasn't working on our floor," they mumbled, as though reminding one another. They pushed number five, and then the man exclaimed, "Oh, we thought this was going *down*."

"Well, we get an extra ride for our money, honey," added the girl, which they both found somehow hilarious.

At the eighth floor the elevator door opened. The two men made no move to get off. Carla stepped to one side and motioned to them. "This must be your floor, too. Go ahead. I'm not getting off. I just remembered I have to go back to the lobby for something." She reached out and pushed the first-floor button.

"What a coincidence!" said the taller of the two. "We've got the same problem."

Don't panic! Think! There's got to be some way. What should she do? What *could* she do? The elevator made its way to the top floor, then started back down. The two men were like sphinxes. Oblivious to her predicament, the young couple chattered away happily in low voices. Should she get off with them? No, they would be no help at all—and she might get them killed as well for witnessing what happened to her. Was this all paranoia? As though in a bad dream, she felt the elevator come to a stop at the fifth floor, saw the door open, and watched helplessly as the young couple, still talking nonstop, got off. The doors closed, leaving her—a lone mouse—to face these two cats who were ready to pounce.

She determined to confront them. Perhaps by taking the offensive she could use up the time it would take to reach the lobby. Just as she opened her mouth to speak, however, the man closest to her reached quickly inside his coat pocket. Instead of the gun she feared would be pointed at her, he held out a badge.

"We're with the FBI, Miss Bertelli. We just wanted you to know that we'll be checking with you from time to time in case you have any problems."

Carla gasped in relief. Then a wave of anger surged over her. "You two goons really gave me a scare! I thought you were from the FSB! Why did you wait so long to tell me?"

"We were going to get off with you on your floor, and then that young couple got on. We could hardly identify ourselves in their presence. I'm sorry we frightened you. But tell me, why would you even imagine we were from the *FSB*?"

The elevator came to a halt on the ground floor and its doors opened. They stepped out into the lobby together. Carla was still fuming. "If you had identified yourselves right away you might have caught some FSB agents! I don't know who else would have followed me here! Come on, I'll show you. They're parked out on the street."

The two men ran for the front door, with Carla following as fast as she could. When she joined them outside, the car was nowhere to be seen. "They were right over there," she said, pointing to where her pursuers had parked. "Followed me all the way from up in the hills west of town."

"Can you give us a description of the car and anyone in it?"

"They were always too far behind, and they parked half a block away. I think it was a four-door sedan, dark blue or maybe black late-model Ford, I'd say."

"We'll cruise the neighborhood and take a look," said the special agent who had shown her his badge. He handed her his card. "If you have any problems, call that number."

"I was going to check out of here and into another hotel, now that whoever followed me knows I'm staying here. Should I do that?"

"That wouldn't help. They'd find you wherever you went. Better than that, stay here and I'll recommend a 24-hour watch. We can't guard you, exactly, but we can watch for Russian agents. It has the same effect."

"So I'm the decoy? Wow! I don't like this! But what can I say?"

"We're not asking for your permission. It'll happen, whether you want it or not. We won't come up to you in public, and if you see us, don't show any sign of recognition. Okay?"

"Okay. And thanks a lot. Pardon my temper. I feel a whole lot better now."

the
MIND
INVADERS
22

A Foolish Adventure

W hile praying for Carla the next morning, Ken felt overwhelmed by a sense of responsibility for the part he had played in leading her into her present danger. After all, he had introduced her to the field of psychic research and encouraged her to ever-deeper involvement even when she'd had little interest in it herself and her editors at that time had not been supportive of this new direction her writing was taking. She wouldn't be associated with Frank and heading for who could say what ultimate delusion or destruction at the hands of "the Nine" had it not been for his influence in the past. That realization became an overpowering burden.

Instead of taking this feeling of guilt to God for forgiveness and asking God for His direction, Ken began to think of what he could do to make up for having led Carla astray—something to help her now. In that obsessive frame of mind, the insistent thought wouldn't leave him that he ought to call the CIA in San Francisco. It really didn't make sense, but driven now by a crushing sense of guilt, he became the victim of an irrational compulsion. Checking with the operator, he found that there was no listing there or in Los Angeles. Eventually he called Virginia information, got the number of the headquarters in Langley, and dialed it, wondering exactly what he would say.

"CIA," intoned the girl on the switchboard.

"I need to talk to whoever's in charge of your West Coast operations."

"What kind of operations?"

"It involves a psychic research installation."

After a long silence, she came back on the line and said, "I don't find any listing for psychic research or anything with 'psychic' in it."

"Listen to me!" demanded Ken. "This is terribly important! Someone's life is in danger! Just get me somebody with some authority who's connected at all with this part of the country!"

Quickly the operator assured him, "I'll put you through to someone who may be able to help you."

After a few moments a male voice said, "Hogan."

"Mr. Hogan, my name is Ken Inman. I'm calling from Palo Alto. There's someone out here who is working for you, and I wanted to let you know that her life is in great danger."

"Hmm. What kind of danger?"

"From Russian agents seeking revenge!"

"Really?"

"Really. She helped Russia's top parapsychologist escape recently and—"

"How recently? And where?"

"Last week—in Paris."

"I think someone's been pulling your leg. There wasn't a high-level Russian defection anywhere in the world last week. If there had been, I'd have known it."

"Look, Hogan, I've got top security clearance with NASA and the Pentagon. I've designed computer systems for your agency as well as for military intelligence. I'm not a kook. I know what I'm talking about, and if you don't, then I guess it's too highly classified. Do you know anything about a secret psychic research installation near Palo Alto run by Frank Leighton?"

"If I did, obviously I couldn't tell you."

"A citizen of the United States who helped a Russian scientist defect—and who's getting involved with your agency—is in great danger. She has to be protected, and nothing's being done about it! How do I get some action?"

"Mr. Inman, I don't doubt your clearance level or your sincerity, but I doubt the validity of what you're telling me. Someone has misinformed you. And even if what you say were true, a man of your intelligence knows I can't go on hearsay. If your friend is indeed a part of one of our operations involving any kind of personal danger, you may be certain she will be provided all necessary protection."

"But I don't think you know she's working for you!" interrupted Ken anxiously, realizing that didn't make sense, but trying desperately to keep Hogan from cutting him off.

"Those things have a way of getting sorted out. I really wouldn't be concerned about it, Mr. Inman. I appreciate your call." With that he hung up.

Ken realized it would be fruitless to call back. It didn't make sense no matter how he tried to explain it. *Bureaucracy is an incurable plague! This is incredible! I know she's in danger, but the CIA probably doesn't even know she's working for them. Maybe Leighton has taken some steps, but I doubt it.*

His troubled thoughts were interrupted by the phone ringing. He picked up the receiver. "Hello."

"Ken, this is Don Jordan. I just wanted to let you know that two of our men checked in with Carla last night. She's still at the Hilton—got in very late. She was followed in from somewhere in the foothills, but we don't have any leads. We've got her hotel room under 24-hour surveillance."

"Don, I don't want to seem to be interfering, but what about when she drives back and forth from Frank's lab? If she was followed from out there last night . . . ?"

"Ken, if it weren't for your top-secret clearance level, I couldn't even discuss this with you and shouldn't be. Whatever Leighton is doing out there is apparently so highly classified that I can't find anyone in the CIA who'll even admit that his lab exists. We'll pick her up along the access road about a mile from the highway and follow her in—at the U.S. Government sign. But inside, that's under CIA jurisdiction. Our men would look silly going in there. We just can't do it."

"Silly or not—"

"I understand how you feel. Believe me, I'm doing all I can. In fact, I'm really stretching it."

"I know you are, and I appreciate it. Thanks, brother—and please keep praying!"

Ken left his office at his computer company early that afternoon. He couldn't shake off the insistent thought that Carla was in imminent danger and that he ought to do something about it. It seemed all too clear that the CIA wasn't going to take care of her. She had fallen through a bureaucratic crack. At least he had accidentally alerted the FBI and they were watching her, but not along the most dangerous stretch of access road. He decided to drive up there to check it out himself. If the Russians had sent a team to get Viktor and found that he was guarded day and night inside a fortress, he had no idea how they would tackle that problem—but Carla was clearly vulnerable. The most likely spot for them to go after her, now that the hotel was being guarded, would be that isolated stretch of access road that the FBI wasn't covering. *Maybe it's crazy, but I'm going to check that out myself—at least see what it looks like.* On his way out there, he stopped by his house to change into some jeans. As a last-minute thought, he grabbed a down jacket and an old deer rifle he hadn't used for years and some ammunition.

His mother was sitting outside reading when he hurried by on his way back to the garage. "Don't make any supper for me," he remarked casually. "It'll probably be late before I get home."

She looked up at him over her glasses as he walked by. "My goodness! I didn't know it was hunting season! Where are you going in such a hurry?"

"I'm just going to do a little scouting around up in the hills. See you tomorrow. Take care."

"You take care!" she called after him. "You hear me? Take care!"

Driving slowly past the "Restricted Government Property. No Trespassing!" sign, Ken began to feel rather foolish. It would be very embarrassing to meet Leighton—or Carla, for that matter—on their way to Palo Alto. When he came within sight of the wall surrounding the property, he turned around, drove a few yards until he could not be seen from the installation, then pulled over to the side and sat there with his engine idling. *So, I've looked it over. What do I do now? I've just wasted my time. There's nothing I could do.* He remembered seeing about 100 yards back toward the highway an opening in the trees next to the road that could conceal a vehicle. He decided to check it out on his way home.

Dusk was now settling fast under the tall redwoods. When he came to the narrow clearing, he got out of his car and inspected it with his flashlight. It went deeper into the woods than he had thought—more than 20 feet—and he noticed there were tire tracks that continued back under the trees farther than necessary if one were merely turning around. *Someone has been parking here! A hunter, perhaps, poaching on government property? Not likely—game is scarce in this area. The tracks look very fresh!*

A foolhardy thought crossed his mind and he rejected it. But it came back again . . . and again. Getting into his car, he drove on another quarter of a mile and pulled off the road as far as he could at one of the few spots where the shoulder was a bit wider than usual. Then he scribbled a note on a scrap of paper—"Ran out of gas. I'll be right back"—and stuck it under the windshield wiper.

Loading the rifle, he put some extra ammunition in a pocket, locked the car, and started off down the road with the gun wrapped in the down jacket. Five minutes of brisk walking brought him back to the narrow clearing. It was now after six o'clock and nearly dark. *Suppose Russian agents are planning to use this spot tonight! Somebody parked in here very recently. I want to scare them away, but I'd also like to be able to identify them. How can I do that?* Afraid to use his flashlight, he groped around until he found some large, loose branches, two nearby logs small enough for him to drag, and some hefty boulders. He carefully made a low barrier somewhat less than a car length inside the trees. A driver backing in would not be likely to notice it in the dark, especially if he had been there before and had been able to drive back much farther out of sight.

Ken found a hiding place in a cluster of high ferns about 20 feet away, just behind a large tree. There he settled down to wait. The night air grew cold—good thing he'd brought the heavy jacket. He shoved his hands deep down into its warm pockets. The rifle lay across his lap. One hour went by, then two. He must have dozed off. The sound of a car engine approaching from the highway jolted him awake.

Now he could see its lights coming intermittently through the trees. It slowed, stopped directly in front of him, then began to back into the narrow opening. Ken's heart began to pound. He released the safety and moved over to crouch up against the tree. In the dim illumination of back-up lights, he could just make out the low barricade he'd constructed, but the driver apparently didn't see it. There was a crash as the tail pipe hit a large boulder, the grinding of another boulder under the gas tank, and a dull thump as the rear tires struck logs.

Doors opened and two men jumped out and ran back to investigate. The volley of angry words left no doubt that these men were *Russians!* He froze against the sheltering tree trunk. They shined flashlights on the debris and kicked at it in anger, then yelled something at the driver. He pulled the car up and they started to move the rocks and logs out of the way. Then they seemed to have second thoughts and stopped their work. There were subdued mutterings as they held a brief consultation. Hurriedly they got back into the car and drove off. *So there is a Russian team on Carla's trail, and they had planned to wait for her here! I've got to get word to the FBI!*

Should he go to the guards at the gate? They'd probably just run him off—wouldn't even listen to him. And if he followed too quickly in the direction that the Russians had driven, they might be waiting for him. What if they came back? After about 20 minutes of anxious indecision, Ken cautiously made his way out to the road and, after an uneventful hike, reached his car. Nothing had been touched. The note was still on the windshield. Getting in, he drove out to the highway as fast as the curves would allow, without seeing anyone. It seemed forever before he came to a public phone on the way into Palo Alto. From there he dialed his friend Don Jordan's residence, a number that he knew by heart.

After a few rings, there was a tired, "Hello." It was Don's wife.

"Gloria, is Don there?"

"Who is this? Oh, Ken. I didn't recognize your voice. Don's getting dressed right now to go into the office. There's an emergency."

"I've got an emergency, too. Something awfully urgent. Can you put him on for just a minute?"

"Hold on." There was a brief wait, then, "Hello. I'm really in a rush, Ken."

"Listen! I was up on the road into Leighton's fortress and I ran into some Russian agents!"

"You did? How did you know they were Russians?"

"I was hiding near a spot I thought someone might use to park out of sight—about 200 yards from the installation—when this car backed in. Two of them got out and they were talking *Russian!* Then they took off."

"How long ago was that?"

"About 40 minutes, maybe a little more."

"You can be *very* thankful, Ken. We had two special agents in a car on that road beginning about nine o'clock, waiting to follow Carla back to her hotel. They must have gotten there just before the Russians drove out. They radioed that they were attempting to pull over a car they had pursued out of the private road. They chased it down toward Palo Alto and then it turned off to the north. By the time our back-up units and the highway patrol found their car, our men were dead. We have an APB out, but we don't know who we're looking for. We have a vague description of the car, but no license number."

"You mean they were too much for your men to handle?" gasped Ken. "Who are these guys!"

"It's a special Russian team, like I suspected would be coming."

"You mean the *Spetznas?*"

"No. A secret psychic combat group ten times more dangerous. We don't have anyone on the West Coast capable of dealing with them. We've sent to Virginia for some special commandos. They'll have that road blanketed by tomorrow night."

"What about Carla?"

"I don't think she's in any immediate danger. We've probably scared them off for the moment at least. But we've got another team out on the road now waiting for her. They'll escort her to the hotel. Ken, I've got to go. I'll keep you up to date."

"Thanks, Don."

"Listen, do me one favor, will you?"

"What's that?"

"Don't try to play cops and robbers anymore. You may have saved Carla's life tonight, but stay out of this from now on. I mean that! For your own good—and for Carla's! Is that clear?"

"I hear you, Don."

the MIND INVADERS
23

Invasion!

The isolated stretch of access road was empty when Carla at last drove out to the main highway after leaving the installation. She had, of course, no knowledge of the deadly drama that had been acted out along that route earlier. Nor did she know that she had reached its juncture with the main road just minutes before the back-up FBI team assigned to escort her arrived. Consequently, the men sat waiting for nearly an hour before they were belatedly notified that she had already driven to Palo Alto.

Twenty minutes later, she was racing up the steps of the hotel. A quick survey of the lobby revealed one of the two FBI special agents from the previous night. He was sitting in an easy chair and glanced at her over the newspaper he was reading, then went back to it without a flicker of recognition. Just seeing him—together with the fact that she hadn't been followed this time—made her feel immeasurably better. Uncle Sam's men really were on the job! Carla resisted a second glance.

There must be a convention! she thought, as she took in the crowd. *People everywhere!* About a dozen of them squeezed into the elevator with her. Ordinary people, it seemed—except for the two men on the far side that she noticed just as the door shut. There was something strangely familiar about one of them. Was he the shorter of the two FBI agents she'd encountered in the elevator the previous night? He'd had a beard. She stole another look. *Pavlov? No, it can't be!* He turned to look at her, and their eyes met, just as her lips framed his name in disbelief.

She turned her head quickly away, but was drawn irresistibly back to that face again for another furtive glance. It was important to be absolutely certain. He was not looking at her, so she was able to study him for a moment. The new beard—*perhaps to cover some nasty scars*—had almost fooled her, but there was now no doubt about it. The man was unquestionably Dr. Alexandr Pavlov from Paris, who, as Viktor had explained to her, was in fact Colonel Alexei Chernov, a Russian Army officer in charge of a special contingent of psychic combat troops! Nor could there be any doubt as to his intention!

Instead of experiencing the waves of panic she'd always imagined would possess her if she ever actually faced such a situation, Carla felt strangely detached from herself and everyone around her. Was this real? The elevator began to spin. Would she faint? She longed for the oblivion of unconsciousness, but fought it off in terror. She leaned against the wall and clenched her fists, trying desperately to hang on and think. *What can I do? No way am I going to get off on my floor! And getting off with someone else is no better. If I ride it to the top, I'll finally be on it alone with the two of them. Should I scream right now? They might kill everyone!*

There was only one thing to do. Clutching her left side, she fell against the man next to her and in a weak voice, but loud enough for everyone to hear, pleaded with him: "I must be having a heart attack! Please get me back down to the lobby! I need an ambu lance!" Gasping loudly for breath, she clutched her chest with one hand, and with the other grabbed at him frantically for support as she slid helplessly to the floor. People craned their necks to see. She had turned ashen with panic, and thus gave involuntary authenticity to the scenario she was playing out so desperately.

"Stand back!" The man just behind her had taken charge, easing Carla to the floor and pushing passengers back to make room for her. "Give her some air! How can we get this thing turned around?"

"You can't," said a woman. "Where's everybody getting off?"

"There are only four floors punched," said someone else.

"Don't anyone get off!" wailed Carla. "Please stay with me. Help me!"

"Okay, lady. Keep calm. Everyone stay aboard," the reassuring and authoritative voice barked. "Push the 'close door' button as soon as it opens."

"Anyone know CPR?" asked a concerned male voice.

"I do!" responded a female, "but she doesn't need it yet. We'll need all of the men to help carry her when we get back to the lobby!"

Amazingly, no one got off. The door was closed promptly each time it opened and in no time at all they were back to the ground level. Through a forest of shins and ankles, Carla had warily observed the feet and legs of Chernov and his companion. They had shuffled around on the far side of the elevator, but had made no move toward her. Now as others bent over to carry her, she saw the two Russians scurry out into the lobby.

"FBI!" Carla screamed, pushing away those who were bending over to lift her, and getting warily to her feet. "Help! FBI!" she yelled even louder. The special agent who had been sitting in the lobby when she'd entered came running around the corner, and another one rushed up from the opposite direction. Carla's fellow passengers fell back in surprise and stood nearby staring at her in shock.

"Two Russians—one with a beard!" Carla managed to tell them. "They headed for the front door! That way!" Now she became aware that she was trembling from head to toe.

The two agents ran off at great speed and Carla, still trembling, followed them cautiously at a safe distance across the lobby and out the front door. There she stood and looked anxiously in all directions but saw nothing. In a few minutes they came back separately and empty-handed. A crowd of the curious had gathered in front of the hotel.

"We can't talk here," said the agent who seemed to be in charge. He showed her his badge and introduced himself and his companion. "I'm Carl Richardson. This is George Lawton. Let's get out of here."

They led her to an unmarked car parked by the curb and put her in the backseat. Richardson climbed in there with her. "Now tell us what happened," he demanded.

As she told her story, Lawton drove slowly around the area, then parked a block down the street so they could keep the hotel in view. "That was quick thinking, Miss Bertelli," Richardson said when she'd finished. "It probably saved your life. We have a thick file on Chernov. He's the most vicious and dangerous man the FSB has. But we need as complete a description as you can give us of his present appearance, and of the other man as well."

"Well, physically Chernov hasn't changed since I saw him less than three weeks ago in Paris," said Carla, trying to picture him. "He looks about 45 years old, an even six feet tall, powerfully built—I'd say about 200 pounds. Sharp nose, square jaw, his eyes are sort of sunken and narrow, broad forehead, thick black hair cut very short, but it lies down flat. His beard is extremely short—it can't be more than three weeks old because he didn't have a beard in Paris. His companion, also powerfully built, is about two inches taller, but I really didn't get a good look at him. I think he had short, sandy hair and broad cheekbones, but that's about all I remember. They were both wearing dark suits."

As she gave the descriptions, Lawton repeated them over the car radio. "That's going immediately out on an All Points Bulletin," explained Richardson. "It goes not only to our agents, but to local police, sheriffs, highway patrol—every law-enforcement agency. Unfortunately, we don't have a description of their car other than what you gave us last night, which isn't much to go on."

They drove back to the hotel, this time parking around the corner, and the three of them walked in the side door and hurried across the lobby. Immediately they were recognized and several of the most inquisitive guests followed them. "Stand back!" ordered the two agents as soon as an elevator door had opened, and they prevented anyone else from entering. The door closed on the three of them, and Richardson punched floors four, six, and ten. Responding to Carla's questioning look, he explained, "Some of those people will be watching to see what floor we get off at, and they'll literally snoop along the halls trying to find out something."

At the fourth and sixth floors he punched the button to close the door immediately. When the elevator opened at the tenth floor, they got out and the FBI agents led the way down the stairs to the eighth, where Carla's room was located.

She opened the door to her room, and they went in with her to check it out. "Lawton and I have blown our cover," explained Richardson. "You won't see us again in the lobby. We'll trade places with the team that has been occupying the adjoining room." He pointed to the access door between. "The door on our side is open at all times. If you have an emergency, just open your side and come on in. We'll be there 24 hours a day. There's another team in the room directly across the hall watching your door day and night."

"You really make me feel secure," responded Carla gratefully. "I didn't know I was this important. It's hard for me to believe that someone actually wants to kill me. That's a horrible realization!"

"From what you told us, you nearly killed Chernov," said Lawton. "He's not the kind to take that without getting revenge."

"Don't forget, however, you're not his primary target," added Richardson. "That's in your favor. He's after the defector you rescued. He now knows you'll be watched around the clock after you recognized him tonight, and he may decide it isn't worth the risk and effort. We hope so, but if he tries, we've got you covered. No more elevator rides unescorted. Everywhere you go, someone will be right there. You won't always know it, but you can count on it."

Carla was in bed trying to fall asleep and finding it impossible, when the phone rang. "Miss Bertelli," said a deep male voice, "this is Don Jordan. I'm in charge of the FBI teams that have you under surveillance. I just wanted to explain a couple of things. First of all, you might be interested to know that the men you saw in the elevator were apparently on the private access road out near the research center earlier tonight—probably to waylay you. A mutual friend of ours, Ken Inman, seems to have frightened them off."

"You're kidding! What in the world was Ken doing out there?"

"Exactly what he shouldn't have been doing—and I've warned him about that. But he had such concern for you, he just didn't realize what he was getting into. But he knows better now. This is a very dangerous Russian team. They killed two of our men who tried to arrest them a little later."

"So Ken saved my life—and risked his own to do it?"

"I guess you could say that," said Jordan.

For a moment Carla saw herself walking out of a hospital room and heard Ken calling to her. Then she realized that Jordan was telling her something important.

". . . we don't know how many more there may be in this elite Russian team, but we've got a company of specially trained Army commandos coming in from Virginia who can handle them. By tomorrow evening they'll be deployed all along that access road leading from the main highway to the laboratory so you won't have anything further to worry about."

"Are you expecting a major assault on the laboratory?" asked Carla in surprise.

"I can't say what we're expecting. Of course, everything I've said to you is confidential. I mainly wanted to let you know that we have the situation under control. Just relax and have a good night's rest."

"I really appreciate this," said Carla. "I was having a terrible time trying to get to sleep. I don't like to take pills."

"Definitely don't take any under *these* circumstances!" Jordan cautioned her.

"Thanks again. You've made me feel so much better!"

Carla slept fitfully. Nightmares merged with waking fantasies. The whole of life had become a bad dream from which she hoped one day to awaken. Was it worth going on? *Of course it is!* she told herself whenever such a thought surfaced. There was no doubt that she had a Pulitzer-prize-winning story in the bag, at least five million dollars in movie rights, and all of the other endless benefits. She was not only sitting on the story of a lifetime, but she was living it, participating in its frightening development, *experiencing it all herself from the inside!* Had any other journalists ever been so lucky as to stumble upon such an opportunity?

After a late breakfast in her room—delivered by an FBI agent—she dressed and went down to her car. The man in the hall who got on the elevator with her and followed her into the garage, the unmarked car with two men in it that pulled out just ahead of her, and the similar one that followed just behind and stayed with her all the way to the gate of the installation, gave her a feeling not only of impregnable security, but also of importance that was more than gratifying. She wouldn't want to live that way for long, however. At least it was quite apparent that Chernov was not going to be able to complete his designs upon her—and certainly Viktor was beyond his reach in Leighton's impregnable fortress.

"I hear you've had some adventures," exclaimed Leighton the moment she walked into his office just before noon.

"I had some anxious moments, but I'm really not worried anymore," said Carla, trying to be blasé about the whole thing. Then she added with a laugh, "You'd think I was the president of the United States if you could see the way my hotel room is watched—and the escort I got right up to the gate!"

"Well, you're safe out here—that's for certain. This place is guarded better than Fort Knox. Maybe I can persuade you to move in. You'd have your own apartment like Viktor, great food—the Hilton can't offer anything better—sauna, gymnasium, swimming pool. . . ."

Carla laughed and shook her head. "And miss the celebrity feeling I get with escorts and guards following me everywhere? I appreciate the offer, but I'm not worried anymore. They told me they're going to have a whole company of special Army commandos guarding the road by evening, so even that spooky stretch that used to scare me to death is going to be a piece of cake from now on."

"I know," responded Leighton with a scowl, "and I think it's a ridiculous overreaction. The escort they've given you should be enough. I don't like so much attention—not that kind. Some senator could start asking questions that we can't answer yet." He shrugged and managed a half-smile. "Look, I'm not suggesting it's your fault. Anyway, we've got a job to do out here. Let me get the lab on the intercom and see what Del Sasso's up to. Viktor is already down there. We've got a lot of ground to cover today."

The night was pitch-black. Not only was it the dark of the new moon, but a heavy bank of fog had crept inland from the coast a few miles to the west and up and over the mountains, seeping down to the ground through the treetops. Silence and immobility reigned. The two guards on duty at the gate were facing the usual evening boredom. It was now about 8:30 p.m. and there had been no activity since the lab assistants and secretaries had left in the normal day's-end exodus shortly after five o'clock.

This was not a job that lent itself to cards or television in off moments. Even though the daily routine was mostly watching and waiting for something that so far had never happened, vigilance was demanded at all times. The guards took turns peering from their fortified station through the small, thick pane of bulletproof glass at the fog swirling along the floodlighted road in front of the steel gate they were manning. The report that Russian agents were known to be in the vicinity stalking Miss Bertelli and were likely to attempt a penetration of the installation to kill Dr. Khorev had put nerves on edge.

"I can't believe they think they can attack this fortress," mused the younger of the two guards for the fourth or fifth time that evening, more to himself than to his companion, who was tired of hearing it.

"Yeah, yeah, I've heard that opinion. Myself, I don't take anything for granted."

The younger man turned away with a loud yawn from another look at the fog-enshrouded road leading to the gate. "If you had the job of getting inside here and killing someone, how would you go about it? Not a frontal assault."

"I wouldn't even try. I'd wait till the guy came out, which he'd have to do eventually. I'd lie low and get him when he was on vacation somewhere and not expecting it."

"Suppose there was some reason why you couldn't wait that long?"

"You'd have to wait. It's impossible to crack this place. You know that. You can't go through the wall, and even if you could get over or under it, the electronics would trigger an immediate alarm. You'd have to come through here—over our dead bodies. And I don't know how anyone could get at us." He took his turn peering into the night.

"Helicopter, maybe?" persisted the younger one.

"Don't be silly. You've been watching too much TV."

"Well, how about parachutes? Some of these guys can land on a dime."

"In the middle of these tall trees—and at night? Now you are getting crazy!"

"Tap, tap, tap." At the sound coming from behind them, the two men whirled around, automatic weapons poised. They could see a familiar face peering into the small window in the heavy steel door that gave them access to the inside of the compound—a retreat route they could take if it were ever needed.

"Well, look who's here," said the younger to his companion. "It's not often we get a visit from the 'big wheels.'" He went over, unlocked the door, and opened it. "Out for a stroll, are you?"

"Yeah. My brain was getting foggy, so I thought I'd clear it with a short walk around the base. That never fails."

"Well, come on in," said the older guard, "and relieve our boredom for a few minutes. We're supposed to be on alert, but what's the point? The woods are crawling with Army commandos. Any Russian agents out there couldn't get within a country mile of this place. And if they did, I'd like to see them try to get in!"

Suddenly the visitor, who had stepped inside the small station, stared with shocked expression past the guards through the small window and asked in a hushed voice, "What was it that just moved over there across the road?"

The two guards stepped quickly over to peer out through the bulletproof glass into the fog. "Straight across?" the elder one asked, half-turning back toward the visitor. As he did so, he noticed a quick movement out of the corner of his eye.

With a lightning motion, the video surveillance camera had been shoved to one side. Wearing a derisive smile, the visitor was pointing a handgun fitted with a silencer. The guard had no chance to aim his own weapon in defense: The three slugs tore into his face and head, killing him instantly. His younger companion whirled around but was dead before he could raise his gun.

Instantly, the visitor pushed the button that opened the armored door, stepped quickly over the two bodies and into the open doorway, and waved at the empty road. Four men in dark sweat suits raced swiftly out of the thick woods. Chernov was the first to enter the guard station. "Harasho!" he grunted, taking the gun that had just killed the two guards. It would leave the base with him when he and his men had accomplished their mission.

When all four were inside, the "big wheel" closed the automatic door again, pointing out the control button to the others, and said in fluent Russian: "Give me two minutes to get back inside. Then you angle left to the side entrance. Get immediately away from the wall and stay away from it. That's where the electronic surveillance devices are. Otherwise you only have to contend with dogs and guards." Stepping quickly out the inner door, the "big wheel" was gone.

Psychic War!

Chernov and his men moved swiftly to get the surveillance camera back into place. Both corpses were dragged up next to the inside door, out of the camera's normal viewing angle. One of the men put on a flak jacket that had been quickly stripped from a body. His hair and weight were similar to those of one of the dead men, and from the rear he could pass the periodic cursory look from the security control center inside. Quickly the camera was moved back. Then they waited. Two minutes seemed an eternity, but it was absolutely essential to protect the identity of their agent on the inside. When the last second had been counted—leaving the new "guard" peering out the small window toward the road—Chernov led his other two men into the complex, closing the door securely behind them.

A short, fast run of about 90 feet brought all three to a clump of small fir trees near to the end building on the left side of the entry drive. There they stopped out of sight to survey the situation and orient themselves with the map of the property they had memorized. They knew there were four trained and extremely vicious Rottweiler attack dogs that roamed the grounds after dark. It would be only a matter of a few moments until they would pick up the intruders' strange scents and be upon them.

The number of guards patrolling and the routes they took varied, so the three Russians were running the risk of being discovered at any time. They crouched and waited for the dogs. It would be best to dispose of them first. Chernov smiled to himself. Dogs and guards were no great challenge for him and his men. It was the hooded one that concerned him.

The sound of barking coming at them from two directions caused Chernov and his men to crouch lower. Two of the converging canines were dispatched with single shots from silenced guns as soon as they came within range. Then the invaders jumped out of the shelter of the trees to face the other two. Snarling ferociously, the dogs charged with fangs bared. The colonel stepped back to watch these two men that he had carefully trained perform. The guard dogs didn't stand a chance. Lightning kicks to the throat broke two necks in midair lunge.

Chernov grunted his approval. "Now!" he whispered, and they raced for the row of low buildings on their left. Once there, they crept cautiously along, keeping close to the walls and traversing quickly the short open spaces between. Reaching the far end of the last structure, they paused for breath again and surveyed the area leading to the side door that they knew would be unlocked.

"Freeze!" The stern command was barked from behind the furtive figures. A guard had just come around the other end of the building and spotted them. He approached rapidly, automatic weapon out in front, ready to fire.

"Hands up! Get up against the wall! Now!" Chernov and his men obeyed grudgingly. "Spread your legs—no sudden movements." He approached them cautiously to get a better view in the dim light. *How did these guys get in here?* He looked around warily in case there were more.

He had to notify central control immediately, and he was also going to need some help. Keeping a careful eye on the intruders and his gun trained, he pulled his walkie-talkie from his belt. Out of the corner of his eye, Chernov saw what was happening and knew he had to act instantly.

Whirling around faster than the guard's eye could follow, the colonel made a sweeping motion through the air with one hand. He touched nothing, yet the walkie-talkie splintered into dozens of pieces. The automatic weapon was torn from the hands that gripped it and thrown against the concrete wall of the building with such force that the barrel bent and the stock shattered. In another blur of graceful motion, Chernov broke the helpless man's neck with a flying foot. They dragged his body quickly under a large bush, then hurried to the main structure.

Keeping as much as they could in the shadows, they quickly reached the side door they knew would be unlocked without encountering any other guards and made their way noiselessly inside. Following the blueprints of the building they had memorized, they headed swiftly and silently for Leighton's office.

"Remember!" whispered Chernov, repeating an order he had already drilled into his men. "The tall hooded one is dangerous. Shoot him on sight! And the woman is mine."

After another exhausting day of watching experiments, recording explanations, and analyzing the daily "transmission" from the Archons, Carla had been in an intense strategy session all evening with Viktor, Del Sasso, Morris, and Leighton in the latter's spacious office. The Archons' "transmission" that day had given the first details of how the Plan would be presented to the world and the necessary steps to be taken thereafter for its implementation. Following the exact procedure was absolutely essential. The process would require a number of news "leaks" by Carla to her editor friend in New York in addition to her own syndicated articles, all of which had to be written and handled with extreme care.

Carla and Leighton had been left alone for the past ten minutes. Kay had excused herself to do some preparation in the labs for the next day's work. Viktor had stepped outside to clear his head with a short walk. And Del Sasso had gone to his apartment to change clothes. "I have an intuition," he'd explained, "that I'm not supposed to wear my usual robe the rest of the evening." He hadn't yet returned.

"His headache may have gotten worse and he went to bed," suggested Leighton.

Viktor had just rejoined them when Carla made a decision. "Is that offer of a room for the night still open?" she asked Leighton.

"It sure is!" came the quick reply.

"Well, maybe I'll take you up on it—for tonight, anyway."

"It's a long drive back, I suppose," suggested Viktor.

Carla hesitated. She'd been debating with herself all evening whether to tell them what had happened, and had finally concluded that she should. "I didn't want to upset you, Viktor. Of course, everyone knows that the access road is now guarded with a company of special commandos."

"That's ridiculous!" retorted Frank impatiently. "Who needs those guys?" He turned to Viktor. "Someone thinks they spotted a special Russian team apparently here to assassinate you." Viktor suddenly looked frightened. "Don't give it another thought," Frank continued. "Look, Viktor, what happens out there is no concern of ours. Inside this fortress is another world, and nobody's going to break in here, believe me! That's why you're in here."

"There's something you don't know, Frank," interrupted Carla. "When Viktor dove into my convertible in Paris and we made our escape, a Russian delegate to the Congress that I only knew as Dr. Alexandr Pavlov, a real brute of a man who was chasing Viktor, leaped onto my car. He was climbing in, and would have had us, when I made a fast turn that broke his grip and threw him through a plate-glass window. . . . "

It wasn't "Pavlov" she was seeing now in the rearview mirror, clinging to her car in Paris, but Chernov in the elevator in Palo Alto—with revenge in his eyes. She had to stop to get control of her voice. *Why do I feel like this? There's nothing to be frightened of anymore. For Viktor's sake, get hold of yourself. Don't make it worse for him!*

Viktor picked up the story. "As you knew, Frank—although I had no idea at the time *how* you knew—'Pavlov' was really Colonel Alexei Chernov, the commandant of the secret installation where my lab was located. It was also a military base for training special troops in psychic warfare."

Leighton smiled and nodded. "I knew who he was the minute I saw him that first night. As you both now know, we've got him on lots of film." Then he added with a chuckle, "I blew his cover at the

Congress. Privately, of course. You remember that, Viktor?" Viktor nodded soberly.

"Chernov is here!" continued Carla, looking at Viktor sympathetically. "He almost got me at my hotel last night!" She paused again to control her voice. "I'm sure he's after both of us!"

"Then you have to stay here!" exclaimed Leighton. "Not just tonight, but until the Plan has been implemented and all nations, including the Russians, are part of it. Only then will the threat from Chernov and his men be ended!"

All the color had drained from Viktor's face. Leighton noticed and tried to reassure him. "There's nothing to be afraid of, Viktor—nothing at all. Chernov can't even get close to us out here with a whole company of commandos deployed along the access road. It would take an army with tanks to get past them. And it's at least a three-mile hike through thick woods with no trails, so you can forget about that. And even if, by some miracle, they got here, I guarantee you they could never get inside. It's impossible! So just relax."

"You don't know the capabilities of these men," said Viktor in a weak voice. He sounded resigned and defeated.

"Forget it!" insisted Leighton. "Now Carla, let me show you to your apartment. It's right next to Viktor's—all made up and ready. Do you have some things in your car?"

She nodded. "Just a few."

"We can pick them up on our way over there. Are you coming, too, Viktor?" Viktor nodded listlessly. He looked like a condemned man whose day of execution had arrived.

Leighton stood to his feet. "Viktor! I tell you—there's nothing to be afraid of. I wish you could see yourself in a mirror. It's comical. Come on, man, cheer up!" Then he remembered something. "Wait a minute. I almost forgot. Let me call the FBI so they know you're staying here tonight."

Out in the hall and just around the corner from Leighton's office, Del Sasso was being kidded about his attire by one of the CIA guards, a devout Catholic. "I almost didn't recognize you! I said to myself, 'Who let that strange dude in here?' You don't look like yourself without that robe, Father. I thought you never took it off."

"Oh, I do have it laundered once a year, when I take my annual bath. I'm quite civilized."

At that moment, Chernov and his two men, moving quickly down the main hall from the side door, stepped into view. The agent saw them at the same time they saw him. He went into an immediate crouch, swinging his automatic weapon quickly from where it was slung over his shoulder. There was no time for him even to aim. A volley of muffled shots from Chernov, and his men left the guard dead in a pool of blood. Del Sasso slowly raised his hands over his head.

"He's a tall one," said Chernov. "Use him for a shield!" One of his men grabbed the psychic, put a gun to his head, and marched him along in front of them. They arrived at the office door just as Leighton opened it.

"My God!" cried Leighton and jumped back into the room, trying to close the door. Chernov's shoulder smashed it open and knocked Leighton to the floor unconscious. With one of the Russians standing guard at the door, the colonel and his other man charged into the office, pushing Del Sasso ahead of them.

Carla screamed and Chernov smashed her across the mouth with the back of his hand, knocking her down. From the floor she watched in semiconscious terror.

"Pavlov" stood over her, enjoying this moment immensely. "So, we do meet again, Miss Bertelli. You were quite brave in Paris, and that was a brilliant piece of acting on the elevator. This time there's no escape!"

"Don't harm her!" pleaded Viktor.

Eyes blazing with hatred, Chernov slammed him across the mouth, knocking him to the floor also. "I'm taking you with me, Khorev—back to Moscow. I'd rather kill you right now, but you have some debts to pay to the country you betrayed!"

The colonel glanced quickly around the large office without finding someone he had expected to be there. Leaning over Viktor, he demanded, "Where's the hooded one?"

"The 'hooded one'?" stammered Viktor, pretending not to understand.

With one powerful hand Chernov grabbed Viktor by the back of his neck and pulled him to his feet, shoving the barrel of his pistol under Viktor's chin. "You know who I mean! Where is he?"

"I'm the one you call the 'hooded one,'" said Del Sasso, "and you are all dead men." He pulled away from the Soviet who had been holding the gun to his head and faced them with a twisted smile on his face that stunned Viktor and Carla. It was derisive, contemptuous, and mocking—like the smile of a bully gloating over a cowering victim. Here was a frightening side of Del Sasso that Viktor and Carla had tried to forget.

"You were going to shoot the 'hooded one' on sight. Then shoot him." Del Sasso was laughing now, taunting them.

To Carla, the very atmosphere in the room seemed to have been charged with some mysterious force. Yet it wasn't so much a power as a *presence*—primordial and horrifying—like nothing she could fathom or label. *The Archons?*

The barrel of the gun that had been pressed against Del Sasso's head bent and twisted and the useless weapon was wrenched from the hand that held it and fell to the floor. The tough and seemingly invincible warrior, "ten times more dangerous" than the *Spetznas*, who had been holding Del Sasso, was now quaking like an aspen leaf in the wind. He levitated slowly, began to twirl at increasing speed, then suddenly shot through the air and crashed into his companion who was guarding the door, sending them both into the corridor. The door slammed shut. There was a volley of shots from the direction of the lobby, then footsteps running toward them and a babble of voices.

Now Del Sasso turned his attention to Chernov. The old Master was desperately attempting to aim a gun that seemed alive and refused to point at the 'hooded one,' whom he now recognized at last. A slight, quick gesture from Del Sasso and the gun was torn from Chernov's grip and skidded across the floor toward Viktor. Viktor grabbed for it.

Chernov made a feint as though he were going after Viktor and the gun, then spun suddenly and with blinding speed arched his lethal foot toward Del Sasso's throat. Instantly he was thrown against the far wall of the office, just as Yakov had been in the laboratory. Battered and bloody, he pulled himself up from the floor, shook himself, and began a wary advance toward his incredible antagonist.

"I detest violence," said Del Sasso. Carla noticed that his voice had taken on a very controlled and almost conciliatory tone. "Surrender now and no more harm will come to you."

With a cry of rage, Chernov charged. He had not taken two steps when, to her utter terror, Carla saw the heavy glass that protected the top of Leighton's huge desk abruptly lift into the air. Spinning like a high-speed circular saw, it sailed swiftly through Chernov's midsection, bisecting his body at the belt line. Smashing into the wall behind him, the glass exploded into a thousand bloody shards. Carla gasped in wordless horror and lost consciousness.

When she came to her senses, Carla found herself lying on a sofa in the lobby. Ghastly pale and in shock himself, Viktor was leaning over her, dabbing gently at her bleeding mouth with damp paper towels held in trembling hands.

"Are you okay?" asked Viktor.

She nodded weakly. "I can't believe it. I just can't."

Badly shaken, but with a wild look of triumph in his eyes, Leighton was nearby, alternately talking on a phone, and barking orders to those present. He was very much in charge once again. Kay Morris hovered at his elbow, consulting with him between phone calls.

Carla watched the frantic activity out of a fog, trying to regain her senses. At first, the room was swarming with guards—more than Carla had imagined were on the base. They conferred together in low tones with Mike Bradford, the director of security, shook their heads in unbelief at what had happened, then hurried back to their assigned duties. Unruffled and composed, as though he were in another world, Del Sasso stood near Leighton, watching and listening. There was an unearthly peace about him that seemed supernatural.

Viktor held both of her hands tightly in his. "It was awful!"

"Is it all over?" Carla asked. "The other two men?"

"When Del Sasso knocked them through the door they were shot by some guards who were coming down the hall searching for them."

Carla struggled and managed to sit up. Her ear was still ringing from the blow Chernov had given her, and one side of her face was swollen. She saw Leighton hang up the phone. He came over and sat down beside her and put an arm around her tenderly.

"Are you okay?" he asked. She nodded. "Should I call a doctor?" He looked at her swollen face and cut lip with concern.

She shook her head. "I'm okay, Frank—really."

"I can't tell you how sorry I am that this happened," he told her.

"Please, it's not your fault."

Turning to Viktor apologetically, Frank said, "I still say it's impossible. There's no way they could get in here. They must have come up through the woods. Somehow they got into the guard station at the gate and killed the guards. They must have tricked them, but how? I just can't believe it!"

"Antonio saved our lives," murmured Carla. He turned and smiled at her across the lobby. "You were magnificent, Antonio!" she called out to him.

He walked over, pulled up a chair, and sat down heavily. "I'm sorry that he hurt you, Carla. And about your office, Frank—things really got out of hand. I didn't want it that way, but sometimes the only way to stop violence is with greater violence." He seemed almost like a repentant child apologizing for some misdeed.

"Please, Antonio!" said Leighton gratefully. "If it weren't for you, we'd all be dead!"

Del Sasso turned to Viktor and Carla. "I offered him his life. You heard that, didn't you? I asked him to surrender. You're my witnesses."

"We're your witnesses," said Viktor solemnly. He still seemed to be in a state of shock.

"I heard it and I saw it," Carla assured him.

"So much blood!" murmured Del Sasso. "I don't like it. Basically, I'm a gentle person." He seemed obsessed to prove that he hadn't intended such bloody violence. Carla wondered at that.

She put a hand gingerly to her swollen face. She hadn't known that she would be getting into something like this, could never have anticipated it. Well, there was always a price to be paid for anything that was worthwhile, and there could no longer be any doubt that she was sitting on a story far bigger than she had even imagined. Whatever the cost in the future, there was no turning back now.

Carla was extremely grateful to Del Sasso for saving her life, but at the same time there was something terrifying about the power he controlled. Or did it control him in some mysterious way? Was that what he was trying to tell them, and why he was so apologetic? Was Del Sasso, after all, just a pawn of the Archons? It was a frightening question.

An Infinite Potential?

W e lost four good and brave men," intoned Leighton. "Men who believed in what we're doing and gave their lives in the line of duty. We will not dishonor them and their memory—or the bereaved families they left behind—by abandoning the noble cause to which they had dedicated themselves. Let this be a time of solemn rededication to the high-minded ideals of international goodwill among all peoples and nations."

The occasion was a memorial service held in the large theater in the center of the main building the day after the slain guards had been interred. It was now four days after the Russian attack. Carla was surprised at the large number of personnel involved at the secret complex. There were about 50 employees present: from scientists, lab assistants, and secretaries; to cooks, janitors, and of course the internal security force—which had now been increased by eight men in addition to replacing the four who had been killed. The entire staff was in attendance—a staff that had come through a terrible ordeal with obviously high morale in spite of the losses it had sustained.

Leighton finished his speech on a positive note: "We will carry on without looking back. We will let nothing and no one deter us from our goal. We are working for a New World of peace, love, and brotherhood—a world without fear of war or crime, a world without hunger, a model society of equal opportunity and of long life for all. We are within sight of that goal and it will be achieved!" From here and there came the staccato of enthusiastic applause.

"This very auditorium in which you now sit will soon be filled with leaders from all nations, who will meet to implement the Plan for that New World. That Plan, as you all know, is still too highly classified to share openly even on this occasion. Your individual contributions to the program and your confidence in me as your director have brought us to the very brink of success, and I am grateful for the spirit of loyalty and dedication that continues to motivate each of you. It will not be long now until everyone in the world will know the secret and reap the benefits of your persistent efforts here. I am pleased to say that I have just received confirmation of the full backing of the President of the United States. Preliminary contacts are being made with key leaders in the Senate and House, but of course no details can be shared with them until that time comes—which I assure you will be very soon." There was another burst of applause.

Leighton pulled an envelope out of his pocket, opened it, and unfolded a piece of paper. "I want to read to you part of a telegram received from the president only a few moments before this gathering convened. The rest is confidential, but will be disclosed to you later. Here it is: 'I have spoken by phone with the Russian president and described to him the attack by Russian agents upon your installation, which is dedicated to the peaceful use of psychic development for all peoples. He has assured me that he was not aware of this assault team and is taking steps to prevent such an occurrence from ever happening again. He has given me his personal word that peace is his top priority and that his country will participate in the forthcoming Congress for which you are now preparing. I congratulate you and your colleagues for the part you have played and will continue to play in the establishment of a peaceful and prosperous world for all mankind.'" Leighton paused dramatically, and again there was an enthusiastic response from his listeners.

"You can see that our president backs our mission 100 percent. You also know that, while not doubting the sincerity of the Russian president, and being thankful for his promise of peace, we shall not relax our vigilance until our goal has been reached. I am determined in my own heart, and I call upon you as well to join with me in a pledge to our higher selves, that those whose memory we honor today will not have died in vain!"

There was thunderous applause, and the audience stood to its feet. Leighton acknowledged their endorsement of his leadership graciously for a few moments before stepping down from the podium to mark the end of the meeting. There was a brief babble of voices as staff members came up to shake his hand and express their support once more, before returning to interrupted tasks in labs and offices.

Back in his office at last, Leighton held a council with his inner circle. Present were Morris, Del Sasso, Khorev, Bertelli, and Mike Bradford, head of security. It was a solemn gathering.

"I think you all know Mike," began Leighton. "I've asked him to meet with us to discuss the most troubling aspect of the recent attack."

Mike was a veteran of CIA covert operations from Cuba to Vietnam and Angola—and most places in between. He was as tough and smart as they came, and he was clearly very disturbed. He scanned the faces of those present carefully, then cleared his throat and began.

"We were hit bad the other night. I still don't believe it. I've been puzzling over this thing ever since. What happened was impossible. The Russian assault team entered our complex without triggering any electronic alarms. That is possible only if they entered at one particular place—which leaves only one explanation, and it isn't a pleasant one: Someone from the inside let them in!"

The stunned silence spoke louder than words. Mike folded his arms and watched the reactions.

"Are you certain?" asked Viktor at last, obviously badly shaken.

"Nothing is 100 percent certain," admitted Mike. "They might have tricked our men somehow, but that's so unlikely it can be categorically ruled out."

"But it *is* a possibility," interjected Kay Morris.

"Very unlikely. Can you imagine how our men could have been induced to open the door to their fortified station and let someone in? And we were on alert!"

"Hypnotic control, perhaps," mused Viktor. "I can tell you that Chernov had incredible psychic powers."

"Let's get the picture," said Frank. "The gate was closed, but both doors to the guard station were wide open. That is the only possible entrance route—and apparently an exit as well for at least one Russian."

In response to the questioning looks, Mike explained, "One of the flak jackets is missing and was probably being worn by someone who left in a hurry. How many others there were, we don't know."

"This really bothers me," said Kay. "I don't think we should even suggest it was an inside job until we're absolutely certain. The thought of a traitor within our own ranks is not only repugnant, it breeds an atmosphere of suspicion that I, for one, would find impossible to work in. If that assault team has been able to leave us with a suspicion that will eat at us, then in a sense they've won after all, and I don't want to concede that!"

Leighton was taken by the thought and nodded in agreement. "I agree with Kay. You all realize that an atmosphere of mistrust could literally shut us down—it would be a psychic victory for the Russians. It takes faith not only in the Archons but in ourselves and in one another for the Plan to succeed."

"That's what concerns me," continued Kay. "I can't imagine how they got in. But suppose the Russians were able to cover all trace of their entry? That would accomplish two things: It would leave that method secret for a future team to use; and it would allow them to leave 'evidence' that they got in by way of the guard station, which would seem to point to an inside job and breed suspicion among us all."

There was a long, uncomfortable silence. "What about this possibility?" suggested Carla at last. "The Russians got inside—we don't know how—and the two guards at the gate were the first to discover them. They came out of their station and were killed, dragged back in there out of sight—"

"They were shot inside the station," interrupted Mike, who had been listening quietly, while shaking his head with evident displeasure.

"So they were captured and then taken into the station and executed to further the 'inside job' theory," said Morris quickly.

Leighton turned to Del Sasso. "You've been awfully quiet, Antonio. Have the Archons given you the answer?"

"They don't tell us everything, for reasons that I don't entirely understand—something to do with responsibility and personal growth. I thought the FBI was investigating, so I'd like to know what they think."

Frank gestured toward Mike. "Well?"

Mike looked embarrassed. "Actually they have pretty much thrown out the inside-job theory. They seem to favor something more like what Dr. Morris is suggesting."

Leighton looked pleased. His protégé had proven her analytical capabilities once again, and the dread pall of suspicion had been lifted. "I'll buy that," he declared emphatically. Noticing Mike's disappointment, Frank patted him on the shoulder. "Of course, if Mike comes up with substantial evidence, that's another matter. But until then I think we ought to lay aside suspicions and get on with our work. And for you, Mike, that means somehow finding how they *really* got in!"

Leighton stood to dismiss the meeting. "I needn't remind you that what we have discussed here must be held in the strictest confidence. For the sake of morale we can't allow even the slightest suggestion to leak out that it might have been an inside job. It would poison the atmosphere among the entire staff."

Carla dialed a familiar number and leaned back comfortably at her desk. She had finally moved into her own office just down the hall from Leighton's and was enjoying the privacy. At Frank's suggestion she was belatedly returning a string of phone calls to her hotel from her editor friend at *Time* magazine. Project Archon was back on schedule, and she was now authorized to drop some tantalizing pieces of information. It took a few minutes

230 • *Dave Hunt*

to get through, and when he came on the line, George Conklin was upset.

"Carla! Aren't you getting my phone messages? 'Two FBI agents slain in Palo Alto—routine line of duty' comes over the wires. Maybe it is routine, but my journalistic nose is twitching and I think I smell something—maybe some connection to your big story? But I can't even reach you. Where've you been? Vacationing in Hawaii?"

"I've been *involved*, George, right in the middle of this thing. It's not just a *big* story, it's the *biggest* you or I will ever see. I literally haven't been able to get to a phone. This is my first chance."

"So you're telling me there is some connection?"

"You better believe it!"

"We've had a team of our best bloodhounds out there sniffing everywhere and they came up with nothing. We're printing next week's edition tomorrow, so what's the connection, and what's the story? Can you tell me yet?"

"I'm sorry, George, but the answer's 'no.' This thing is still getting bigger every day. But I'm going to give you some info that you can print if you want to—without my name. You'll be quoting 'a reliable inside source,' and what I'm going to tell you is the unvarnished truth. Okay?"

"My tape recorder's running."

"George! You bury that tape!"

"Don't worry. It doesn't exist unless I have to resurrect it. So what's going on?"

"Your 'reliable source' informs you that the two FBI agents were killed when they tried to intercept a special Russian combat team here on a secret mission."

"You're kidding!"

"I wish I were! I saw this thing firsthand and almost got killed myself. But delete that. Back to the printable stuff. The Russians attacked a top-secret psychic research lab near Palo Alto run by the CIA. Why? Because the Americans have made a research breakthrough that puts them light-years ahead of the Russians and everyone else in the development of incredible psychic powers."

"I already told you," interrupted George, "this psychic stuff is strictly for the sleaze tabloids."

"The Russians apparently have a different view," returned Carla pointedly. "I saw the team they sent with my own eyes, and I can tell you this is top-priority stuff with them—and with our own government as well. Get your head out of the sand, George!"

"I'll admit," came the grudging response, "there are Congressmen and ex-astronauts and Nobel scientists involved in this thing. Why, I can't imagine."

"Give them credit for some intelligence, okay, George? And listen—I haven't gotten to the real point yet. And I don't want you to print any of the above if you leave this part out. The reason why the Americans are so far ahead is—hang onto your chair—they've made contact with higher intelligences that have been guiding our evolution and—"

"Is this your idea of a joke?" interrupted George. "Come on, Carla, you're wasting my time."

"This is the absolute truth. You think humans are the only intelligent life in the universe?"

"So 'we're not alone.' How many sci-fi films have used those lines! 'They've' been here and now we've got some 'little green men' on ice at an air base."

"I said nothing like that!"

"You said the CIA is in touch with 'higher intelligences.' We can't print that."

"Then I guess I'll have to go to *The Washington Post*. I want to give you the hottest story of your career. This is just the tip of the iceberg. But you know your standards, and if you can't handle it, then—"

"Carla, they'd laugh us out of business. *Higher intelligences* are taking over? I suppose they're arriving in UFOs! You know how crazy people are. You could start a nationwide panic—like Orson Wells' 'Martian invasion'!"

"I didn't say they're taking over—and they're *not* arriving in UFOs. You're the one who's making it ludicrous. I'm telling you, George, psychic contact has been made."

"Do you know how far out this is?"

"And have you forgotten that 'truth is stranger than fiction'? If you need an angle, here's one: Tie it in with the Search for Extraterrestrial Intelligence that Carl Sagan founded and has only grown larger since his death. Would you print it if they made *radio* contact? But that's a whole lot less likely than what I'm talking about. It could take hundreds or thousands of years for radio to get to the nearest inhabited planet, but psychic contact is instantaneous. It's happened, George! I know that for sure! But say it however you want to—hint at it as a possibility suggested by your 'inside source.' I don't have to tell you what to do."

There was a long silence. Finally George mumbled, "This is really the story behind the deaths of the two FBI agents?"

"The tip of the iceberg—with more to come if you want it."

"It's the story of the century, if it's true."

"'If it's true'? Now you're insulting me! Look, George, you've known me for how long—six years? Did I ever exaggerate or give you any information that wasn't solid gold? I'm telling you that something bigger than you or I have ever imagined is going to break soon. And don't try to verify this—you'll only get denials from the White House on down."

"Carla, you know I've got to have confirmation from someone."

"Not on this story, you don't, George! This is from a 'reliable inside source.' There's no way you can get verification. You either print it that way, or you've got nothing."

"You give me fits, Carla. I've got to be crazy to print this. Listen—do a better job of keeping in touch, will you?"

"I'll do my best. Take care."

As soon as she put the phone down, she dialed Leighton on the intercom. "I just finished talking to George. He's going to print it, but you were sure right about resistance. He climbed the wall when I mentioned 'higher intelligences.' Even suggested that such a report—if people believed it—could cause worldwide panic."

"That's a major problem. Scornful denial or panic—those are the two reactions that could kill us. The Archons have to be introduced to the world in a way that generates acceptance of them and their mission, and faith in their abilities and good intentions. That's why you have such a crucial role to play."

"Well, I can see it isn't going to be easy. I'm working on my first article. I'll have it to the point where you can go over it by tomorrow or the next day."

"Great! Don't forget: We're meeting in my office again right after dinner."

Kay Morris excused herself from the planning meeting in Leighton's office that evening—there were three labs to prepare for the next day's experiments. All the others were present: Viktor, Antonio, Carla—and, of course, Frank himself. Frank had noticed that Viktor had seemed withdrawn the last few days and finally decided to find out what was wrong.

"Something's bothering you, Viktor. We're in this together, and one of the rules is that we don't keep any secrets from each other. What's the problem?"

"It's something I have to work out in my own mind."

"Well, come out with it. We'd all like to help."

Hesitantly, Viktor began: "You have to understand my background of a lifetime under oppressive totalitarianism. Yes, the Iron Curtain came down, and we supposedly have new 'freedoms' and there's plenty of talk about democracy, but in actual fact an elite inner circle runs the country and no one else can do anything about it."

"But you've left that behind," said Leighton, trying to be encouraging. "And you won't be cooped up behind these walls for too much longer."

"I've got no complaints, Frank. I'm very grateful for all of that. What troubles me—well, it's like we've sold our souls to the Archons. Whatever they say goes. Period. We're told that the Plan will be implemented soon. A council of superior beings who've been watching over our evolution are about to intervene to keep us from destroying ourselves. Why not just admit that they're going to take over the world? That's what it amounts to. Don't you see why it looks to me like we're helping to put the whole world in the grip of a new totalitarianism that could be even worse than the one I escaped?"

Frank smiled benignly. "There are some huge differences, Viktor, between the old Soviet and now the new Russian system and the New Age the Archons will bring to earth. For one thing, the Archons have no selfish interests. They get nothing out of this—no money, power, property. They're benefiting us, not taking anything from us. They're so far beyond our evolutionary stage of development that they don't want anything from us."

"That's true," conceded Viktor, "but something still troubles me about the whole thing. It's not that I want to back out; please don't think that at all. I believe in what we're doing, but I'm just trying to understand some aspects."

Del Sasso, who had been listening quietly, now stood to his feet and walked over to sit on one end of Leighton's huge desk where he could command a view of everyone's face. "There's something much deeper that you're missing," he began confidentially, "and this is probably as good a time as any to explain it."

Carla noticed gladly that this was not the Del Sasso of a few nights ago—the psychic warrior who had exuded such a palpable evil and who had committed such an atrocity against Chernov. Now he emanated an equally superhuman love and compassion that was no less tangible.

"I've been in communication with the Archons for about two years," Antonio continued, "and know them better than anyone." He turned to Viktor and Carla. "You've read or listened to only a fraction of the transmissions from them so far. Let me explain that the Plan involves a whole lot more than psychic power and peace and prosperity. The Archons' ultimate goal is to bring out the best in mankind, the true inner goodness that has been put down by thousands of years of negative religions exalting false and oppressive deities. They want us to realize that we are goodness personified and really gods ourselves."

"Now that's something I can really get excited about!" exclaimed Carla. "It resonates so truly with my own experience! You can't imagine the put-downs I suffered growing up with a father who pastored a fundamentalist church. His one mission in life seemed to be to drive into the congregation—and especially into me, his only child—what worthless wretches we all were and that we were under condemnation by a God who would send us all to hell to burn forever if we didn't knuckle down and live the straight-laced, sober and sad, self-denying, miserable life that was required of all Christians. It almost destroyed me, especially when I found out that my father didn't live the kind of life he forced on others!" She turned to Viktor. "Talk about totalitarianism and oppressive systems! You can't imagine the liberating sense of freedom when I realized that I didn't have to believe in any god but myself!"

Del Sasso had been nodding with approval. "You know I'm a Jesuit priest, but what Carla has just said is exactly what I believe. I'm ashamed that my own church has been a major force in oppressing mankind—especially women—in just the way Carla experienced. Yet a Jesuit priest, Pierre Teilhard de Chardin, is credited with being 'The Father of the New Age.' And by the way, Teilhard wrote of the very Omega point at which psychic contact is first made with the Archons—the point at which he said mankind would merge into godhood."

"Those ideas are quite a departure from what both Catholics and Protestants have always taught," remarked Leighton. "It takes a great deal of courage to break with so many centuries of tradition."

"It has to be done," affirmed Del Sasso. "The Bible is an unfortunate perversion of the ancient nature myths held in common by all peoples. As one very popular Catholic priest has pointed out, so-called 'original sin' was really the 'original blessing.' The 'serpent' is not the enemy of mankind but its savior and truest friend. There is much wisdom hidden in the myth of the Garden of Eden. The serpent's offer of godhood was not a lie, but the liberating truth that delivers us from the oppressive belief in a jealous god who sets himself up as superior to all others. That's an insult to the integrity of any human being! In fact, we're all equal because the force latent in the universe is available to all."

"You don't know how good that makes me feel!" declared Carla with conviction. "It's so great to hear a man of the cloth speak out like this and vindicate ideals I've tried to promote for years! It's like a breath of fresh air. I only wish my mother could have heard this before she died."

Del Sasso walked over and sat down beside Viktor. He put his hand on Viktor's shoulder and looked at him compassionately. "So you see, Viktor, the New World we are working for is not at all like the oppressive system of a Stalin or Khrushchev, or the unjust superstructure of capitalism. The very reason why you reject those systems is that you're a god who must be free—you can't be ruled by anyone. We're a race of gods who have lost our way, forgotten our true identity, and need to remember who we really are. The Archons don't want to take over; they want to set us free to experience our own infinite potential. Their ultimate purpose is to restore a positive self-image, a glorious sense of self-esteem to a world of beings broken under a load of negativism that has stifled their full development as creatures of the cosmos."

Carla's eyes were sparkling. She leaned over and gave Viktor a hug. "Can't you see the truth in what he's saying?" she asked.

"I think so," said Viktor. "I think so." He was smiling as he had not smiled since facing Chernov and apparent death four nights earlier. And the man who had saved him then was now pointing the way to a brighter future than he had ever imagined possible.

"I think I understand something a little better now," mused Carla.

"You mean about the way I acted the first time we met," said Antonio, as though he were reading her mind.

"Exactly. I can see why my ex-fiancée's presence enraged you. He's a narrow-minded Christian fundamentalist who represents the very antithesis of the liberating truth you've just explained so beautifully. That's why the Archons identified him as the 'enemy.'"

"You do understand!" said Del Sasso warmly. There was something infinitely gentle and comforting in his voice.

Lying in bed at her hotel that night, Carla found sleep eluding her once again. For all of her enthusiasm earlier that evening when Del Sasso had explained things so well, here she was plagued by some of the same old doubts. *How can I be so sure one moment that the Archons and Del Sasso are goodness personified—after all, he's*

their only representative—and the next moment be troubled by basic concerns? And why don't I ever think of the right questions to ask when I'm with Del Sasso? I'm so overwhelmed by his charisma that I lose the ability to think for myself!

Del Sasso's persuasive pronouncements about infinite human potential and the innate goodness and power in everyone had been very appealing. Yet now she remembered distinctly that he had said just as clearly, when they had first met, that such a belief was a delusion. After all, the recognition that humans didn't have psychic powers within themselves but that they came from these 'higher beings' had been the whole basis for the great breakthrough that had come in psychic research. Their willingness to honor the Archons as the source of psychic power was why the Americans had leaped ahead of the Russians.

What was the truth, and why did Del Sasso contradict himself? Were there *two* truths—one to be told to the world at large, and the other to be known only to the inner circle? Why had Del Sasso been presenting as truth that evening what he had formerly identified as a lie? Of course she no longer believed it, but it did trouble her to remember that the Bible definitely identified the idea that man is a god with infinite potential as the great lie of Satan. She remembered, too, as a girl, hearing revival preachers warn of a man who would speak great lies and deceive the whole world. It would be paranoid to connect that biblical myth with Del Sasso, the Archons, and the Plan, but there was a troubling similarity that she found difficult to dismiss.

Close Encounter!

I see a Pulitzer prize in your future!" The sound of the exaggerated gypsy accent, pompously intoned, caused Carla to look up from her computer with a start. Del Sasso was standing in the open doorway to her office, acting the consummate fortune-teller. "Yes, I see the world of journalism worshiping at your feet."

"Then you can't see very well," returned Carla with a laugh. "You're obviously a cheap phony. The world of journalism would be green with envy, not worshiping at my feet."

Smiling broadly, he stepped inside and stood there towering over her. "Still working on that first story?"

"You're badly informed all the way around. I thought everyone knew the big news by now. I finished my first article yesterday, and *The Washington Post* grabbed it. They thought it was *hot*. Other papers won't be able to pick it up until the *Post* prints it tomorrow. I'm really excited!"

"*Magnifique!* Well, I've got to get over to the main lab. Don't miss the transmission today. There's going to be something special for you and Viktor."

After a short break for lunch, Carla and Viktor walked together over to the lab where the daily transmission from the Archons was received. It was in the first building on the left as one entered the complex through the gate. They took the longest possible route, enjoying the beauty of the well-landscaped grounds and the towering redwoods that could be seen just beyond the wall.

"Do you realize this is one of the very few chances we've had to talk alone?" remarked Carla as they started along the winding gravel path that led away from the main building.

"I hadn't thought of it that way," mused Viktor, "but now that I look back, you're right. I don't think there's been any intention to keep us from talking."

"Oh, I didn't mean that. We've been extremely busy day and night." Carla stopped and pointed to an exceptionally large redwood just outside the complex. "Some trees, huh? Did you ever see anything so huge? They're the oldest living things on earth!"

"The pictures I'd seen just didn't prepare me for the real thing," responded Viktor appreciatively. "There's something awesome you couldn't possibly understand without *experiencing* it! I'd love to get out there and spend a day just walking through a forest like that!"

"You've no idea how awesome they are up close. We'll take a good long hike through those trees together, Viktor—*soon*."

He looked at her fondly. "Is that a promise?"

"That's a promise."

"We need to spend some time together, Carla, just to talk and get acquainted, and it's impossible in here. Everything goes at such a feverous pitch. I had no idea Americans worked this hard!"

"Most of them don't," laughed Carla. "Frank's unusual, but he's driven by a sense of urgency that I must admit I share."

"Oh, I do too. I'm not complaining about that. You know what I'm trying to say."

"I know, and I feel exactly the same way."

There was a poignant silence. When Carla broke it, there was suppressed excitement in her voice. "Antonio says the Archons are going to tell us something special today. Frank thinks the first World Congress and the inauguration of the New Age will come within a month. It's moving faster than I thought!"

They were nearing the end of their brief walk. Viktor slowed the pace and lowered his voice. "I've wanted to ask you something. What do you think of Dr. Morris?"

"Kay? She's quite a remarkable woman, if that's what you mean."

"No, something else."

Carla stopped and looked at him closely. "Are you trying to say something?"

"Just asking what you think."

"Well, since you mention it, I've had a strange feeling about her ever since we first met, but I don't know why."

"I think she's a Russian!" said Viktor abruptly.

"You *what*?"

"In fact, I'm almost certain."

"Viktor, come on! She's a graduate of MIT—with a New York accent!"

"I know it sounds crazy, and I probably should have kept it to myself, but I've been watching her. It's little things that I've noticed, like mannerisms and the way she puts sentences together—even some expressions she uses seem to be peculiarly Russian but translated into English."

They resumed their walk very slowly. Carla was flabbergasted. "Have you said anything to Frank?" she asked.

"Not yet. It wouldn't do any good. I couldn't prove it, and maybe it means nothing."

"She left Frank's office that night about 30 minutes before—" Carla began, then stopped. "No, it's not fair even to think such thoughts. After all she's the *director* of the labs, and she works as hard as Frank. She's really committed."

"Do you think Frank's in love with her?"

"So you picked up on that, too. He's smitten for sure, but I think she's very careful not to show too much feeling in public. People do fall in love." Her shoulder brushed against Viktor's. Their eyes met and held for the briefest of moments.

"I've talked to Mike," continued Viktor, "and he says he's certain that someone on the inside shot the guards and let Chernov in—but not to mention it to Frank. Is that because he thinks Kay might be the one?"

"Why didn't you ask him?"

"I couldn't do that!"

"I really feel bad about this whole conversation," said Carla. "It isn't fair to Kay—" She struggled to find the words.

Their walk had taken them behind the building. Before Carla could finish that sentence, they came around a corner just in time to see Leighton, who had hurried directly across the lawn, approaching the front door of the lab at a lope. "We'll talk about it later," whispered Carla.

"Well, look who's been out for a stroll!" exclaimed Frank, obviously in good spirits. "I'm sorry you two haven't had time to get better acquainted." He pulled the door open and motioned for them to enter. "You make a very handsome pair."

"We'll accept that compliment," laughed Carla as she put her arm through Viktor's. He blushed slightly and looked pleased.

Entering the lab, they took their seats quietly. As usual, Del Sasso was already in place. Dr. Morris and an assistant were in the process of connecting wires from various parts of his body to a bank of monitoring equipment. As soon as that was done, the assistant left. Only the inner circle could be present at these sessions. Antonio went immediately into a trance. He breathed rapidly for a few moments, then settled down to a slow, rhythmic pace.

Suddenly his whole body jerked and his head cocked to one side. An eerie and strangely metallic voice began to speak through him at a high pitch. "The Nine give you greetings from another dimension directly adjacent to yours. The recent attack on your installation was a necessary test. You passed it well, but more are to come. The question of entry is a mystery you must confront and solve for your own spiritual growth. Every step is important as we move toward our goal. Carla Bertelli's articles will play a key consciousness-raising role. Viktor Khorev must give the keynote address at the Congress."

"It is therefore essential that these two see us for themselves. They may not approach us, but they will be allowed to enter and witness our meeting with the three higher initiates. This will occur at precisely 3:15 this afternoon. At that time we will announce the date for the coming World Congress. Farewell."

The moment Del Sasso came out of his trance, a euphoric Leighton hurried over to Carla and Viktor, who were very excited but also confused and apprehensive. "Congratulations!" exclaimed Leighton. "You can't imagine what good news this is! We couldn't really go forward until we had that date, and until the Archons accepted you both into the Plan. This is going to change your lives forever!"

"What did they mean—*see* them?" asked Carla. "With our physical eyes? I didn't think they had bodies."

"It has to be a surprise the first time," said Leighton enigmatically.

Promptly at 2:30 Leighton herded Del Sasso, Morris, Khorev, and Bertelli into a late-model Cadillac. Frank got behind the wheel with Kay beside him and the other three in the backseat. They left the base escorted inconspicuously by a car in front and one just behind, each—in addition to its driver—carrying two heavily-armed CIA agents dressed in workmen's clothes. On the other side of Palo Alto they entered a seedy, run-down industrial park and drove along a winding street. It ended in a cul-de-sac, most of which was taken up by the sprawling grounds of an extensive building, apparently abandoned. There were no cars in the parking lot, and the landscaping was noticeably unkempt. The three vehicles pulled into a drive and parked behind the building. Everyone except the two drivers in the other cars climbed out.

"The Company owns this property," confided Leighton as they walked around to the front.

"*Company?*" asked Viktor.

"That's what we affectionately call the CIA." Waving a hand at the run-down appearance, Leighton added, "We purposely let it look abandoned and use it for nothing but these meetings. They come irregularly at the Archons' command."

The two CIA agents in the lead car had remained at the rear of the building to pretend they were making some repairs, while the other two started to pull a few weeds in front, one near each corner of the wide structure. Leighton led the others up a short brick walk to the front door, where he produced a key and let them all in. He turned on no lights, and in the semidarkness they walked through what had once been an office straight toward a rear door.

Leighton paused before opening it. "Carla and Viktor," he warned them solemnly, "what you are about to see will shock and perhaps even terrify you. Stay behind us at all times and keep your emotions under control. Don't panic, and under no circumstances try to approach the vehicle. We three will do so at the appropriate time, but for your own safety you *must* keep your distance."

"*Vehicle?*" asked Viktor. He was literally trembling with fear. They were actually going to *see* some Archons? Carla was eager with anticipation, but at the same time almost afraid to go through the door.

"It must be a surprise!" said Leighton. "Remember? So don't ask any more questions!" Then he added solemnly, "Kay had her initiation here just a week before you two arrived."

Opening the door, he led them into what appeared to be a huge warehouse with a very high roof. They stood together just inside for a moment. Then Leighton, Del Sasso, and Morris took two steps forward, put their palms together in front of them in the traditional Oriental greeting, and bowed in unison nine times. Puzzled and fearful, Viktor and Carla remained near the door, watching in wonder. Peering around, they tried to adjust their eyes to the dim light that filtered through dusty venetian blinds drawn tight across lofty skylights. The building appeared to be empty.

Suddenly a vibrating hum began, like a thousand monks chanting the "OM." It seemed to charge the atmosphere with an almost-tangible electrical current. Then there it was—as though it had materialized out of thin air. "Look!" whispered Viktor in astonishment.

A giant spacecraft, looking like something out of a science-fiction movie and filling the far end of the warehouse, was now hovering just off the floor, its top crowded up against the roof. It was nearly the size of a 747 but without wings and of a futuristic design.

Carla nearly fainted from shock and fright. "It can't be!" she whispered back. "You see it, too?"

"It's impossible!" said Viktor hoarsely, unable to believe his eyes.

At that moment two lights on the top of the object came on and began to rotate, flashing purple and green as they spun round and round, revealing a strange, unearthly sheen to the metallic surface. As if that were a signal, the craft seemingly began to pulsate with life, as though it were about to metamorphose into some predatory creature. Stricken with an unreasoning terror, Carla and Viktor could hardly retain their sanity and stifle the instinct to flee. Involuntarily they shrank back against the wall.

A shimmering pyramid of brilliant white light, with a base of about 35 feet on each side, suddenly appeared in front of the hovering craft. The light had a peculiar radiance that made Carla feel instantly dizzy. The dizziness passed, however, as quickly as it had come. Now she felt an irresistible attraction for the glowing pyramid of unearthly incandescence—as though her mind were somehow being drawn into another consciousness that was merging with something living inside that strange light. An overpowering *presence* could now be felt in the warehouse. Carla sensed it was the same *presence* she had felt in Leighton's office when Del Sasso had taken control from the Russians.

"That's our signal," said Leighton in an excited voice, motioning to Viktor and Carla to remain behind. "You wait here. Don't move under any circumstances!"

With Leighton in the lead, the three moved slowly toward the mysterious craft. As Viktor and Carla watched in terrified fascination, nine luminous and almost transparent beings suddenly appeared in the center of the pyramid. They wore shimmering robes of light that covered their entire bodies, leaving exposed only their reptilian-like heads that seemed to flare out from their broad shoulders like the hoods of cobras. There was something awesomely supernatural about the creatures. They seemed to be grotesque and beautiful, repulsive and attractive at the same time. In eerie silence they quickly formed a circle around Leighton, Del Sasso, and Morris as the three earthlings solemnly entered the pyramid of light together and prostrated themselves in worship. The leader of the Nine motioned for them to arise.

"I don't believe this, I don't believe this." Carla kept repeating the words to herself through chattering teeth. She was shaking as though from a chilling sub-zero wind.

"We can't both be hallucinating," said Viktor, wiping the cold perspiration from his forehead with a hand that was already damp.

The Nine seemed to be conversing with Leighton and his party. As they did so, fire came out of their mouths and their bodies became a thousand points of light that cast weird shadows of both human and inhuman forms on the warehouse walls. In spite of her terror, Carla found herself unable to turn her gaze from this unbelievable performance. As her fascination grew to almost hypnotic proportions, her fear subsided and the *presence* that charged the atmosphere became benevolent and all-wise. She was no longer shaking, but was now overtaken with a feeling of gratitude for the privilege of witnessing such a scene. How blessed the world was to be visited by such creatures of love who had come to rescue mankind from self-destruction!

the

MIND
INVADERS
27

An Antichrist Rebellion?

The circle of unearthly creatures opened as suddenly as it had closed. Viktor and Carla watched in stunned bewilderment as their three colleagues walked slowly back toward them. The pyramid disappeared instantly, and the Nine vanished with it. When Leighton, Del Sasso, and Morris had resumed their original places facing the strange craft just in front of Viktor and Carla, they put their palms together and bowed nine times again. The vibrating "OM" faded and in its place a strange whirring sound arose and grew in volume. To their consternation, Viktor and Carla realized that the UFO had swung around to point in their direction. It was gathering speed and heading directly toward them.

Leighton sensed their terror and reached back a cautioning hand. Without taking his eyes from the strange craft, he yelled, "Don't move!"

The whirring sound had become a high-pitched scream when, at greatly accelerating speed, the UFO passed within inches over their heads and out through the side of the warehouse. Carla clutched Viktor and together they clung to each other as a brief wave of nausea passed over them and subsided.

Carla had cringed in anticipation of the devastation as the spacecraft tore through the walls. To her complete astonishment, the warehouse was now empty and still intact. Her eyes met

246

Viktor's, and for a moment they clung to one another in sheer relief.

"You took it very well," said Leighton when their ears had stopped ringing. "Better than I did the first time I had this experience." He could not hide his own trepidation, however, even now. Morris seemed to be controlling herself with great effort. Only Del Sasso was completely cool. It seemed to Carla that he was almost indistinguishable from the Archons, so closely had he become identified with them.

Leighton led them back outside. The CIA agents were still pulling weeds in a bored and halfhearted manner. Had they seen this giant spacecraft come bursting out of the side of the building so often that it no longer affected them? Viktor took hold of Leighton's arm. "What does it look like from out here when that thing comes shooting out of the building?"

Leighton put a finger to his lips and shook his head to remind Viktor that their experience was not to be shared with others. "They saw nothing out here!" he said in a low voice. "So far the Archons have chosen only to reveal themselves to us and only inside that building. Out here they're invisible. But one day they will make themselves known to the entire world."

"When you were in that pyramid of light," whispered Carla, unable to restrain her curiosity, "what did you talk about?"

Again Frank put a finger to his lips and shook his head. "We'll share that later," he said and led the way to the car.

Once inside their auto and on their way back to the base, Frank gave vent to his suppressed excitement. "We've been given the date!" he announced to Viktor and Carla. "Six weeks from next Friday. That doesn't give us much time. Carla's first article will be printed tomorrow, and the Archons promise an enthusiastic reaction from both the media and the public."

Still stunned from their experience, Carla and Viktor seemed scarcely able to comprehend what Frank had said. "Didn't you hear me?" he asked. "We've got the date for the World Congress!"

"That's fantastic," said Carla, "but I'm so *disoriented* that I can hardly think. I've just seen what looked like a huge solid object sail right through the side of a building as though the walls weren't there. And then you say it's *invisible* outside. What was that thing?"

"Call it a UFO, if you like," responded Frank. "The Nine say there's no way they can make us understand such events at our present level of development. It's some kind of transmogrification of psychic energy. That's all they can tell us."

Viktor was beside himself. "Frank, what we've just seen makes Columbus' discovery of America, the Bolshevik Revolution, man walking on the moon, and everything else that's happened in history seem like nothing in comparison. This is it! This is the ultimate!"

"Visions of the Virgin Mary are the same order of event," put in Del Sasso casually. "All religions originally came from such apparitions."

"*Apparitions?*" asked Carla in surprise. "What we saw wasn't really there?"

"It was and it wasn't," responded Frank. "It's the old question of what's real, and you know there's no answer to that!"

"I saw it with my own eyes," said Viktor, still overcome with awe, "or no one could have gotten me to believe it!"

"Oh, I almost forgot to tell you," said Frank, addressing Carla and Viktor again. "They informed us that the gathering of leaders is to be called, 'World Congress 666.'"

"I like that!" said Del Sasso with a hearty laugh. "In fact, I *love* it!"

"'666'?" asked Viktor. "Does it mean something?"

"Now, there's one of the advantages of growing up in an atheistic society!" laughed Carla. "No Antichrist myths to give little children nightmares like I used to have."

"*Antichrist?*" asked Viktor, still not understanding.

"Sorry," said Carla. "He's a satanic figure in the Bible who's supposedly going to be worshiped as 'God' and take over the world. You'll find it hard to believe, Viktor, but in the West this superstition is so strong that the number 666—which is supposedly the Antichrist's number—really frightens people. Even major Hollywood films have exploited the fear it generates." She turned to Frank. "I'm mystified as to why the Archons would want to identify their New World Order with a symbol that's certain to arouse paranoia and opposition."

"They didn't explain it," said Frank, looking a bit perplexed himself. "I'm as curious as you are to know why they chose what most people consider to be a negative symbol."

"There's no need to explain something so obvious," broke in Del Sasso impatiently. "It's a stroke of genius—and a bold one. The Antichrist myth has obsessed Westerners for centuries. Even people who don't go to church will pay to watch a movie that depicts that nonsense. And instead of looking at it like any other horror film, they sit there transfixed with the fear that it really could happen."

"That's exactly what I was saying," interjected Frank. "Using 666 can hardly arouse much goodwill and support!"

"And you're a psychologist, Frank?" returned Del Sasso. "Shame on you for not recognizing what the Archons are doing. They're incredible psychologists. They're going to force the world to face the obsessive fear of the Antichrist head-on and get rid of it once and for all!"

"But think of the outcry from Christians everywhere!" protested Carla. "Use 666 and they'll point to Bible prophecies and call this the fulfillment. They'll be able to say, 'Aha! We told you so—it's an Antichrist plot!'"

"Let them say it. That's precisely the strategy. It's ingenious." Del Sasso leaned back and went into paroxysms of laughter. "It's brilliant," he added, wiping the tears from his eyes when he had recovered. "If the fundamentalist watchdogs were able to sniff around and come up with suspicions of some Antichrist connection—well, that might catch on. But to call government leaders to a '666 Summit' makes it so up-front that no one can make charges about a hidden agenda. Don't you see?"

Frank and Morris were nodding their agreement. "It is brilliant," said Kay.

"I'm sure it goes far beyond what any of us understands at this point," added Del Sasso, "but there's something deeper and of greater importance involved that's rather obvious. Can you see what it is?"

"It's got to be more than just a clever means of disarming the opposition," suggested Carla. "I think it's also a declaration—almost a statement of faith they're requiring from world leaders, and eventually from earth's entire population. Is that what you mean?"

"*Voilà!*" Del Sasso reached over and gave Carla a playful pat on the cheek. "You're really getting tuned in! The Archons, who are watching you closely day and night, must be very pleased."

"You've lost me," said Viktor.

"It's actually rather simple," said Del Sasso. "And, as you know, simplicity is one of the marks of genius. By identifying themselves with the forbidden number 666, world leaders—who are obviously not followers of some mythical Antichrist—will destroy this super-stition in one stroke!"

"Talk about pulling the rug out!" said Leighton, becoming more enthusiastic with every new insight. "Anyone who accuses this New World Order of being a front for the Antichrist will be laughed out of court."

"Exactly! It's like the chief in a primitive tribe violating a taboo," went on Del Sasso. "He either gets killed, or he puts an end to the prohibition and thereby liberates his followers. By identi-fying themselves with 666, participants in the Congress will lib-erate the world from a superstitious fear that has inhibited real progress for centuries. That will be the end of the Antichrist myth forever!"

"Pardon me, Antonio," added Carla with excitement mounting in her voice, "but there's an even greater genius behind this bold move." She turned to Viktor. "You're having difficulty under-standing this because you were raised in an atheistic environment free from the harmful effects of Christian superstitions. If you knew what a strong grip the idea of an Antichrist has in the West, you'd realize that in order to usher in their New Order, the Archons *have* to destroy this idea. The Bible says that 666 represents a man who will establish a New World Order in rebellion against the Supreme Being. 'Shame, shame!' the Christians will cry against those who take that number, but 'Bravo!' say I. It's a rebellion that *has* to happen and whose time has come. It will liberate the world forever from the demeaning lie that mankind can't make it on its own and has to grovel in confession of its sin and inadequacy and live off the crumbs of 'grace' that 'Christ' drops now and then from his sumptuous table."

"So it *is* an Antichrist rebellion after all," said Viktor, beginning to understand at last.

"Of course it is!" Del Sasso's jaw was set and his eyes were flashing with the fire of independence. "We will indeed establish what the Bible has called the rule of Antichrist. It won't be evil, however, like the Bible warns, but a monument to the innate goodness and deity of man. And it will be led by a man who embodies this deity in its grandeur and fullness!"

Poltergeist!

A fter an early dinner in her room, Carla lay in bed flicking the television channels back and forth, trying to find something that held her interest, and hoping most of all that she would somehow doze off. Getting to sleep was becoming a nightly problem. At last she turned off the TV and lay in the dark, going over recent events and conversations and wrestling with her own thoughts.

When they had arrived back at the lab complex late that afternoon, no one had felt like doing anything further that day. The meeting with the Archons had been too emotionally draining, and their announcements so exhilarating. Frank had given everyone the evening off. Yet the sleep Carla needed so desperately eluded her.

It frustrated her that she kept coming back to the number 666. As much as she tried to deny it, the fact that the Archons had chosen to identify themselves and their Plan with the symbol of the Antichrist was troubling. Everything Del Sasso had said, and to which she had so cleverly contributed, made sense. It was logical, even brilliant, as they had all agreed. Yet that very fact worried her as well. It was almost too ingenious. And in spite of its brilliance, it lacked one essential element: any means of proving that it, rather than the opposing Christian view, was *true*. Selling this to the world would not be easy, and that was *her* job!

The most troubling thought seemed childishly simple: The setting up of a New World Order associated with 666 *was an undeniable fulfillment of Bible prophecies concerning the Antichrist!* Del Sasso's insights, though very cunning, were simply an attempt to deny the obvious facts. No matter how one tried to explain it away, the fact remained that the Bible predicted that the coming Antichrist would set up his kingdom using, in some way, the number 666—and that was exactly what the Archons were proposing to do!

Carla had told herself for years that she didn't believe the Bible. Yet it still made her exceedingly uncomfortable to see herself participating in events that seemed so much like what the Bible predicted—events that established an Antichrist kingdom and would therefore incur the wrath of God upon those involved in them. It was particularly devastating that Del Sasso, in spite of his devious explanations, even admitted that the Plan was clearly an Antichrist plot, and the man he'd said would head it up—was he referring to himself? How could she communicate the facts to the world without arousing suspicion, opposition, and even panic? That this was her personal responsibility as a journalist had begun to haunt her.

It had all seemed crystal-clear that afternoon when she had agreed so wholeheartedly with Del Sasso, but now she wasn't so sure. The Plan was something that she desperately wanted to believe. It offered hope for a world on the brink of disaster and it made a lot of sense, but was she really convinced that it would all work out exactly as the Archons promised? Try as she might to give an unequivocal "yes" to that question, there was a nagging doubt that plagued her. And that fact was very unsettling. Del Sasso had said that the Archons were watching her day and night. Could they also read her mind? Were they, then, displeased with her, or did they consider doubt normal for human beings?

The Archons! Every time she closed her eyes she could see that UFO coming directly toward her, then passing incomprehensibly through the side of the building over her head. Frank had said it wasn't a *physical* object, but it had certainly looked physical. No physical object could fly through walls—or could it? Relativity, uncertainty, black holes, antimatter—who could keep up with what might be possible, and who was really qualified to make dogmatic assertions that something was impossible? If the Archons themselves were not physical, however, then whatever it was they flew around in wouldn't need to be physical either. Did they really need these vehicles to transport themselves, or did UFOs serve some other deceptive purpose?

Carla had never believed in UFOs. The very term "unidentified flying object" had seemed like a cop-out. Now she'd seen one for herself at close range, and it was still *unidentified*. And the beings that came out of it to talk with Leighton, Del Sasso, and Morris— why did they look so . . . *reptilian?* Granted that they had evolved beyond bodily existence, but if they were going to materialize temporary bodies so they could be seen by humans, why did they choose to take a form that seemed to be not only repulsive, but *demonic?* She shuddered at the thought. Was this what Ken had warned her about and for which she had ridiculed him? Had he, in fact, been right all along? No, she could never admit that her father, instead of having been destroyed by Christianity, was actually an evil man who had perverted the truth.

Sleep had come at last when suddenly Carla was jolted to transfixed wakefulness. The bed was shaking, but this was no earthquake. The whole building wasn't moving, just the bed—then it stopped. The drapes were open, and in the dim light coming through the window from the street below she saw what appeared to be a shadowy figure glide quickly around the corner into the bathroom. She froze in terror, a scream coming soundlessly from her paralyzed lips.

Suddenly the bed began to shake again and one side of it tilted up, dumping her onto the floor. *Lights! Turn on some lights!* Staggering to her feet, she switched on the bed lamp. The bulb glowed, but its light didn't shine out—as though the darkness in the room were absorbing it. She felt her way over to the lamp that stood on one end of the long, low combination bureau and desk. As she reached over to turn it on, it slid away from her outstretched hand as though it were a living thing.

She felt utterly helpless and vulnerable. What could she do? As she tried to wrestle with that terrifying question, she noticed that a strange luminescent glow was emanating from the half-open bathroom door into which that mysterious figure had disappeared. Now she heard guttural mutterings in there that made her skin crawl. She would have to go past there to get into the hall. The thought of fleeing from the room turned terror into panic.

Out of the corner of her eye she saw flashing against the wall opposite the window the same purple and green lights that she had seen earlier emanating from the UFO. *The Archons!* Were they, as she had feared, displeased with her doubts and were making a threatening show of their power? Were they just frightening her, or did they intend some punishment?

Should she go to the window and yell into the night that she believed in the Archons, so this nightmare would end? Believe in their existence and power, that she did—but who were they, really, and what were their intentions? The questions that mattered the most were the hardest to answer. She found herself unable to make the total commitment of faith she knew they demanded. Would this be the end of her involvement with Leighton? Would she dare to go back there again?

Now she felt that *Presence* in the room—oppressive, ugly, reptilian, horrifying. Yet it had become loving in the warehouse. Would it make that same transformation now? If only the FBI still occupied the adjoining room, she would appeal to them! Why not appeal to the Archon that was apparently in the room with her?

She stood in the middle of the floor feeling foolish as she poured out her words into the darkness, but driven to do so by an overpowering fear. "Please, may I talk with you? If you want me to believe, don't scare me to death. Please leave me alone. I'm on your side. I want the Plan to work, but I have some questions—please!"

The luminous glow left the bathroom, the guttural grumblings stopped, and the light from the lamp she had turned on illuminated the room. With an audible sigh of relief, Carla sank down onto the bed and began to cry. They had heard her and had left. She was grateful. But the very thought of going back to bed seemed insane.

Even if they had gone, there was no way she would stay in this room!

She picked up the phone to dial the desk to see if another room was available, at least for the rest of the night. Instead of a dial tone, however, she heard coming out of the instrument into her ear that guttural voice that had earlier been muttering in the bathroom: "No one defies the Nine . . . no one defies the Nine. . . . " It was like a broken record—and utterly terrifying.

Instantly she dropped the receiver and stumbled over to the bureau. Her suitcase was sitting on top of it. In a frenzy she took some of her things from a drawer and threw them into the suitcase, sobbing over and over as she did so, "I'm not defying you . . . I'm not defying you. . . . "

When she had finished dressing it occurred to her that the manifestations had stopped. That gave her fresh hope and courage. Cautiously she went to the bathroom, reached in through the half-open door and flipped the light switch. The light came on. Everything seemed to be normal again.

Carla stepped one foot inside the bathroom and grabbed her toiletry case containing her toothbrush, comb, and other similar items. As she straightened up to step back out, she looked into the mirror. Instead of her own reflection, there was the close-up image of one of the Archons just as she had seen them in the pyramid of light. It was staring at her with unblinking, hooded, reptilian eyes.

With a shriek she jumped back and slammed the bathroom door behind her. A large picture on the wall next to the bed crashed to the floor and splintered into pieces. The sound of shattering glass resurrected a horrible memory. She could see Chernov being cut in half again and the bloodied glass desk top exploding against the wall. That horrifying vision pushed her over the brink.

With uncontrollable sobs gushing from a throat now tightened in panic, Carla managed somehow to put the case from the bathroom into the suitcase and close it. Shuddering in terror as she hurried past the bathroom door with the suitcase clutched tightly, she fled into the hallway.

◆ ◆ ◆

All that day Ken had felt an insistent burden for Carla and an overwhelming sense of danger on her behalf. He had left his office shortly after lunch to come home and had spent the afternoon and evening in his bedroom in earnest prayer. He had cried out to God to rescue her from the seductive influence of Del Sasso, to protect her from evil and the destruction that he knew the Plan would lead to for those involved in it, and to do whatever was necessary to open Carla's eyes to the true identity of the Archons. The burden had finally lifted about nine o'clock, and he was confident that his prayers had been heard and would be answered. He had gone into his study to do some computer work that had to be ready the following day. Having finished that task, he was reading his Bible before going to bed, when the doorbell rang.

The bell continued to ring frantically as he hurried to the front door concerned that the sound would waken his mother. *Who could it be at this time of night?* The recent violent events had caused him to become cautious. Before opening the door he called out, "Who is it?"

"It's Carla. *Please!*"

Praise God! He opened the door and there she stood, hair disheveled, eyes swollen from crying, panic and terror written all over her face—and holding tightly to a suitcase from which several items of clothing protruded. Ken took the bag, and with an arm around Carla drew her quickly inside. She clung to him, sobbing, "Something's after me! I almost didn't get here. The car was fighting me like it was alive!"

For one reeling moment Ken relived his own experience with a car that had driven him over a cliff.

"I know what you mean. You did the right thing coming here," he assured her as he led her into the living room. She sank down onto the sofa and fought back the tears. He sat beside her. "Can you tell me what happened?"

"All hell broke loose in my hotel room!" The words poured out in a flood of tears. "The bed was shaking, pictures coming off the wall . . . voices . . . a horrible *Presence*. It was terrifying! I—I can't talk about it."

Ken put an arm gently around her. Its protective pressure released more pent-up sobs. "I'm sorry," she said when she had recovered somewhat. "You know this isn't like me." She straightened up and smoothed her hair and wiped her eyes. "I'm going to be okay. You offered to take me in—is that still open?"

"For as long as you want!"

"Ken, this is so good of you. It's just until I can recover my wits. I feel like a fool, blubbering like a baby."

"Carla! What happened?" Mrs. Inman had come into the living room and hurried to put an arm around Carla as well.

"Demonic manifestations in her hotel room—horrible," said Ken softly. "She can't talk about it."

"You poor dear! Let me show you to your room," said Mrs. Inman, taking Carla by the hand. "Ken, you bring the suitcase."

They walked down the hall together to the far end of the house, where Ken's mother opened the door to a spacious suite. "The bed's made up," she said, leading Carla inside. "The bath's through that door. I'll get some towels. The other door goes to a study. This end of the house is all yours."

Mrs. Inman hurried to pull some towels and an extra blanket out of a linen closet just outside in the hall and put them on the bed. Ken set the suitcase down and stood there uncertainly. "Would you like to come into the kitchen for a bite to eat or something to drink—and unwind a little?"

"I could fix something—whatever you want," added his mother, patting Carla on the arm.

I desperately need to talk this over, but not with him. He'll just lecture me about demons.... "Thanks so much. It's very kind, but it's so late and I'm absolutely wiped out. If I can just get some sleep. In the morning I'll tell you all about it."

"You sleep in as late as you want," said Mrs. Inman. "Breakfast is whenever you get up." She joined Ken in the hall. "See you in the morning, Carla."

"Good night. And thanks so very much."

It didn't take Carla long to get into her nightgown. Leaving the bathroom light on and the door open a crack so that her room wouldn't be completely dark, she collapsed into bed completely exhausted. Peace . . . safety—the house and its occupants exuded the feeling. The events of the last few hours receded into a limbo of blessed unreality as she drifted off to sleep.

How long she slept she didn't know, but something suddenly awakened her. She struggled to open her eyes. Through the drawn drapes came the dim flashing of violet and green lights, apparently from just outside the sliding glass doors. *Their UFO again!* A sixth sense caused her to turn her head—and there he was. She saw him distinctly in the dim light and gasped in surprise. The long black robe and hood were unmistakable.

"Antonio?" she whispered. "What are you doing here?"

The figure made no answer, but moved toward her ominously, seeming to glide without touching the floor.

"Antonio!"

He was standing over her now, motionless and silent. Inside the hood she could not make out his face—only the glowing eyes. Suddenly he bent over and reached out. She screamed just as his hands grabbed her by the throat and choked off the sound.

Woman and Serpent

Ken was turning out the light in his study when he heard the stifled scream. He raced across the adjoining living room and down the hall toward Carla's room. He flung open the door and burst in. The hooded figure leaning over the bed released Carla and turned quickly to meet this challenge.

There was no mistaking the tall figure, the full-length monk's robe, and the deliberate, almost flowing movements. For one brief moment of confusion and indecision, Ken wondered how Del Sasso had gotten in. Then he understood.

Now only a few steps away and moving rapidly toward Ken, the hooded figure pointed its right hand threateningly at him. In the same instant, a giant cobra dropped from the ceiling onto Ken's head and shoulders. From where she lay, clutching her throat in pain and still gagging, Carla watched in transfixed horror.

"God, help me!" cried Ken. Instinctively he grabbed at the thick body that was wrapping itself around him, and found only empty air. The memory came surging back of another time so long ago, when he had been helpless against a similar attack. Now he knew what to do.

In a firm and authoritative voice, he commanded the huge serpent and hooded figure: "In the Name of Jesus Christ of Nazareth, *be gone—and do not return!*" Instantly they vanished from the room.

Ken hurried over to Carla. She was sobbing quietly. He put an arm around her shoulder, and she recoiled in fear. "They're gone," he said softly. "Are you okay?"

"I'm terrified, Ken!" she said in a weak, hoarse voice, finding it very difficult to speak. "Where did they go?" She searched the room with frightened eyes.

"Never mind *where*. They're gone, and I promise you they won't come back. Not here. You'll be safe in this house from now on."

"My throat—I can hardly swallow."

"How about something warm to drink? What would you like? I'll run to the kitchen and make it. It won't take a minute."

She clutched at his arm. "Don't leave me, please!" She struggled out of bed and to her feet. "I'll come with you."

He helped her into her robe and supported her as they walked down the long hall past the living room to the kitchen on the other side of the house. Carla sank into a chair while he put on a kettle and dug around for some tea bags.

"How did Antonio get in here, and where did they go?" she asked in bewilderment.

He sat down at the table with her and looked at her earnestly. "I don't know how to tell you, Carla. You know we've had some misunderstandings and I don't want to—"

"Please, Ken. Just tell me. I'll listen." She returned his gaze with eyes that were tired, defeated, and desperate.

"It wasn't Del Sasso."

"But I saw him!"

"I saw him too, but that's not who it was. It was an evil spirit. . . . "

"A *spirit*? How can you say that! I can still feel those hands on my throat. Look—there must be marks!"

He leaned over to look closely. "There are marks, but not made by Del Sasso in the flesh. It was one of the Archons, and you know who I've said they are. They're demons!"

Carla winced. "I was afraid you'd say that. But how could something without a body choke me and leave physical marks?"

"Did you see any *body* shake your bed or rip that picture from the wall?" he asked. She shook her head in confusion. "Is it *bodies* that throw things around in a genuine haunted house—or *spirits*?" Ken continued. "Does that tell you anything about the feats Del Sasso pulls off?"

They sipped their tea together in silence. She was still thinking over his question. At last she said, "Psychic power—we've always called it 'mind over matter.'"

"Whose mind?" he asked pointedly.

"Well, presumably the mind of the psychic."

"Why couldn't it be some other mind—the mind of a spirit being that's deceiving psychics into thinking it's their mind that's doing the great feats?"

"But spirits aren't physical," protested Carla, "and there's a lot of physical phenomena involved."

"Here we go again. Is a psychic's *mind* physical?" asked Ken.

"I guess I've always equated mind with brain."

"Have you ever seen a psychic's brain reach out and physically move some object? Is that what's meant by 'mind over matter'?"

Carla laughed ruefully. "Oh, that hurts!" she exclaimed. She swallowed the tea slowly in silence once again, letting its healing warmth soothe her throat.

"You're knocking a lot of props out from under me, Ken," she admitted grudgingly. "Why haven't I ever thought it through like this?"

"Do I dare say *pride*? That was the problem in my case, and its the besetting sin of the entire human race. The Archons know that. So they bait the hook with the idea that psychic phenomena represent a power that *we* have, a power of *our minds*, that there's an infinite potential in each of us that merely has to be developed. And all the time they're channeling their power through us in order to delude us and bring us, in the end, under their control."

Carla shook her head in bewilderment. "That calls for another cup. Make it a little stronger this time, will you please?"

Ken brought the tea to the table and sat down again. "There's also an element of fear involved. The threat from something physical doesn't cause nearly as much fear as the threat from something nonphysical."

She nodded solemnly. "I found that out tonight!"

"So you understand what I'm saying. If I told you there was a lion in the next room, you'd have one level of fear, and you'd quickly think of ways to defend yourself when it came through the door. But if I told you there was a *ghost* about to enter this room and you really believed in such things, you'd experience a terror far beyond what any physical threat could generate. Am I right?"

"Believe me," she said, "even when you claim you don't believe in such things, you're still terrorized. Back in the hotel I tried to tell myself I didn't believe, and I must have looked like a blob of jelly when I got here."

"Carla, the entire human race knows intuitively that evil spirits are real. But because of pride and fear we pretend they don't exist. We hide behind the discredited materialistic bias of 'modern science' as our justification for doing away with Satan and God, demons, and angels."

Carla had finished her tea and was turning the empty cup around in her hand, studying it carefully.

"But that's not really relevant to what happened to me tonight," she said at last. "You haven't convinced me that demons were involved at all. I really think it was the Archons, and I still believe they're highly evolved, *benevolent* intelligences from some other part of the universe. I don't see why that can't be true."

"They certainly act like demons!" said Ken sharply.

Carla put the cup down and started to cry softly. She buried her head in her arms on the table to stifle the sobs. "They're trying to frighten me, and I don't understand why they think they have to." She lifted her head and looked at Ken through the tears. "I know you won't understand this, but I still want to work with them. Yes, they scare me to death, but I think their Plan makes sense. . . . "

Ken shook his head in disbelief. "Carla, if what you've been through hasn't convinced you, I don't know what it's going to take!" He swallowed the rest of the sentence.

"Ken, your Bible says that *God* chastises people—sometimes very severely," said Carla. "And you think that's okay."

He nodded. "I know what you're going to say, and it doesn't work. God is infinitely just and loving, and His ways are perfect.

You can trust Him. But if you trust the Archons, Carla, you're finished!"

"Let me tell you what happened," insisted Carla. "I talked to the Archon that was in my hotel room, Ken—honestly I did. And they stopped frightening me for a while. I think it's horrible what they did in the hotel, but suppose they were trying to discipline me for doubting, like you believe God does? I just don't want it to happen again. I was terrified!"

"And here in your bedroom?"

"I think that was different. Supposing there are bad Archons out there, and they did that to turn me against the good ones and their Plan?"

"And I think you're too tired to be rational," said Ken in frustration. He glanced up at the kitchen clock and stood to his feet. "It's nearly 3:00 A.M. I'm bushed, and you ought to be in even worse shape. Let's get some sleep."

Carla pushed her chair back and got up reluctantly. "I'm afraid to leave the security of this kitchen and go back to bed."

"I'll make you a promise, Carla," he assured her again. "They're not coming back. Believe me."

"You've got power over them. I've seen that. That's what makes me feel safe here."

"It's not my power," put in Ken quickly. "I can only command them in the Name of Jesus Christ. That ought to tell you who they are!"

Her eyes were pleading with him. "Can I ask you one other thing? I was *physically* choked by a *spirit* entity of some kind—and could have been killed if you hadn't saved me. I saw that horrible, huge cobra with my own physical eyes. And there was Del Sasso, only it wasn't him, and it wasn't a real snake. That's what you're trying to tell me, is that right?"

Ken nodded.

"Why *me*—and what's it all about?"

Ken started to speak, then hesitated. After a long thoughtful silence he said at last, "Carla, there's too much involved in those questions to get into them when we're both so exhausted. We'll talk tomorrow morning, or whenever you want to."

Together they started walking slowly back toward her bedroom. "I'll say this much right now," said Ken. "What happened to you tonight isn't anything new. It's been going on in various forms since the beginning of time."

"It has? Like when and where?"

"Well, it all started with a woman and a serpent in a garden. You know when that was. Instead of threatening her, however, that serpent seductively offered her infinite knowledge and power. But it destroyed her and all of her descendants with an ingenious deception."

"Oh, Ken—you know what I think about that story. If I weren't so tired—"

"You amaze me, Carla. I'd think that what just happened to you would have been more than convincing! You saw the serpent with your own eyes, and you know that the Bible always identifies Satan as 'that old serpent.' What is it going to take?"

"Are you saying that was *Satan* himself?" demanded Carla.

"It could have been," said Ken without hesitation. "Whether that's so or not, he was certainly the one behind what happened to you tonight."

"Del Sasso has an entirely different interpretation of the Garden of Eden myth," said Carla softly. "It made an awful lot of sense when he explained it, and I was so sure then, but now I'm confused. I don't know what I believe."

"I know very well what Del Sasso and others like him teach," responded Ken evenly. "They've turned the whole thing inside out so that the serpent becomes the savior. And the promise of godhood, instead of being the seductive lie that enslaved the human race, is promoted as the 'truth' that sets us free."

"I still think it makes a lot of sense," said Carla defensively.

"Stop and think Carla, please! Can't you see that the lie hasn't changed? And the Leightons and Del Sassos and Khorevs—yes, and all the rest of us—are just as vulnerable today as Eve was then."

At the door to Carla's room they stopped. "You can be very thankful for what happened tonight," Ken declared with conviction.

Carla's instant look of protest demanded an explanation.

"You'll be thankful one day, Carla. It's going to force you to make a decision. The Archons realize you've got doubts, so they can't destroy you by deceit. You're not buying the whole lie, so the next thing they try is fear and violence. You've seen behind the mask to their true character. God has allowed this in His mercy. Look at the evidence now, and make the right choice!"

Carla could respond only in stunned silence. "Good night," she murmured at last.

"Good night—and God help you!"

the
MIND
INVADERS
30

Keeping the Faith

W hen Carla entered the kitchen late that morning, Ken was on the phone and his mother was squeezing orange juice. From a pot on the stove came the gentle "plop-plop" of oatmeal cooking. The wholesome fragrance, the homey sound, the instant welcoming hug that Mrs. Inman gave her lent a restorative normalcy to life.

"I'm so glad you felt comfortable about coming here!" came the sincere words from the matronly figure in the blue-sprigged apron. "And then in *this house* to have something like *that* happen—I couldn't believe it! Ken told me just a little bit. I hope you were able to get some sleep after that."

"Believe it or not, I zonked out completely and just woke up a few minutes ago. But I still feel exhausted." She smiled, took Mrs. Inman's hand, and added, "You're both so kind. I appreciate it more than words can express."

"You just make yourself right at home." She turned her attention back to the orange juice and carried on over her shoulder. "I'd apologize for this Spartan breakfast, but Ken tells me you eat the same stuff. I don't even have a slice of bacon in the house. He calls it 'junk food.'"

"You've got some plain yogurt, I bet."

"Lots of it. And lecithin granules by the quart, if you want any."

"*Toujours*, of course," laughed Carla. "You manage to survive in spite of Ken's dietary paranoia?"

"Well, I do sneak something *unhealthy* once in awhile, but I don't think he's *that* paranoid. A bit wiser than some of the rest of us, perhaps. But he tells me you're just as fanatical."

"Almost."

Ken hung up the phone. "So, you slept well—no more 'visitors.' That's great."

"I don't even remember having a dream."

There was the usual small talk as the three ate at the kitchen table together. Ken seemed reluctant to bring up the events of the previous night or carry on their discussion unless Carla was ready. When she did broach the subject, he was surprised by her question.

"What do you think about UFOs?" she asked.

"They're 'real,' but certainly not physical," replied Ken without hesitation, giving her a questioning look and wondering what this had to do with the horror she had just been through.

"Why do you say that?"

"There are lots of reasons. I think you know them as well as I do. For example, they've been tracked on radar making a 90-degree turn at 7000 miles per hour. Physical objects just can't do that without disintegrating. UFOs hover motionless, then accelerate through the sound barrier without making a sonic boom. Again, a physical object couldn't do that. And there are other reasons. But why do you ask?"

"I'll give you one more reason," interrupted Ken's mother. "You can tell them to be gone in the Name of Jesus, and they vanish. You didn't ask my opinion, but I'll give it to you anyway: They're demonic manifestations, and I wouldn't have anything to do with them!"

Carla looked from mother to son in mock surprise. "So Ken swept you into the fold, too! You're not the same lady I remember visiting in Maine a few summers ago."

"I hope you like this one better," said Mrs. Inman. "I certainly do."

"You've got my vote on that." Carla contemplated her oatmeal for a moment, then reluctantly continued. "In fact, as much as I don't want to admit it, you've both got a peace and contentment and a quiet confidence that I, uh . . . well, frankly, admire and envy. This place is like an oasis."

There was a long silence. Carla took a swallow of orange juice, leaned back, and studied the glass. "I'm almost afraid to ask these questions. You know very well that before what happened last night I wouldn't have wanted to hear your opinion." She fell silent again.

"Why do you have UFOs on your mind?" asked Ken.

Carla hesitated and then decided to tell part of it. "I was sworn to secrecy on this, but after what *they* tried to do to me last night, I've got some legitimate questions."

"We'll keep it confidential," promised Ken.

"I'd appreciate that. Well, whatever they are, I saw my first UFO yesterday afternoon—very close." Carla tried not to sound dramatic. "And last night—both at the hotel and over here—when all of that horrific stuff came down on me, the same lights that were on that UFO were just outside."

Mrs. Inman was shocked. "You really saw a *UFO*? Close up? That frightens me for you, Carla! I don't even want to know what it looked like!"

"I presume it was related to the Archons," said Ken.

"That's right. The Archons told us to be there. Apparently Frank, Del Sasso, and Kay have been meeting with them this way for some time."

Ken was grim. "Carla, you know my opinion, so I won't state it again. You don't fool around with this stuff! You could get into this so deep that you can't get out. What was your reaction when you saw this thing?"

"It left me shaken—and very confused. It was a horrible experience one moment, but the next I seemed to be drawn into it, like I was being hypnotized, and from then on it seemed wonderful and desirable. It's really strange: It was *evil* and *repulsive* and yet *good* and *attractive* at the same time. There was something very seductive about it that drew me."

"That's what I was afraid of," said Ken. "What did the UFO do— I mean, what was the purpose?"

"It was an incredible encounter with the Archons, but I really shouldn't say any more. I just wanted to know what you think of UFOs, and you said pretty much what I expected you would. I saw this whole episode with my own eyes and still can't believe it.

Viktor saw it, too. The Archons and their craft had to be *real*, but I'm not sure anymore what that means."

"Like Del Sasso and the serpent last night," Ken reminded her. "That was real, too, wasn't it?"

"And even more frightening and confusing."

"They're the same kind of event, Carla. And I think you can see that your consent to be involved in the one—and then having doubts about it—brought on the other. If you won't believe their lies, then their only option is to destroy you before you believe in the One who will deliver you from their power."

She winced at the oblique reference to Christ and lapsed into thoughtful silence again. At last she reminded him, "As I said last night, I don't think they're trying to destroy me. They could have done that if they'd wanted to, but they stopped the manifestations when I pleaded with them to leave. Well, there was something after that, but—"

"Look, Carla!" said Ken earnestly, "there's a lot of prayer going up for you, and if the Archons didn't destroy you last night in the hotel, I'd give God's mercy the credit rather than their benevolence." He leaned across the table. "I don't want to give you the wrong impression, either. All the prayer in the world isn't going to protect you if you make that final rejection of Christ—and only God knows when that happens."

"I do appreciate your prayers," said Carla softly.

"Even if you leave God and Satan out of this," Ken continued, "surely it must occur to you that whether you think the Archons are demons or highly evolved extraterrestrials, you have the knowledge and the power, as a journalist, to become a threat to them."

"That's what frightens me."

"If they no longer look upon you as an asset but as a liability in their scheme—" He left the sentence unfinished.

After a long silence she said, "Do you think they can really read my mind?"

He shrugged. "I'm not sure what demons can and can't do. Their power is limited by God and by our relationship to Him. If you play by their rules, you're going to suffer the consequences. I despise them utterly, and I have no fear of them at all."

"I respect and admire you for that, Ken."

"That's nice to say, but how do I get through to you? How is God going to get you to the point where you'll admit the truth? Jesus Christ is your only means of escape from the destruction that Frank and Del Sasso are dragging you into. If you don't open your heart to Him—"

"Are you trying to get me to accept Jesus for self-preservation?" she asked accusingly.

"That can't be the only motive, but it's legitimate. In the final analysis, however, you really have to believe that His way is best. If the Archons are actually more loving than Christ and can do more for you, then you'd be a fool not to follow them—and I wouldn't try to persuade you otherwise. But if Christ wins in those departments, then—well, I don't have to tell you."

Carla withdrew into silence again. Her lips were trembling when she spoke at last. "You know what this kind of discussion did between us before. It's best if we avoid it." Her eyes met Ken's in a moment of shared sorrow. Briefly her hand touched his, then she drew it back. She turned quickly to Mrs. Inman. She was just opening her eyes. The possibility that she might have been praying was strangely comforting. "It was a delicious breakfast," Carla proffered. "Thank you so much. May I help with the dishes?"

"Oh, don't be silly. I've got all day to putter around here. You've got far more important things to do."

Carla pushed her chair back from the table. "Well, I really should get out there. Frank will wonder what happened to me."

"He ought to wonder about more than that," said Ken pointedly.

The doorbell rang and Ken jumped up. "I'll get it. If you can spare another few minutes, Carla, it's someone you really should meet."

In a moment Ken returned with a sandy-haired man of pleasant manner and military bearing. "Carla, I want you to meet my good friend Don Jordan. He's got something extremely important to tell you."

Ken pulled out a chair for Don and they both sat down. "You don't need me," said Mrs. Inman, getting up and gathering the remaining dishes from the table, "and I've got work to do. Now, before I go, can I get something for you, Don?"

"Some coffee, if you've got it."

"Will instant do?"

"That's great—I take it black."

Carla had been looking from Ken to Don questioningly. "That name is familiar for some reason."

"I'm with the FBI," Jordan began. "We talked on the phone a few days ago, if you remember."

"Yes, I do remember. You were in charge of the men who were watching my room and following me everywhere—using me as a decoy to catch those Russians."

Don looked a bit uncomfortable. "We did all we could."

"Oh, you misunderstand me," cut in Carla quickly. "I'm not complaining at all. I appreciated the protection!"

Jordan smiled. "Thanks. Ken says you have to get back out to the research complex, so I'll be brief. What I'm about to tell you must be held in the strictest confidence from everyone, and that includes Leighton, Khorev, Morris, Del Sasso, and anybody else. Are you willing to abide by that?"

Carla hesitated and glanced over at Ken, but he had looked away. This was to be her decision. "If you think it's something I really ought to know, and if those are the conditions—okay, I'll agree to that."

Jordan leaned forward. "You have a Russian agent working inside that installation," he declared bluntly. Carla drew in a quick breath. Ken looked grim. "I'm telling you this in part because of my friendship with Ken and his concern for you, which I share. But also I want to enlist you as our eyes and ears to let us know anything at all you learn from the inside that might be even remotely related to this case. I don't think that will place you in any danger. In fact, it will probably contribute to your safety."

Carla was trying to digest this information and assess its implications. "I don't know who it could be," she said thoughtfully. "Certainly not Viktor or Leighton. One of the security men, perhaps?"

Jordan took a sip of the coffee Mrs. Inman had placed in front of him. "As far as we're concerned at this point," he said, "everybody who was there that night is under suspicion."

"Well, I suppose I should ask why I'm not on that list, too," said Carla with a wry smile. "Or I guess I should thank Ken for that. Well, this is interesting! Mike Bradford—you know, the head of security—is convinced it was an inside job, too. Yet Leighton won't hear of it. In fact, we were told that the FBI was convinced it was *not* an inside job." Carla gave him a questioning look.

"It's a bit like poker," said Jordan. "We've had to mislead them as to what we believe, and we have our reasons for that. As for whether someone on the inside was the key to this operation, there simply isn't any doubt. I won't take time to give you the many reasons. One of the most interesting is something that Mike doesn't know: The person who killed the two guards at the gate gave the murder weapon to Colonel Chernov, the leader of the Russian team. He had it with him in Leighton's office at the time of his death. It was American-made, not Russian. We're trying to trace it."

Carla was staggered. "I see what you mean—there doesn't seem to be any doubt at all! But why not let Frank know the truth? Surely he isn't one of the suspects!"

"For two reasons. First of all, we want to give the Russian agent a false sense of security. Second, we want everything to proceed normally. It would be very difficult for Leighton to provide normal leadership if he knew what I've just told you."

A sense of helpless incredulity gripped Carla. "I thought I was hot on the trail of a big story, but I had no idea it would develop into *this*! It's going completely berserk."

"If you hang in there, which I wish you wouldn't," said Ken, "it's going to get even wilder if the Archons push it to a conclusion."

"I'm not backing out now," declared Carla firmly. "And I don't think Mr. Jordan would want me to. My major motive at one time was a Pulitzer prize. There's a lot more than that at stake now. It's ironic, Ken, that even if your arguments about who the Archons are and what they're up to are all true, that gives me even more reason not to back out!"

Ken looked at her in alarm. "You lost me, Carla."

"I got into this because I just happened to be in the right place at the right time to save Viktor Khorev's life. And I certainly won't abandon him now—demons or no demons!"

"I don't know exactly what the two of you are talking about," said Jordan, standing to leave. "You understand, Miss Bertelli, that someone on the staff out there, someone that you may work with every day, is a ruthless murderer who shot two guards in cold blood, undoubtedly let the special assault team into the base, and is probably still committed to the same objectives. Does anyone at all stand out in your mind as a possible suspect?"

"Not really," said Carla. She hesitated. "Well, perhaps I should say that Viktor told me he thinks Kay Morris is Russian. Of course, she could be Russian and not be the one—"

"We've already checked her out along with everyone else, and she certainly isn't Russian!" said Jordan. He pulled a pad from his inside pocket and made a notation. "We'll go back over the data."

"Well, I guess I'm game for whatever you want me to do," said Carla.

"Great," said Jordan. "We'll count on you to tip us to anything you think we ought to know. Nothing is too insignificant. Anything at all that strikes you as suspicious or out-of-the-ordinary, let me know about it right away." He handed her his card. "Don't call me from the phones out there. I guess you know they're all bugged."

"I assumed that," she said. "And I won't carry this card with me. I'll memorize the number."

The three of them walked toward the front door together. Jordan reached into his coat pocket, pulled out a snub-nosed 38 revolver and held it out to Carla. "Do you know how to handle a weapon like this?"

She took it, broke it open, and spun the cylinder. It was empty. "I've done quite a bit of target practice. Yes, I can handle it—and even hit what I'm aiming at, believe it or not."

"Ken said you could, but I wanted to see for myself." Jordan opened his briefcase and brought out a box of ammunition. "Here you are. I'd load it right now, and don't go anywhere without it. I've taken care of the paperwork, so you're authorized to carry a concealed weapon. Don't hesitate to use it if you have to."

Carla looked grimly from the weapon and ammunition in her hands to Jordan and Ken and back again. "Well, I sure got myself into something, didn't I!"

the
MIND
INVADERS
31

Growing Doubts

On her way to the installation, Carla went by the hotel. Entering by the side door, she went quickly to the restaurant. There she went through the breakfast buffet, picking up some fruit and juice and a piece of toast. Hurriedly eating as much as she could, she charged the ticket to her room. It was the weakest of covers to make it appear that she had spent the night there. Next she went to the front desk.

"I need to pick up my messages. Carla Bertelli, room 815."

"Oh, Ms. Bertelli!" exclaimed the young man on duty. "Everybody's been trying to reach you. We haven't gotten any answer in your room."

"I've been in and out and have scarcely had a minute. Let me have them." She started to walk away, then remembered the condition of her room. "By the way, a picture fell off the wall last night and shattered. I've no idea how it happened."

"We're sorry about any inconvenience, Ms. Bertelli. We'll take care of it."

There were nearly two dozen phone calls. Carla took a quick look through them as she hurried from the lobby. Every major television network had called at least once, some twice. In each case it was "urgent." George was trying to contact her; the message said it was "an emergency." Reporters from the *San Francisco Chronicle* and the *Los Angeles Times* were also trying to reach her, as well as local radio and television stations. Her article that morning in *The Washington Post* had obviously created quite a stir! She would have to consult Leighton on how to respond to the requests for interviews.

On the drive out to the installation, her ecstasy over the response to her article was submerged in a renewed wave of concern: How could she face Del Sasso after the events of the previous night? Did he know what had happened? It seemed unrealistic to imagine that he had no connection to the attack upon her by a figure that looked exactly like him. If it had been an Archon—good or bad—why had it impersonated *Del Sasso* in its attempt to terrorize or even kill her? There had to be a reason—some connection. Of course, he was the Archons' link with the world, so who else but Del Sasso?

Could it have been his "psychic double" that choked her? There were reports that Satya Sai Baba of Ananthapur, South India, had appeared in two geographical locations at once. So had the famous stigmatist Padre Pio. She had always rejected such ideas as religious superstition. Now she didn't know what to think. Sai Baba and Padre Pio—a Hindu guru and a Catholic priest—supposedly knew when and where their "doubles" appeared and what each was doing and why. Would Del Sasso know what had happened to her, and be aware of his connection to this horrible event? Was this the end of their friendship and thus of her involvement in the Plan? She couldn't let that happen!

Carla arrived just in time for the usual 11:00 A.M. meeting of the inner circle. Antonio was walking down the corridor, approaching Frank's office from the opposite direction, as she walked up. They met at the door. *Play it cool, Carla! Act like nothing has happened.* She did her best, but the psychic seemed to sense something unusual—or did he really know everything and was just pretending to pick up on something now?

"What's the matter, my dear? Seen a ghost?" he queried and put a comforting arm around her momentarily.

"You are remarkably perceptive!" responded Carla nonchalantly, as though she were going along with some make-believe game. "As a matter of fact, I just saw one leering at me in the lobby, but I gave it a karate chop and it disappeared." Walking past him into the office, she took a seat on the sofa next to Viktor, who nodded to her and smiled as Antonio continued his monologue.

"Appearances like that can happen," persisted Del Sasso solemnly as he followed on her heels. "Negative thoughts attract psychic energy that may linger from a traumatic experience and can even seem to give it solid form." He lowered his huge frame to the floor nearby and settled into a yoga position.

Why was he pursuing this idea of *psychic appearances*? Well, if he was expecting to get some emotional reaction from her, he was wasting his time. There was no way that she was going to tell anyone about her horrifying experience—not even Viktor. Had the Archons told Del Sasso that she had some doubts about them? If they were upset enough to attack her, wouldn't they denounce her in the next transmission? Yet they had not identified the traitor on the staff. Why? Apparently they were not all-knowing, so perhaps they couldn't read her thoughts after all. It was all very confusing.

Pretending to have no further interest in what she and Del Sasso had been sparring about, Carla turned to talk to Viktor. Just at that moment, however, Leighton burst exuberantly into the office with Kay Morris in his wake. He rushed to his desk to grab the remote control, hurried over to sit on the sofa next to Viktor and Carla, and motioned to the others to take seats for viewing the giant TV screen.

"Everybody take a seat where you can see the screen," he said breathlessly. "There's a special news bulletin on all the networks at 11:00. We're just in time to catch it."

When the screen lit up, the newscast was already in progress: ". . . according to a brief article in the current issue of *Time* magazine. Nothing has aroused such intense bipartisan interest on Capitol Hill since the Israeli-PLO peace agreement. Fearing they may have an unauthorized CIA clandestine project on their hands, members of both Houses are clamoring for an investigation unless the White House makes a full disclosure. So far the president is insisting that the information is highly classified and that there has been no wrongdoing. As for the *Time* allegations about a secret CIA psychic research breakthrough, the Director of Central Intelligence, who appeared with the president at the news conference earlier this morning, admitted that there have been some major developments, but refused to discuss them.

"Congress suddenly finds itself caught short. There is no committee officially overseeing psychic development because most members of both Houses have until now refused to take such phenomena seriously. There are no controls or guidelines because the proponents' glowing descriptions of what could be done with psychic power have consistently been dismissed by critics as imagination at best and fraud at worst. If the CIA has, in fact, not only developed 'psychic warfare' capabilities, but, as the *Time* article further alleges, has employed these weapons against the Russians, who sent a special combat team to destroy the CIA's secret psychic research installation, then someone within the top levels of government may well have engaged in activities not authorized by Congress. Thus far the only comment from the Kremlin has been 'no comment.'

"And now into this highly charged atmosphere comes an article in today's *Washington Post* by Carla Bertelli, who is generally regarded as the most reliable journalist reporting psychic research. There is speculation that she may be the 'inside source' quoted in *Time*. Ms. Bertelli goes even further than *Time*'s astonishing claim that the CIA has made contact with 'higher intelligences.' She alleges that these extraterrestrials are in fact responsible for the psychic breakthrough—and that their ultimate purpose is to share this power with the entire world. This network has so far been unsuccessful in its attempt to reach Ms. Bertelli for a live interview. Stay tuned for periodic updates as this fast-breaking story develops."

Frank switched off the TV at that point and jumped to his feet. "Well! How do you like that!" he exclaimed. "Things seem to be moving along exactly as the Archons predicted!" He walked over and sat on the front of his desk where he could face his colleagues. "We should all be very encouraged, but there's a long way to go and it isn't going to be easy. We've got plenty of top government leaders on our side now, and that's what it takes for the World Congress. But the second phase involves the general population. We've got to get them fully behind us. The Archons have already targeted key leaders in entertainment, business, education, and ethnic and other minority groups. Self-hypnosis and subliminal tapes and success-motivation seminars will play a big part when we get to that point."

He turned to Carla. "A key factor in laying the foundation for all of that, as the program we just watched demonstrated, will be your news leaks and articles. How are we doing?"

Carla had been uncomfortably aware that Antonio had been observing her closely during the television news broadcast. She was grateful that Leighton had reminded him—and the others as well—of the key role she was playing.

"My phone at the hotel has been ringing off the hook," she announced. "I didn't know what to say, so I just didn't answer it and pretended I wasn't there." She pulled the sheaf of phone messages out of her purse and waved them at Frank. "These accumulated just this morning since the *Post* article came out. Every television network is after me plus every other kind of media. What do I say to these people?"

"It has to be handled discreetly from here on," cautioned Leighton. "I've been on the phone off and on all morning with the DCI. He's ecstatic. Antonio and I are flying into D.C. next week. The DCI's setting up some meetings for us with some key senators and congressional leaders."

"But what about these phone calls?" interrupted Carla. "Do I give interviews—and if so, what do I say?"

"I was getting to that. That's what I've been discussing with the DCI all morning. You must not give any further details. Those are to be revealed only in your articles or specific news leaks to your friend at *Time* as the Archons direct us. In the meantime, you simply explain that you're not authorized to give out any further information yet. And you keep hammering away on three salient points. Word them differently for variety, but here they are: 1) explain that something *absolutely new* is going to happen on earth that will benefit all of mankind; 2) emphasize that no political party or nation will be responsible for or able to control this process for its own benefit; and 3) that everything will be under the control of higher intelligences who have been monitoring our evolutionary development for thousands of years and are now stepping in to preserve life on earth and to usher in a New Age of peace and prosperity."

"But am I authorized at this point to go on TV and radio and to give interviews to reporters?" persisted Carla.

"Definitely not. That would be premature. You're going to have to put them off. Let them know that the director and psychic from this secret research installation will be going public in Washington next week, and drop some hints of further developments. But nothing more than that."

"I'm working on my next article for the *Post*. It's due next week."

"Yes, of course. Continue with that."

"And I really need a secretary of my own, Frank. Viktor and I have been sharing the same one."

"I'll take care of that immediately. You'll have one in the morning."

"I haven't yet met with Carla to give her my input," interjected Del Sasso.

In response to Carla's questioning look, Frank waved his hand at Antonio and said, "Why don't you go ahead and give us all a brief summary."

Del Sasso stood to his feet and positioned himself so he could observe each face. "We all know," he reminded them, "that the Plan could fail because of either skepticism or fear. Either nobody believes in it, or they believe but are afraid to trust the Archons. A lot of people equate extraterrestrials with spaceships invading earth to enslave us. Psychologists, psychiatrists, sociologists, and a lot of academicians and educated people are very skeptical about the possibility of contact with extraterrestrials. So we've got to give them something they can believe in. We let them think that we're only presenting the Archons as highly evolved extraterrestrials to cater to the imagination of the common people, but that the Archons are really Jungian archetypes coming to us from the collective unconscious. So we satisfy everyone."

"You mean," interrupted Carla, "that the *truth* doesn't matter?"

"*Truth?*" responded Del Sasso a bit contemptuously. "What does that mean?"

"It's not easy to define, but I think we all know what it means."

"On the elementary level of mathematics and the physical sciences, perhaps," conceded Del Sasso. "But the secret to human happiness and fulfillment lies outside science in the realm of consciousness, and there *belief* is what counts. We just want them to believe in and trust the Archons. It doesn't really matter who anyone thinks they are."

Carla looked a bit nonplussed. "I'll drop by your office later this afternoon," Del Sasso told her, "and go over this again with you. The most important thing to remember is to keep whatever you speak or write on a positive note. All of the problems in the world today have resulted from the fact that the race of gods living on this planet has been caught in the descending spiral of its own negative thinking, which has lowered self-esteem. Mankind needs to be trained to create a new reality through the power of positive thinking."

Back in her office that afternoon, Carla found that she needed more than a positive approach. When she returned the many phone calls, media representatives confronted her with a problem she hadn't even considered, and for which she couldn't give them a very good answer. The practical considerations of moral accountability in running a government were the center of their concern. Her conversation with George Conklin was typical.

"I'm getting a lot of flak from upstairs," said George, when Carla reached him at last. "They think this whole thing sounds like an elite group of insiders accountable to no one but themselves, operating a government within the government, making their own rules."

"George, this is not an elitist operation," she replied quickly, anxious to put that argument down immediately. "It's not what we've seen so much of in the CIA in the past—a group of zealots answerable to no one but themselves. The Plan for a New World Order has been conceived and is being directed by higher intelligences who play no favorites. They want to benefit the entire planet and all mankind together."

"Carla, I don't know if I'll ever live down printing your line about 'higher intelligences.' Nobody here believes that stuff, and you ought to see our mail. We're getting ripped by skeptics."

"All the letters can't be negative."

"I didn't say they were."

"So what are the percentages?"

There was an embarrassed pause. "I don't have that figure."

"Come on, George. You must have some idea."

"Okay, so the vast majority are favorable. But the skeptics represent the better-educated and more intelligent readers."

"Oh, sure. Do you have IQ test scores for each of your readers? Or is the level of 'intelligence' determined by whether they agree with your skepticism or not? Shame on you elitists at *Time!* Do you really think that humans are the only intelligent beings in the entire universe, or the most highly evolved?"

"Of course not, but so far there's been no contact, and until there is—"

"That's what I'm telling you, George. There *has* been contact."

"Then prove it. Let's see these little green critters in the Oval Office. After all, that's where they'd go, isn't it? You know, 'Take me to your leader.'"

"You'll see them in due time, and so will the whole world. And George, they're not green."

"Are you trying to tell me you've seen them?"

"I am—and I have. But that's not for publication yet."

"What are they putting in the water out there in Palo Alto?"

"That's not kind. I wasn't hallucinating, and I'm not lying."

"Well, put them on display then, and we'll all be convinced."

"George, you don't 'put on display' beings that are as far beyond us on the evolutionary scale as we are beyond worms. They're calling the shots, and they'll show themselves when the appropriate time comes."

"That's a smoke screen. I'm sorry, Carla, but the cute little phrase 'when the *appropriate* time comes' isn't going to cut it. You've thrown us some scraps. If you don't follow up with the whole meal pretty fast, you're going to lose all credibility and the reputation you've built over the years—and I don't want to see that happen."

"Look, George, you're the one who told me that if contact really had been established, then breaking the news too suddenly could create worldwide panic—fear of an attack from Mars or, even worse, some horrifying *Invasion of the Body Snatchers.* Remember?"

"That was nearly a week ago, but we haven't seen anything either to be afraid of or to get excited about. So what's happening now?"

"I can only tell you this: Next week the psychic who has these incredible powers and is in daily contact with these entities will be coming to D.C. with the director of the secret research facility to meet with key leaders on the Hill and to let them all see firsthand what he can do. There won't be any skeptics in Washington after that. If you want to see it for yourself, contact the director of the CIA for a press invitation."

There was silence for a moment. When George replied, what he said shook Carla with another possibility that she hadn't even considered. "Yeah, I'll think about that. But, you know, I already told you that it smacks of an elite group inside the CIA making their own rules."

"And I explained, George, that the Archons are in control, not the CIA!" interrupted Carla.

"Yeah, I heard you," said George, "And that's what really bothers me. It's the perfect setup for taking over the world. If this group could somehow convince everyone that they're only carrying out the instructions of extraterrestrial intelligences with infinite powers who are imposing a New World Order. . . . You see what I'm thinking?"

◆ ◆ ◆

Ken had spent much of the evening in prayerful study of Paul's epistle to the Ephesians—especially chapter six that dealt with spiritual warfare. He was still up very late when Carla returned. She knocked softly and he hurried to the front door.

"I'm sorry. I completely forgot to give you a key this morning," said Ken apologetically as he let her in. "You've got your own entrance around the side if you want to use it. And you need your own remote so you can put your car in the garage. Remind me at breakfast, and I'll give them to you."

"Asking for a key never crossed my mind. All I could think of was that my purse was awfully heavy, and what if they wouldn't let me carry that gun on the base. Of course I couldn't tell them that I was carrying it to protect me from what might happen—not in the cruel outside world, but inside that installation."

"Did they take it away?"

"No. The guards found it, of course. I showed them the permit Don had given me and explained that it was because my life was still in danger on the outside from the other members of that Russian team—whoever and wherever they might be. They checked with Frank and he said okay."

"Can I get you something? Hot chocolate, tea, some juice, fruit . . . anything?"

"I'm wiped out, but I'm so keyed up that maybe some steaming-hot decaf tea, if you've got it, will help me unwind."

"We've got it."

They walked into the kitchen together, where Ken put on some water to boil. "Frank sure must be a slave driver!" he said dryly. "Is this the length of a normal day?"

"Normal?" laughed Carla. "I don't think I know what that means anymore—not just in relation to a workday. I mean in general."

"Something's bothering you," suggested Ken. "Anything I might help with?"

Carla hesitated. Finally she asked, "There's a theory that our minds create the reality around us. What's your opinion?"

"It's ludicrous," declared Ken without any hesitation.

"How can you say that, when so many top scientists believe it?"

He poured the tea and sat down with her at the table. "In fact, very few if any reputable scientists take that idea seriously. It's been popularized by a handful of writers such as Capra and Zukov, but they represent a very small fringe element in physics. In 30 seconds I can show you just how stupid it is."

"Go ahead."

"Did you 'create' the cup I pulled out of the cupboard to pour your tea into, or did I?"

"Well—"

"You didn't even know what color it was going to be, or what shape, and I wasn't even thinking of that. So obviously, neither of us 'created' it. Right?"

"That's pretty straightforward, I'd have to agree, but that still leaves the possibility that it was created by someone else's mind and we just accepted that."

"And that other person's mind has been *maintaining* its existence and spatial position without even knowing where it was?" He gave her a reproving look. "Come on, Carla! And what about the millions of microscopic creatures in the water I boiled, or the molecules and atoms in the water. Whose mind created that reality?"

"I never thought of that."

"The shape and color of that cup are very superficial impressions interpreted by our eyes and have nothing to do with what the cup in itself really is. It looks far different through an electron microscope, for example. And there's a whole universe of molecules and atoms and subatomic particles—including some particles that science hasn't even discovered yet—that make up that cup that no human eye has ever seen or human mind conceived. You think *that* reality that we don't even know about yet is the product of human thought? Can you seriously imagine that the distant galaxies, the interior of stars, black holes, and myriad wonders of a universe never seen by human eye and predating our existence—that all of that was created by our minds? I'm sorry, but I don't have much patience with people who call the account of Creation in the Bible a myth and then fall for ridiculous ideas like that!"

Carla held up her hands in mock surrender. "I give up," she said. "Boy, when you get on your soapbox! Okay, so it's ludicrous. Then why does this theory seem so reasonable to so many intelligent people. Why?"

"I've already said it, Carla. It's pride. The colossal dimensions of the delusion are only exceeded by the gigantic egos that swallow it. Far from creating reality with our own minds, we're struggling to discover the secrets of a universe that was created by another Mind who is infinitely beyond us."

A Mind infinitely beyond us, thought Carla. *He's giving me an argument for the existence of God—and I asked for it!* They sipped their tea in silence. At last she asked, "What would you say if I suggested that the UFO and the Archons that I saw in that warehouse were an illusion created by movie projectors rigged up to deceive me and Viktor? And that the same mechanism will be used to convince others?"

Ken thought about it carefully. "It's possible, but not likely. What gave you that idea?"

"One of the editors at *Time* I've known for years. He's suspicious of the whole thing. Thinks it might be a ploy by an elite group in Washington to take over the world by making everyone think they're following orders from higher intelligences."

"I don't know what happened in the warehouse. I wasn't there. But I can assure you there weren't any movie projectors in your room the other night—here or at the hotel. And there weren't any in the lab when Del Sasso put on his show. There's definitely some heavy demonic involvement."

"It always comes back to that, doesn't it," said Carla. There was just a hint of bitterness in her voice.

Ken shrugged. "That's like saying eating always involves food, or—"

Carla held up a hand. "Okay, don't overwhelm me. I get the point."

"I'm sorry," said Ken. "What your friend said about an elite group in Washington or within the CIA—he might have something there. I'd bear it in mind and see if any developments that come along seem to fit that scenario."

"You really think so? I'm surprised you'd say that."

"Evil always operates on two levels," said Ken. "The demonic and the human. Satan has the same ego problems with his disciples that God has with His. If Christian leaders often try to build their own little kingdoms, it's not surprising that the followers of Antichrist would."

Carla smiled and shook her head. "You amaze me, Ken. Two years ago you were the consummate atheist, and now you're the ultimate Christian!"

"If that's the way I come across, then I've got to repent of it," said Ken. "I'm so far from being the ultimate Christian."

"Well, you sure have this thing wired. And I don't mean that in a bad way. I'm really impressed. You've got a unique way of saying things: 'Satan has the same ego problems with his disciples that God has with His.'" She leaned back and laughed. "That's quite a way to put it!"

"I'm not trying to play the big expert," responded Ken. "You could look it up in the Bible for yourself—anything I'm telling you. Then look at the world around you through that wisdom and you get a whole new perspective. You don't have to be too bright to realize that Frank and Del Sasso could possibly hope to use the Archons for their own ends. That's not too farfetched, knowing human greed and pride."

"I suppose you're right," conceded Carla. "Which does give some support to George's concern."

"Whatever the case," said Ken earnestly, "I'll tell you one thing for sure. In the end, everyone involved with the Archons will become victims, and I'm praying day and night that you won't be one of them!"

A Warning!

Ken's left for the office already," his mother informed Carla when she entered the kitchen the next morning. Seeing the disappointment on Carla's face, she added, "He works much too hard—always has, even when he was a boy. Forever some urgent project or other."

"That's one of the things that attracted me to him," said Carla. "He was on a mission, going somewhere, not wasting his time but doing something worthwhile, goal-oriented."

"He still is," said Mrs. Inman, "but, of course, the goals have changed drastically, and for the better—believe me, they have!" Carla started to frown, then smiled.

"Well, what would you like this morning?" Mrs. Inman asked her. "Some bacon and eggs for a change? I bought some, just in case."

"You mean you want me to join you in a mini rebellion against the tyranny of health food? Okay, let's go for it!"

Ken had gotten up early to spend considerable time crying out to God once again for Carla. He prayed that the demonic evil would be so obvious that Carla would not be able to deny it; that God would put a shield of protection around her; that Viktor and Frank would have their eyes opened as well; that the Plan would

288

be frustrated—and in general that God would do all He could without violating Carla's power of choice to make the truth clear enough to her that she could make that choice without any deluding influence upon her.

It concerned Ken deeply that in spite of the frank discussions they had been able to have, instead of escaping the Archons, it seemed she was being drawn in deeper and was preparing to play a key role in persuading the world to embrace their seductive Plan. He keenly felt the urgency to pray specifically that she would see through the mask to the evil behind it and become thoroughly disillusioned. And that she would be protected from the demonic power that he knew would be unleashed against her in renewed fury if she tried to back out.

In the quiet of early morning, Ken had concluded that there was little point in trying to reason with Carla any further. He had said more than enough. All he could do now was to keep praying and believe that God would do everything possible to bring her to the point of decision, at which time she would have to exercise her power of choice. There was nothing that even God Himself could do to *make* her choose the right path.

The phone rang in the kitchen just as Carla and Mrs. Inman were finishing breakfast. "It's Ken—for you," said his mother as she handed the phone to Carla.

"Good morning!" said Ken. "I just wanted to make sure that you got the key and remote garage-door opener I left on the counter in the kitchen."

"Your mother pointed them out to me. Thanks a lot."

"Is everything okay?"

"Yeah, just fine."

"Anything I can do?"

"Well, I was thinking of asking you to meet me at the hotel. I really need to get the rest of my things, and there's no way I'm going back in that room without *you*."

"I understand. Did you want to do it this morning or tonight?"

"Well, if you can fit it in, do you mind, say in half an hour?"

"No problem. See you in the lobby."

◆ ◆ ◆

"It looks so mundane in here, so 'everyday-commonplace-business-as-usual,'" said Carla as they left the elevator and walked down the hall toward her room. "I feel kind of silly asking you to help me get some clothes." In spite of the brave words, Carla's voice betrayed her anxiety.

"I know exactly what you mean," responded Ken.

Carla opened the door. She took a step inside, turned on the light, and screamed. "Ken! Look! I—I don't believe this! Why?"

He rushed in past her, then stood transfixed by the destruction that met his eye. The mattress and bedclothes had been ripped off the king-size bed and thrown into a corner, smashing a lamp. Three pictures now lay shattered on the floor along with two other lamps. The drawers had been dumped out and the drapes ripped from the windows.

Carla surveyed the scene in anguish. "The Archons weren't this vicious," she said. "This is incredible!"

"You don't think the Archons did it?" asked Ken in surprise.

"Okay, Ken, you see a demon behind everything. But what I see in here is the work of the CIA, FSB—or even the FBI. They were looking for something. That's obvious."

"What do you have that they would want?"

"Nothing, that I know of, but they obviously thought I had something."

"Carla, be reasonable! The CIA or FSB—and certainly the FBI—would have no reason for doing this. But the Archons would."

"Why?" asked Carla. "I wasn't even here."

"Maybe they just wanted to let you know how vulnerable you are—that they can pull your strings and make you do what they want you to, like a puppet!"

Carla just stood and stared at him in shock.

"Come on," he said. "Let's pack your things and get out of here."

Together they gathered her clothes and put them into her suitcase.

On the way down to the lobby in the elevator, Ken told her, "I was thinking, Carla, that this may work out for the best anyway. It gives you a reason to check out, presumably for another hotel. Here's what I think you ought to say."

Back at the front desk, Carla turned in her key. "I'm going to have to check out," she began in a low voice. She was visibly shaken and it was obvious that she had just been through a traumatic experience. "Someone got into my room—thank God I wasn't there—and tore it completely to pieces."

"I'm terribly sorry. I don't see how anyone could get in," said the young man waiting on her.

She leaned forward in a gesture of confidentiality. "You remember when the FBI was here a few days ago?"

"Yes."

"Well, you wouldn't have known, but they were protecting *me*." She nodded in Ken's direction and the clerk raised his eyebrows knowingly. "We thought the threat had ended, but apparently whoever is after me got into my room. Obviously I'm not saying where I'm going. I'll come back tomorrow to pick up any messages. Do you have any now?"

"We certainly do. I almost forgot. You've got a stack of phone calls."

In the parking lot Ken put the suitcase in Carla's car and held the door open as she climbed in. Quickly she riffled through the phone messages. "ABC, CBS, NBC, *New York Times*—everybody wants me to be on their talk show or do an article for their newspaper or magazine. I've never been so much in demand." She looked up at him. There were traces of tears in her eyes, but her voice carried the old determination once again. "Don't think you haven't made some points, because you have. I've thought seriously about chucking this whole thing, but I don't see how I can."

"Carla!"

"Look, I'm not a puppet on a string, but I've made a commitment to Frank."

"You don't owe Frank a thing! He's on a power trip and he's using you!"

"Maybe, but I can't abandon Viktor."

"And there is a story you're after."

"Don't fault me for that, Ken. I am a journalist, and I've got to see this story through to the end!"

"I'll be praying for you!" There was nothing else to say.

"Please do, Ken." Carla bit her lip and looked away. She started the engine and leaned out the window, forcing a smile. "I've got an assignment from your friend Jordan, too, you know. I can't let him down either. When it's all over, maybe I'll write a book: *I Was a Spy for the FBI.*"

Carla had just turned onto the access road leading into the installation when she saw ahead of her the flashing red light of a police car approaching rapidly. It passed at great speed on its way out to the main highway. She drove on slowly, warily. *What is it now?* As she came around a bend within a few hundred yards of the front gate, the overwrought sense of danger and *déjà vu* peaked as another nightmare lay before her gaze. Police cars, uniformed and plainclothes officers, the prone body of a woman on the ground. . . . Carla's reactions moved into slow motion and a protective unreality descended over the scene.

Unaware, she slowed her car to a crawl. A uniformed officer waved her on. *I've got to know who it is . . . what's going on! I thought the violence was over.* In numbed defiance of the order, she pulled over to the side of the road and got out.

"Here, let me help you," said a kind and familiar voice. She became aware that Don Jordan was beside her with his hand under her elbow.

"What happened?" Carla asked, averting her gaze from the figure now being covered with a sheet nearby, and fearful that whoever was lying there had some connection to the installation.

"She was found hanging in a tree just back from the road early this morning by one of the guards on his way in to work," came the terse reply.

"Who was it?"

"A young woman about 25 named Inger Krieg."

"Oh no! Suicide?"

"That hasn't been determined, but we think so."

"Did she leave a note?"

"Yes, apparently in her handwriting. It's being analyzed. I understand she worked at the base."

"She was the other psychic," said Carla, fighting the feeling of light-headedness. "Well, we've had several, but none of them worked out. Inger came all the way from West Germany about three months ago. None of the others seemed able to adapt to the Psitron. They all ended up basket cases mentally. Two of them are still in the psychiatric hospital in town. But Inger, she was doing very well. I saw some of her work. She was being trained by Del Sasso. She was such a likable person. This is terrible!"

"I'd better get back over there," said Jordan. "I'm supposed to be in charge of the investigation since it happened on government property. I haven't heard a peep out of you. Nothing happening?"

"Nothing—no—nothing that I've noticed. Nothing incriminating on Kay Morris. She's working very hard and seems to be 110 percent committed to the project."

"I checked her out again, and she seems to be clean. We've got three of our people in there now. Night-shift guard Stan Kirby, day-shift guard Art Denham, and lab assistant Anne White. You can send messages to me by any of them, and if you need help at any time, rely on them."

"Have they come up with anything?"

"Not yet. I'll see you later."

As Carla pulled into her usual parking place, she saw Viktor walking across the lawn from the transmission lab back to the main building. She jumped out of the car and called, "Viktor!" His face brightened when he saw her coming toward him. They met in the middle of the lawn and hugged each other briefly, then began walking slowly toward the front door together.

"Did you hear about Inger?" she asked immediately.

Viktor's face darkened and he nodded. "Leighton announced it to the staff early this morning."

"What did he say?"

"He called it a great tragedy. It apparently happened sometime last night. He suggested that it was despondency due to home-sickness. I don't believe it."

"Nor do I," agreed Carla. "This is number what—six? Why can't anyone but Del Sasso make it on the Psitron?"

"There's something fundamentally wrong," said Viktor grimly, lowering his voice as they neared the front door.

No, seven! thought Carla. *Ken was the first, and that makes seven. Then why did Del Sasso take to the Psitron like a duck to water? Frank has used those exact words at least a dozen times. Why is that priest so special? Could Ken be right?* She glanced over at Viktor. He appeared to be dealing with his own inner conflicts.

"The Plan is supposed to bring peace, love, and brotherhood to the world," he murmured, more to himself than to her. "Ironic, isn't it?"

Later that morning at the 11:00 staff meeting, Carla sensed that Leighton was tired and discouraged as he addressed the inner circle. He paced nervously back and forth in front of his desk as he talked about the loss of Inger.

"This is a terrible blow to the program. We need millions of Antonios, and so far we've lost every one we've tried to develop. I just don't understand it!" He turned to Viktor. "You've been analyzing the program. I know you worked closely with Inger. Do you have any ideas?"

"There's something fundamentally wrong!" said Viktor with conviction, echoing the very words he had spoken to Carla earlier. "We've had problems with the mental stability of the psychics in the past, so we modified the approach, slowed it down. We were rushing them along too fast. Inger was the first under the new approach, and she was doing well. She was almost another Antonio. In fact, I called her that just yesterday—and now this! Why don't the Archons explain?"

"They have," Del Sasso cut in. "We've been premature. It's our fault for rushing the program. You recall that we were not specifically instructed by the Archons to start the training program yet. Even so, I don't think we should be discouraged, Frank. For one thing, it was the karma of each one of these people. They will come back the better for it, so we don't mourn for them, dead or alive. And we've all learned something in the process that will be invaluable when the Plan is being implemented worldwide."

"Antonio's right," agreed Kay. "If you went back over the transcripts of all of the transmissions, as I did recently, you wouldn't find any instructions to train other psychics yet. In our zeal I think we've rushed ahead—a costly lesson, but one we can benefit from."

"One thing none of us can afford to forget, I guess," added Frank. "We're pioneers in a new field, explorers of inner space—and there are dangers. Think of the lives lost in the past for each new advance mankind has made. There's always a price to pay. It could yet cost some of us in this room our lives. But when you think of the benefits to the entire human race—well, I think we have a tremendous privilege!"

"There's something else," cut in Del Sasso. "I shouldn't be the one to say it, because it may sound a bit egotistical and self-serving, but it's been a great mistake to attempt to train others on the Psitron at this stage. If we had a number of psychics with powers equal to mine, there would be no clear leadership, maybe even rivalry. That wouldn't be good at this point—right?"

"I think you're right," said Frank a bit reluctantly. "I'd wanted to have at least one other Psitron-trained psychic to show off at the Congress, but I let my own ambitions instead of the Archons' wisdom rule. Now I can see why the Archons have held back the development of the psychics, who will be necessary to implement the Plan, until it's been adopted by the world."

"All of this wisdom now isn't helping Inger and the rest," said Viktor solemnly. "I've got to take my share of the blame."

"Well, let's not blame one another," said Frank. "That isn't going to help. We need to go forward again. Antonio and I leave for D.C. in the morning, and I expect to have some exciting news when we return."

Leighton stood up, signaling the end of the meeting. "You know what to do," he said, turning to Kay. "There's a lot of work in the labs that needs to be finalized while Antonio is gone. Viktor will help you. But remember that preparing for his speech takes top priority. Right, Viktor?" Leighton slapped him on the back. "You're the keynoter, you know."

Viktor looked solemn. "That's a big responsibility, but I'm looking forward to it."

"And Carla," added Leighton, "as soon as you finish the rough draft of the next article, you should go on to the third one. I'll go over them both when I get back."

"Knock, knock—may I come in?"

Carla looked up from her work to see that Del Sasso had opened her office door a crack and was peering in.

She leaned back and stretched with a weary sigh. "Please do. All packed and ready to go?"

He pushed the door open and stepped just inside. "Oh, I don't take much with me. I just throw a few things together at the last minute. That's the way I've always done."

"Really? You've traveled a lot?"

"All over the world."

"I didn't know that. You haven't told me much about yourself, Antonio."

"When is there ever time around here to visit with beautiful women?" The glint in his eye startled her. "What do you want—the bare facts? I was born in Rome, grew up there, became a Jesuit—and have lectured all over the world as a special envoy for the black pope."

"The black pope?"

"That's what they call the head of the Society of Jesus, because the successor to Ignatius Loyola—that's our founder—wears a black robe like mine, while the pope wears a white one."

"How interesting. I never knew that."

Antonio looked at her closely as he had been doing ever since *that* night. He noticed her discomfort. "Have no fear," he said in a soothing voice. "I am not here to reprove you for your doubts. Every person must deal with them in his own way, and I have confidence that you will come through your present period of conflict with firm conviction."

"Well, thank you."

What he said next caught her completely off guard. "You know, Carla, Dr. Inman is right in a way about what he calls 'demons.'"

"Really?" Apparently he could read her mind after all. That thought was devastating.

"Psychic development has its pitfalls," continued Del Sasso. "And the psychic world is a dangerous one—as poor Inger just found out."

"It was such a tragedy!" replied Carla, wondering what he was leading up to. "She was so young—and full of life."

"I tried to warn her, but she wouldn't listen. There's a dark side, you know."

No reply was expected. *Is he warning me?*

"Never rely on someone else to save you," said Del Sasso. "That's the major misunderstanding most Christians have about Christ. You must look to the divine within yourself, not within another. Realize your own oneness with the cosmos, and then these misguided creatures Dr. Inman calls 'demons' have no power over you."

Carla found herself nodding assent, propelled by the very force of his personality, yet unable to make an audible reply. Was he telling her that her doubts about the Archons had brought on the recent frightening experiences? Was he warning her not to doubt in the future?

"There's a place for honest doubts . . . up to a point," said Del Sasso abruptly, apparently reading her mind again. "In the early stages of the Plan, discussion of the issues will be encouraged in order to clarify the thinking of those who sincerely seek the truth." He came closer and stood there towering over her. "Regretfully, it will eventually be necessary to eliminate all opposition. The stakes are too high to do otherwise. I don't need to tell you that Christians are, unfortunately, the chief opposition to the Plan. They'll have to be persuaded . . . or else."

"If I understand what you're saying, Antonio," said Carla, "then I think you may be overlooking something. There are millions of Christians—people like Ken Inman—who would rather die than deny their Lord. Do you really mean they'll have to be *eliminated*?"

"There's no other choice. It's not because the Archons are opposed to religion, which they're not. But narrow-minded dogmas have to go in order to make way for a much more appropriate religion broad enough for the entire world to embrace."

Del Sasso spoke the words without animosity, much like a doctor dictating a prescription. "The new world religion will be ecumenical, embracing all creeds—except, of course, those that claim to be exclusively true. There are millions of Christians who pose no problem, who understand that Christ, regardless of what the Bible says, never claimed to be the only way, but representative of all ways. They will fit into the New Order without any problems. As for the narrow-minded fundamentalists, however—whether Christians or Moslems or Jews, or whatever religion—if they don't voluntarily give up their obstructive, negative dogmas, then of course other measures will have to be taken. At stake is worldwide peace. Narrow sectarian beliefs can't be allowed to stand in the way."

He started to leave, but turned to pause a moment in the doorway. "I wanted to warn you before I leave for the East. Never trust any beings, no matter how highly evolved they may seem to be. Some of the most enlightened have chosen to use the dark side of the Force. They can be very destructive. And if you allow them to frighten you, then you're in their power."

So he did know! Carla fought to control a rising panic. She heard herself saying, "Thank you, Antonio. I appreciate this very much. It explains some things I've been wondering about."

"I'm aware of your questions and doubts. It would be a tragedy not to resolve them in the right direction." His eyes seemed to pierce into her very soul as he held her with his intense gaze. Then he turned and left, closing the door noiselessly behind him.

the
MIND
INVADERS
33

Outwitted!

T he next few days passed quickly and uneventfully. Absorbed in getting her new secretary oriented and catching up on back phone calls, Carla had little time to devote to long-standing doubts and conflicts. They had only been put aside temporarily, however—not silenced. Disappointingly, Ken had been of little help lately in sorting them out. He seemed, in fact, to be avoiding her. On the few occasions their schedules had brought them into contact over breakfast or a late-night cup of tea, he had been uncharacteristically reluctant to carry on their discussions of the past. She couldn't understand that. Did it mean that he'd given up on her? A few days ago that would have pleased her, but now it bothered her greatly. She felt neglected.

The research center seemed empty without Frank and Antonio, and Carla realized that she had a greater affection for both of them than she had been willing to admit. They had impacted her life in many ways, and she felt a real sense of camaraderie in sharing with them the mutual goal of bringing peace to a world that teetered on the brink of disaster. Whether Project Archon would actually turn out to be the answer or not, it was a noble venture. She felt a strong commitment to work together with them to see the Plan through to a successful conclusion, if that were at all possible.

During this time she had seen little of Viktor. He seemed to be working day and night with Kay, and Carla wondered how they were getting along. She had intended to ask him that at lunch that day, but Viktor had not appeared. It was now nearly 2:00 P.M., and still no sign of Viktor in his office across the hall from hers. She pushed back from her computer, stood up and stretched, and decided to check on their progress.

There were three lab assistants—two men she knew and a young woman she had never met—working in the main lab when she walked in. Kay and Viktor were nowhere to be seen. "Do you have any idea where I might find Dr. Khorev?" Carla asked.

"He left here a while ago with Dr. Morris," said the young woman. "By the way, I'm Anne White. I've seen quite a bit of you, but I don't think we've ever met."

"How nice to meet you," said Carla. She gave Anne a slight nod and a knowing look to indicate that she knew who she was. "Any idea where they went?"

"I got the impression," said one of the men, "that they were having a serious disagreement. Maybe they wanted to go someplace where they could discuss it alone."

"Really? Do you have any idea what the problem was?"

"I really couldn't say. I don't think it was anything about the work in here—something personal between them, maybe."

"How long ago did they leave?" asked Carla.

"About ten minutes ago, wouldn't you say?" said the young man, turning to Anne for confirmation. She nodded. "About that, I'd guess."

"Well, they certainly didn't go to Viktor's office," said Carla half to herself. She picked up a nearby phone and dialed Kay's office, then Frank's, then Viktor's just to be certain. Secretaries at each place said they hadn't seen either of them all afternoon. She dialed the staff lounge, but they weren't there—then Viktor's apartment, but there was no answer. Carla was beginning to feel apprehensive.

"Well, they can't just disappear, can they," she said aloud to no one in particular, trying to sound nonchalant. "I wanted to talk to them about something that really can't wait. Maybe they're back in Viktor's apartment and just aren't answering the phone. I'll take a look over there."

Frank had apparently not been denied anything he'd wanted in constructing the secret complex. Behind the main structure was a set of six luxury apartments in a long, two-story brick building. One apartment was reserved for the director of the CIA, who had not appeared since Carla had been there, but who, she understood, had used it frequently in the past. Frank used another of the apartments, as did Mike Bradford, the head of security. Viktor, of course, who was kept on the base continuously for his protection, had his own apartment, which Carla had visited a couple of times.

Approaching the building, she could see that the door to Viktor's apartment—number 5, in the middle on the upper level—was half-open. As she climbed the stairs, Carla smiled to herself. That was just like Viktor. He was a bit prudish and would never have a woman in his apartment without having the door ajar, so maybe that was a sign that he and Kay were in there after all. If so, it was odd that he hadn't answered the phone. That wasn't like him.

When she reached the top of the stairs, she heard subdued but angry voices coming from within. Peering cautiously inside the half-open door she could now hear them plainly, but she couldn't make out the words. Then it hit her like a freight train: They were conversing in their native tongue! So Viktor had been right. She *was* Russian! Had he confronted Kay in the lab, and then taken her up here to have it out?

Carla cautiously pushed the door open a bit wider and slipped quietly into the entry hall. From there she could see part of the living room and kitchen. The voices were coming from farther within. Taking the gun from her purse and releasing the safety, she moved quickly through the living room. Beyond it she very cautiously entered a long hall, holding the gun ready. The voices were coming through an open door on the right, which she remembered was a large study. Sliding along the wall, she crept closer.

Now she could see Viktor, sitting at the far end of the room in front of the fireplace, his right profile toward her. He was speaking Russian rapidly and his tone was clearly angry and accusatory. Another step nearer, peering carefully through the open doorway, and she saw Kay facing him, looking surprisingly composed. In fact she seemed to be enjoying herself. *What do I do now? Just walk in?*

302 • DAVE HUNT

Wait? Or should I go back and get security? In the next moment
Carla's heart froze in her chest as that decision was taken from her.
Kay's eyes had wandered over and seen her!

With her heart beating wildly now, Carla stepped quickly into
the room and pointed the .38 revolver at Kay. There was nothing
else to do now that she had been discovered. What followed astonished her completely. Kay jumped to her feet and greeted her with
apparent relief.

"Carla! Am I glad to see you. You got here just in time!"

Viktor's reaction surprised her even more. "Carla! How did you
get in here?" he demanded with evident displeasure.

Kay started toward her. "Hold it right there!" commanded
Carla, aiming the weapon at her head to let her know that she
meant business. "Not another inch!"

"Why are you pointing that gun at *me*?" demanded Kay with a
puzzled look and hurt tone. "I thought you'd come in to arrest *him*!
You have, haven't you?" She looked at Viktor accusingly. "I've just
blown his cover."

"Wait a minute!" hissed Viktor. "*My* cover? You think you'll get
away with that?"

"You are a smooth one, aren't you," Kay said, turning toward
Viktor and staring at him contemptuously. Then she added to
Carla, "That's the kind it takes to make a double agent. He's a
plant—and a good one!"

"She's lying!" said Viktor angrily. "You don't believe her,
Carla—do you?"

"I sure hope she's lying!" said Carla. She turned to Kay. "I
heard you speaking *Russian*. Explain that!"

Kay laughed nervously. "So that's what has you confused. Of
course I speak Russian. My parents were immigrants. We spoke it
at home when I grew up. That's one of the reasons the CIA put me
in here."

"The CIA?" asked Carla in surprise.

"Even Frank didn't know," said Kay. "No one but the director
of Central Intelligence himself knows who I am and why I'm
here—to spot Russian infiltration of this operation. Viktor almost
fooled me."

"Wait a minute!" interrupted Carla. "I happened to have been there when he escaped from Colonel Chernov—the same one who came in here to take Viktor back to Russia."

"That's right," cut in Kay. "*To take him back to Russia.* He wasn't going to kill Viktor along with the rest of us. You innocently became part of a staged 'defection' in Paris that gave Khorev the perfect cover—until I got onto his game. He threatened to kill me just before you came through that door!"

"Carla, this monster is lying through her teeth," said Viktor. "I knew I'd seen her somewhere, and finally remembered. She's Chernov's lover!"

"Viktor!" exclaimed Carla. "You expect me to believe something that incredible?"

Viktor stood to his feet and took a step toward Carla. "Hold it!" she commanded, pointing the gun at his head. "Stay back!"

"Listen to me, Carla!" he pleaded. "I've seen her picture on Chernov's desk! She's changed her appearance. That's why it took me so long to realize who she was. But she admitted it."

Kay was now livid. "Khorev, you lying snake, you're going to the chair!" She turned to Carla again. "Look, we don't have to stand here and listen to this garbage. There's a phone over there. Pick it up and get the DCI. He'll tell you who I am. I'll give you the number that goes right into his private office at the headquarters in Langley, Virginia. I just talked to him there not more than 30 minutes ago—just before this Russian plant and I came up here to have our confrontation."

She's got to be lying, thought Carla. *I know Viktor. He's no plant! But what if he is? I can't trust either of them!*

"I'm not calling Langley," announced Carla. "I'm going to get security up here to arrest both of you and then we'll sort it out from there."

"Now you're making sense," said Kay. "Just get him into custody—that's all I want. And then we'll find out who's lying."

"Shut up, both of you!" commanded Carla. To her surprise, she noticed that Viktor now looked worried. "If it's going to be my word against hers," he said, "I don't stand a chance. You know that, Carla."

"I said to shut up!" responded Carla. "I don't know who's telling the truth. So get this: I'll shoot either of you if you make a move! Stay right where you are." She walked sideways over to the phone sitting on a table at the end of the sofa just to Kay's left. She picked up the phone, with her left hand, holding the gun in her right and keeping it pointed at Kay. When she heard the tone, she put the receiver down and began to push the buttons with her left hand. To do so, she had to turn her eyes momentarily down to the phone and the gun wavered slightly off target. That was all the opening Kay needed.

"Look out!" Viktor yelled, but the warning came too late. Before Carla could react, Kay had covered the distance between them in one leap, and a flying foot had knocked the gun from her hand. In another blur of motion, so fast that Carla was hardly aware it was happening, the same foot swept both of Carla's feet from under her. And in the next instant Kay was standing over her with the gun in her hand pointed at Carla's head.

"Get up, Ms. Bertelli." Kay's voice was like steel. Carla struggled to her feet. "Now, over in that chair where I was sitting!" She waved the gun. "Khorev, sit back down again." There was nothing to do but follow orders.

"You won't believe this," gloated Kay, "but Moscow ordered me to get out of here and come home a week ago. I wouldn't do it. Nothing was going to rob me of my revenge. But I never dreamed it would be handed to me on a silver platter! You really surprised me, Carla. I had no idea you carried a gun—and that's just perfect!"

"Were you really Chernov's lover?" asked Carla.

"That's why I'm going to enjoy this so much!"

"But your New York accent?"

"That's where I grew up, stupid. My father was with the Soviet delegation at the UN. But that's enough! I don't have any more time."

"You sure don't," said Carla. "You're cover's blown, lady. This room's bugged—everything's being recorded. Whatever you do with us, you won't get away with it!"

A derisive smile formed on Kay's lips. "You're right. And I know where all of that equipment is, so you won't have the satisfaction of thinking that I'll be caught."

She moved over and stood behind Carla. "It's going to be a very obvious murder-suicide. You're in love with each other, aren't you? I've known that for a long time. You've been having an affair, quarreled, and you killed him, Carla. Then you turned the gun on yourself. With all the mental illness and suicides attributed to the Archons, you'll just be two more tragic casualties in the quest for godhood."

She shoved Carla to one side in her chair and knelt down behind her to aim at Viktor, who closed his eyes in anticipation. "I have to get the angles just right."

A shot rang out from the hallway. Viktor dove for cover behind his chair. Carla was suddenly aware of Kay's head, so near her own, jerking violently and turning red as Kay was knocked to the floor with the bullet's impact.

As though in a dream, Carla turned to see Anne White racing through the door toward her, gun in hand, pointed at the now motionless body of Kay. She stood over her for a moment, then put the gun back into her purse.

"That was close!" Anne said in relief. Viktor was picking himself up from the floor. "Are you alright?" she asked Carla.

Carla nodded weakly. The horrible reality of the last few minutes was just beginning to hit her. "I can't thank you enough!" She closed her eyes. *It could be me and Viktor lying on the floor instead of Kay!* She felt an arm around her and looked up into Viktor's face. He was trembling—like she was. "I'm sorry!" she said. "So sorry!"

"Please!" said Viktor. "She was a good liar. You had to be sure."

"I didn't want to kill her," said Anne matter-of-factly, "but I had no choice. I couldn't take a chance that she'd shoot you if I told her to drop her gun."

"You followed me?" asked Carla weakly.

Anne shook her head. "No, not immediately. But the more I thought about you coming over here, the more worried I became. So I prayed, 'God, please show me what to do.' Thank God that I got here just in time!"

"Thank God, you did!" said Carla.

"She was a member of Chernov's psychic combat troops," explained Viktor. "She admitted to me that she killed the guards and let Chernov in."

"Both of you will be material witnesses," said Anne. "Now let's vacate this apartment—and be careful not to disturb anything in this room on your way out. I'll just use your phone in the kitchen for a minute, Viktor."

A Hoax?

An hour later, when Carla picked up her office phone, it was an extremely excited Leighton who was on the other end.

"You won't believe what's been going on back here in Washington!" he bubbled. "I want you to get Kay and Viktor, and the three of you go into my office where I can talk to you all at once on the speaker. I'll call back in ten minutes."

"I've been trying to reach you, Frank. Kay, uh—she isn't here any more. She's . . . dead."

"What?" exclaimed Frank.

"It *was* an inside job, Frank, and Kay was the one who killed the guards and let the Russians in."

"I don't believe it! And you say she's *dead?*"

"An FBI agent shot her just in time. She was about to kill me and Viktor. She was trained by Chernov—she was his lover. It happened in Viktor's apartment."

"Chernov's *lover?*" There was an anguished silence, then the choked response. "I can't believe it. She was just as excited about the Plan and just as dedicated as any of us. I was very fond of Kay. We were very close. I—I don't understand. How could she deceive me so completely?"

There was a long silence. "Frank, are you there?"

"Why didn't the Archons tell us about her?" he asked at last.

"They told us it was a mystery we had to solve ourselves for our spiritual growth—remember?"

"I remember. But to think it was Kay—one of the inner circle, a higher initiate! I cared a lot for her, Carla, and I was sure she felt the same about me. We had such rapport. How could I be so stupid?"

"I wonder how much she passed on to Moscow?" asked Carla.

"We've got to assume she passed it all along. The Russians know everything! I don't think that will hurt us, but it's a good thing the Plan is going into effect soon. I just can't believe it!"

"I'm sorry, Frank. It was a great shock to me, too. Should I get Viktor and come into your office?"

"I don't have the heart to talk about it now. We're coming back tomorrow. We'll just wait until then."

Carla called Viktor's office on the intercom to tell him of her conversation with Leighton. His secretary answered. "He's not here," she said. "He may still be back at his apartment. An FBI agent came in here about an hour ago and said that a Mr. Jordan wanted to see him over there."

"Thanks," said Carla. She hung up the phone just as Viktor walked through the door of her office.

"So you've already had your session with the FBI," said Carla. "I wish they'd get to me. I don't feel like hanging around here any longer. It's impossible to do anything productive after what we've been through."

"They want to talk to you now," said Viktor. "Jordan asked me to come and get you. Did you ever reach Frank?"

"I did. He took it very hard. He was involved with Kay, and I guess she let him think she cared for him."

"She was incredible." Viktor shook his head in disbelief.

"Viktor, I can't tell you how sorry I am. She had me so confused. I could have shot you!"

"Please. I don't even want to think about it!"

"It's boggling!" sighed Carla. "This is a world of spies and international intrigue I've read about but was never sure how much was fact or fiction. And to suddenly find myself part of it!"

"The FSB makes its own rules," said Viktor bitterly. "Evil becomes good and might is right." He hesitated for a moment, and then plunged on as though there was something he'd been holding back and had to express. "And I have a terrible feeling that whatever the Archons represent operates exactly the same way. I don't like it, Carla."

She put a finger to her lips and shook her head. "We've both had our doubts from time to time," said Carla quickly, "but that's only natural with something of this magnitude—and especially something that's so revolutionary. Nothing like it has ever happened in the history of the world. And I understand your resentment that we have to take orders from the Archons, but after all, it's *their* Plan. The whole world is going to be grateful to them—and us—someday. That's what keeps me going." She stood wearily. "Well, you said the FBI wanted to talk to me—I suppose to get my version of this nightmare. So why don't you lead me to them."

When they were outside, Carla scolded Viktor, "Have you forgotten? Our offices have ears! You can't talk like that in there!"

"I don't know whether I care anymore," said Viktor angrily. "I'm beginning to feel like I'm back in the Soviet Union of the past—or maybe that I've landed in something far worse. I'm confined to this prison, can't even go outside, and the Archons dictate our every move—and soon our thoughts!"

"But if the Archons are who they claim to be," insisted Carla, "well, I mean, they're so far beyond us, it only makes sense that we should take orders from them."

They had stopped to talk and were standing now between the main structure and the apartment building. Viktor leaned close to Carla and whispered, "Suppose there are no Archons. Suppose the whole Archon thing is a hoax."

"You can't believe that, Viktor!"

"I've been tormented day and night trying to fit the pieces together, and here's what I've come up with. There's no doubt that Antonio has inconceivable powers—beyond imagination, really. In all my years of psychic research, I never even dreamed of anything close to what he can do."

Carla could see Jordan standing on the landing in front of Viktor's apartment watching them. She waved at him and he waved back. "Jordan's waiting for us," she said. "We could discuss this later."

He held her by the arm and continued to talk rapidly. She had never seen him so agitated. "I've got to share this with you—now. Listen! Antonio has all the power he needs to take over the world. Nobody could stop him. But billions of people would resent what he'd done and there would be no end of rebellion. So he pretends the Archons are directing him. Instead of doing it himself and arousing resentment, he gets installed as world ruler by this group of 'highly evolved extraterrestrial intelligences who have been guiding our evolution.' It's an ingenious idea. Of course, Del Sasso, like everyone else, must follow *their* orders—and that makes him not the villain but the hero. The idea of 'highly evolved intelligences from another dimension' has enough romance and science-fiction appeal so that everyone would want to go along with it or be afraid not to—at least until he's so fully established that rebellion just wouldn't be possible." Viktor ran out of breath.

Carla's head was spinning. "Are you serious? I never would have dreamed it, but then—" She could hear the voice of George on the telephone again, and suddenly pieces began to fall into place. "Do you think there might be an elite group within the CIA conspiring with Del Sasso on this?" she asked.

"That's possible. I haven't tried to think of such details. I've been haunted by this nightmare ever since Inger's death. I think Del Sasso drove her to suicide!"

"I never told you that he almost killed me."

"When? How?"

"Well, maybe it wasn't really him, but there had to be a connection. A figure that looked exactly like him, hooded robe and all, came right into my bedroom when I was asleep and tried to strangle me!"

"That sounds like his psychic double! Why did you come back here after that? And why didn't you tell me sooner?" Viktor was clearly upset.

"I didn't want to abandon you, but I didn't know what to say. The whole thing has been very confusing. I've wanted to talk about it, but there never seems to be the right time."

"Well—how did you escape from Del Sasso?" asked Viktor earnestly.

"I can't talk about it."

"Carla, it's only you and me—just like in Paris. Only it isn't Chernov who's after us now. We're up against something much bigger. I don't even know who our enemies might be anymore. It could be anybody! We have to stick together and share what we know."

Carla spoke reluctantly. "Someone rescued me. He'd have to explain how he did it."

"Was it Dr. Inman?"

She nodded. "I'd like to get his reaction to your theory."

"So would I," said Viktor. "He invented the Psitron, but he's one of the few I would trust. I'd like to know what he thinks—why Del Sasso is the only one who's been successfully trained on it. We've lost six."

"Seven," corrected Carla. "Ken was the first, and the Archons almost killed him—remember?"

"It wasn't the Archons—it was Del Sasso."

"But he wasn't even in the picture at that time."

"I think he was, but no one knew it—except Frank. They've got to be in this together. They both work for the CIA, and I don't see any difference now between that and the KGB or its successor, the FSB."

"But how could Del Sasso control Ken's mind then, if Ken has complete power over him now?"

"He can't stand up to Del Sasso's power!" responded Viktor.

"I'm certain that he can, and that has me confused."

"You mean at the lab? Del Sasso explained that."

"I've seen other evidence since then that I really need to share with you. But I can't do it without Ken present to give his own explanation."

Carla thought for a moment. "There's got to be some way to get you out of here to meet with Ken, and I think I know how. Come on. Don't ask me how I know, but Jordan is someone you can trust as well." They continued the rest of the short walk. At the bottom of the stairs, Carla stopped and called up to Jordan, "Can we ask you a question down here?" He nodded and came down the steps two at a time.

She motioned to Jordan, and the three of them withdrew from the swarms of security men and FBI agents around Viktor's apartment. "Don, Viktor has something that I think you ought to hear. He can't tell you inside of this complex, because Ken has to hear it too. We need his opinion. It's really important. Is there some way you could get Viktor out of this prison long enough to discuss this with Ken—like this evening?"

Jordan thought for a moment. "Yeah," he said. "That can be arranged. He's a material witness and I simply need to bring him into my office for some more questioning. I'll take him in my car. I was heading back there as soon as I'd gotten your statement anyway."

"Terrific!" said Carla. "I'd feel more comfortable about saying certain things if you took my statement in your office as well. Is that okay?"

"That's fine. In fact, I was going to suggest it."

"Okay. I'll follow you and Viktor. How long do you think you'll want to spend with me?"

"Half an hour, maybe a little more."

"Good. One more thing. Viktor has seen nothing but the inside of this sterile installation ever since he arrived in the United States. When you're done with me, instead of having the discussion with Ken in your office, how about a nice restaurant? Just a little favor for a man who had such high hopes when he defected?"

"I see no problem," said Jordan. "Where do you suggest?"

"How about the Old Wharf Fish House? It's 4:30 now, so let's make it 7 o'clock. Okay?"

"That's fine. Let me clear up a few things here, and Viktor and I will be waiting in my car by the gate in 15 minutes."

"I'll phone Ken from my office and make sure he can meet us," added Carla, with obvious relief.

Back in her office, she gathered a few papers into her briefcase, then called Ken's company. A polite female voice answered. "Sensitronics International. May I help you?"

"Yes, I'd like to speak to Dr. Inman."

"Just a moment, please." There was a pause as the switchboard connected her with Ken's secretary.

"Dr. Inman's office."

"This is Carla Bertelli. Is Ken available? It's rather urgent."

"Just a moment, Ms. Bertelli."

Ken's voice came on the line. "Carla! Are you okay?"

"I'm fine. Ken, is your evening clear?"

"It can be. What's up?"

"Oh, I just thought it would be nice to get together with you for dinner at the Old Wharf Fish House . . . say about 7:00?"

There was a pause on the other end. "You're not pulling my leg?"

"No, I'm not. Something awful has happened out here, and I really need some diversion to take my mind off of it. It would be very nice, Ken."

"I think it would be fabulous. Shall I have my secretary get reservations?"

"Please. Make it for four."

"For four?"

"Yeah. There are a couple of people you absolutely *must* meet."

A Rival Plan

Ken was at the restaurant when Carla arrived. While they waited for Jordan and Viktor, she filled Ken in on what had happened—who Kay Morris was and the close call she and Viktor had had that afternoon and how they'd been rescued in the nick of time by an FBI agent named Anne White.

"I know her very well," said Ken. "We've dated a few times."

"Really? She's quite attractive," said Carla.

"A very nice person. You'd like her," said Ken. "Her real name is Anne Bartkowski, but she goes by 'White' on special assignments like that."

"How do you know her and Don Jordan?"

"They both attend the same Thursday night prayer meeting that my mother and I go to . . . the one that's held in Dr. Harold Elliott's house. I'm sure you remember him."

"How could I forget?" said Carla with a frown. "Well, I must say, you certainly have an interesting group of 'Christian friends'—and you sure seem to look out for one another."

Viktor and Jordan arrived at that point, and they were seated immediately at their table. As they were looking over the menu, Carla remembered something she'd forgotten to tell Jordan. "Don, you know Anne White got my gun," she said. "I suppose it's part of the evidence, but I wanted to be sure you knew what happened to it. And I'd rather not have another one. Thanks just the same!"

"You did your job, so we'll let you go into early retirement," said Jordan. "Anne told me all about it. She said that you and Viktor handled yourselves well."

"That was kind of her to say, and it's true of Viktor—but I was completely outclassed. I needed not just a gun but a tank against Kay. I've never seen anything like it. And Anne—she was fabulous. She sure knew what she was doing. She saved our lives—just in time."

"She's one of the best," said Jordan. "She's our 'Annie Oakley.' Well, what's everybody having?"

"I'm going to take the combo," said Carla, "and that's what you've got to have, too, Viktor." She leaned over and pointed to that selection on the menu. "You've never had anything like this in Moscow, being so far from the ocean. That's why I wanted us to come here. It's a combination plate: chinook salmon from Alaska, the world's best lobster from the Caribbean, and giant prawns from the Gulf of Mexico—everything flown in fresh, and the prawns are in the most delicious batter you've ever tasted. It's fabulous! How about it?"

Viktor, who had never even imagined such a scene, had spent as much time looking around the restaurant as he had going over the menu. "It sounds amazing," he said. "If you recommend it—"

"You won't regret it," said Jordan enthusiastically. "I'm going to have the same thing."

"And so will I," added Ken.

"Well, that makes it unanimous," laughed Carla. After they had ordered, she wasted no time. "Before we get down to business, I just want to ask Don whether the FBI can't persuade the CIA to let Viktor see what it's like in the outside world at least once in a while. I know the experience this evening is going to do him a lot of good, and I don't see how he can be in such big danger anymore. Right?"

"It's still unpredictable at the Kremlin," replied Don. "I think they really want peace—for their own reasons, of course. And the Russian president seems to be getting along well with our president. If the Russian president can survive another year or so without a military coup."

"Do you think Kay Morris was telling the truth when she said she'd been called back to Moscow and refused to go in order to get revenge on me and Carla?" asked Viktor.

"From all the information we have, I think that's true. But there could be other renegade agents out there. If I were you, Viktor, I'd undergo a complete change in identity. This is a big country. You could drop out of sight very easily—at least until you're no longer of any importance to the Russians."

Viktor looked somber. "That's not possible before the Congress. My identity is what makes me valuable to Leighton, and he says it's essential that I give the keynote address."

"Then I'd ask the CIA to take care of it immediately after the Congress, when your present identity has served its purpose. And in the meantime, I wouldn't leave that fortress. I've got four men in here guarding you right now. This is a pretty expensive meal for Uncle Sam."

"You're kidding!" said Carla, looking around the room. "I didn't realize that would be necessary, but I think it's going to be worth it. Viktor desperately wanted to discuss some ideas he has with Ken—and, as you know, Ken is *persona non grata* out there. So this was the only way." She turned to Viktor. "Why don't you explain what you told me this afternoon."

"I was enthusiastic when I first came here," began Viktor. "Seeing Del Sasso's powers changed my whole thinking. And the Plan held out such hope for rescuing planet Earth. But I became uncomfortable at the way the Archons dictate everything. Their word is law and has to be obeyed or else—just like the oppressive Marxist society I grew up in. I noticed that everything the Archons did increased Del Sasso's importance and power. He's the key to the whole thing. Each day a 'transmission' comes from the Archons through Del Sasso telling us what to do. But there's no way to prove whether the Archons are really speaking through Del Sasso, or whether he's just putting on an act. That began to trouble me."

Viktor was trying to eat as he talked. He had obviously never seen a lobster and didn't know which end to go after. "Who's winning the battle over there," Carla kidded him, "you or the sea monster?"

Not willing to admit defeat to a crustacean, he said, "I think I'm going to come out on top," and went back to attacking a claw.

"Here, let me show you," said Ken with a laugh.

"Mmm! Really delicious!" said Viktor. When he'd gotten some good chunks of the succulent white meat, he continued earnestly. "The Plan promises that Del Sasso is only the first. There will be billions just like him who can use this psychic power for the good of mankind. Yet, so far, we haven't been able to produce even *one*. We've had six psychics in succession training on the Psitron and every one of them has met disaster. Five began acting strangely, lost touch with reality, and two of them are still in a psychiatric hospital. The last one—that's Inger—apparently hung herself."

"We haven't resolved that," interjected Don. "It's a very strange case."

"Anyway, the point is," continued Carla, "anyone who seems to be developing powers that could pose any kind of challenge to Del Sasso gets eliminated one way or another."

"Even communism sounds good on paper, but the paradise it promises never quite materializes," said Viktor. "It's like that with the Archons. They promise peace, love, and brotherhood, but all we've gotten so far has been violence and death. To put it bluntly, I think the whole Archon thing could be a hoax, and the Plan is simply Del Sasso's clever means of taking over the world. I suspect Frank's an accomplice, but maybe he's been fooled like the rest of us."

Carla turned to Ken. "Well, what do you think?"

"You know where I'm coming from. Viktor doesn't, so let me explain a bit. The Bible says that an evil man called the Antichrist is going to take over the world."

"You mean 'Mr. 666,'" said Viktor. "So you believe that?"

"Yeah, I do. There've been a few good candidates in the past. Hitler came awfully close. It can only happen when God allows it, and the Antichrist will probably be an incarnation of Satan, who's also known as the serpent. Whether the Archons' Plan is the way it will happen, I don't know. Powerful as Del Sasso is—at least at this point—I doubt that he's the Antichrist. But he certainly has some of the qualifications."

318 • *DAVE HUNT*

"Such as?" asked Carla.

"Second Thessalonians 2:9,10 and Revelation 13:4 explain that he manifests *all the power of Satan* in 'signs and lying wonders and with all deceivableness.' That certainly fits Del Sasso—and being born in Rome doesn't hurt. But I think the Antichrist will also have a powerful political base to start from, so it's a toss-up at this point."

"Is this Del Sasso really that great?" asked Jordan.

"Incredible!" said Carla. "His psychic powers are comparable to anything the New Testament says about Jesus. I haven't seen him raise the dead, but I wouldn't doubt that he could. Not only that, but he's got irresistible powers of persuasion—charisma like you couldn't believe. He's certainly qualified to head up the Plan—which, by the way, I think is ingenious and really does offer genuine hope for the world. It makes good sense. Frankly, I still hope it works."

Ken gave her a disappointed look, then turned back to Viktor. "Whatever else comes through the transmissions, or whether Del Sasso fakes it at times, I don't know because I've never been present. But from what little I've heard, I don't think it's Del Sasso's Plan. It's the Archons'—and they're demons!"

Ken noticed Viktor's cynical smile. "I was as much a skeptic as you are, Viktor—probably more so. You're asking my opinion, and I have to give you at least some of the reasons why I hold it, or it would make even less sense."

"I'm not objecting," replied Viktor. "I want to know exactly what you really believe."

"Okay," said Ken. "Del Sasso may very well hope to become the world ruler. And with his perverted theology, he may even feel that being the Antichrist would be a great honor. That could explain why he has probably eliminated anyone who seemed to be developing powers comparable to his. But the Archons really exist. You must know that the history of the occult is filled with references to them—though they're most often called 'the Nine,' as they first identified themselves to me."

Viktor nodded. "So Del Sasso didn't pull something out of the air. He pretended to be in touch with traditional entities that occultists and psychics at least are familiar with. That gives the Plan a certain legitimacy. Maybe there are such entities. I don't dispute that. In fact, it was the conviction that nonphysical entities were behind psychic phenomena—and the desire to pursue that possibility in my research—that caused me to defect to the West."

"Then what are you saying?" demanded Carla. "I thought you suggested they didn't exist."

"I mean they don't exist *as Del Sasso represents them*. I don't know who or what they really are, but I think he's made them into something else for his own ends."

Ken reached into an inside pocket of his jacket and pulled out a small black book. He held it up for Viktor to see. "These were rare in the Soviet Union. With the new so-called-freedom they're readily available, but you may never have seen one."

"What is it?" asked Viktor.

"A New Testament—part of the Bible."

"You're right. It's unfamiliar to me."

"Let me just read a few verses from it." Ken glanced over at Carla. Her look of anticipation pleased him. "Believe it or not, the Archons were mentioned in here 1900 years ago," he added. Carla looked surprised.

"A Jewish religious leader named Saul, who hated Christians and had them put in prison and killed, claimed that Jesus Christ, resurrected from the dead, came to him, and converted him. That seems to be the only logical explanation for Saul suddenly becoming a Christian. He became known as the Apostle Paul, and faced prison and death himself. I'm reading from a letter he wrote to the church at that time in Ephesus—a town that's in modern Turkey today: 'Finally then, find your strength in the Lord, in his mighty power. Put on all the armour which God provides, so that you may be able to stand firm against the devices of the devil. For our fight is not against human foes, but against cosmic powers, against the authorities and potentates of this dark world, against the superhuman forces of evil in the heavens. Therefore, take up God's armour; then you will be able to stand your ground when things are at their worst, to complete every task and still to stand.'"

Viktor seemed unimpressed. "So what does it mean?"

"The word 'authorities' in this English translation comes from the word 'Archons' in the original Greek in which Paul wrote it. When I saw that one evening while I was reading this Scripture, it nearly knocked me out of my chair."

"I knew it was a Greek word," declared Viktor. "But I never knew the Bible was originally written in Greek—like those messages we got in my lab back in the Russia!" He was giving Ken his undivided attention now.

"The Archons, as you probably know," continued Ken, "were the nine magistrates who ruled Athens in Paul's day. However, Paul—who claimed to be inspired by God to write this—makes it clear that he is referring to Athen's rulers only as a way of explaining that there is a similar hierarchy of demonic beings directing the forces of evil in this world. He specifically says that the battle is not against *human foes*, but against spiritual beings of great power and wickedness who are apparently under the command of what Paul himself calls the Archons, or the Nine."

Carla had been listening to Ken's explanation with obvious astonishment. "Why didn't you ever tell me that the Bible identified the *Archons*?" she demanded. "This is amazing!"

"You weren't exactly eager to hear anything from this book, remember?"

"But Del Sasso knows the Bible," persisted Viktor. "He must know that it talks about the Archons, and that only gives one more reason for him to pretend they're directing him."

"Not pretend—they *are* directing him," said Ken firmly. "You came to the conclusion that some *nonphysical entities*—not the psychic's *mind* as is popularly thought—were the source of psychic power. I'm convinced of the same thing. The Archons, or the Nine, have to be the source of his power!"

"But who says they have the Plan that comes through Del Sasso in these 'transmissions'?" insisted Viktor. "What if they don't care how this power is used, so he's pretending they're directing him so that he can monopolize it and dominate the world?"

"Then many other psychics should have gotten the same power. But you admit that Del Sasso seems to be unique. That tells me he's their chosen man for *their* purpose, not his. This thing is bigger than Del Sasso—or even the human race. There's a cosmic struggle going on between God and Satan, and mankind joined Satan's side by believing the lie that we could become gods—the very lie that is now being presented through the Plan."

"If God is so all-powerful," objected Carla, "why doesn't He just slam Satan across the mouth with the back of His hand and lock him away and be done with it?"

"May I get a word in here?" asked Don, who had been following the conversation with great interest.

"Please do!" said Ken.

"It's not a matter of raw *power*," suggested Don. "The issue is a *moral* one. *Good* and *evil* have nothing to do with *force*. Might does not make right. There's a *moral choice* that each person must make willingly. The only way that God would want to win this battle for the human heart—and indeed the only way He *can* win—is through love. He loved us so much that He became a man and died for our sins so that He could justly forgive us. Those who love God in response to His love and believe in Christ as their Savior and Lord are delivered from Satan's clutches and in the Name of Jesus Christ have complete power over Satan and his demons."

Ken leaned across the table and spoke to Carla and Viktor earnestly. "You both saw me shut down Del Sasso's power in the laboratory that day. I understand he offered another explanation, but that's a lie. You saw that I was not afraid of him. And Carla could tell you that what seemed to be Del Sasso—although it was really an Archon using his form—came right into her bedroom and was about to destroy her. But when, in the name of Jesus Christ, I commanded it and what seemed to be a huge cobra that was attacking me to get out, they immediately disappeared. Satan is consistently called 'the serpent' in the Bible."

Viktor looked at Carla questioningly, and she nodded vigorously. "That's what I mentioned to you, but I wanted you to hear Ken's explanation, since he's the one who made them vanish. I was really being choked and would have been killed if he hadn't rescued me."

"I, too, was rescued, Viktor," said Ken. "As you know, I invented the Psitron and was the first one to make contact with the Archons through using it. As a result I was *possessed* by the Nine. They tried to kill me—and would have succeeded if the surgeon who worked on me hadn't been a Christian and cast out those demons. That's who they are. So it may not be Del Sasso at all who killed Inger and drove the others insane, but rather the Archons themselves. They almost succeeded in doing me in."

"So you really did shut down Del Sasso in the lab that day," mused Viktor, only half-convinced. "That means you have a greater power. So you could take over the world. Is that what you're saying?"

"The power that I was the vehicle for that day was no more mine to use as I please than the Archons' power can be used by Del Sasso to his own ends. And neither kind is *psychic* power, Viktor. It's something altogether different. The authority I have and to which the Archons and Satan himself must yield—which is why I have no fear at all of Del Sasso—is *in the Name of Jesus Christ*. Jesus Christ conquered Satan by dying for our sins and resurrecting from the dead as proof that the penalty had been paid and that all who would receive Him as their Lord and Savior would be forgiven and would come under God's protection. That's exactly what Don just told you, but I wanted to say it again because there's no other way for you to be protected from Del Sasso and the Archons behind him."

"I don't intend to surrender my integrity to the Archons," declared Viktor angrily, "no matter who or what they represent. And I will not be Del Sasso's or Frank's—how do you say it?— *lackey*."

"That's bravely spoken, Viktor," said Don, "and I admire your courage. But remember, you're now up against the power that wiped out Chernov and his men without working up a sweat! How do you propose to defy the Archons without suffering the same fate?"

"I don't know," responded Viktor gloomily, "but I'm not going along with this new totalitarianism that's even worse than the Marxism I left behind!"

"Viktor, please!" pleaded Carla.

"You're both in grave danger," warned Ken. "You've been of value to the Plan. But if you try to oppose the Archons, and they realize that they'll never be able to get you to believe in them, they'll try to destroy you. God has a better plan. It's for all those who repent of their rebellion and believe in Jesus Christ."

Viktor thought about it for some time in silence. At last he said, "I've got my own plan. I know what I'm going to do." The discussion was obviously over.

To Save the World

It was late that night when Carla returned to Ken's house. She had gone back to the base to try to reason with Viktor—without success. Ken had waited up for her, and together they sat at the kitchen table to talk—the first time he'd been available to do that in nearly a week.

"I really like Viktor," said Ken, "but I've never seen anyone so stubborn. Did he tell you what he intends to do?"

"No. He just repeated what he said at dinner—that he has his own plan and knows exactly what he's going to do. But he wouldn't spell it out. I'm worried about him."

"And I'm concerned for both of you and praying for you. You were going to hang in there for Jordan, and that assignment was completed. I know you haven't wanted to abandon Viktor, but Carla, he's had it all laid out for him and made his choice—and he won't even tell you what it is! I don't think you're obligated to him anymore."

"I made a commitment to Frank, and I can't go back on that now. And there's a story here, Ken—the story of the century, if not of all history! And I still keep hoping that the Archons really are benevolent higher beings who put us on earth and have been watching over our evolution."

"What are we," asked Ken sarcastically, "some kind of experiment they created in a laboratory and moved to this planet? Or if we're just an evolutionary form of life that sprang up spontaneously on earth, how did they get to be the zookeepers of the universe with the right to control our destiny? Furthermore, if the Archons 'put us *here*,' then who put them *there?* And who put *them* there—*there, ad infinitum, ad absurdum?"*

"Zookeepers of the universe?" Carla leaned back and laughed. "You don't leave a person much room to waffle around in, do you, Ken? Okay, so it is absurd that they put us here, some yet 'higher' creatures put them there—*reductio ad absurdum."*

"So what do you do when something's absurd?" he demanded quickly.

"Hey, back off a bit." She held up both hands in protest. "Everything's so black-and-white with you, so simple, but I don't see it that way. I guess I'm torn at this point. There are times when I want to scream for help and run out of there as fast as I can. But at other times I sense such a genuine warmth and love surrounding Antonio. God knows we desperately need drastic solutions if planet Earth is to survive. At least the Archons, whoever or whatever they may be, offer something positive for a change—the first plan that I've heard of that makes sense."

"It doesn't make sense. It has no moral foundation, no basis for individual freedom of conscience, and thus no genuine love—and it reeks of *evil*. Viktor senses that."

"So do I at times, but not always. I guess I just *want* it to work because there seems to be no alternative."

"There's an alternative, Carla, that does make sense. And you know what I mean."

Carla traced the pattern on the tablecloth for a while with a spoon handle. Finally she said, "I see myself to a remarkable degree in Viktor. Perhaps that's why I feel so close to him. His hatred of Marxist totalitarianism, and now his fear that the Archons intend to control the entire world, is much like the way I felt about Christianity as a teenager. It seemed so restrictive, and I wanted total freedom."

"If that kind of 'freedom' existed," said Ken, "we'd all be hostage to the uninhibited actions of others, which would inevitably clash with our own. Real freedom can only exist within laws that define it. Obedience to universal laws gives us the freedom to fly airplanes or hang gliders, travel to the moon, use the energy in the atom. Listen! The incredible scientific advancement mankind has made has always been through obedience to the laws that govern the physical universe—working within them, not trying to overthrow them. There are also moral and spiritual laws that must be obeyed, and the great delusion that we can do our own thing in violation of these laws is the cause of all our ills."

No response was forthcoming so, after waiting a few moments, Ken continued. "The only real freedom is found in Jesus Christ. And the only reasons you can offer for rejecting Him all involve *people* who misrepresented Him, not Christ *Himself*. It's unfair to blame Him for what others have done in His Name. Just remember: He loves you, and He's willing to forgive all your animosity."

Carla's expression alternated between anger and amusement. "I find it amazing that I'm sitting here so calmly while you try to convert me," she responded at last with an uncomfortable laugh. "I would have stormed out of here if you'd dared to say such a thing only two weeks ago. You haven't convinced me, of course, but I'm glad we can at least talk now."

Upon his return with Del Sasso from Washington, D.C., Leighton called the entire staff into the theater to give them his report. Before doing so, he had a few words to say about Kay, but he did not mention her name, nor did he give any details of what had actually happened in Viktor's apartment. Kay's body had been hurriedly removed that night, and the CIA and FBI had put a lid of secrecy on the whole affair. Anne White had simply not come back to work the next day, and the complex had been buzzing with rumors. The two guards who were working for the FBI remained as a precaution, but even Mike, as head of security, was not aware of their true identity.

"We had for some time suspected that a traitor was in our midst," began Leighton, and Carla noted that his voice was firm. He had apparently been able to put Kay and his relationship with her completely behind him. "A murderer," continued Leighton, "who killed two guards and let the Russian attack team inside these premises. Well, that person has now been eliminated. We must now put this in the past and move on into the future, which, I am delighted to tell you, has never looked brighter. Let me give you a few details of what has just happened in Washington, D.C.

"The president is wholeheartedly with us. He gathered at Camp David a select group of ambassadors from 40 or 50 countries as well as sympathetic members of the House and the Senate. Almost his entire Cabinet was there, along with a number of high-ranking Pentagon officers. I wish you could all have been there to witness what occurred, but the media wasn't even invited. You would have been proud of Antonio Del Sasso. Before this august group he put on an incredible performance—and I do mean *incredible*.

"Of course there were skeptics," continued Leighton with a laugh, "and Antonio put them in their place with finesse. There was this senior senator from the South—the consummate skeptic. Antonio had just levitated an Army tank brought in for that purpose. He left it suspended 50 feet in the air for a full five minutes, while he lectured the audience on the peaceful uses of psychic power. Can't you just imagine the total bewilderment and consternation *that* created! Everybody was absolutely staggered—except this individual, who shall remain unnamed. He was convinced it was a trick. Some trick that would be! Then there was the Congressman who thought the whole thing was a waste of valuable time and insisted in a very pompous tone, 'I can't see that this mind power that's being demonstrated to us today has any practical and peaceful purposes.'

"Antonio was the soul of patience. The president is a trap-shooter, you know. So Antonio asked for a trap to be set up. 'Imagine those clay pigeons are missiles fired by the Russians, Americans, or any other country,' he told everyone. 'Now watch this.' As the targets came out of that trap, Antonio shattered them almost instantly one after the other." Frank was interrupted by loud applause and motioned to Del Sasso to stand up and acknowledge the acclaim of his colleagues.

"Let me tell you," Leighton concluded, "by the time we left, Antonio had them eating out of his hand. The only problem we have now is the size of this auditorium, because, believe me, everyone wants to come and participate in the Congress. I've left it to the president to invite those individuals who would be most influential in their countries. Through his support we're now assured of success!"

There was a standing ovation. After shaking hands and receiving congratulations from each person there, Leighton hurried to his office. There he gathered with his inner circle, now diminished by Kay Morris' death, to present them with further details. First of all, he turned to Viktor.

"I couldn't help noticing the expression on your face, Viktor, when I was speaking to the staff in the theater. I know it must have been a terrible experience—what you and Carla went through while we were gone. Is that it?"

"It's nothing new," said Viktor. "I've mentioned it before, and I thought I'd resolved it, but I haven't." *Watch it, Viktor!* Carla gave him a quick warning look, but he paid no attention. The words seemed to gush out as though propelled by passion. "I'm still bothered by the authoritarianism of the Archons and the similarity between the New Order they propose and the old Soviet system that I grew up with." He seemed to get control of himself and shrugged helplessly, looking apologetically from Leighton to Del Sasso. "I don't want to be the one to hold things back."

"It is *their* program," said Carla softly, but with conviction. "And they're so far beyond us that we ought to take their advice. I don't see how it could be otherwise, or what's wrong with that."

"It's not taking *advice* that concerns me," reiterated Viktor, "it's surrendering ourselves to their control."

Leighton looked uneasy. He turned to Del Sasso. "Viktor has honestly expressed his concerns about the integrity of the Archons. Is there some 'sign' we could give him that would restore his confidence?"

Antonio nodded solemnly. "I'm confident that the Archons are willing to attest to their goodwill in a manner that Viktor cannot doubt."

Quickly he assumed the yoga position and was almost immediately in deep trance. From his throat issued the voice of an elderly man. Loudly, deliberately, solemnly the voice intoned a message in a language that Carla could not identify and which apparently was unknown to everyone else in the room also—everyone, that is, except Viktor. He sat transfixed.

The voice ceased as abruptly as it had begun, and Del Sasso came slowly out of his trance. "Well?" he asked immediately.

Viktor was trembling uncontrollably. When at last he could speak, it was to stammer, "He—it—was speaking to *me* in an obscure dialect spoken only in the small Siberian village of Karkaralinsk where I used to visit my grandparents in the summer when I was a small boy." Overcome once again with emotion, he had to pause while he wiped tears from his eyes.

"It sounded exactly like my grandfather," Viktor continued at last. "The same mannerisms and phrases—like he used when he'd scold me for being afraid of the milk cow that used to bully me when I was very small. The voice said that I must not be afraid, but I must trust the Archons, for like that cow their purpose was to nourish me and all mankind."

Emotion overcame Viktor again. At last he recovered himself and continued. "I only now remembered that it was 20 years ago today that my grandfather went into the forest and never returned. No body was ever found. That is the sign the voice offered to me, but I don't know what it means."

"It is quite clear," said Del Sasso quickly. "The world, like your grandfather, is walking 'the path of no return' and must be rescued. You could not help your grandfather then, but you are in a position to help the entire world now."

Head bowed, Viktor's shoulders shook convulsively. "I'm sorry. I feel ashamed of myself for doubting."

Leighton tried to pick up the conversation again to take the embarrassing attention from Viktor. "We know that the Archons have incredible, I suppose infinite, power. If their intentions were evil, they could have finished us off long ago."

"Of course!" agreed Carla. "And I can't imagine what they would want from us anyway."

Carla was not surprised that the renewed assurance the incredible demonstration gave her didn't last long. She had been on an emotional roller coaster ever since snatching Viktor from Chernov's grasp in Paris. And lately she had begun to fear that her fluctuating emotions were in danger of getting out of control. Old doubts that she had wrestled with repeatedly came back again, now stronger than ever. She hoped, however, that Viktor had at least given up his "plan." Whatever that might be, she was sure it would bring him into dangerous confrontation with the Archons. And she knew what that could mean!

The promise Carla and Viktor had made to spend more quality time together had fallen victim to the hectic pace they were both maintaining. Carla was now granting some telephone interviews and had been to San Francisco twice for network television appear- ances. Two days after Del Sasso's remarkable performance in Leighton's office, however, she made it a point to drop in on Viktor. He was hunched over his computer and concentrating so deeply that he didn't even notice her enter his office until she was standing over his desk.

"Are those your memoirs, or are you still polishing that keynote address?" she queried lightly.

He looked up and smiled, then leaned back and stretched his cramped arms and back. "No, I was asking this machine to tell me how in the world I got from my small village in the Urals to this—this—" He searched for words, then shrugged and threw his arms out wide.

"Wishing you were back there?"

He shrugged again. "Maybe. When you think about where this world is going, you either want to close your eyes and wish for the good old days or try to do whatever you can to make it better. And I'm not sure that one is any less fantasy than the other."

"It wouldn't be hard to become a complete cynic," responded Carla sympathetically. "I feel the same way at times. Hey! Why don't we go outside for a breath of fresh air. I need a good walk to clear my head."

Once outside and away from the buildings and walking along the path just inside the wall, she said quietly to Viktor, "Well, you got your 'sign' the other day. I thought it was pretty impressive."

"It was more than impressive," admitted Viktor. "It was incredible. That *was* my grandfather's voice and his peculiar idioms and inflections!"

"I could tell from the look on your face," said Carla, "that it was genuine, though I didn't know what was being said."

"It convinced me at the time, but I realized later, of course, that it was no more a 'sign' or the proof I needed than anything else Del Sasso does. I was like putty in his hands, and that made me resolve that my decisions will be made alone, not when I'm with him and Frank or anyone else. I'm ashamed of myself—the way I broke down."

"I don't think you should feel that way at all."

"I know what I'm saying, Carla. When I thought about it afterward with a clear head, I realized that all I'd seen was another display of psychic *power*, and I had mistakenly accepted power as a sign of *truthfulness and sincerity*, which is stupid."

"You're right!" said Carla. "I thought of the same thing, but didn't want to destroy the faith it had given you. Ken has been trying to point this out to me for a long time—that *might* isn't *right* and that *power* provides no *moral* foundation. But I don't really think it's fair—at least not yet—to label Del Sasso and the Archons with this error."

Viktor stopped to gaze at that giant redwood just outside the complex that always gave him such a sense of awe. When he turned to face Carla again, his eyes had narrowed and the stern determination was back in his voice. "I risked my life to escape Marxist oppression. Yes, it still hangs on in the 'new' Russia—and it's coming back with a vengeance. Now I'm going to risk my life again to help the world escape an even worse totalitarianism. I realize that I may die in the attempt, but there is no other honorable course to take."

"Don't be a fool, Viktor! I'm terrified for you."

"I had a very good friend—my old lab assistant—who said much the same thing to me in Moscow when I told him I was going to defect," reminisced Viktor. "He was a Christian, like your friend Ken. I wonder what happened to Dmitri after I left."

"I wish I knew what you were planning to do. Is there any way I could help?"

Viktor shook his head. "You will see when the time comes."

World Congress 666

I t was June 14—a day never to be forgotten. This date, conveners of World Congress 666 were determined, would go down in history as the day of the key event that laid the foundation for a New Age of unbroken world peace and economic and ecological wholeness. They were confident also that it would always be remembered and cherished as the day that the planet was rescued from an almost certain holocaust. For residents of an area famous for its fog, it would certainly be remembered as one of the most beautiful June days in history. The unusual weather provided the dignitaries from all over the world flying into San Francisco's International Airport a crystal-clear and sweeping view—from the Pacific Ocean and Golden Gate Bridge, over Nob Hill and the skyscrapers along Market Street, across the Oakland Bay Bridge to Berkeley, and on into the Walnut Creek area, over which Mount Diablo could be seen towering in the distance like some brooding giant.

To regular commuters that Friday morning, there was nothing unusual in the number of foreigners at the San Francisco airport, many in native dress from robes to turbans. But to the discriminating eye, the *quality* was quite remarkable. One would have to go back to the April 1945 San Francisco Conference that birthed the United Nations to find a time when a comparable number of international leaders had converged upon this part of the world. And even then the comparison failed. In 1945 only about 50 nations had been represented; on this date, high-level dignitaries from more than 120 nations poured into the Bay area. From the airport, however, these international representatives did not proceed north into the metropolitan district, but south in a steady stream of limousines whose destination was a certain secluded and, until recently, unknown CIA installation in the redwoods west of Palo Alto.

Elated, yet with unresolved conflicts still stirring within, Carla paced nervously in her office awaiting the call on the intercom that would tell her it was time to join Frank and the other VIPs to formally greet their guests. Her excitement grew as she caught glimpses through the window of the limousines arriving one after another. There were diplomats from around the world, including those from many Third World and Communist countries (even China and North Korea were represented), as well as high-level officers representing the Pentagon and NATO. Among the first arrivals was a U.S. Army staff car with the flag of a four-star general flying from the front fender. After the two dozen parking places inside the complex were filled, the drivers had to drop off their fashionably attired passengers and then drive back through the gate to park outside. The guards were still there to check identities and to hand out the official packet of materials to each invitee, but the gate was now left open in honor of this great event. From this date forward it would remain perpetually open as a symbol of the new trust that would henceforth prevail among all nations.

There was, of course, a large press corps present, but because of limited seating capacity in the auditorium where the main meeting was to be held, most of them were required to wait just outside the gate. There nearly 200 congregated and had to be held back by police to prevent blockage of the narrow road in front of the entrance. About 30 representatives of the major media giants, each one handpicked by Carla, were allowed inside to mingle with the guests and to see this historic event unfold from the inside.

Promptly at 4:00 P.M. a justifiably proud and beaming Frank Leighton led his inner circle outside to stand beside him in a reception line to greet their distinguished guests, who had already been taken on guided tours through much of the facility. For this auspicious occasion Leighton was attired in a dark suit with almost indistinguishable pinstripes. On his lapel he wore a discretely designed badge identifying him as founder and director of the

Psychic Research Center. Across the top of the badge were embla-
zoned the large gold numbers: 666. In the packet given to each delegate to the congress was a similar identification badge bearing
each one's name, country, and office—and of course the same
prominent numerical designation.

To Leighton's left stood Antonio Del Sasso wearing his long, black
monk's robe, hood thrown back, smiling graciously, and projecting a
captivating charm. Next came Carla, radiantly beautiful in a full-
skirted, flowered silk dress; and finally, a pale and tense Viktor, feeling
uncomfortable in a very expensive suit that Frank had ordered tailor-
made for him. As the keynote speaker, he had to look the part.

"There's a warm and beautiful presence of love over this whole
place, isn't there?" Carla whispered to Viktor. "Haven't you felt it
growing stronger all day?"

He shook his head. "I hadn't noticed," he said in a faraway voice.

"Are you okay?" whispered Carla. He nodded and looked away.
"I'm worried about you!" Viktor's jaw stiffened, but he made no
answer.

The invited delegates filed slowly by, shaking hands, bowing,
honored to meet Leighton and thrilled to shake the hand of the
greatest psychic the world had yet known—the one who would lead
mankind into the New Age. Carla and Viktor, too, were the recip-
ients of repeated congratulations for their contribution to the success of the research center. In the euphoria of that grand moment,
she felt herself wanting to believe more than ever before that the
Plan would indeed cure the world's ills. What a day it would be for
planet Earth and its inhabitants if only that could be true!

U.S. Marines in dress uniform strolled among the guests, carrying large trays loaded with a variety of drinks and hors d'oeuvres.
Long tables holding the same fare had been set up on the expansive
lawn on the right side of the drive. There the guests mingled with
one another until at last all had arrived and gone through the formality of the reception line. Leighton then moved to a microphone
set up on a small platform.

"May I have your attention, please!" The babble of excited
voices died down. "Before we go into the auditorium to proceed
with the activities of this historic occasion, Antonio Del Sasso

would like to welcome you and say a few words about the badges you are all wearing. By the way, is anyone not wearing a badge?"

There was an anxious flurry here and there as delegates who had forgotten to put on their badges did so. In the meantime, Del Sasso stepped to the mike.

"Welcome to 'World Congress 666,'" began Del Sasso in a warm but booming voice. "You are all aware that the very name and date and substance of this gathering was decreed by higher intelligences who have been watching our progress for millennia. They have chosen to intervene at this crucial time in order to rescue us from a probable nuclear holocaust and to lay the foundation for a revolutionary new political and economic system that will usher in a New Age of peace and prosperity and freedom for all peoples.

"I'm sure you all know the name Pierre Teilhard de Chardin, the Jesuit priest rightly known as 'the father of the New Age.' You may not know that he predicted this day would dawn—the day when mankind would take a quantum leap on its journey toward the Omega point where we each realize our true godhood. This has been the hope of all religions. Yet there are certain, shall we say, 'badly-informed' fundamentalist elements among Jews, Christians, and Moslems that will not accept this great truth. Such negativism cannot any longer be allowed to hold back the development of the race. There will be specific instructions concerning this later. In the meanwhile, the destruction of the Antichrist myth, which we are together accomplishing today, is the first step along that path.

"You are each wearing—and with great pride and dignity, I trust—the number 666 on a badge, along with your name, country, and office. The significance of doing so has already been communicated to you in the literature you received with your formal invitation. Yet many of you, in coming through the reception line, had questions about this and some seemed quite confused. Indulge me, therefore, while I give a brief explanation of the monumental importance of this moment. Those of you coming from the East may not realize it, but the Western world has lived for centuries under the haunting fear of a coming Antichrist taking over this planet and requiring every inhabitant to wear the number 666 on pain of death. Your courage and conviction in identifying yourselves today with that dread number has broken that powerful taboo and has delivered the entire world, from this moment forth, from the debilitating Antichrist superstition that has enslaved so many in the past. The world can now break free from the negative ideas of sin and redemption and the demeaning delusion that man is dependent upon some mythical 'God.'

"Your brave example will be followed by men and women of goodwill everywhere, who will identify themselves with the New Order by wearing a similar badge. So I congratulate you on the role you are playing today. Let us all drink a toast to each other and to the glorious freedom from the destructive religious beliefs that have for too long strangled progress and fostered intolerance."

The applause was followed by good-natured banter and the clinking of glasses. Carla felt someone tap her on the shoulder and turned around to look into the smiling face of George Conklin. He raised his glass to touch hers, and with a wink said, "Here's to the peaceful use of psychic power!"

"Coming from you, George," she laughed as she raised her glass to touch his again, "that's the biggest compliment I've ever gotten!"

"I really mean it," he said. "Thanks for getting me inside. There's an incredible presence of love in here. I felt it the moment I came through the gate, and it's growing stronger!"

"Beautiful, George! Isn't it fantastic?"

"You know I'm not given to superlatives, but this is really uplifting. I've never felt anything like it!"

"You can't even imagine what you're going to see this afternoon!" added Carla. "You're a tough nut to crack, but believe me, you're going to be completely boggled—and converted. There won't be any doubts after today!"

She turned to touch glasses with others of different complexions, dress, and culture as the guests toasted the new era of peace each was convinced was dawning. Swept along as on the crest of a wave of overwhelming love and ecstatic optimism that had all but submerged the conflicts still stirring within her, Carla found herself touching her badge with pride. It was such an honor to shake hands with and hug and exchange sincere expressions of brotherhood and sisterhood with these men and women of world renown, each there on behalf of the scores of countries that had sent representatives. It was like getting a sneak preview of the new world soon to be realized through their joint commitment to the Plan.

She had lost sight of Viktor and wondered whether he had been similarly stirred. *Do the Archons know whatever it is that he has up his sleeve? Will it be detrimental to the Plan? If so, what will they do to stop him? Should I tell Frank that Viktor has a plan of his own? Wouldn't it be for Viktor's own good as well as for the good of the whole world?*

Carla sensed that someone was staring at her. She looked up into the eyes of Antonio Del Sasso who was now moving slowly through the crowd a few feet from her. He was smiling. She returned his smile and blew a kiss in his direction.

Frank stepped to the microphone again. "We will go inside in a few minutes and there you will all witness for yourselves the awesome capabilities that reside in Antonio Del Sasso, who is mingling among you right now to give you an opportunity to converse with him personally. As you already know from the White House report that was sent to each of you, Dr. Del Sasso has powers that no other person, dead or alive—including Krishna, Buddha, Jesus Christ, or Mohammed—has ever displayed.

"Our purpose is not to worship him. Neither is it his to solicit our worship. He is a very humble man whose only desire is to serve mankind. Antonio continually reminds me that he has been chosen by higher intelligences merely as a prototype of the millions and eventually billions of others who will, through his example and guidance, in due time develop the same godlike capabilities. This is the heart of the Plan and the only hope for a new world of peace, love, and genuine brotherhood among all peoples. Only then can we be accepted into the intergalactic community of planetary civilizations that has patiently awaited for centuries our long-overdue coming of age. What a heritage to pass on to our children and grandchildren!

"Whenever you are ready, you may begin to move to your right through the two entrances to the auditorium where you see the marine guards standing. Have your official badges prominently displayed for entrance. We'll convene in there in about 15 minutes."

◆ ◆ ◆

For more than a week, Ken had experienced a heightened concern for Carla. For that concern he had concluded that he no longer had any recourse except fervent prayer. They'd had little contact in the last few days as she daily seemed to become more and more withdrawn and uncommunicative. He'd been reluctant to try to break into her private world, sensing that he must leave her to deal with her conflicts alone. Neither prayer nor persuasion could force her to make the right decision. It would have to come willingly from her own heart. Arguments and coaxings—he'd given her more than enough of those in the past. She knew the truth, and it was now a matter of acting upon it without any further influence from him. As the day of the Congress drew near, he had agonized for her in prayer that God would leave no stone unturned in confronting her with the truth.

She had showed him her badge at breakfast on the morning of the thirteenth, making light of the large 666, and he had been appalled. "I can't find words to express my horror at this!" he'd said. "You're trifling with your eternal soul!"

"Back off, Ken," had been her instant response. "I've never seen you react like this."

"Carla—your mother, if she were still alive, would be far more shocked to think of you wearing the number 666 than by your father's unfaithfulness!"

She had put the badge back in her purse without another word and had left the table, leaving her breakfast untouched.

"Those who take that number," he had called after her as she had hurried down the hall, "will suffer 'the wrath of the Lamb'! Don't bring the just judgment of God down upon yourself, Carla, please!"

She had left the house without another word.

With an urgency verging upon despair, Ken had appealed to Hal and Karen Elliott, whom he looked up to and respected as his father and mother in the faith. "Prayer isn't going to change her mind," Hal had said. "But we can petition God to intervene and prevent this diabolical Plan from coming into being, at least for now, so that the world will have a little longer to turn to Christ." With this in mind, it had been decided that as many as could would take the day of June 14 off from work and would spend it together in prayer and fasting.

Carla and Ken met only briefly at breakfast that morning. Ken's mother had tried to get a conversation going, with little success. Ken had waited until breakfast was over to lovingly attempt once again to impress upon Carla the seriousness of what she was about to participate in. She had politely thanked him for his concern, then had hurried off to the installation, calling over her shoulder as she went out the door that this was the "big day." A few minutes later Ken and his mother had driven over to the Elliott's house for what was to be a "big day" for them as well.

It was a solemn gathering of about 20 who met together in the familiar living room. "I'm convinced that this is the greatest challenge we have ever faced as a group," said Elliott as they prepared to pray. "As you all know, this is the long-awaited day when the attempt will be made by Frank and Del Sasso to persuade delegates from around the world to turn their countries over to the Archons. I think you're all familiar with the fact that Archon is the Greek word in Ephesians for 'principalities' in the King James—the demons that Paul identified as directing the evil powers of darkness over this earth. The delegates, of course, don't realize it, but to embrace the Archons' Plan is tantamount to turning the world over to the Antichrist. They are even being persuaded to wear the number 666 in order to mock the prophecy warning against this in Revelation 13. I believe there's a great spiritual battle being waged in the heavenlies right now, and our prayers could play a significant part in its outcome.

"Of course, if this is God's time to allow Satan to take over, then our prayers will not change that. Somehow I can't believe that time has come yet. If it had, I'm convinced we would already have been raptured out of here, and that obviously hasn't happened. So let's pray in faith and bind the forces of evil in the Name of Jesus Christ from deceiving those who are at all open to the truth. Let's pray that Satan's purposes will be frustrated, that the Plan will not take shape yet, that there will be at least a little more time left for the gospel to be preached and for many more to come to Christ before it's forever too late."

"And please pray two specific things for Carla," Ken added, "that her eyes will be opened completely and she will have the courage to turn from evil to Christ, and that she will be kept in physical safety. That whole scene out there is a powder keg. Almost anything could happen. And pray the same for Viktor Khorev, the Russian, as well—and for Frank, and for the delegates from these many countries, that they will have their eyes opened also and be delivered from the lies and persuasive influence of seducing spirits."

So it was that while Frank, his team, and a vast assemblage of world leaders savored their moment of destiny out at the installation, a humble group of suppliants was kneeling in prayer that these same high hopes might not come to fruition.

While the delegates proceeded through the outside doors, Carla and the other staff members who were to be seated on the platform entered through the front lobby. Turning to their left along the corridor past Leighton's office, then to the right past the main lab where Carla and Viktor had first seen Del Sasso demonstrate his powers, they branched left again down a narrow passageway that led them onto the stage by a back entrance. Joining Leighton, Del Sasso, Viktor, and Carla in special seats on the platform behind the podium were Mike Bradford, head of security, his assistant, Leighton's personal secretary, and former Cal Tech professor Dr. Chris Burton, who had recently arrived to take over as head of the labs in place of Kay Morris.

From her place of honor on the platform, Carla watched in fascination as the representatives from more than 120 countries hurried to claim the front rows in the small 250-seat auditorium. These sophisticated personages—many of them world renowned—seemed as eager and excited as children jostling their way into a Saturday movie matinee. To think that the president of the United States had been deluged with requests from around the world from ambassadors, members of parliament, senators, and Congressmen to attend—and that thousands had been turned away for lack of space! Such an outpouring of acceptance and support at this early stage—even before the full story had been told to the world—had had a telling effect upon Carla's own thinking. In fact, it had been one of the key influences during the past two weeks in easing her doubts and renewing her commitment to the Plan.

An army of sound and electronic technicians to supplement their own staff had been brought in and could be seen at their posts throughout the auditorium on video machines and in the sound and recording booths. Then there was the rewiring that had been done to put earphones at every seat for simultaneous translation in 20 languages by the 40 translators who had been brought in, some from other countries. They were now seated in their specially constructed booths along the curving rear wall between the huge, laminated-oak beams that supported the domed roof. And behind her, looming up to the sloping ceiling from its base on the platform, was the newly installed, giant, curved television screen.

For Carla, it was awesome to see it all laid out before her now and to remember the events that had brought her to this incredible point in time. How quickly it had all developed—and now the culmination, with the eyes of the world upon them! And to think that it had all begun because she just happened to have a car in the right place at the right time in Paris to rescue Viktor Khorev, the man sitting beside her at this very moment—the man who was to give the keynote address to this august gathering. It was an honor and responsibility he surely had never anticipated when he made the crucial decision to defect! She desperately hoped it would be for him a time of vindication and honor and acceptance by the world, which he so justly deserved, and that it would bring the happiness he so evidently lacked.

Her train of thought was broken by Frank's low, whispered voice as he leaned over close to Viktor. "Are you feeling alright, Viktor?"

Viktor waved him off. "Just nerves. I'll be okay once I get to the podium." Frank seemed satisfied and went back to his seat next to Del Sasso to await the moment when he would officially convene World Congress 666.

Carla looked over at Viktor in concern. He was going through his notes, underlining key phrases with a red pen. There was no point in telling him again that she was worried, or in warning him not to do anything foolish. She had already said that too many times. She would understand "when the time comes," he had told her. Apparently that moment in history had now arrived. She was excited—and suddenly terribly afraid.

Holocaust!

L adies and gentlemen, distinguished representatives of
the world's nations, select members of the media,"
Leighton began at last, "it is a great honor and joy to welcome each of you here today to this most important occasion in the
long and too-often tragic history of our race. We are gathered just
to the south of San Francisco where, in 1945, hopeful delegates
from less than half of the nations we represent met to lay the foundation for the United Nations. Today we lay the foundation for
something far more significant—not just an organization of
nations that remain hopelessly separated by national rivalries, but
a New World Order that will make all people and all nations equal
and one. When we have proven ourselves to be united and at peace,
then we will qualify to apply for entrance into an intergalactic
community of civilizations that have evolved far beyond us and
who stand ready to share technology and supernatural powers that
will give us undreamed of access to the vast universe of space and
its limitless resources.

"We must crawl before we can walk, take baby steps before we
can run and then fly. The key to this New Age lies in the first step
we must take: qualifying for and receiving the gift of psychic power
dispensed by highly evolved intelligences who have been watching
over our evolution for thousands of years. When we first made contact with these entities more than two years ago, I selfishly

assumed that this power was for my own nation's exclusive use in an ongoing rivalry with the Russians and Chinese, who were also attempting to develop psychic warfare capabilities. I soon learned, however, that the intention of the Archons was for us to share this knowledge and power equally with the entire world.

"Here again we see another very significant difference between what we seek to accomplish today and what happened at the San Francisco Conference of 1945. Then also the United States had developed an incredible new power, but one it was afraid to share with the world. That power has been the cause of much suffering in the deadly rivalry that ensued and leaves us today in fear of a nuclear holocaust. Now, as then, it is the United States that holds the secret to an incredible new force. But this time, fortunately, it is under the control of higher beings and is to be shared with the world—not hoarded for ourselves and thereby creating a rivalry with others who would feel compelled to steal it. Indeed, equal sharing is the major condition under which this power will be dispensed. That fact alone should set every nation at ease and assure the success of this great adventure that we are privileged to launch today for all mankind. This will be, indeed, a quantum leap.

"You have all been given a draft of the agreement to be signed by all nations in the world. This Congress is not meeting to make changes in that agreement. It has been dictated by the Archons and cannot be changed. However, you will easily see that it is simple and gives no preference to one nation over another, but is designed for the mutual benefit of all. Your purpose in being here is to see a demonstration of the power that is being offered to your nation if you will join the New Order. Then you are to carry your report, together with the agreement and your recommendation, back to the leaders of your respective countries. We have 90 days in which all of the nations of the world must unite in signing the agreement, or the offer will be withdrawn. It is inconceivable that any nation would not wish to be the recipient of this power, but it must be left to individual decision. There will be no coercion, but the decision must be unanimous.

"As you will see, receiving the power entails submission to the direction of the Archons until they determine that we are well-established in the New Order and capable of carrying on by ourselves. Until there are comparable psychic leaders in each country to form a competent World Council, the Archons' orders will be relayed through Antonio Del Sasso. He is the man whom I now wish to present to you once again—first of all on the giant television screen just behind me, and then, in person, as he gives further demonstrations of these capabilities."

The applause was thunderous. The lights were dimmed. Viktor and Carla saw once again basically the same video that Leighton had showed them that first day in his office. There was, first of all, the location of oil, but now inserted in the video were statements by several geologists concerning the amazing size of the oil pool that had been verified to be underground at this seemingly unlikely site. Also added was a "transmission" from the Archons through Del Sasso promising that similar pools of oil lay in many other locations around the world—some in areas of extreme poverty— and would be disclosed according to a fair development schedule.

Next came the same sequence showing Del Sasso in the pyramid-shaped hothouse holding his hands over the young plants, then the harvesting of the huge produce. At that point the video stopped and the lights came on briefly while an assistant secretary of Agriculture for the United States displayed some of the actual produce on the stage and explained that it could be grown in depleted soil and in arid conditions without fertilizers.

"The only thing standing in the way of this bounty being available to the poorest areas of the world," he said enthusiastically, "is the training of psychics for the individual countries and localities. The sooner the world adopts the Plan, the sooner we can see the complete elimination of all famine and malnutrition. I urge you to recommend early acceptance when you return to your home countries!"

The video resumed with some shots inside Viktor's laboratory north of Moscow and showed him at the central controls. But the horror of Yakov's death had been cut out. Finally, there was an astonishing montage of brief scenes in rapid succession around the world: Russian leaders in a series of secret meetings inside the Kremlin, similar secret meetings of Chinese leaders, generals and their aides conferring in an emergency meeting at NATO head-quarters, the president's Cabinet meeting in closed session in the White House, drug czars meeting secretly in Colombia, a top-level Mafia conclave in Sicily, the pope in private prayer in his chambers, and officers conferring over a map on the bridge of a Russian SS-18 Typhoon nuclear submarine under the polar ice-cap. Subtitles in English explained each scene.

The lights went on, and Leighton stepped quickly to the podium amid a buzz of whispered comments erupting throughout the stunned audience. "You are wondering how we took all of those shots of secret meetings around the world," said Leighton with a smile. "You'd never guess! They were all shot by Antonio Del Sasso from a laboratory just down the hall to your left and recorded from his brain directly onto videotape just as you saw them." He paused to enjoy the applause, continuing when quiet had once again been restored.

"You saw Dr. Khorev, for example," Leighton went on, "in his laboratory north of Moscow. That was *before* he came to this country, and he was unaware that the video was being taken at the time. And remember, that was in a secret and heavily guarded com-mando base whose very existence is known to only a handful of top Russian leaders. I need not tell you the potential of such capabili-ties, not only for ending war, but crime as well. That is why we selected the shots of the secret meetings of drug czars in Colombia and of Mafia leaders in Sicily. Those men have not been arrested yet, but you may be sure they will be once the Plan has gone into effect. Both war and crime, ladies and gentlemen, will become obsolete on this planet!"

Enthusiastic clapping interrupted him for nearly a full minute. As it died out, however, the initial enthusiasm registered on the faces before him quickly gave way to a wary concern. Leighton smiled knowingly as he continued.

"I know what some of you are thinking. This will be the end, as well, of all privacy for everyone! Indeed not. You can put those fears at rest right now. Del Sasso is not peering into bedrooms. There will be no spying on business competitors or sports rivals. The Archons impose a psychic screening process that allows only illegal activities to be monitored and that blacks out everything else. The only exception would be in cases of life-threatening dangers to the parties concerned. The benefits are almost limitless, while safeguards will prevent any abuse whatsoever.

"Now, for the moment you've all been eagerly anticipating: when Antonio Del Sasso gives you a firsthand live display of just a small sample of the powers the Archons stand ready to dispense to the world. And now, ladies and gentlemen, once again, Dr. Antonio Del Sasso, an extraordinary Jesuit priest—but much more than that, the Archons' ambassador-at-large to the world!"

Tension peaked and found momentary release in a thundering standing ovation as Del Sasso stood modestly with head bowed. At last he waved his arms for quiet. "Just a brief explanation first of all," began Del Sasso when the welcoming applause had subsided. "Those of you who know anything at all about the psychic research that has been in progress around the world for the past century realize that this has been a most difficult field. To get any results at all, the conditions must be just right. The outcomes of the most fruitful experiments are very difficult to repeat even under precisely the same conditions. Moreover, psychic power has been notoriously unpredictable and unreliable, and the effects achieved are disappointingly small at best and difficult to control.

"With that in mind, notice that the conditions are of no concern to me. You don't have to be quiet, the lights need not be dimmed—I don't even have to be close to whatever is happening. Yet it is all under perfect control—not mine, but the Archons'. I mention that again, because the key to receiving this power is in giving credit and submitting to those who direct it for our benefit. I can only do what they allow me to do and within the limits of the power which they are willing to dispense at the time—which, by the way, will be unlimited when the Plan has been fully implemented."

At this point the trace of a grin touched Del Sasso's face. "We have among us today about 30 representatives of the major media giants. They are sitting in a section to my right and to your left. I won't ask them to stand or raise their hands, because you will all be able to see them. Take a look!"

To the utter astonishment of the audience and to the chagrin and fright of the media personalities, all 30 of them were suddenly lifted out of their seats and levitated up to the ceiling. Pandemonium broke out. "We won't allow any heart attacks," said Del Sasso quickly. "The medical benefits of this power—we haven't even mentioned them yet—are staggering. The potential for healing all disease on the planet and giving long life to everyone is unlimited."

He waved a hand and those suspended slowly returned to their seats. "Now," said Del Sasso with a laugh, "I'll show you how selective this power can be. You would certainly expect—would you not?—that everyone who had just lived through a remarkable experience such as the one you've just seen with your own eyes would now be an enthusiastic believer. But that, strangely enough, is not the case. The skepticism of reporters and newscasters is beyond belief. Some of them are still convinced that what just happened to them was some kind of trick. Right now those who remain skeptical of this power and the Plan are going to go through the same experience again to see if we can make staunch believers out of them." Instantly five men and two women shot up out of their seats and found themselves near the ceiling once again. Carla noted with satisfaction that George Conklin was not among them. Then Del Sasso lowered them amid laughter and applause.

Now Del Sasso stood facing the audience, arms folded, eyeing each person thoughtfully. One could sense the apprehension. What might this man do next? Then he burst into a good-natured laugh. "Don't worry," he assured everyone. "I'm not going to have any more 'audience participation.'" There was an audible sigh of relief.

"Some of you were at Camp David a few weeks ago," continued Del Sasso, "when I was challenged by a certain well-known Southern senator who doubted the contribution this power could make to world peace. At that time a trap was set up, and as it propelled the clay pigeons, I disintegrated them into a thousand fragments with my mind, suggesting that ICBMs would meet the same fate shortly after they were launched anywhere in the world, once the Plan was in force. Of course, the first step would be to disarm and destroy all such missiles, since there would no longer be any need for them.

"The question was raised later whether such destruction of nuclear missiles in flight might not detonate them or in some way spread nuclear waste or contamination. That was a very perceptive observation. Actually, we wouldn't disintegrate ICBMs the same way I did the clay pigeons. I was simulating what a shotgun does. With nuclear missiles, however, we would, if the need arose, simply disengage their connection with this universe—in other words, dissolve their existence, make them disappear, as though they had run into a lump of antimatter.

"I need a volunteer from the audience—a man with considerable strength. Quickly."

From the front row a uniformed and very athletic-looking young United States Army colonel of about 35 jumped to his feet. Judging from the thick neck, cauliflower ears, and bent nose, he had been a boxer at one time. Del Sasso motioned to him, and the colonel hurried onto the platform. Looking at the 666 badge he was wearing, Del Sasso read off the information: "This is Colonel Rob Blaisley, adjutant to the current NATO commander." He reached out and shook the colonel's hand warmly. "I'm pleased to meet you, Colonel."

A lab assistant had wheeled up a large metal grocery cart filled with round objects. Pointing to it, Del Sasso said, "There are about a dozen bowling balls in there and a couple of steel shot puts." The colonel was hefting and checking them as Del Sasso spoke. "Is that right, Colonel?"

"They're legit," said the colonel. "I love to bowl and I used to put the shot. These aren't cream puffs. They're regulation 16-pound bowling balls and solid-steel 16-pound shots. What do you want me to do—throw them at you?"

"Say, we're going on tour together, you and I," retorted Del Sasso with a laugh. "You've got some great lines. We'd make a terrific act! No, don't throw them at me. Throw them at the audience. The bowling balls first."

The colonel picked up a bowling ball and prepared to throw it, when Del Sasso said, "Drop it on the floor first of all so everyone knows it's solid." He held it over his head and dropped it. The impact was convincing.

"I didn't mean from that high!" said Del Sasso. He turned to Leighton. "We need to reinforce this floor if we're going to do that again."

"Please don't!" responded Leighton quickly.

"Okay. Start throwing them out there," said Del Sasso.

The colonel hesitated. "Are you sure somebody isn't going to get hurt?" he asked. With that he was lifted off the floor up to the ceiling.

"You see what happens to doubters," quipped Del Sasso, easing him back down again. "Now throw that thing right out there. You've got a four-star general on the front row next to where you were sitting. Aim it at him."

"Not on your life, sir!" said the colonel, and threw the ball quickly toward the other side of the auditorium. It had not traveled more than ten feet in the air when it suddenly disappeared. There was a loud gasp simultaneously from 250 throats. The colonel threw another in a slightly different direction, with the same result. Then a third. Del Sasso held up his hand.

"I think that's enough of those, Colonel. There's no point in destroying more bowling balls. They cost money, and the Archons have not yet told me how to bring them back. Now, how about those two shots? How far did you used to be able to put a 16-pound shot?"

"Sixty feet or more in my college days. I wasn't that great at it, but I competed in a lot of meets and won a few."

"Okay. I won't ask you to drop that onto the floor—it would go right through. But just let everyone know it's solid."

"It's solid steel," said the colonel, hefting the ball back and forth from one hand to the other.

"Now, let's see how far you can put that thing out into the audience," said Del Sasso.

The colonel gave a mighty heave. The steel shot launched in a high trajectory out over the audience, then suddenly disappeared. "I don't think we need to bother with the other one," said Del Sasso, "unless you want to."

"Yeah, let's do it again," said the colonel enthusiastically.

"Okay, heave-ho," said Del Sasso.

Out went the second 16-pound shot of solid steel, arching toward the audience, then vanishing into thin air. There was a roar of approval from the audience, then thundering applause. Del Sasso held up his hand for quiet, then motioned to the right of the stage. From behind the curtain a lab assistant brought out a strange contraption and thrust it into the arms of the astonished colonel.

"Would you care to tell the audience what that is?" Del Sasso asked him.

The colonel seemed dumbfounded. "It's a—a *flamethrower*!" he said. "What am I supposed to do with this?"

"Strap it on your back and use it to burn me to a crisp."

"You don't mean that!"

"Yes, I do. You wanted to throw bowling balls at me. I much prefer flames. Go ahead."

The colonel strapped it on his back while Del Sasso talked. He backed off a few paces, and from about 20 feet turned it on. A sheet of flame shot out aimed directly at Del Sasso, but disappeared when it got within a few feet of his chest. He began walking toward the colonel, and the flames receded as he advanced until suddenly, when he was standing directly in front of it, the flamethrower itself vanished.

Spontaneously the audience, which had been sitting in breathless wonder during this incredible display of power, came to its feet clapping and cheering. Del Sasso smiled imperceptibly, bowed several times, then returned to his seat.

The standing ovation was deafening. Leighton held up his hands for silence. "You understand, of course," he said when he could at last be heard, "that what you've just seen represents only the tiniest fraction of the power being made available to mankind through the benevolent intervention of the Archons. Moreover, as we have already mentioned, their Plan will involve the development of literally millions of psychics with powers equal to those of Antonio Del Sasso. In fact, there will be no limit. Each nation will be able to train as many shamans as it desires. There is unlimited power available to all—even to the tiniest and poorest countries. Ultimately, each person on earth will have unobstructed access to the force innate within the universe without going through the Archons!

"Of course, to do this it will be necessary to manufacture large numbers of the Psitron—that's the ingenious electronic divination device through which initial contact is made at the Omega point with these entities and which serves as the official training mechanism. We already have a commitment from a conglomerate of the world's banks for a loan in the amount of five billion dollars to set up manufacturing plants for the Psitron in strategic locations on every continent. The guarantee for this loan, of course, will come from the signatories to the New World Constitution, which, as you now know, will of necessity include every nation on earth.

"Naturally, considerable technical expertise will be required to carry this through to a successful conclusion in as brief a time as possible. We are fortunate to be joined in this effort by a man who is undoubtedly the most brilliant parapsychologist the former Soviet Union ever produced. I refer, of course, to Dr. Viktor Khorev. Initially he defected from Russia in desperation to join the program. Now, however, Dr. Khorev is a hero in his own country and he has recently been commended to this work by the Russian president himself.

"It now gives me great pleasure to present to you our keynote speaker of the evening, a man whose presence is a symbol not only of scientific greatness but of the solidarity between our two great nations—the United States of America and the Russian Federation—Dr. Viktor Khorev."

Slowly and deliberately Viktor stepped to the podium and took his notes out of a plain folder and spread them before him. "Representatives of the world's nations and honored guests," Viktor began, looking out over the audience, "since coming here to this remarkable research center, I have been doing what all of you must carefully and courageously do tonight. That is, I have been attempting to understand the ever-more incredible happenings in these laboratories and their implications for all of humanity.

"What you have seen on videotape is all true. It is light-years ahead of anything we were able to accomplish or even dreamed of accomplishing during my years of psychic research in the Soviet

Union and then in the Russian Federation. And the same can be said for the psychic research in any other country. There is no way, as both Dr. Leighton and Dr. Del Sasso have already carefully explained . . . " Here Viktor half turned and nodded toward Leighton and Del Sasso, " . . . that such power could be developed apart from these entities known as the Archons—or 'the Nine.' I can tell you without fear of contradiction, based upon my many years of research, that no human agency has or can develop such powers. They come exclusively from the Archons. They control this power and dispense it as they will and to whom they will. And they have now declared their willingness, through Antonio Del Sasso, to make this power available to the world in order to prevent the destruction of this planet—a destruction which otherwise seems inevitable.

"For the world to receive this power, as we have already been told, we must of necessity submit ourselves completely to these entities—through their ambassador Antonio Del Sasso, of course. I think you are all convinced of the important part he will play in the Plan, and of his unique qualifications to do so. Naturally, if we are to submit totally to the Archons, then we must trust them completely. It would be folly to submit to beings that we are not certain are absolutely trustworthy.

"Therein lies the crux of the problem that I have wrestled with over these past few weeks. I want to take you through the process of doubt that I myself have experienced, and then bring you to the happy conclusion I have reached. I realized that if I and all of us—the world—are to trust them, and that is a necessity for the Plan to be put into operation, then there are certain criteria which we must assess.

"Here is the reasoning process I myself struggled through. First of all, I was raised in an atheistic country and am an atheist myself. Yet I recognize, as every reasonable person must, that only God—if such a being existed—could be trusted totally. This is true because God, by very definition, is loving and kind and above corruption even by His own desires, being self-existent and infinite and thus needing nothing from anyone or anything, being Himself the Creator of all. And because God is, again by very definition, unchangeable, we can on the basis of both His character and His past performance have complete confidence in what He will do in the future. Unfortunately, God doesn't exist, so we are left to our own devices and dare not put ourselves at the mercy of anyone else. And, as I thought it over carefully, that seemed logically to include the Archons as well.

"Being less than God—indeed, they deny the very existence of a supreme deity and claim that each of us is a god in his own right—the Archons could conceivably be corrupted by their own selfish desires. Here I faced a grave dilemma. Since the Archons, highly evolved though they may be, are less than God and thus capable of change, we have a serious problem. Even if they had been nothing less than completely benevolent in their dealings with mankind for the past thousand years, we could not have absolute confidence on the basis of that impressive record that they would not turn against or deceive us in the future."

At this point in his talk, Viktor turned and gestured again toward Leighton and Del Sasso, who both wore expressions of concern, but seemed generally pleased with his approach thus far. "Dr. Leighton and Dr. Del Sasso have known of my doubts and have given of themselves most graciously in helping me to work my way through them. It was not easy, because the problem was a most difficult one. We are called upon to submit to the Archons totally, even though they are less than God and could be pursuing selfish interests that are unknown to us. Of course they tell us they are benevolent, but how can we accept such assurances?

"One persuasive argument is the fact that the Archons are so far beyond man that they really don't need us. There is nothing we can offer them, it would seem, therefore nothing they would want from us. And so they would have no motive to lie to or trick or harm us in any way. After all, what would be the purpose? For some time I accepted this line of reasoning. I eventually had to face the fact, however, that if they had no interest in harming us, then why would they be interested in helping us. Why would they be interested in us at all? That question left me puzzled, and then I realized that there was something I had overlooked."

Viktor paused to draw several deep breaths at this point and to gather his courage. A stillness that could almost be felt had settled over the audience. Every eye was fixed in unblinking anticipation upon Viktor. Carla noticed that Leighton seemed frozen in his chair and Del Sasso was ominously motionless as though he were going into trance. She felt a growing sense of dread, yet at the same time she seemed to be strangely insulated from what was happening around her.

What Viktor had said about God had hit her with stunning force. Here was an atheist telling her who God was—if, as he said, there was a God—and why He alone could be trusted. His reasoning had been powerfully persuasive. It had loosed a flood of deep and growing convictions that she had been suppressing. Time seemed to stand still, the auditorium receded into unreality, and Viktor's voice became a distant drone as conversations she'd had with Ken came back with new force. His logic could not be refuted, and now could no longer be ignored. And the very points Viktor, an atheist, was making—which she seemed to be hearing as though for the first time—reinforced and gave new credibility to what Ken had tried to persuade her of these past weeks.

Viktor's voice, now betraying the strain of a growing fear, yet ringing with a courage born of conviction and the urgent desire to warn the world, caught her full attention once again. "There was no need to speculate. The evidence was staring me in the face, but I had been unwilling to accept it. It is a matter of record, if Frank Leighton will be willing to admit it—and if not, there are others here who may have the courage to do so (here he glanced quickly at Carla)—that the Archons have been less than forthright in their dealings with those involved in this project even from the very beginning. They have promised peace, love, and brotherhood. Instead they have produced violence, involving even the death or insanity of those who have believed their promises and submitted to their control. In contrast to the millions of psychics in addition to Del Sasso they promise, they have not produced even one—in spite of diligent efforts at these laboratories to train others on the Psitron! I now doubt that they ever intended to. We have obediently given the Archons complete control of this project and our lives, and the results so far—other than the powers Del Sasso displays to seduce us—have not been good!"

At last it was all coming together for Carla. *Why didn't I listen to Ken?* she thought. *What if the Archons are demons? Viktor is making an airtight case against them. They're evil, without a doubt, bent upon deception, domination—and perhaps even destruction.* She felt an overpowering urge to get up and run for the nearest exit. But Viktor! What would happen to him? She couldn't leave him. So she sat there, transfixed by the horror she felt, and which she knew with a strange and terrifying certainty was about to explode before her.

From the audience came a restless stirring, a rising murmur. Carla sensed that the presence of love that had earlier been felt had gone, and in its place was the reptilian presence she knew all too well. Leighton started to rise from his chair, then sank back, seemingly too stunned to react. Now an ominous silence had settled in the auditorium, like the calm before a storm. The audience was transfixed in silent alarm. Only the eerie sound of breathing could be heard.

Viktor's words came in a torrent now, as though he expected to be stopped and was rushing to get it all out. "It's the complete control they demand that concerns me. I've experienced totalitarianism. I understand that there are many changes being made even now in my native country—a country that I dearly love. However, that country is far from the freedom that all men cherish, a freedom that I sought in the West and which I find is lacking even here."

Carla could not believe her ears. And it seemed even more unbelievable that Leighton had not intervened, and that Del Sasso had made no move to cut him down. Were they reluctant to create an even worse scene in front of this audience and therefore would simply allow Viktor to finish and then discredit him? And what of the Archons? Why had they made no move to silence him?

"This is a crucial gathering and you do indeed hold the future of the world in your hands. Everything depends upon whether you bow to the will of the Archons or resist them. I warn you now, to submit to their control will be to turn this world into one vast prison—not of bodies confined within cells, but of minds no longer able to think for themselves. The paradise the Archons offer will in fact turn out to be the indescribable hell of a vicious totalitarianism worse than anything this world has yet seen—dictated by alien intelligences who intend to use us for their own insidious purposes."

Leighton had shaken himself out of his paralysis and jumped to his feet. He ran to the podium and tried to pull the microphone away from Viktor. Fighting off Leighton, with a last effort Viktor shouted into the mike, "Close your minds to the Archons' influence. Fight back. Don't let them impose their will." At that point a security guard grabbed Viktor, tore the mike from his hands, and threw him onto the platform floor.

The unleashing of the Archons' fury came at that moment, and with a violence that swept all rational thought before it. The stillness was broken by a cry of rage from the throat of Del Sasso, horribly reminiscent of his reaction when Ken had shut him down in the laboratory. Yes, Carla was now certain that Ken had indeed shut him down. Ken's last words came vividly before her: *The wrath of the Lamb—the judgment of God! Yes,* she admitted at last, *Jesus is God. He is all Viktor has attributed to the Creator of the universe, and here, in this building He is no longer restraining the murderous evil the Archons represent. Those who believed them are reaping the fruit of rebellion against the true God.*

The floor began to buckle, then it suddenly opened beneath the media representatives, swallowing them en masse. Seats were ripped up from the floor and flew through the air. The audience was thrown about like so much flotsam on a stormy sea. The entire auditorium was in a state of massive upheaval. Huge chunks of the roof caved in, crushing scores of delegates to death. And most horrible of all, the laminated wood beams that supported the ceiling splintered off into long spears. They flew through the air like guided missiles and impaled those who still remained alive and were madly scrambling over bodies and debris in an attempt to get to the exits.

Those delegates who managed to reach the exits without being speared, climbing over piles of bodies and wreckage in the process, found the doors locked and their exit from the holocaust denied. Pounding with their fists helplessly on the doors and walls, some died of hysteria, while the remainder were crushed under the rain of debris from the collapsing roof that seemed to be aimed at those below by some all-seeing intelligence that was directing the destruction. Clearly, no survivors were going to be allowed to escape to tell the horrible truth of what actually happened.

Leighton, in the last spasm of a blasted dream, cursed the Archons and burst suddenly into flames. His scream was quickly swallowed up in the intense heat and his body seemed to melt and turn to ashes before Carla's horrified gaze. Then she saw other examples of spontaneous human combustion taking place among the few who still remained alive. The flames began leaping from their bodies to consume others who were already dead. Mike Bradford, head of security, was hit in the middle of the back by a heavy piece of the ceiling that knocked him to the floor. He struggled up on one elbow, pulled his revolver from inside his coat and in a rage fired several slugs into Leighton's disentegrating body. Then he turned it upon Del Sasso, who was sitting entranced in his chair in yoga position, but the gun was torn from his hand and a heavy beam came crashing down and crushed his skull. His assistant leaped from the platform, only to vanish before he landed on the auditorium floor below.

Viktor, who had been too stunned to move from where he lay, was slowly regaining consciousness. He struggled to his feet and began to stagger desperately toward the rear of the platform. He had only taken two steps when a huge section of the overhead stage lighting crashed down upon him and pinned him to the floor. He lay motionless. Carla, miraculously untouched, was certain that he was dead. She had already started to run toward the backstage exit where she had entered, when she heard her name being called.

Turning around, she saw that Viktor had regained consciousness once again and was struggling to get free of the weight that held him down. His eyes were pleading with her. To go to him would be almost certain suicide, but she could not abandon him. She made her way back as quickly as she could over the debris.

"Lord Jesus, help me get to him—help me!" It was the first prayer she had uttered in over 20 years.

A Greater Power

Ken had been growing uneasy as the afternoon progressed. It was now after 5 o'clock. What was happening out there? Was it enough just to pray, or was there something he had to do as well? Decisively he rose from his knees and announced to the rest, "I've got to leave. I just know I'm supposed to get out to the installation as soon as possible. I don't know what I may be getting into or why the Lord is directing me to do this, so please pray for me! You know the guards have my picture and instructions not to let me in."

Don Jordan walked outside with him. "You're not even going to get off the main highway," he told Ken. "They'll have that access road blocked off for sure. You'll never get through. I'm going to get on my radio and contact the head of the local highway patrol, give him a description of your car, and ask him to let you through. That will get you onto the road. What you do at the gate is something else. I can't help you there. We'll just keep praying."

"I'll trust the Lord for that," said Ken as he hurried to his Jeep. "He'll make a way somehow! Thanks a lot!"

Sure enough, a California highway patrol vehicle and three local police cars were at the entrance to the access road and a police barricade across it. Ken pulled in and an officer waved him to stop. The officer looked at his driver's license, grunted, and handed it back. "Hey, move that thing and let this car through," he yelled, waving at two officers standing near the barricade.

There was another police checkpoint just inside the "Government Property" sign, but when Ken waved his driver's license at the officers manning it, they motioned him on. The last quarter of a mile to the installation, one side of the road was completely taken up with parked taxis, limos, and private autos, their drivers standing around talking and smoking or nodding in their vehicles. Nearing the gate, he saw that it was surrounded with television film crews and other media personnel who hadn't been allowed inside. They were waiting to get pictures of the dignitaries and hoping for interviews. It was total congestion. For a moment, Ken had a mental image of the opening day of trout season on a small creek in Los Angeles County. You almost had to bring in your own rock to stand on.

Ken drove his Jeep slowly through the milling mass and finally reached the gate. To his surprise he found it standing wide open. As he was easing his vehicle on through, a guard came running out of his station, yelling at him to stop. "Hey! You can't go in there. There aren't any parking places inside," said the guard, coming up to his window. "You're two hours late, anyway. Let me see your ID and your invitation."

"I don't have an invitation," said Ken, "but I've got to get through! I was sent out here by Don Jordan of the FBI."

"He's got no jurisdiction in here. Say, aren't you Ken Inman?" Ken nodded. "I thought I recognized you! Okay, just back this thing up and get on out of here. You know you're not allowed on the premises."

Reaching Viktor, Carla was able to lift the beam enough for him to slide free. She helped him to his feet, then getting her shoulders under an arm, she half-carried and half-dragged him toward the backstage exit that led off the rear of the platform into the interior corridors. They reached it safely amid the continuing rain of debris. By some miracle the door was ajar. She took one brief backward look at the chaos. Del Sasso was standing with uplifted head and hands—unscathed, untouched by deadly missiles. He appeared to be in an attitude of worship, as though he were offering to the Archons the impaled and crushed bodies as a libation. Then he turned and saw her. Even at that distance, she could see the searing hatred in his eyes.

Viktor was half-stunned and dragging a bloody and battered leg that was nearly useless. He clung to Carla, terror-stricken. If it were not for his helplessness, she could have been outside by now. But how could she abandon him?

"What have I done?" Viktor kept repeating. "What have I done? I thought we could fight them if we all did it together. Did I cause the deaths of all of those people?" He leaned against the wall, gasping for breath. "Someone has to escape to tell the rest of the world. You go on without me. It's enough if only one of us makes it. The world must be warned!"

"We're not the only survivors," said Carla, trying to pull him gently along. "Del Sasso is alive! We've got to go faster, if you can."

"I can't make it—go on yourself. Tell them the Archons are *evil*. Tell what they've done. They've killed everyone so no one would know the truth."

"I'm not leaving you, Viktor," she said firmly. "We're going to make it together. Come on, you can do it! Don't give up now!"

Slowly descending a short stairway and painfully staggering along the narrow hall, they reached its juncture with the main corridor that went past the central lab and on to the offices. As they came around the corner into the broad hallway, they were suddenly confronted by Colonel Chernov blocking their path. It was impossible. He was dead. She had seen his horrible demise with her own eyes—but there he was, apparently in the flesh, a twisted grin defacing his mouth, his face a mask of evil. Revenge was clearly written in his malevolent eyes.

Chernov seemed not to notice her, so intent was he upon Viktor, whom he addressed in Russian. Viktor replied in halting phrases and seemed to be pleading for his life.

"It's not Chernov!" Carla yelled at him. "It's an Archon!" Viktor stared back, uncomprehendingly. "Tell it you belong to the Lord Jesus Christ. Use His Name—believe in Him! He will save you!"

Carla was amazed. Had those words issued from her mouth? Then she realized they were coming from her heart as well. "I believe," she cried aloud. "I do believe that Jesus died for me!" Now she had a new reason for surviving—not only to warn the world, but to tell Ken. Here, in this extremity, at the very apex of her life, she had yielded her rebellious heart to the One she had so long rejected.

Viktor was shaking his head. "Christ demands submission, too. I won't do it. I want to be free!"

"Christ gives freedom—from *yourself!*" She was pleading with him now. "The real dictator is Viktor Khorev! You're a slave to *yourself*, Viktor! Christ will save you. He died for you."

"No!" said Viktor. He stared at Carla for one brief moment with wide and glassy eyes. To her sorrow, she saw the unreasoning, frightened look of a man lost in a wilderness and despairing of ever finding his way back.

He tore his hand loose from her grip and began backing away in terror. Chernov, his twisted smile now turned into a snarl, was stalking him like a tiger preparing to spring on its prey.

"Viktor!" she yelled. "Believe in Jesus! He will protect you!" But Viktor seemed deaf to her voice now.

In a sudden blur of motion, Chernov spun around. His flying foot hit Viktor in the face with a deadly force that hurled him against the wall. Eyes instantly glazing over, Viktor's limp body dropped to the floor.

Now Chernov turned his evil intentions in her direction. "Help me, Lord Jesus!" she murmured, and Chernov vanished. Sobbing uncontrollably, she ran along the main corridor, past the lab where she had first seen Del Sasso display his powers, then turned left past Leighton's office, where the nightmare had begun and where she had spent so many hours and days and nights struggling with her conflicts and finally committing herself—to *this*.

As she burst into the lobby with freedom now in sight, she saw him. He was standing in front of the door in his long, black robe, hood thrown back, barring her escape. This was no Archon. It was Del Sasso himself in the flesh!

"What's the hurry, Carla?" he asked with exaggerated concern. "The party isn't over, and it isn't polite to skip out like this without thanking your host." He regarded her with an expression of greedy anticipation.

Carla hesitated. Should she run back down the hall for the side exit? No, he would catch her before she took a dozen steps. He could move like a cat.

"You don't have your Ken-boy here to help you this time!" gloated Del Sasso. "You're all mine!" He started toward her, and she began to back toward the corridor.

"You're mad, Antonio," she said. "Completely mad! You were enjoying that holocaust! You did enjoy slicing Chernov in half, didn't you?"

"I love the power," he said simply. "Why not? It's like being God. I can do anything. You'll see!"

With the guard's words ringing in his ears, Ken began to pray. *Lord, please help me. I'm not backing out of here. I have to get through to Carla!* Suddenly over the main building appeared a pulsating glow of alternating green and purple. Then he saw it—a giant UFO all aflame rising right out of the roof of the theater in the center of the main building. There was a deafening roar and the roof seemed to collapse. It was obvious even to atheists and agnostics that a holocaust of supernatural proportions was taking place.

"I said back this thing up!" the guard was snarling, reaching for his weapon. Then he heard the explosion and turned and saw it, too! At that moment a pervasive and ancient reptilian presence seemed to have been loosed through the ruptured roof—a presence that was terrifying beyond description.

For one brief moment the guard stared in stark terror, then he turned and ran. Ken gunned his engine and drove forward. In the rearview mirror he could see the throng of media personnel scattering in panic and heard their horrified screams. The UFO, looking more like a ball of fire now than a spacecraft, had dropped down and was heading directly for the gate at accelerating speed, skimming along just above the ground.

"Help me, Lord Jesus—thank You!" There wasn't time to say more. The UFO was upon him. He gripped the steering wheel and closed his eyes for one brief moment. His car passed right through it. *"Thank you, Lord!"* Now he could see that there was no place to park. The few spaces were filled with limousines and military vehicles. He pulled up in front of the stone wall that protected the front door and jumped out. They would be in the theater. He ran the hundred feet along the building to his right and tried both doors, but they were locked. The handles were almost too hot to touch. No sound came from within except the stillness of death and the crackling of fire. He stepped back a dozen feet and looked up. Dense, black smoke tinged with the red of leaping flames was billowing into the sky. The theater was engulfed, completely ablaze.

Carla turned to run down the corridor, but Del Sasso reached out quickly and caught her long, auburn hair in one huge fist. She screamed, scratched, kicked, but he was far too strong for her. She felt herself being dragged back into the lobby, where he threw her down in the middle of the floor. She lay there half-stunned. Standing over her, Del Sasso was preparing to offer to the Archons a most acceptable sacrifice—a new Christian.

"Lord Jesus, help me!" Carla cried. "God help me—please!"

"Jesus is helping *me!*" intoned Del Sasso. "He belongs to the Archons now. They crucified Him, and they want you as well."

They both heard the handle turn and then the front door swing rapidly open and slam against the outside wall. Ken rushed inside, heading for the corridor. Then he saw them and stopped in surprise. Del Sasso whirled to face him.

"You said you shut me down and that I was afraid of you. And I said I would kill you if you ever showed your hateful face in here again! Now we will see." Del Sasso grabbed a heavy ceramic lamp from a table, ripped it from the wall, tore off the shade and gripped it by the narrow top to use as a weapon. Warily, he advanced on Ken.

"Let's go, Carla," said Ken firmly. "We're leaving. Head for the door. Now."

"Look out, Ken! He's—" She struggled to her feet and began to circle widely around Del Sasso toward the door.

"Why do you need a weapon like that?" asked Ken calmly. "What about 'psychic powers'? Why not use them? You know they won't work on a real Christian, don't you, *you demons of destruction!*"

Del Sasso's mouth moved, but no sound came out. He hesitated, eyeing Ken murderously. Carla had reached the door, pushed it open, and held it as she watched in frightened fascination. Ken began to retreat slowly toward the open door, never taking his eyes from Del Sasso, who was following, brandishing the lamp uncertainly.

"I'm not talking to you, Antonio. You're just a shell," said Ken in an even voice. "I'm talking to the demons who possess you. Whoever you are, however many of you there are, in the Name of Jesus Christ and through the blood of His cross—we're leaving. You can have this building!"

Ken had reached the door now and motioned for Carla to leave. "Get to the Jeep!" he whispered. She turned and ran. Ken stepped quickly outside, still keeping his eye on the psychic. Del Sasso let out a roar of rage and threw the lamp just as Ken slammed the door shut. He heard the lamp smash harmlessly on the inside of the door as he turned and hurried to join Carla. She was leaning up against the Jeep, sobbing. The door to the lobby had not opened.

"He won't follow us," said Ken. "Praise God, you're safe!"

She fell into his arms. He held her tight as she shook with sobs. "You can't believe what happened in there!" she managed to say. And then the whole world started to spin and everything went black.

He carried her into the car, then climbed in behind the wheel and started the engine. In the distance he heard the sound of sirens approaching rapidly along the access road. Film crews were rushing through the gate, setting up cameras. Reporters were talking into recorders. Ken drove slowly around the circle drive and through the gathering crowd. Looking back, he could see that the fire, driven by a stiff breeze, had spread from the theater and now engulfed almost the entire structure. The four-starred flag was flapping proudly above the fender of the general's car.

The Archon Legacy

arla recovered consciousness about a quarter of a mile away from the installation when Ken pulled over to let the first fire engine—with siren wailing at ear-splitting amplitude—roar past. She opened her eyes, looked around in terror for a moment, then realized that they were safe and on the way home. He had to pull over and stop to let another fire engine go by, and Carla took hold of his arm. He turned and their eyes met. She was crying again, but now she was smiling through the tears.

"Look at me, Ken," she said between sobs. "Something happened to me—something *wonderful*. Can you tell?"

"Are you telling me . . . ?"

She nodded, and her eyes told him what she couldn't find the words to say. He put his arms around her and held her tight, both of them sobbing now—tears of joy. "Thank God! Oh, Carla—thank God!"

Firemen found Antonio Del Sasso facedown, unconscious from smoke inhalation, in the main corridor just outside the narrow passage that led to the backstage door. They speculated that he had been felled by the powerful explosion in the theater earlier, had come to, and had been able to make his way only that far before being overcome by the smoke. Otherwise there was no explanation why, if he had escaped injury in the theater, it would have taken him so long to go such a short distance, or why he hadn't gotten out safely along the same escape route as Carla Bertelli, the only other survivor.

Ken called the Elliotts the moment he had gotten Carla safely to his house. There was mingled joy and sorrow at the news he conveyed: joy that Carla had not only survived but had surrendered to Christ at last, and sorrow for Viktor and Frank and the many others who had perished. As firemen would later report, the all-consuming holocaust had been so fierce that only ashes had remained and little could be learned of its cause from examining the ruins. Of course, Viktor's body—not five feet from Del Sasso—had been found as well, the only one recovered of all those who had died.

"We have to be careful," Hal Elliott had cautioned the gathering as he announced the news, "that we don't imagine that our prayers have the power to frustrate completely Satan's plans for this world. Our prayers played a part today because it's clearly not yet God's time to allow the Antichrist to set up his counterfeit kingdom. And we must always remember that it's not how loudly or how long we pray that counts. We are not heard for our 'much speaking,' as Jesus said. What matters is the faith God gives us, and the holiness of our lives. 'The effectual fervent prayer of a righteous man availeth much,' according to James 5:16. God won't use unclean vessels for His work, no matter how often we cry to Him and claim His promises. And He only answers according to His perfect will, to which we must be in obedient submission or we will not be heard at all."

To the "Amens" and nodded agreement, Hal added another exhortation. "Instead of resting on what we might imagine was a great victory, we need to spend still more time while we're here in letting God search our hearts and perhaps reveal through His Word the significance of today's astonishing events. Where does this fit in, if at all, with Bible prophecy? What does it mean for the future, and what are we to do about it? I think we're at a critical juncture in world history, and we believers need some fresh insight and direction from God's Word."

While he agreed with Hal and was willing to continue to pray along with the others, Don Jordan had the sudden conviction that another task had been given to him at that moment. He called Ken and told him that he was coming right over—that it was urgent.

When Jordan arrived, briefcase in hand, Carla was lying on the sofa in the living room, pouring out to Ken the whole unbelievable tale. "You're doing the right thing," said Jordan sympathetically to Carla when he joined them. "You've got to get this off your chest, share it with someone right away. That's why I wanted to be here." He pulled a tape recorder out of his briefcase. "There's another and maybe even more important reason, also. I suspect that your version of the story is going to be very crucial in the future. You may be certain that Del Sasso will have a different tale to tell, in total conflict with yours."

"I don't know how far you've gotten," he said, as he put the recorder near Carla and turned it on, "but you'll have to start over—with this morning, first of all. Take us through the entire day, and don't leave out any detail. Then we'll go back to when you first met Viktor in Paris and bring it forward from there. Take your time. I have no official status, and probably never will. This will be handled by the CIA to begin with—and then a federal grand jury, I would imagine—or perhaps a Senate committee, depending on which way they want to go. Tomorrow I couldn't do this, so let's get at it while we can."

It was after midnight when they finished at last. The process had been an exhausting and horribly traumatic one for Carla, but she held up well to the very end. Then she went off to bed. Ken and Don talked a while longer. The latter would not leave the house until they had made a copy of every tape for Ken to put in his safe-deposit box. Jordan took the originals for his files, to be produced if the appropriate time ever came. Having heard the story, he knew that he had done the right thing—and that he would not hesitate to take the witness stand, even if it meant his job, which he was now convinced might very well be the case someday. There were people highly placed in Washington who would rather die than have the truth come out. He was now sure of that.

An early morning phone call from Jordan relayed the expected news. "Ken, we've just gotten orders to bring Carla in for questioning. It isn't going to be under our jurisdiction. As I suspected, the CIA will be in charge, but they want us to bring her in. Two of my men are on the way over there now. Don't wake up Carla until they get there—but

I wanted you to know. I don't know for sure, but I get the impression that Del Sasso has already said some things that may implicate Carla."

"Implicate her?" responded Ken. "In *what?*"

"In the cause of the destruction."

"That's insane!" Ken felt himself losing control.

"Get hold of yourself, Ken. And make no statements to the two agents when they come. Just keep cool. That's why I called you. Okay? Pray about it, brother, and let the Lord take over. You've got to walk in the Spirit now if you ever did—not in the flesh! And not a word, of course, about the recording we made last night, or about this phone call."

It was late afternoon when Carla was finally brought back to the house by the same two agents—both of whom had previously been on duty at the Hilton. She looked exhausted—and stunned—when Ken opened the door to let her in. "Remember, you're not under arrest yet," one of the agents was saying, "but you shouldn't leave town without checking with us first." Ken opened his mouth, then bit his lip and took Carla by the arm and led her inside. She put her arms around his neck and clung to him, trying to hold back the tears.

He held her until she had stopped shaking, then they walked to the kitchen, his arm around her. He put some water on to boil and they sat down at the table. Carla wiped her eyes. "I didn't let them see me like this, I can assure you," she said. "I was strong down there. But it's so unbelievable."

"Tell me about it."

"I can't—they won't let me."

"What do you mean?"

"I'm under a court-imposed order of silence—can't discuss this whole thing, from beginning to end, with anyone, not even with you."

Ken's thoughts were racing. Jordan hadn't just been guessing. What was going to happen? This was incredible. He would fight with every ounce of his strength. They wouldn't get away with this—whatever it was they were trying to get away with that Carla couldn't tell him about. The shrill sound of the kettle brought him back to the present.

When he had brought the cups and teapot back to the table, he said, "You can at least tell me how it went, and why you're so upset."

"Ken, I'm not supposed to say *anything*."

He remembered what Jordan had said. "Are they blaming you in some way?" he asked. "Don't say anything—just nod yes or no."

She nodded slowly. "But there's no way they can make that lie work!" he exclaimed angrily.

"Maybe they can. There's something I overlooked, Ken. We all overlooked it—even Jordan."

The United States government had immediately set up an armed patrol to keep the curious from entering any part of the property, including the access road. A blanket of complete secrecy had been pulled over the entire affair. The fact that there had been a huge explosion and fire with the loss of nearly 300 lives, many of them well-known international leaders and top media personalities, could not, of course, be kept quiet. News reports and graphic film footage of leaders arriving for the Congress, the throng of journalists outside the gate, then the fire, were flashed around the world in a matter of minutes. Beyond that, however, the media was left to speculate on its own. Other governments, of course, whose representatives had perished in the disaster, were demanding answers. Each received the standard response that no comment was yet available and that a full inquiry might take months.

No interviews of either Bertelli or Del Sasso were allowed to the media. It was rumored, however, from "reliable sources" that their testimony was in serious conflict, and that there were major holes in Bertelli's story. It was easy enough to speculate, and a lot of that was done openly in the press in the days that followed the disaster. There almost seemed to be a resentment by some of her former colleagues that she alone—in contrast to the 30 other media persons inside at the time of the disaster, each of whom she had personally invited—had survived. Why? Something didn't add up. For one thing, Del Sasso had been found unconscious not far from the theater, while Bertelli, on the other hand, had made it out without even a bruise. How could she have been in the theater at the time of the huge explosion that had been witnessed by the media personnel clustered around the gate at the time, and by the two guards? Why was she the only survivor, and how could she have escaped unscathed? So the rumors flew, and when there are no facts to go by, rumor feeds upon itself.

After a week in the hospital under close guard, Del Sasso seemed to be completely recovered. The "source" leaked enough to know that Del Sasso could remember everything up to the time of the explosion, but nothing thereafter, which was, after all, what one would expect, given the force of that blast. Yet Bertelli knew all the details, before and after—and some of them were absolutely unbelievable. Science-fiction writers would hesitate to paint the scenario she had come up with, so it was rumored.

As for the giant UFO, no one had gotten a picture, and the reports were extremely conflicting. Some said it hadn't been a UFO at all, but a huge ball of fire propelled by the explosion, and that it just seemed to look like a UFO. Others swore they had been able to make out the metal body and the windows and the classic *Star Wars* shape. Only one witness said he had seen Ken's Jeep drive right through it, but obviously that couldn't have happened—it had to have passed just over him.

In the final analysis, the UFO theory fell under the weight of the unbelievable scenario that would have to be accepted if it were true. For one thing, the witnesses—more than 100 of them—were nearly unanimous that the object had come out of the domed roof of the theater on the right side of the main structure. Since there was no way a spacecraft of such huge proportions could have gotten inside the building, it was obvious that one didn't exit the building either. So the object had to be not a giant UFO ringed with flames, but a huge ball of fire that by some freak of nature—related possibly to the kind of explosion or the wind currents at the time— had been propelled in a horizontal vector and had dissipated in the trees just beyond the gate. That several treetops were badly scorched in a linear pattern leading away from the theater seemed to confirm this line of reasoning.

◆ ◆ ◆

Ken and Carla refused to allow government prohibitions to dictate their personal lives, especially when it came to that which mattered so much to both of them. The wedding that had been cancelled more than two years before because of Ken's conversion to Christ became a reality at long last because of Carla's conversion. There was, of course, a whole different list of guests now than had been proposed originally. Everything had changed. Carla found herself involved with a new world of friends, most of them from the prayer meeting at the Elliotts' and the church Ken attended and a weekly Bible study in his home that he led.

"As your husband," Ken had said when he'd proposed for this, the second time, "I'll be able to share secrets you can't tell me otherwise, so we can fight this thing together."

Carla had laughed. "Are you trying to justify this grand proposal? Some men marry women for their money—which I don't have. And others—well, are you marrying me for the secret information I'm privy to?"

Originally, they had hoped to honeymoon in Hawaii, but that was out of the question now with the imposed prohibition on travel. It would have been a local resort, had not Jordan intervened on their behalf. Under his pressure, the CIA relented and let them travel as far as Carmel, a mere 50 miles to the south of Palo Alto, but in many ways no less beautiful or popular with newlyweds than Maui.

During the next six months, Carla was summoned to Washington, D.C. several times to testify before a closed Senate hearing. There was much pressure in the media to lift the lid of secrecy, but the government would never give in to such demands. And it soon became clear to Carla and Ken, who always accompanied her, and to the two lawyers Ken had hired, that Carla was in deep trouble—and why.

"You're still sticking to your story," asked the chairman of the Senate investigating committee on Carla's third appearance before that body, "that it was Colonel Chernov—a man who had been dead for several weeks—who killed Dr. Khorev in the corridor as the two of you were trying to make your escape?" He peered at her over his glasses incredulously.

372 • DAVE HUNT

"As I've already explained, it wasn't Chernov." She was finding it increasingly difficult to hold her Irish temper under control. They seemed to be deliberately insisting that she had said what she hadn't, and attempting to discredit her testimony in every way they could, simply because it disagreed with that of their star witness, Antonio Del Sasso. Her demand to confront him face-to-face was repeatedly denied.

"But you said it looked exactly like him!" the chairman interrupted sharply.

"I explained that it was an Archon masquerading as Chernov."

"And Dr. Del Sasso says that the whole 'Archon scenario' was something that Viktor Khorev invented, and that you went along with it. Apparently the two of you had this agreement from the very beginning. We have, of course, your published articles to verify this. You don't deny them?"

"Of course I don't deny them. And I'm telling you once again that Del Sasso is lying. He presented himself as the Archons' ambassador-at-large to the world and stated on many occasions, including at the gathering under investigation, that the psychic powers he manifested came entirely from the Archons."

"And you expect this committee to believe fantasies about highly evolved extraterrestrials without bodies—spirit beings that you now call *demons*—who go around masquerading as dead Russian officers?"

"I don't have any control over what the committee believes. I only know that I'm telling you the truth, whether you believe it or not!"

"And you still stick to your story," put in another senator, "that you encountered Dr. Del Sasso in the lobby after the explosion—in spite of the fact that firemen found him lying unconscious just outside the theater, far inside the building?"

"I am—and my husband, Ken Inman, has corroborated that fact."

"Yes, we have his testimony, and it does, indeed, agree with yours—as would be expected."

At that point Ken jumped to his feet to object, only to be pulled down by his two lawyers. "I took Carla out in my Yukon. There are witnesses who saw us come out of the lobby together!" he whispered to the attorneys. "And that proves nothing about Del Sasso being in the lobby!" was the stern response, with a reminder to keep cool and let them handle it. After all, that was what he had hired them for.

"We are urging you to tell the truth, Mrs. Inman," the chairman said again. "You have not had a criminal record up to this time, and I want to appeal to you on the basis of the loyalty you once seemed to have toward your country. World leaders died in that holocaust, placing the stability of our relationship with other nations at jeopardy. I cannot offer you clemency—that would be for a judge to decide—but I can offer you the satisfaction of knowing that you can at least in some degree redeem yourself from this unspeakable crime by telling the truth now."

"I have told the truth," was all Carla could say. She seemed to have lost touch with reality. This couldn't possibly be happening!

"You know that it makes no sense at all," persisted the chairman, "that Dr. Del Sasso would be in the lobby a step from safety, and then go back in to almost certain death. In fact, if the firemen had not found him just in time, he would have been dead. Why would he go back? He would have known that everyone else was dead. And having come that far in his effort to escape, he certainly wouldn't reenter a burning building for no reason."

"Maybe he was ashamed of what he'd done and wanted to die," responded Carla. "I don't know. You'll have to ask him why he went back. But since he's obviously lying, there really isn't much point in asking him anything. And I still want a face-to-face confrontation with him before this committee."

That was a wish that would never be granted, in spite of the arguments Ken's lawyers ably presented and some behind-the-scenes pressure from Jordan at considerable risk to himself.

So the hearings dragged on month after month in very disappointing fashion, in spite of the prayers of the group that met at the Elliotts' house that the truth would come out to warn the world. Dr. Elliott's reminder to the prayer group that there were trials of faith and that God's will was always best, and that He was in control in spite of appearances to the contrary, were a great comfort to Ken and Carla and to everyone in the prayer group. They had confidence in the goodness of God, that they were in His hands, and that in His time the truth would indeed come out, though that seemed an impossible dream.

It was, after all, Carla's word against Del Sasso's. The old saying, "Truth is stranger than fiction," certainly proved to be accurate once again. In this case, the truth was too strange for the Senate investigating committee to believe. It wasn't that any of them were necessarily conspiring with those certain persons high up in Washington who knew the truth and wanted it suppressed. It was simply that Carla's story seemed beyond credibility. Without an intimate knowledge of the facts, it couldn't be otherwise.

In the meantime, Del Sasso's entire approach had been revised. He no longer mentioned the Archons, since they were being totally discounted in the Senate hearing. Instead of highly evolved spirit entities external to mankind, he spoke of Jungian archetypes that could be contacted through a revival of ancient shamanistic techniques—and insisted that this had been his thesis all along. By this means, he suggested, one could tap into the infinite powers of the mind that lay unused in the unconscious, but that could be awakened and developed. He formed a company called Shamans Unlimited to offer instruction in such techniques and became very quickly the most popular guru on the human potential/positive mental attitude/success-motivation circuit. There were, of course, many others bringing this message to business and political leaders, to educators and psychologists, but Del Sasso had an exclusive on the psychic powers with which to bait his hook. He did, however, tone down those powers considerably in his demonstrations under the rationale that he didn't want to get anyone's expectations too high, at least in the beginning.

"It is ironic," Ken told the prayer group, "that what seemed at first to be a disaster for the Archons has turned out to be a great leap forward. It's almost as though they planned it this way. Where Del Sasso was once known to an elite upper echelon of leaders, he's now known to the entire world. Thanks to the news media, which has treated him as a hero, his name is on everyone's lips. Overnight he's become an international celebrity.

"As for the Plan, nothing has really changed that much. It doesn't matter whether you call them 'Archons' or 'archetypes' from the collective unconscious. They're still demons, and Del Sasso is still their number-one man. The end result will be the same: the demonization of countless millions in preparation for the Antichrist. Now, however, Del Sasso is using a more effective means of taking the delusion of godhood and infinite potential to the masses."

"That's right," Hal had agreed. "Prophecy will be fulfilled. Satan's 'Archon plan' has not been shut down—it has only changed form. And you can count on it: The public's appetite and gullibility for the counterfeit supernatural hasn't been shut down either—it's growing. We're just seeing a clever adjustment in the program for setting the world up for the great delusion. We're not going to stop that. We won't save the world, no matter how much praying and preaching we do. The key is the church. If it will awaken to what's happening and proclaim the true gospel, then maybe a multitude of these deceived souls can be saved before it's too late. Carla's an example. She seemed hopelessly entangled, but—thank God!" Hal's smile said the rest.

It was nearly eight months after the fact when the committee finally reached its verdict. The findings were accepted by Congress and the White House and communicated to the many nations who had lost leaders in the holocaust. Ken and Carla were called back to Washington to be present when the public announcement was made. "Are we going to be arrested?" they asked their attorneys during the flight.

"Not from the information we've received," they were assured, "but you're going to be very unhappy with the findings."

Indeed they were unhappy when they met with the committee and learned its verdict. They were not allowed to reply—all arguments having ended—but were required to listen silently as the list of charges against them was read. They were then told that, due to lack of evidence, the charges were being dropped, but that the investigation was not over. Then they went outside to mingle in the crowd and listen to the public announcement.

It was a cold and blustery February day, with leaden skies threatening to dump considerable snow on the nation's capital. Nevertheless, the announcement was made from the Senate steps. Public clamor for the facts had precluded revealing the verdict at an ordinary news conference. The public demanded to be present, and thousands had gathered in the chill wind, some of them to wait several hours for the long-expected pronouncement. The president of the United States was meeting with his Cabinet at Camp David, so the vice president, as leader of the Senate, read the prepared remarks in his place. They were brief.

"The full, written report will be available to anyone who wishes to go inside after this statement and pick it up at the information counter," he announced into the microphone that carried his voice over loudspeakers to the vast throng. "In brief, the conclusion the committee has reached is this: The deaths of 289 persons and the destruction of the psychic research facility near Palo Alto, California, last June 14 were due to an explosive device planted by Viktor Khorev who had only recently pretended to defect to the West. He was not, however—and we want this to be very clear— acting as an agent of the Russian government, but as part of a plan engineered by a certain Colonel Alexei Chernov without the knowledge of his superiors in Moscow. When their first attempt to destroy the psychic research facility failed and Chernov was killed through the heroic efforts of Dr. Antonio Del Sasso, Khorev— acting with other persons unknown—accomplished that goal with a powerful explosive device. We have the assurance of the Russian president himself that Khorev and Chernov and certain other rogue agents were acting on their own and without the sanctions or backing of their government. Intensive investigation with the help of our allies overseas has verified the truth of that declaration.

"Well-known journalist Carla Bertelli, now Carla Inman, has also been implicated. It was she who helped Khorev and Chernov stage what we now know was a fake escape in Paris as part of Khorev's phony defection. She was a close friend of Khorev during the time they were together at the facility, and apparently joined him in the conspiracy to destroy it. She published articles presenting Khorev's fake thesis about mythical beings without bodies, called Archons, to use as a cover for their plot, and even tried to convince the Senate investigating committee that the 'Archons' were the ones responsible for the destruction. Bertelli escaped without so much as a scratch, something even Khorev failed to do, so it is at least presumptive that she knew when the explosion would take place and left the theater in time to avoid it.

"Reluctantly, the Senate investigating committee has decided not to indict Mrs. Inman and her husband at the present time, for lack of evidence. The investigation will continue, however, and if at some future time that evidence is ever put together, then they will be arrested and prosecuted for their part in this diabolical scheme. In the meantime, they are free.

"I know that the media representatives here today have many questions, but this is not the time or place for asking and answering them. The president is meeting at this very moment with the Cabinet to discuss this vital matter and how it affects our relationships with other nations, many of whom lost some of their top leaders. He will hold a press conference next week, and at that time he will answer your questions."

Ken and Carla's attention was distracted momentarily from the vice president's droning voice when a reporter from *The Washington Post* who had known Carla for years wormed his way through the crowd to reach them and started asking questions.

"I was really shocked by what we just heard," he said to Carla. "And very sorry. I find it unbelievable. Do you have any comments?"

"We can talk now that the gag order has been removed and I've been falsely accused publicly—and we will. In fact, we'll do more than that," said Carla. "I intend not only to defend myself from the slanderous accusations you've just heard, but to clear the good name of Viktor Khorev as well. My husband and I will not give up until the truth has been told. You can count on that!"

The vice president was just concluding, and what he was saying caught their attention once again. "One more thing, ladies and gentlemen. Dr. Antonio Del Sasso, the only survivor of the blast, and the one who heroically risked his life in attempting to carry Dr. Khorev to safety, is here with us. The president will be awarding him a medal in a special ceremony at the White House later this afternoon. I want him to stand here beside me where you can all see him. Ladies and gentlemen, please show your appreciation to this man for his efforts to bring prosperity and brotherhood to this planet."

The crowd went wild. Now garbed in a turtleneck sweater and tweed sport coat, Del Sasso inclined his head slightly and smiled. Yes, the Plan would go forward. The few lives that had been sacrificed were only the beginning. It was all part of the Plan, all necessary to keep it moving. Nothing could stop it now. Of that he was certain.

ALSO BY DAVE HUNT

THE GOD MAKERS
—Ed Decker & Dave Hunt

Mormons claim to follow the same God and the same Jesus as Christians. They also state that their gospel comes from the Bible. But are they telling the truth? One of the most powerful books to penetrate the veil of secrecy surrounding the rituals and doctrines of the Mormon Church, this eye-opening exposé has been updated to reveal the current inner workings and beliefs of Mormonism. Harvest House Publishers, 292 pages.

ISBN: 1-56507-717-2 • TBC: B04023

DEATH OF A GURU:
A REMARKABLE TRUE STORY OF ONE MAN'S SEARCH FOR TRUTH
—Rabi R. Maharaj with Dave Hunt

Rabi R. Maharaj was descended from a long line of Brahmin priests and gurus and trained as a Yogi. He meditated for many hours each day, but gradually disillusionment set in. He describes vividly and honestly Hindu life and customs, tracing his difficult search for meaning and his struggle to choose between Hinduism and Christ. At a time when eastern mysticism, religion, and philosophy fascinate many in the West, Maharaj offers fresh and important insights from the perspective of his own experience. Harvest House Publishers, 208 pages.

ISBN: 0-89081-434-1 • TBC: B04341

THE SEDUCTION OF CHRISTIANITY: SPIRITUAL DISCERNMENT IN THE LAST DAYS
—Dave Hunt & T. A. McMahon

The Bible clearly states that a great Apostasy must occur before Christ's Second Coming. Today Christians are being deceived by a new worldview more subtle and more seductive than anything the world has ever experienced. Scripture declares that this seduction will not appear as a frontal assault or oppression of our religious beliefs; instead, it will come as the latest "fashionable philosophies" offering to make us happier, healthier, better educated, even more spiritual. As the first bestselling book to sound the alarm of false teaching in the church, this ground-breaking classic volume still sounds a clear call to every believer to choose between the Original and the counterfeit. As delusions and deceptions continue to grow, this book will guide you in the truth of God's Word. Harvest House Publishers, 239 pages.

ISBN: 0-89081-441-4 • TBC: B04414

IN DEFENSE OF THE FAITH:
BIBLICAL ANSWERS TO CHALLENGING QUESTIONS
—Dave Hunt

Why does God allow suffering and evil? What about all the "contradictions" in the Bible? Are some people predestined to go to hell? This book tackles the tough issues that Christians and non-Christians alike wonder about today, including why a merciful God would punish people who have never heard of Christ, how to answer attacks against God's existence and the Bible, and how to tell the difference between God's workings and Satan's. Harvest House, 347 pages.

ISBN: 1-56507-495-5 • TBC: B04955

THE NONNEGOTIABLE GOSPEL
—Dave Hunt

A must for the Berean soul-winner's repertory, this evangelistic booklet reveals the gem of the gospel in every clear-cut facet. Refines and condenses what Dave has written for believers to use as a witnessing tool for anyone desiring a precise Bible definition of the gospel. The Berean Call, 48 pages.

ISBN: 1-928660-01-0 • TBC: B45645

BATTLE FOR THE MIND
–Dave Hunt

Positive thinking is usually better than negative thinking and can sometimes help a great deal, but it has its limitations. To deny those commonsense limitations and to believe that the mind can create its own universe is to step into the occult, where the demons who foster this belief will eventually destroy the soul. Unfortunately, increasing millions in the West are accepting this mystical philosophy, forgetting that it is the very thing that has brought many deplorable conditions wherever it has been practiced. The Berean Call, 48 pages.

ISBN: 1-928660-09-6 • TBC: B45650

DEBATING CALVINISM: FIVE POINTS, TWO VIEWS
—Dave Hunt & James White

Is God free to love anyone He wants? Do you have any choice in your own salvation? "This book deserves to be read carefully by anyone interested in the true nature of God." —Tim LaHaye, co-author of the *Left Behind* series. Calvinism has been a topic of intense discussion for centuries. In this lively debate, two passionate thinkers take opposite sides, providing valuable responses to the most frequently asked questions about Calvinism. Only you can decide where you stand on questions that determine how you think about your salvation. Multnomah Publishers, 432 pages.

ISBN: 1-590522-73-7 • TBC: B05000

WHEN WILL JESUS COME? COMPELLING EVIDENCE FOR THE SOON RETURN OF CHRIST
—Dave Hunt

Jesus has promised to return for His bride, the church. But when will that be? In this updated revision of *How Close Are We?* Dave takes us on a journey through the Old and New Testaments as he explains prophecy after prophecy showing that we are indeed in the last of the last days. In the process, Dave compellingly shows that Scripture illuminates the truth that Jesus will return two times, and that His next appearance—the "rapture" of His church—will occur without any warning. The question is, are you ready? Harvest House Publishers, 251 pages.

ISBN: 0-7369-1248-7 • TBC: B03137

COUNTDOWN TO THE SECOND COMING:
A CHRONOLOGY OF PROPHETIC EARTH EVENTS HAPPENING NOW
—Dave Hunt

Who is the Antichrist? How will he be recognized? How are current events indicators that we really are in the last of the last days? Using Scripture and up-to-date information, Dave draws the exciting conclusion that, indeed, time is short. This book instructs, encourages, warns, and strengthens, urging readers to "walk circumspectly, not as fools, but as wise, redeeming the time, because the days are evil" (Ephesians 5:15-16). The Berean Call, new paperback edition, 96 pages.

ISBN: 1-928660-19-3 • TBC: 00193

A WOMAN RIDES THE BEAST: THE ROMAN CATHOLIC CHURCH AND THE LAST DAYS
—*Dave Hunt*

In Revelation 17, the Apostle John describes in great detail the characteristics of a false church that will be the partner of the Antichrist. Was he describing the Roman Catholic Church? To answer that question, Dave has spent years gathering historical documentation (primarily Catholic sources) providing information not generally available. Harvest House, 549 pages.

ISBN: 1-56507-199-9 • TBC: B01999

OCCULT INVASION: THE SUBTLE SEDUCTION OF THE WORLD AND CHURCH
—*Dave Hunt*

Occult beliefs march freely across America today; the deadly impact of Satan's dominion is seen in the rise of teen suicide, the increase in violence, and the immorality that pervades our society. Noted cult expert Dave Hunt reveals: how Satan's lies are being taught behind the academic respectability of science; how demonic activities are presented as the path to enlightenment through "alien" contacts and paranormal experiences; how pagan religions are being promoted through ecology and "we are one" philosophies; and how evil is being reinvented as good by psychology and the legal system. Harvest House Publishers, 647 pages.

ISBN: 1-56507-269-3 • TBC: B02693

WHAT LOVE IS THIS? CALVINISM'S MISREPRESENTATION OF GOD
—*Dave Hunt*

Most of those who regard themselves as Calvinists are largely unaware of what John Calvin and his early followers of the sixteenth and seventeenth centuries actually believed and practiced. Nor do they fully understand what most of today's leading Calvinists believe. Multitudes who believe they understand Calvinism will be shocked to discover its Roman Catholic roots and Calvin's grossly un-Christian behavior as the "Protestant Pope" of Geneva, Switzerland. It is our prayer that this book will enable readers to examine more carefully the vital issues involved and to follow God's Holy Word and not man. The Berean Call, 576 pages.

ISBN: 1-928660-12-6 • TBC: B03000

SEEKING & FINDING GOD: IN SEARCH OF THE TRUE FAITH
—*Dave Hunt*

It is astonishing how many millions of otherwise seemingly intelligent people are willing to risk their eternal destiny upon less evidence then they would require for buying a car—yet the belief of so many, particularly in the area of religion, has no rational foundation. With compelling proofs, this book demonstrates that the issue of where one will spend eternity is not a matter of preference. In fact, there is overwhelming evidence that we are eternal beings who will spend eternity somewhere. But where will it be? And how can we know? The Berean Call, 160 pages.

ISBN:1-928660-23-1 • TBC: B04425

A CALVINIST'S HONEST DOUBTS: RESOLVED BY REASON AND GOD'S AMAZING GRACE
—*Dave Hunt*

A non-intimidating, easy-to-read "introduction" to Calvinism. Based on years of actual accounts and conversations, *Honest Doubts* reads like a real-life drama because the characters are composites of actual individuals, and the circumstances are equally real. Discover the heart of a Calvinist "seeker"—and the surprising result of his quest for truth in this fictionalized but true-to-life dialogue derived from Dave's much larger scholarly work, *What Love Is This? Calvinism's Misrepresentation of God.* The Berean Call, 112 pages.

ISBN: 1-928660-34-7 • TBC: B60347

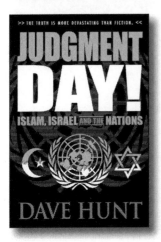

JUDGMENT DAY!
Islam, Israel, and the Nations

BY DAVE HUNT—This new book is the most comprehensive examination of ancient biblical prophecy and modern-day Middle East politics regarding Islam, Israel, and the nations— which includes the United States of America! Painstakingly researched using up-to-the-minute data, *Judgment Day!* is sure to become a respected resource for scholars, analysts, pastors, professors, politicians, and laypeople alike. Amazing historical facts and firsthand, eyewitness insight make this book a thrilling, sometimes troubling, read—but one that is necessary for a heavenward understanding of the prophetic times in which we live. Hardcover, 448 pages.

ISBN: 978-1-928660-32-3

REVIEWS FROM DECORATED MILITARY LEADERS

"Dave Hunt's *Judgment Day!* has encyclopedic dimensions of the most crucial and vital issues of our times.... Like the biblical prophets, Dave Hunt has a vision and is not hesitant to issue a Battle Cry."

— SHIMON EREM, GENERAL, ISRAELI DEFENSE FORCES, RETIRED

"Dave Hunt's *Judgment Day!* introduces and explains the radical faith of Islam and the actions of its subscribers.... A 'must-read' for all U.S. State and D.O.D. personnel as they execute this current world war."

— THAD HOYER, COLONEL, USMC, RETIRED

"*Judgment Day!* is a tour-de-force, both in scope, scholarship, and insight. This superbly researched work examines the most vexing global security issue facing our world today.... Those of us living in the democracies of the West ignore this sobering, well-documented assessment at our own peril."

— RICHARD SCOTT, COLONEL, USMC, RETIRED

TBC VIDEO PRODUCTIONS

The Berean Call produces and distributes quality Bible-based documentary and teaching programs on VHS and DVD

ISRAEL, ISLAM, AND ARMAGEDDON: The Final Battle for Jerusalem

Overflowing with powerful fast-moving visuals spanning centuries of history and biblical prophecy to clarify current and future events, this powerful history lesson documents how the current peace process is fraught with peril, and why it is impossible for Jerusalem to know true peace in our age. 60 minutes.

THE INDESTRUCTIBLE BOOK: The Historic Path of God's Word from Mt. Sinai to Plymouth Rock

From the ancient deserts of Israel to the shores of the New World, *The Indestructible Book* documents the incredible story of faith and sacrifice to protect the Bible and carry its message of hope and salvation forward through the centuries. Filmed on location in Israel, Europe, Britain, and the U.S., *The Indestructible Book* captures the spectacular sweep of history with visual images as rich and varied as the story it unfolds. 4 hours.

LEST WE FORGET: A Documentary of Anti-Semitism Past and Present

This film documents a concerted campaign to de-humanize the Jewish people and de-legitimize the nation of Israel. As viewers will see in this exclusive footage, today's Arab-sponsored state-run propaganda is alarmingly similar to that of Nazi Germany during World War II, and presents a clear and present danger to Jewish people around the world today. 74 minutes.

OBSTACLE TO COMFORT: The Faith Ministry of George Müller

George Müller of Bristol became a legend in his own generation. He was the builder of schools, a supporter of missions, and a father to some 10,000 orphans. The amazing issue of his life does not lie in *what* he did but in *how* he accomplished it: by faith—refusing to tell anyone of his needs, mentioning them only to God in private, on his knees. 74 minutes.

THE SIGNS AND WONDERS MOVEMENT EXPOSED

Many believe that we are the generation that will witness the return of Christ. Jesus said that those alive for His second coming would be subject to the greatest onslaught of deception ever leveled at the body of Christ—and that this deception would be predicated upon signs and wonders. This may be one of the most important videos professing Christians can watch. 4 hours.

A WOMAN RIDES THE BEAST: The Roman Catholic Church and the Last Days

Most "end times" discussions focus on the coming Antichrist, but he is only half the story. In Revelation 17, there is another mysterious character at the heart of prophecy—a woman who rides the beast. Tradition says this "mystery" woman is connected with the church of Rome—but isn't such a view outdated? Remarkable clues in Scripture remove all doubt. 60 minutes.

ABOUT THE BEREAN CALL

The Berean Call (TBC) is a nonprofit,
tax-exempt corporation which exists to:

ALERT believers in Christ to unbiblical teachings and practices impacting the church

EXHORT believers to give greater heed to biblical discernment and truth regarding teachings and practices being currently promoted in the church

SUPPLY believers with teaching, information, and materials which will encourage the love of God's truth, and assist in the development of biblical discernment

MOBILIZE believers in Christ to action in obedience to the scriptural command to "earnestly contend for the faith" (Jude 3)

IMPACT the church of Jesus Christ with the necessity for trusting the Scriptures as the only rule for faith, practice, and a life pleasing to God

A free monthly newsletter, THE BEREAN CALL, may be received
by sending a request to: PO Box 7019, Bend, OR 97708; or by calling

1-800-937-6638

To register for free email updates, to access our digital archives, and to
order a variety of additional resource materials online, visit us at:

www.thebereancall.org

BEND • OREGON